CR

America is caught in the middle of a drug war when a powerful Bolivian goes up against the Mob for control of the lucrative cocaine trade. As part of a Justice Department strike force, Mack Bolan refuses to wait on the sidelines of this war for the final confrontation . . . because he knows it's not just the players who can get burned.

DON PENDLETON's
MACK BOLAN

TROPIC HEAT

A GOLD EAGLE BOOK
London · Toronto · New York · Sydney

Special thanks and acknowledgement to
Charlie McDade for his contribution to this work.

*First published in Great Britain 1988
by Gold Eagle*

© Worldwide Library 1987

*Australian copyright 1987
Philippine copyright 1987
This edition 1988*

ISBN 0 373 61409 8

25/8807

Made and printed in Great Britain

All spirits are enslaved which serve things evil.
— Percy Bysshe Shelley

When bad men combine, the good must associate; else
they will fall, one by one, an unpitied sacrifice in a
contemptible struggle.
— Edmund Burke

From where I stand, the struggle appears to be
uphill all the way. But no matter how futile
it looks, I shall persevere until the end.
— Mack Bolan

To all Americans who are involved in the never-ending fight against the drug trade.

La Paz _____

CHAPTER ONE

The sun sat on the edge of the Andes, as if impaled. The snowcapped purple spikes, ragged as a broken saw, seemed to hold the blazing ball for an instant. It glowed bright orange, seemed to swell, and then, like a balloon suddenly pierced, was gone. The shadows that had loitered in the alleys of La Paz for more than an hour took command.

The city was a hodgepodge of lavish estates, government buildings and the standard-issue Third World hovels. Like most large South American cities, its numbers had been swelling steadily for years. Displaced by crumbling economies, or drawn by a modern version of El Dorado, the poor streamed into La Paz from the mountains and the jungles. Dirt farmers, Indians, mestizos and—as to most large cities around the world—fast-buck artists, con men, smugglers and prostitutes.

Low in the bowl-shaped valley, off to the east, directly beneath a ridge where the sun had been just moments before, a paler glow sprang into view, just visible against the line of trees that was the last green of any substance. Casa La Paloma was a mix of the modern and the Spanish colonial. It was tasteful and not ostentatious, but there was no hiding the fact that it took money to build such a place, lots of it. But unlike many such estates, this one was not a barrier against the people, but a citadel that housed their aspirations. It belonged to Camillo Rogelio Rodriguez y Yanez, the current president of Bolivia.

This night, it drew the attention of a stranger, a tall man, dressed in black, who seemed more at home in the sudden darkness than he had been in the fading light. From a small house on the western rim, high above the Plaza Murillo, he had been watching the estate for three days. Tonight, he would take a closer look. He sat in the dark house, the colorful woven curtains little more than shades of gray bunched in one hand.

Outside, the streets were slowly emptying. The hustlers and peddlers, both running out of clients, were making their way home, straggling through the winding streets and disappearing into alleys and aging buildings. La Paz had grown out rather than up, and instead of teeming in the aggressive towers of tenements that lined the mean streets of North American cities, its poor lived in tumbledown huts and sheet-metal shacks. The rats were there, and the stench of human waste and cheap food, the latter drenched in oil, its marginal edibility bolstered by spices. But none of this concerned the stranger.

His eyes, fixed on Casa La Paloma through powerful binoculars, saw nothing but the slowly shifting array of lights as its residents moved from room to room, preparing for sleep. For the past three days the owner of the estate had been away. It had not been pleasant, waiting, waiting, waiting. At night, the scurrying feet, the occasional squeaks and squeals conspired to remind him of his own origin, a time and place he preferred to forget. It was all behind him, but it never left him. It was something he had surmounted but not conquered. Like a small boy playing king of the hill, he relished his precarious perch on the pinnacle, but never forgot for a minute that there were others, some bigger, some faster, all meaner than he, willing and eager to pull him down.

As long as he was the best at what he did, he was secure, but that security was ephemeral. It could vanish as quickly and completely as the sun he had just seen disappear. One day, he knew, it would. But when was up to him.

A strolling band of musicians drifted into the alley outside his window, their instruments droning in a high, plaintive melancholy. He had seen them earlier in the day, sweating under the hot afternoon sun, their music brisk and lively, passersby gathering in small knots—some even dancing a minute or two before moving on. It was no different from the Chicago ghetto, where he had grown up. The music on the South Side was harsher, harder edged and electrically driven, but the spirit was the same. Even its themes were the same, love lost and love found, momentary joy and lifelong suffering.

The silent stranger thought for a moment that he was on the wrong side. The man who lived in Casa La Paloma mattered to these people. He stood for something they needed: dignity. But the doubt was gone, willfully rooted out before its cancer could spread. He couldn't afford such thoughts in his business. He had a job to do and a living to make. Reflection had no connection to either, and no place in his life.

When the musicians reached their homes, the music thinned as, one by one, they closed the door on another day until only a single instrument continued, its high, resonant melody drifting back through the tangled alleys like a strand of rope its creator would follow back to civilization and sunlight in the morning. Then it, too, was gone.

As if the last note were a signal, the silent observer let go of the curtain. Putting down the binoculars, for a long moment—he continued to stare at the window now obscured by the rough cloth—then got to his feet. His movements were slow and deliberate, with the studied grace of an athlete. He crossed the small room to a wooden table and took a compact attaché case by its handle, hefting it as if to make sure it was not empty. The handle creaked as the case swung back and forth until its weight brought it to a halt. Satisfied, he turned and opened the door.

A sliver of moon hung pale and silver against the high, dark blue of the sky. Rags of cloud drifted in the glow, pale violet barely perceptible against the dim light. He stood in the alley, nearly as tall as the building he'd just left.

The outline of Casa La Paloma was dim against the bottom of the valley, spiky trees here and there and, towering behind it, the mountains were a ragged fence against the stars. The alley was empty and light almost nonexistent. Like a river of darkness, it stretched downward, through the terraced hovels, bending now and then to slide past a misaligned shack. The dull clay and rusted metal walls were uniformly black, the floor of the alley not much lighter in the pale moonlight.

Avenida de la San Martin was a more direct route, but attention was something he didn't need. A solitary shadow in the angular darkness of the sprawling maze would attract no notice. His clothing, black as the obsidian path before him, was little darker than his skin. The dark attaché case, its brass handle and clasps painted flat back, dangled from his left hand. He began to walk, his black hightop sneakers making no sound against the hard-packed clay of the alley.

His destination loomed ahead of him, constantly visible against the trees, bobbing gently with the motion of his gait, almost ghostly in the night. Once, a dark cloud obscured the moon, and he paused for a moment to get his bearings. The estate was almost dark now, one window on the left still lighted, and the few scattered security lights winking as the breeze riffled through the trees along its stone-walled perimeter. He knew that light was in the library. *El presidente* was working late.

A dog barked behind him, its quick, hoarse rasp startling him. He spun around, but the dog was nowhere to be seen. As he neared the ragged stone steps leading to the next terrace, he heard the click of heels on the paving stones of another alley. He pressed his back against a wall, the briefcase flattened in one extended arm. The footsteps clicked again, this time more uncertainly, as if the person were lost.

He drew in a breath and held it. The footsteps halted for a long minute. When they resumed, they were more certain, this time clicking steadily. Suddenly, from between two houses, a square of light was thrown onto the hard clay as a door opened.

He saw a girl, no more than fifteen or sixteen, wobble through the door on platform shoes. Her bright purple dress seemed out of place here. The door started to close and then, as if she sensed his presence, she turned and peered out into the darkness, her face a garish mask in the flickering light of an oil lamp. The makeup and aggressive décolletage of the flamboyant dress told him all he needed to know about her, and about her life. This, too, he had seen in Chicago. Poverty was one of the eternal verities, its few desperate escape routes predictable and universally pathetic.

The door closed, and she was gone. So was the tug at his memory and the vestigial conscience lingering at the bottom of his consciousness like the sludge in a cup of Turkish coffee. As he looked again at Casa La Paloma, he remained splayed against the wall, as if afraid to move. The estate was about a mile away now, partially obscured by the low roofs of the terraced squatters' homes on the highest level of the hill. Below the terraces was a broad park, mostly open sweeps of grass and bunched knots of shrubbery, a full, flowing fountain at its center. On the far edge of the park, a stone wall with a brook at its base—like a medieval moat—marked the end of the slums and the beginning of the wealthy area.

He found it hard to imagine why the landed gentry would want to look up at the sky over the crowded slum, but realized they didn't have much choice. Their homes dated back to the early nineteenth century. Pride of place and tradition kept them there. Mostly old families, their owners had been at the summit of Bolivian life since independence. They were not about to be driven out by the rabble, no matter how distasteful, no matter how ominously poised above them.

Besides, he knew conditions were so fluid, the rabble could be gone in a year, or two, or three. Their hopes, slim as they were, were anything but durable. Soured by failed expectations, lured by dreamlike rumor from another place, they would move on. They'd leave behind the ruined hov-

els, the only relics of poverty, and a bulldozer would sweep
away the pathetic detritus. Order would be restored, and
life, for the rich, would go on as it always had. These teeming crowds were a momentary aberration, no more permanent than the clouds that obscured the moon above from
time to time.

As he approached the steps leading down from the last
terrace, the man quickened his pace. His feet shuffled on the
dusty stone steps, and he was nearly to the park. Its clumps
of shrubbery were tangled snarls of darker shadow in the
open, silver-toned sweep of grass. The fountain burbled, its
high, arcing spouts frothy and transparent under the moon.
He passed the fountain on his left, sprinting now, to get to
the base of the wall. The rough face of the stone wall was
perfect for his practiced ascent.

Standing on the top of the wall, he turned to look back.
The cold air was exhilarating, and he breathed deeply as if,
in topping the wall, he had left the ruins above behind him
and the ruined lives that huddled amid the tin and adobe
clutter.

For the moment, he was king of the hill again. As he surveyed the tar-paper roofs and rusted, corrugated tin, which
canted into shadow, he felt as if he had made it, he was on
top, in control of his life. His shadow, long and narrow,
speared out across the park below, an enormous icon of his
achievement. The moon suddenly darkened again, and his
shadow stabbing through the silvery light disappeared. He
knew he had escaped nothing.

Turning his back on the high ridge, he sprinted across the
deserted cobbled avenue and stepped into the shadows along
the wall of Casa La Paloma. The solitary light in the library burned on. He was close enough to see a shadow on
the wall, a man seated, head bent, apparently reading or
writing at a desk. The window was open to the cool night
air. There were four guards, he knew, and they were good.
Not as good as he was, but good enough.

Hurling himself over the wall, the attaché case banging against the stone, he landed in a crouch and listened. Two of the guards would be on the house, and two on the perimeter. Once he got up to the building, he'd have only two men to beat.

And one man to kill.

The moon was starting to fade, clouds thickening and closing in. He moved to the base of a tall tree and hunkered down in the shadows of a small clump of broad-leafed shrubbery. He placed the attaché case flat on the ground, muffled the clasps as they flipped open and assembled his weapon. A custom-modified SP66 Mauser, fitted with a nightscope and flash hider, fell together in seconds under his expert fingers. He slipped spare ammo into his pocket and made sure the weapon was primed. The smell of light machine oil seemed to stabilize his jittery nerves. It had been years since he'd been this spooked on a job, and one thing a mechanic couldn't afford was the jitters.

When the rifle was ready, he turned his attention to the open window. It was high up on the wall, with nothing but stone beneath it. He couldn't climb in without being heard. He couldn't risk assaulting the house because he didn't know its layout, and the man at the desk could disappear in an instant.

Halfway between the tree and the window was another, shorter tree, surrounded by a group of boulders. Flowers clung to the crevices in the rocks and dripped over to the ground below. He would have to work from the tree, despite his distaste for being vulnerable after a hit. There was no way around it.

Duck-walking the twenty yards to the stand of boulders, he paused to listen again. A bird trilled in the woods behind the house, its song echoing among the trees. Just beyond, he could see the very tips of the Andes, snow-white in the pale light. The peaks seemed to turn gray as he watched. The moon vanished again, the darkness almost impenetrable among the rocks. He slipped once, mounting the stone, then grabbed a low limb to swing high and far out, like a gymnast. He grabbed a higher limb and hauled himself up. He was just above the level of the open window now and could see his quarry hunched over a stack of papers on his desk.

The reading man's face was illuminated by the soft glow from a green-shaded banker's lamp. Repositioning himself on the limb, the stranger unslung his rifle and sighted in through the window. Through the powerful scope, he could see the hairs on the back of his mark's left hand, which cradled his chin as he turned pages with his right.

He made a slight adjustment in the scope and sighted in again.

He froze for a second as the man turned toward the window, his eyes gleaming in the dim light, as if he knew he was being watched. For an instant, the bright blue eyes blurred, and the man blinked. The gleam returned, he shook his head once and let his gaze linger on the shadowy tree.

The stranger squeezed once, then again. The sharp reports echoed back among the trees, crisp and brittle in the chilly air. The ruined head vanished from the scope.

Bolivia, once again, was leaderless.

CHAPTER TWO

The house was like those on either side of it. Twenty-one twenty Sunnyland Way was pastel, a pale blue, while those flanking it were yellow. All had Florida rooms and walls of glass facing south. Even in October, the hum of an air conditioner broke the stillness otherwise disturbed only by the flutter of palmetto bugs and the occasional buzz of a bluebottle. To the rear, a channel had been dredged just deep enough to admit the cabin cruisers docked behind each house.

An occasional splash in the dark water testified to the presence of a fish or frog. There were rumors now and then of a stray gator, but no one paid much attention. The story made the rounds as a way to break the sleepy tedium of Florida days, sometimes kicked around over a game of Uno or dominoes. No one would come out and say he'd actually seen the gator, but no one wanted to dampen the modest excitement the possibility offered. So the story kept on going from house to house and dock to dock.

Like so many of the quiet neighborhoods of outlying Miami, this one had seen changes in recent years. The elderly northerners who had once been its principal residents were now giving way to Cubans, Venezuelans, Colombians and Bolivians. The docks were a dream come true for small-time smugglers, and more than one on this particular block had seen a load of grass or a few kilos of coke unloaded.

Small-time, just making a buck, they didn't see much difference between pushing a bit of weed and working in the cane fields back in Cuba. It paid better, of course, and the work wasn't as hard on the back. You kept out of the sun, but it was a job, like any other.

Or so they thought.

Some people looked at it a little differently. To the nay-
sayers, the small-time deals of Sunnyland Way were a pain
in the ass. And pain was something you didn't ignore. You
did something about it. Whatever it took.

No one inside heard a thing. The two men who drifted on
crepe soles to the back door, which was closed but unlocked, wore screaming Hawaiian shirts, short sleeves flapping over their muscular arms. The shirts were half
unbuttoned and draped over belts that struggled just a bit
against the beginnings of early paunches. A trickle of sweat
ran down the cleft between the overdeveloped pectorals of
the lead man, and he paused to pull the clammy shirt away
from his damp skin.

He reached under the shirt and pulled out a small-caliber
automatic, its slender, almost inoffensive barrel made ugly
by the cylindrical extension threaded snugly in place. He
pressed flat against the wall to the left of the door. His
companion, frozen while he waited for the signal, was three
yards behind him. The muscle man waved, and his companion stepped quickly past and positioned himself against
the glass panel to the right of the door. The first man pressed
his ear flat against the wall, listening for some indication
that they had been spotted. There were none.

He held his hand upright and, counting under his breath,
slowly bent the fingers inward toward his palm. When only
one finger remained extended, he took a deep breath. The
rush of air must have covered the soft spit of the weapon
inside. The glass panel exploded and his companion
sprawled facedown in the damp grass. Two small holes,
dark specks against the glistening stains beginning to spread
across the garish cloth, betrayed the point of impact.

He paused, fingers still extended, then turned just as
someone rounded the corner of the house. He dived to the
ground, landing hard on one shoulder, and rolled toward the
wheelbarrow full of flowers that stood to one side of the
boardwalk leading to the dock. He heard a slug rip into the

grass beside him, felt the sting of a second as it bored into the fleshy part of his left thigh. The third slug killed him.

The outraged homeowner sprinted across the lawn to dig in the dead man's pockets for his wallet. It was on his left hip, and he had to roll the body over on its side to yank it out of the snugly fitting pants. When he flipped it open, the soft blue light from a neighbor's TV glinted on the badge.

Satisfied, he tossed the wallet onto the dead man's chest and waved to the house. He was joined by three more men. They each grabbed a limb and, together, hauled the body of Lieutenant Orville Garcia, Metro Dade Police Department, to the small launch docked at the bottom of the yard. Moving swiftly but smoothly, as if well practiced in the maneuver, they returned to the house to get Garcia's companion. When both bodies were on board the launch, two of the men returned to the house, slipping in through the ruined glass panel beside the door. They were back a moment later, each carrying two briefcases. They tossed them into the launch, which started with an earsplitting rumble.

They waved as the launch drifted back away from the dock, then turned in a tight 180 and sped down the channel, its running lights on in observation of the law. When the launch had rounded the first bend and was out of sight, they went back to the house, stopping just long enough to set the timer on the preplaced C-4 plastique in the utility room.

Their green Pontiac Trans Am was five miles away when 2120 Sunnyland Way was reduced to smoking rubble. The Trans Am was eight miles away when it joined the house in oblivion. The launch, as if by a last, fading echo of the first explosion, was ripped from the water for one fiery instant. Then, its roaring engine reduced to a hiss by the cold water, it slid quietly below the surface, leaving Lieutenant Garcia to float facedown among splintered fragments of the hull.

TO THE SOUTH, off Big Pine Key, the *Big Sister* floated on the current. A single lantern swung listlessly from the sailless mast. A soft glow from the cabin below deck tossed spears of dim light onto the rippling water. The coast was a dull gray bulk, barely rising out of the water to the west. Two men sat on canvas deck chairs, smoking and talking quietly.

One man, in an ostentatious cap with gold braid struggling to contain thinning, unruly gray hair, wore binoculars on a strap around his neck. From time to time he lifted the glasses and swept the coast from north to south. Seeing nothing, he'd drop the glasses in his lap and drag on his cigarette.

He was running to fat, and the dirty T-shirt he wore, decorated with a rampant alligator carrying a football, was drawn tightly against broad shoulders. The rough stitching at the neck of the shirt cut into his sun-reddened skin, and he'd reach in under the band to rub away the irritation. He wore holey sneakers and khaki Bermuda shorts a size too large, even for his broad rump.

His companion, several years younger but just as broad of beam, was harder muscled. What he made up in brawn, he lacked in brain, and the dull glint of his piglike, closely set eyes was attributable to alcohol rather than intelligence.

"See anythin'?"

The younger man grunted, rather than spoke, but his boss seemed to understand him.

"Not yet, but it's still early."

"I don't like it, I tell you. I don't trust them greaseballs."

"You don't have to like it, and you don't have to trust nobody but me, Ray. They know better than to mess with me, and if I get paid, you get paid. Don't worry about it."

"You give them more credit than I do, partner."

"Now, that's where you're wrong, Ray. One thing Theron Marr don't give nobody, it's credit. Cash on the barrel head, that's my motto. Them boys will cough up tonight, or they don't get our cargo. It's that simple."

"I sure hope so."

"I *know* so!"

As if to put an end to the conversation, one he'd already had four times that night, Theron picked up the glasses and began to hum as he scanned the low outline of the coast again. This time, to forestall resumption of the discussion, he took his time, moving the glasses back and forth in small increments as he stored the coastline in his memory, like a satellite mapping a continent with overlapping photographs.

There was still no sign of the launch, but he wasn't worried. They'd been late before, and, no doubt, they would be again. He was paid well, and waiting around wasn't fun, but it wasn't all that bad, either. It sure as hell beat dragging a net.

Ray, his nerves beginning to fray, stood up and walked to the wheelhouse, took a Marlboro from his open pack and clicked the cheap plastic lighter twice before it caught. The flame went out almost immediately, and he huddled over his open fist to cup the lighter and cigarette before trying again. This time the flame caught and held. He sucked deeply, drawing the flame into the cigarette, and exhaled a plume of smoke. He caught a glimpse of himself reflected in the Plexiglas windshield and admired his profile. He had taken up cigarettes more for the way he thought they made him look, than for the taste, which he barely tolerated. But Ray Gibbs was more interested in looking cool than almost anything else he could imagine, and he just knew he couldn't look at all cool without a cigarette dangling from his thick lips.

He felt Marr's eyes boring into him, and self-consciously fidgeted around on the small ledge in front of the wheel, finally clicking on the portable radio. He got a burst of static while he twirled the dial, settling at last on a country music station out of Jacksonville. Merle Haggard was wailing about love lost or gone or stolen, and that was good enough for Ray.

He returned to his seat, straining his ears to hear the music.

"You oughtn't have that damn thing on, Ray. How we gonna hear them greaseballs?"

"Hell, Theron, we always hear them a couple miles away, don't we? I'm surprised they ain't been caught before now, the noise they make."

"Maybe so, but I don't want them sneakin' up on me, is all."

"I thought you said you trusted them."

"No, I did not. I said they was gonna pay me or else, that's what I said. Hells bells, I know enough not to trust somebody can't speak good English. Fact, that's one reason I ain't sure I trust you."

"What do you mean? How come you don't trust me? I ain't done nothin'."

"Forget it, Ray. It was a joke, is all."

"It ain't funny, Theron."

"No, I suppose not."

Marr stood up, put the glasses to his eyes yet again and tried to peer through the gloom. He knew the signal by heart and knew it hadn't been given, but his eyes were starting to play tricks on him. Staring long enough into the dark, expecting to see a brief flicker, he knew he'd see one whether it was there or not. He still had some double-ought shot in his behind from making that mistake once before. A married woman he'd been seeing used to signal him with a cigarette when her husband wasn't home. One night his hormones got the better of his eyesight. He responded to a brief orange fireball and walked right up the barrel of a Remington 12-gauge before it dawned on him.

He wasn't going to make that mistake again. Not in this life, anyhow. He walked to the wheelhouse and clicked the radio off. He grabbed a Marlboro from the half-empty pack. He was just lifting the lighter when a shadow in a wet suit climbed over the rail just off the bow.

"What the hell is . . ." The question died in a gurgle. His hands closed over the steel shaft of a fishing spear as blood bubbled up in his lungs, a thin trickle oozing from his open mouth. He wanted to reach for the .45 on his hip, but the pain was too great, and not realizing it was already far too late, he was afraid to let go of the spear.

Ray heard the clatter of the lighter and turned just as a second spear hissed from the black-suited figure's gun. It caught him square in the forehead and drilled through to the plywood bulkhead behind him, pinning him in place like a bug on a velvet board. His eyes rolled up and in, as if to stare at the dull glint of the shaft, but he was already long past seeing anything. The man in the wet suit flashed a quick burst from the diving lamp on his waist, then lowered a rope ladder at the stern. Two minutes later, he was joined on deck by three more men, all dressed in jeans and sneakers. They rushed below and quickly appeared on deck, each carrying two large black plastic bags folded and held closed with silver duct tape.

"They all there?"

"*Sí.*"

"Let's move it, then."

The man in the wet suit, obviously the leader, hurried the other three back into their small launch. Returning below, he reached into a bag at his waist and withdrew a small, flat package. He unwrapped it and placed its magnetic clamp on the engine housing, just forward of the fuel line.

With a twist of his wrist he set the timer to five minutes, then bounced up the ladder to the deck. He could hear the ticking below and knew he had no time to waste.

He glanced around the deck once more, then crossed swiftly to Theron Marr, now lying flat on the deck, his hands still clasped around the base of the spear where it protruded from his chest. Just to be sure, and for no other reason, the man in the wet suit reached down to his thigh for his knife and drew it free of its sheath. With no more compunction than a man cleaning a fish, he slit Theron Marr's throat from ear to ear. Taking chances was not his style. And even if Theron Marr had had more lives than a cat, he still didn't have a prayer.

Satisfied, the man in the wet suit wiped the sticky blade on Marr's T-shirt, replaced the knife in its sheath and briskly saluted.

"Request permission to go ashore, Cap'n." When Theron Marr said nothing, the man snapped off his salute and did a neat about-face. "Thank you, Cap'n Marr, sir. Don't mind if I do, sir."

He was still laughing as he climbed into the launch and pushed off.

CHAPTER THREE

Against the white walls of the huge living room, Diego Cardona was nearly lost. His white-on-white suit couldn't have been more closely matched to the white satin wallpaper of the spacious room. His slender hands, a soft brown in color, their nails gleaming, floated in the air as he gestured to the stark black form of his butler. The latter nodded and moved away, his feet noiseless on the deep-piled white carpet.

Cardona turned to his two companions and leaned back against the white corduroy sofa, placing one foot, which was shod in a white calfskin slipper, on the gleaming alabaster coffee table.

"I hope you don't mind my calling you here on such short notice," Cardona apologized. His voice was soft and low, as if it had lost its way in the white wilderness. "But we have many things to discuss."

His auditors nodded patiently. Cardona wasn't through, and they knew it. He was notorious for his leisurely manner in business conversation, and infamous for his frequent rages, when words tumbled from his lips in frenzy, foam splattering anyone within a dozen feet. Not for nothing was he known as El Perro Demente, the mad dog. Tonight, fortunately, he was not dissatisfied with his listeners.

He ran a hand through his jet-black hair, which shone against the stark white background like a lump of coal, just as dark and, with its sheen of oil, just as shiny.

"Your Mr. Richards has done a magnificent job. He is to be congratulated, as are you."

The two men facing Cardona relaxed a bit. The younger man, Roberto Cabeza, stood up and gestured expansively. "I told you he was good, Diego. The best! And cheap at twice the price, eh?"

"Roberto, you must be getting soft in the head, my
friend. No matter how much money you make, a million
dollars is not cheap. Not even the chairman of General
Motors takes such an expense lightly. Not if he wants to *stay*
chairman."

Roberto smiled. "Well, since you are the chairman of our
little corporation, I will defer to your judgment, Diego. But
I still think it was money well spent."

"We'll see if it was or not. President Yanez was an obstacle to my plans, of course. His elimination, however, does
not solve all of our problems. To think so is to make a very
grave mistake, Roberto. There is much to be done before we
are where we want to be. Besides, the government has been
overthrown before. Don Marino Consuelas thought it was
in his pocket. He found out it costs as much to run a government you own as it does to avoid one you don't. True, he
was a cheapskate. Still, he lives in Argentina now, and not
by choice."

"Maybe, but you have to admit we couldn't have gotten
our plans off the ground with Yanez in office. It was he,
after all, who brought the American helicopters into the
mountains. He was the man who—and you said this yourself, if you remember—cost us five hundred million dollars
so far this year."

Cardona sat up straight, his eyes bulging the slightest bit
as he stared at Cabeza. "Don't throw my own words back
at me. My memory is as good as it has to be, Roberto. But
you are small because you think small and talk big. To be
big, you have to think big . . . and say nothing. And then do
something about it. Do you understand?"

Roberto nodded. He was getting uncomfortable and
turned to look at his companion, who had remained seated
and silent during the exchange. When his companion said
nothing, Cabeza turned back to Cardona. "I understand."
He resumed his place on the couch opposite Cardona. He
realized, as he sat down, that Cardona's sofa was on a platform, raised just enough to give him the high ground when

talking to anyone seated across from him. As many times as he had sat in this very place, he had never noticed it before.

Cardona rose, his eyes still prominent, and leaned toward Cabeza. "Roberto, make sure you do understand. I have given a great deal of thought to my plans, and I won't have any mistakes. Not by you, not by anybody. You seem to think it is easy, sitting where I am sitting. You think, perhaps, that you can do as well as I have done, eh?"

"Of course not, Diego. I don't think that. Not at all." He reached into his pocket for a handkerchief and patted his forehead, which was beginning to bead with perspiration.

Cardona smiled broadly at the gesture. "Perhaps I need to have the air-conditioning checked, eh, Roberto? It doesn't seem to be working. I'll have it looked at tomorrow."

Cabeza said nothing. Cardona continued, the smile gone as suddenly as it had appeared.

"Your Mr. Richards was very good, Roberto. Very good indeed. A thoroughgoing professional."

Roberto nodded.

"You know what it means to be a professional, Roberto?"

"Of course I do."

"It means his services are for hire. I paid him once. I can do it again, if necessary."

The silent man chuckled. It was the first sound he had made since entering the room. Cardona frowned, and the man struggled to control his laughter.

"Our job, *my* job, has just begun, and you idiots don't even seem to understand it," Cardona snapped. "Now I have to take control of the distribution networks, all of them. Everything from extraction to delivery on the street. We are going to cut the other dealers right out of the picture. And when I gain control of the manufacturing, they will have nothing to sell, eh?"

The silent man spoke for the first time. "That's a tall order, Diego. It won't be easy."

"Maybe not, but I have already started."

Cabeza looked surprised. "You've started? Already? But I thought we—"

Cardona cut him off. "You disapprove, Roberto?"

"No, I just thought we—"

Again, Cardona interrupted. "I am not getting any younger, Roberto. If I waited for you, I would be an old man before anything got done. I want to be young enough to enjoy all this." He gestured at the lavish surroundings. "Perhaps even retire, once I have achieved what I want to achieve."

"You can't be serious! Retire? You're not even thirty years old."

"Men, great men, have retired at ages younger than I already am. There are a great many ways to enjoy oneself, Roberto. Something you don't know much about. You are too limited. You have no imagination. And many of those things are best indulged by a man with the physical stamina to explore them fully. To wait too long is to miss them altogether. The genuine pleasure life affords is there for the taking, but one must be vigorous, demanding."

"But you are already the wealthiest man in Bolivia, give or take one or two."

"You see, you've said it yourself, give or take one or two. For you, that might be enough, but not for me. I am the best. I want to be the richest, with no possibility for dispute. I want *everything*, Roberto. I deserve it, and I mean to have it. No one will stand in my way."

Cardona looked as if he were ready to continue the harangue, but the butler returned, momentarily distracting him from his oratory. The servant carried an elaborate silver tray with three glasses and a bottle of champagne in an ornately carved silver salver. He placed the tray on the tabletop, twirled the bottle between his palms with a theatrical gesture, then removed it from the ice. Cardona smiled approvingly, admiring the butler's ritual behavior as if it were a scene in a play.

When the champagne was uncorked, it foamed over the neck of the bottle, a few drops falling on the carpet and darkening the pile. The butler looked apprehensively at his employer, but Cardona either failed to notice the spilled champagne or was too much engaged in the moment to care. The butler poured three glasses and, bowing, stepped back for Cardona to taste the wine.

The sip proved satisfactory, and Cardona gestured to the remaining two glasses. "Gentlemen, help yourselves. I wish to propose a toast."

The two men hastily picked up their own glasses, Cabeza spilling a bit in his alacrity. He reached out to cover the glass with his free hand, holding it rigidly in front of him until the contents settled down. He continued to watch Cardona the entire time, his brow rigid with tension.

Unable to resist the opening Cabeza's clumsiness afforded him, Cardona said, "Lucky for us all your Mr. Richards is not so careless, eh, Roberto?"

Cabeza nodded, squeezing his lips into fine white lines, waiting for the next insult. But it never came. Instead, Cardona hoisted his glass aloft.

"To the future, gentlemen. Yours...and mine." Without waiting for their response, he took a long sip of the champagne and sat down again, ignoring them totally. He reached for a small ceramic container on the table, removed its lid and, with the small spoon inside, scooped a healthy quantity of sparkling white powder onto the smooth surface of the table. He replaced the spoon and withdrew an artist's palette knife. Deftly he composed the small mound into a rough rectangle then, with the assurance of a hibachi chef, split the rectangle into six equal lines.

Cabeza and his companion watched the performance as if they expected some sort of magic show. Cardona reached into his jacket to remove a long ivory tube, its length elaborately carved with naked bodies so hopelessly entangled it wasn't possible to tell which limbs belonged to what trunk. Cabeza was long familiar with the tube and recalled the day Cardona had purchased it, with money from his first real score.

The two men, then little more than teenagers, had spent nearly two hours cataloging the varieties of sexual activity depicted in minute detail. There were more than a few Cabeza had never seen, let alone experienced. He had been astonished that Cardona knew them at all. He suspected then, and now knew, that most of them had been experienced at firsthand by his younger, but more worldly friend.

With almost feminine grace, Cardona bent to the tabletop, coiling himself protectively about the ivory tube. He quickly inhaled four times in succession. When he straightened up, only two lines remained. "Help yourselves," he offered. His lips were contorted into a parody of a friendly smile, his nostrils twitched, and a slight tic was apparent in one cheek. Cabeza had seen it before, more frequently in the past year. Cardona was hitting the coke pretty hard. It was having an effect that Cabeza chose to ignore while Cardona refused to acknowledge it at all.

The visitors, each for his own reasons, declined the offer. With a shrug, Cardona disposed of the remaining cocaine, sniffed twice and waved dismissively. "I'll call you. When I need you."

The two men rose at once and left without a backward glance. At the door, a second butler brought them their coats and opened the fifteen-foot-high walnut doors. Outside, they stood for a moment under the veranda canopy. Cabeza looked at the elaborate garden stretching for more than two hundred yards to the stone wall surrounding Cardona's estate. Halfway across the broad lawn, a fountain burbled, its center occupied by a statue of a reclining nude woman. The water of the fountain hissed as it spurted from her nipples and gurgled noisily as it splashed into the fountain's pool.

Roberto Cabeza was more than awed by the lavish decadence he saw at every turn. It was hard to believe that this all belonged to a man he had known all his life, and harder still to believe that Diego Cardona had once been forced to keep body and soul together by stealing food from vendors in the open-air markets of La Paz. It seemed as if it must have been in an earlier life, so different were the circumstances in which Cardona now lived.

It disturbed Cabeza to think too much about the changes in Diego, because, as much as the money they were now making was what they had always promised themselves they would do, Cardona had changed so much that he was no longer a boyhood friend made good. He was a different person altogether, somehow corrupted more totally than Cabeza had ever thought possible. What could have been dismissed as the excess passions of a wild young man were now too tame for Cardona. Something about his friend was so totally dehumanized that Cabeza not only didn't much like him anymore, but he also didn't feel safe, as if having known Cardona in the old days was some dreadful secret that, sooner or later, Cardona would wish to lock away— permanently. Roberto Cabeza shuddered at the thought.

He shrugged off the morbid reflection when his car arrived, the attendant leaving the door open, then walked around to open the passenger door for Cabeza's companion. Cabeza stepped down the marble stairs to the crushed stone of the circular driveway. Before slipping into the car, he turned to look up at the house.

Diego was in an open window on the second floor. The room behind him was dark, but there was enough ambient light from the security lamps to recognize him. He was naked, a fine white sheen glistening from hips to groin, the only area of his body he protected from the sun. At his side was a woman Roberto had never seen, also naked, her hands gently caressing Diego's flat stomach. Roberto wasn't sure, but he thought Cardona smiled at him.

He ducked into the car and closed the door, harder than necessary, as if he were afraid something in the house might try to leave with him. In a way, he thought, it was too late to worry about such things. In some way he couldn't explain, he was already as corrupt as Cardona. He just didn't revel in it the way his old friend did.

He drove almost entranced. When they reached the huge wrought-iron gates that marked the entrance to the estate,

Cabeza turned to his companion. The latter, although Cabeza had said nothing, sensed the question.

He shrugged, then said, "I know what you're thinking, but as long as we're making money, what do we have to complain about?"

Cabeza let the question hang for a long moment, before answering. "Did he threaten us, or was I just imagining things?"

"I don't know. I guess he did. So what?"

"I'm not sure he is rational, that's what. And if he's not, who knows what he might do?"

"Look, Roberto, he wouldn't be where he is without us. We all know that. Even Diego. You don't think he'd try to cut us out, do you? Be serious!"

"I don't think Diego would do that, no." Cabeza paused, then reluctantly continued. "But I'm not sure I know who the hell is living in that house. I don't recognize him. Not at all."

"You're being too sensitive. He has an ego, sure. And maybe he does a little too much coke now. But we're partners. We're all in this together."

"I just hope *he* remembers that."

Washington, D.C. —————————

CHAPTER FOUR

The big man from the Justice Department looked at the faces before him. As he scanned the room he paused to scrutinize each man, one by one. It never ceased to amaze him how richly varied the human species was, and how vastly different could be the roots of men who shared a common goal. Without exception, the men in front of him had made the same choice he had, but they were all much younger than he, younger even than he could remember being.

He didn't know whether to take heart that yet another generation was willing to forgo the perks of the corporate world in favor of the public good, or to despair that so much time had gone by since he'd made his choice, and so little had changed. Everyone wanted to feel that what he did made a difference, and when he made a sacrifice or two along the way, it was that much more important to see results.

For Hal Brognola, the results had been all too bloodily evident... and all too short-lived. Like bowling pins, he knocked them down, and somebody he'd never seen just reached down without a word and set them all up again. The pattern was always the same, and the challenge never varied. Unlike pins, his targets had faces, but it seemed, more often these days, to be the only difference. Now, almost at the end of yet another year, here he was ready to start all over again. He wondered whether he'd be more successful this time. He doubted it, but hell, what was hope for, anyway?

Stopping at Bolan, he grew a little more hopeful. Here, at least, was a man he could count on, a man who'd been there and back, been places most men wouldn't dream of going. Maybe there was hope after all.

The men, all except Bolan, arranged in a semicircle, sat on folding chairs with Brognola's desk at the focus. Bolan sat in the corner, casually slumped in a battered old leather easy chair. Standing behind the desk, his back against the bright glare of a brilliant Washington October afternoon, Brognola was little more than a shadow. It made no difference to Bolan, who knew the big Fed as well as he knew himself, maybe even better. The others had never met Brognola before, but they'd heard a lot about him, almost as much as they'd heard about the big guy in the easy chair.

Brognola folded his hands behind his back, lacing the fingers together and struggling to make himself comfortable. When it dawned on him that he'd never manage it, he glanced quickly out the window, as if hoping he could adjourn the meeting on account of the weather. The visitors began to fidget nervously in their seats. It wasn't possible to put it off any longer.

Finally, bowing to the inevitable, he spoke.

"Gentlemen, you all know why you're here. Am I right?" He paused briefly until, reassured by the nodding heads, he cleared his throat to continue. "However, you may not know that things have changed considerably since this meeting was first scheduled. The situation is, if anything, more imperative. In case you haven't read the papers in the past two or three days, Camillo Yanez, the president of Bolivia, has been assassinated."

One of the young men raised his hand. When Brognola acknowledged him, he asked, "What does that have to do with the substance of our meeting? I thought this was about cocaine smuggling. I don't think any of us is involved in political affairs."

"You're quite right, Mr. Calabrese. Or rather, I should say, you would have been quite right, if we didn't have reason to believe the man responsible for the assassination was also one of the primary targets of our little project."

"Who?" Calabrese seemed genuinely surprised.

"I'll get to that, but I think we ought to take things in order."

Calabrese nodded his head in agreement.

"As I was saying, things have changed. The targets are still the same, and the facts are still the same, and still appalling. For the past year or two, cocaine has been the largest single commodity produced in Bolivia, and as near as anyone can determine, the amount of money generated by the illicit traffic is more than twice as large as the legal gross national product of that country. The drug used to be the private recreational preserve of the rich and the jet-set types, but technology and taste have changed all that. Crack is now the biggest single narcotic trafficked on the streets of most major American cities. It's cheap, which means anybody can afford it, and it's a hell of a lot more potent than heroin or the snow that used to melt in Hollywood noses. Worse than that, though, is the damage it does to the brain and nervous system. You talk to anybody in a big city police department, and he'll tell you the crime associated with cocaine, particularly crack, is more brutal and more frequent than that associated with any other narcotic. Gentlemen, our mandate is to do something about it."

Another of the young men piped up, without waiting for recognition. "Hell, we just sent Army choppers down there. If they couldn't do anything about it, what chance do we have?"

"Come on, Callahan, you've been to Bolivia. You know what it's like. The military advisers were there in a very limited capacity. They were to render transport and, if necessary, covering fire only. They were not directly involved. Their primary mission was simply to get the Bolivians to places they couldn't reach without the choppers. Hell, some of the *traficantes*, as they're so grandly called, have bigger air forces than the Bolivian government."

"Like I said," Callahan persisted, "what the hell are *we* supposed to do about it?"

"How old are you, Callahan?" Brognola snapped.

"Twenty-seven, why?"

"You ought to be old enough to understand a few things about the way the world works."

"Such as?"

"Channels, Callahan. Channels. When one government asks another for help, there are limits on what can be done. For instance, if they ask for ten helicopters, you can't send five hundred. If they say help us for three weeks, you don't hang around for six months. And when the government lending assistance is as carefully monitored as the U.S., not only by other countries, but by Congress and the media, then your hands are all but tied. Do more than you're asked, and sure as hell, there's somebody all set to jump on your ass."

"I still don't see what that has to do with us."

"I'll make it simple for you. No request, no channels. If nobody knows we're there, nobody will ask us to leave, or complain we're doing too much, or making pains in the ass of ourselves. We call the shots, so we do what we want."

"Where do I come in, then? The DEA doesn't work that way."

"Some people wonder whether the DEA works at all," Brognola responded.

Everybody snickered, except Callahan, his partner, Calabrese, and one other DEA man present, Bob Levine.

"I don't think that's funny," Callahan said, getting to his feet. He turned to face the others. Brognola debated whether to interfere, but thought it would be interesting to see what happened. He glanced at Bolan, but the big guy in the corner was as stony-faced as ever. His eyes were on Callahan, but they were as cold and impassive as those of a predator.

"Every time we get close to one of the big honchos out there, I don't give a shit whether it's Bolivia or Bangkok, somebody puts on the brakes. Half the time, some asshole from the CIA says, 'Wait a minute, you can't touch him, he's one of ours.' And if that doesn't happen, we find out his uncle's the king of Slobbovia, and he's planning a coup. There's always some reason to give these jokers a pass." Callahan looked defiantly around the room.

"You can sit here and laugh, but I'll tell you what. Spend six months in the back alleys of Mexico City and see how funny it is when your best friend gets blown away by a bunch of *federales* on the take."

A thin, scholarly-looking man, his tweed suit a dead giveaway as to his Ivy League background and old money connections, told Callahan to sit down. "I'm the CIA asshole in this room, Callahan, and I just want you to know two things: one, the world is a lot more complicated than you think it is, and two, despite that fact, there are a lot of people in the Agency who wouldn't disagree with you."

Callahan snorted. "See, that's just the kind of bullshit I'm talking about. Notice, he didn't say they agreed. He said they 'wouldn't disagree.' And that's condescending crap about the world being complicated, as far as I'm concerned. It's just the standard Langley apology for the CIA's inadequacies . . . and for the bastards who make a fast buck on the side, all the while telling us how they have to let some animal do what he wants because he's anti-Communist. Who the hell do you think you're kidding? You guys were even flying heroin out of Vietnam on your own planes. In body bags, for Christ's sake. And your buddies really were valuable, weren't they? I mean, we couldn't have won the war without them, right?"

"That's uncalled for," the CIA man said. His voice was quavering, but lacked conviction. His neck was bright pink and Bolan, watching from the rear, knew it was embarrassment more than anger. Callahan was right, and everybody in the room knew it.

"All right, now, hold on," Brognola said. "This is a classic example of the kind of interagency squabbling that we're supposed to get around. As of this moment, you guys work for me. I don't care whether you're from the CIA, like Mr. Andrews, or a DEA hotshot like Callahan. You're all good, or you wouldn't be here. But I got some news of my own for you. As far as drugs are concerned, if your agencies were doing their jobs, there wouldn't be any need for this task force. And I won't stand for any horsing around.

Your loyalty will be to me, and your job will be to do what I tell you to do. Do I make myself clear?''

"Shit, Brognola, what makes you think you can do any better?'' It was Tommy Calabrese again, Callahan's partner from the DEA. He was a few years older than the irascible kid, and hadn't yet made his point to his satisfaction.

"You have a problem with what I said so far, Mr. Calabrese?''

"No. What I got a problem with is what you haven't said. And so far, you haven't said why you think we can do it if the DEA can't, or the CIA for that matter. Shit, Centac has better luck than anybody else. Why the hell aren't they running this show?''

"All right, those are fair questions. I'll take them one at a time.''

"Take them any way you want. But when you're through yapping, if I don't like what I hear, I'm walking. And I don't want to hear a bunch of bullshit about how channels are the problem, and how we can boldly go where no man's gone before, or any of that other science fiction. You might believe the Shadow had the power to cloud men's minds, but I don't. I want nuts and bolts, not words.''

"Why don't you all hold your water and let Hal say what he's got to say.'' The words were soft, barely above conversational tone, but the electricity crackled unmistakably. Mack Bolan had spoken for the first time.

"Oh yeah, and who are you, pal?'' Calabrese turned to face the big man in the corner, a smirk on his face. "What agency are you with, the Boy Scouts?''

"I'm not with any agency.''

"Why not?''

"I don't *need* one." The tone was sharper, and if Calabrese doubted the words, he declined to challenge them. He nodded slightly, then turned back to Brognola.

"All right, all right. Maybe I was out of line. Why don't you just get on with it?''

"I'll make it quick,'' Brognola said. "You men are being asked to participate in this project because you're good, and because you have reputations for getting things done. I'm running it, because I'll make damn sure we get things done. And what we're going to do is nail the biggest drug dealer in Bolivia. We get him, the rest are easy, just like dominoes. Why? That's easy, too. Because there are a lot of people in Bolivia who want him to take a fall, but they can't do anything on their own to make it happen. They need help, the same kind of help he's been able to buy. He owns politicians, generals and cops. He's got more money than God, and some people will tell you he's just as powerful.''

"What kind of budget do we have?''

"No budget. What I have is better . . . unlimited authority. If we need something, I can get it, whatever it is. Cash to set up a buy, guns to take out a small army—and believe me, he's got one—cars, air support, anything at all. No questions asked.''

"I've heard that before,'' Callahan said.

"Not from me, you haven't,'' Brognola snapped.

"Okay, so we take him out. Then what? What about the pretenders to his throne? Nature does abhor a vacuum.''

"We get him, we serve notice. And there's one important thing I haven't mentioned yet. He's in the process of consolidating control over the entire Bolivian drug scene. He doesn't realize it, but he's doing a lot of our work for us. So, when we cut off the head, the snake will die. It's that simple.''

"That's just like the CIA horseshit I was talking about before,'' Callahan mumbled. "What's the difference whether we let some guy build an empire because we want him to do something for us, or because we want to take him out. While he's building, people are getting killed, and other people are killing themselves. Any time you let one of these bastards do business, I don't give a damn if it's just for a week, you've let somebody die who didn't have to. You're just as responsible as he is. Maybe more, because you should have wanted to stop it.''

"We're not going to help him do anything. And we're not going to wait. By the time we get our asses in gear, he'll have all the control he wants. It's started already, and the assassination of Yanez was not only the signal, it was the proof he can do it.''

''You still haven't told us who we're after,'' Calabrese said.

''Diego Cardona is his name. You'll find everything you need to know in the folders under your chairs, which, by the way, I expect you to read before this afternoon's session, and then return to me. I don't want any leaks out of this room. None.''

''What about the Mob? Aren't we just making it possible for them to get back in? The South Americans have pretty much pushed them out of the picture on coke.''

''We've thought about that, but we're ready for it. Mr. Bolan, who will be operating in conjunction with this unit, is more than a little familiar with the Mob. If they try to fill the void, we'll know about it. If we know about it, we'll stop it. Any further questions?''

Brognola looked around the room, again paused at each face. When there were no questions, he said, ''Gentlemen, thank you. I'll see you again at 1:00 p.m. Sharp.''

They filed out, talking among themselves. Brognola rearranged some papers on his desk. When they were neatly stacked, he turned to Bolan, who still sat in the corner. ''Well, Striker, what do you think?''

''I think I've heard of some harebrained schemes in my time, but I never thought I'd hear one like this. And especially not from you.''

''Look, I don't make the rules, I implement them.''

''I know, I know.'' Bolan stood and stretched. ''But that pack of big mouths is not going to get the job done. That kid Callahan might be all right for the DEA, but he's too hot tempered. He can get somebody killed.''

''He's a good kid, and one of the best guys the DEA has. As far as his temper is concerned, you have to cut him a little slack. He's got a personal stake in this thing.''

''Like?''

"His sister. She got into crack pretty heavily. Became a hooker to support her habit. One night one of her friends killed her for her score. And don't ask him about it, because he won't say anything. He'll just try to take your head off. It's personal with him, but he can handle it in the field. He just likes to say what's on his mind."

"Uh-huh."

"You're not convinced, are you?"

"Nope."

"You know it doesn't make any difference, don't you?"

"Yeah, I do know that."

"Some things never change, Mack."

"We'll see."

CHAPTER FIVE

Watching the clouds slide by beneath the left wing, Mack Bolan considered what lay ahead of him. He didn't much like it, and he wasn't impressed with Brognola's team. He knew the big Fed had been given the job and, trouper that he was, would do his best. But Bolan also knew the size of the job, and the limited resources they'd be working with weren't calculated to inspire confidence. Most of the South American coke czars had small armies on their payrolls, a pipeline to the inner chambers of government and unlimited capital. Brognola's assurances that he could get whatever he needed sounded rather thin when measured against that reality.

The plan was bare bones. Levine and Andrews were going to Mexico City and Calabrese to Miami. Bolan was supposed to meet Callahan in La Paz. When they hooked up, Callahan would plug him into the network the DEA had been building for several years with, as far as Bolan could see, indifferent success.

Sitting on the plane, he ignored the blandishments of the flight attendant, a lissome blonde with a name tag that read Valerie Russell. The more he ignored her, the more determined she seemed to keep him a happy flier. An hour out of Dulles, she took the seat next to him and tried to start a conversation. When he ignored her, she left like a spurned hooker, contempt just thinly veiled under the studied smile. She was a looker, but there were more important things to do.

He'd done some checking on Diego Cardona, and the news was all bad. Cardona had been at his trade for only six years, and already was considered to be the boss, the emperor, of the coke traffic. A man noted for his violent temper, Cardona was interested in only two things: making money and spending it.

The dossier Brognola provided just skimmed the surface, but it was impressive. Cardona had one home in Bolivia, a modern collection of glass and rock faces, a nearly impregnable stone monstrosity that loomed over La Paz like a bad dream. In the photographs Bolan had seen, the estate looked like Frank Lloyd Wright's worst nightmare. As modern as now, all lines and sharp angles, it was solid stone and bulletproof glass.

Cardona was also reputed to have a second Bolivian place, somewhere in the Andes. But nobody seemed to know where.

Then there was the estate in Mexico City. More pleasing to the eye, it was no more accessible. In Miami, he had another home, this one doing its best to masquerade as a quiet retreat for a wealthy but inoffensive citizen. All three known places were heavily guarded, and Cardona, a gadget freak, had spared no expense on electronic security. If it beeped or twittered, chances were he had one installed.

Long-lens photos of the Miami location were revealing. A trained eye could detect the camera locations and, beyond the six-foot-high stone wall, Spanish neocolonial in design, the location of no fewer than three security outposts. Disguised as small outbuildings, just the sort of thing a grandee would keep for the hired help, they were wired and featured tinted glass and loopholes for the heavy artillery.

Bolan was most interested in the secluded Bolivian place, but no one had been able to learn much about it. Sure, there were photos, some of them damned good. But the place had been built from scratch instead of modified like the Mexico City estate and the one in Miami. The architect, whoever he was, must have had a siege mentality, because the photos revealed nothing, absolutely zip, about the defenses of the place.

That it was heavily defended was beyond doubt. You didn't get to be a mover and shaker in Cardona's world without making sure you'd be around for the next shipment. And you didn't leave yourself open to attack, either. Too many people wanted a piece of you. They came at you from all sides. The DEA was a gnat, a mere nuisance, when compared to Cardona's compadres in the coke trade. The cocaine cowboys thought nothing of taking out whole families, from infants to grandmothers, just to make a point. If they came at you, they came hard. You had better be ready, and you had better be prepared to move that extra step, take out that extra generation, if you wanted to be the biggest.

Compared to the Mafia wars of the twenties, and Bolan's own shooting war with the latest version of the Mob, these were no-holds-barred affairs. The Mustache Petes were downright genteel when measured against their Latin cousins. Almost weekly, even American papers featured a story on the latest shootout in a parking lot or shopping center. And as exaggerated as the stories of Mafia concern for civilians might be, the cowboys were recklessly indifferent by comparison.

Bolan knew all this, and yet he allowed himself to hope. Just this one time, maybe the government was willing to take the gloves off, let people do what had to be done, no questions asked.

Yeah.

Maybe.

The flight attendant was back, this time with a tray in her hands. The smile was all plastic and a yard wide. "How about a drink?" she asked.

Bolan shook his head. She persisted. "Aren't you thirsty?"

"No, thanks."

"I'm not interrupting, am I?" It was just barely a question. Bolan bit his tongue to avoid being uncivil. Instead, he paused, appearing to think before answering, hoping she would take the hint. She didn't.

"Actually," he said, "I was trying to get my thoughts in order. Sometimes planes are the best place to do that."

"You travel a lot?"

Bolan nodded.

"You in sales?"

"No."

"Advertising?"

"Do I look like I'm in advertising?"

"Not really. I'm just babbling, you'll have to excuse me. I'm a little nervous. I'm pretty new at this."

"Maybe you're pressing, you know? Trying too hard?"

"Is that your polite way of telling me to get lost?"

"If you don't mind..."

"Sorry. I didn't mean to be a nuisance."

"No hard feelings?" Bolan asked, extending his hand.

Her grasp was firm. The soft skin of her hand concealed a muscular grip that was surprising in so delicate a package. She wasn't at all bad looking. "Too bad..."

"What?"

"I didn't say anything."

"You did, you said 'Too bad,' but you didn't finish."

"I must have been thinking out loud."

"Well, are you going to finish?"

Bolan grinned, and her smile lost some of its artificiality. "I was just thinking it's too bad I didn't have more time. You know how it is, things to do, places to go, people to see."

"I know. Still, I can give you my address in La Paz. I've got a two-week layover after this flight. Maybe some other time?"

"Sure, why not?"

"I'd like that." She yanked a ballpoint from a chain around her neck and took a small notepad from her tunic. She scribbled something, folded the paper neatly and tucked it firmly into his hand. "I really would."

She turned to move away, and Bolan reached out to grab her by the arm. "Why don't you leave that drink after all?"

She smiled again, then handed him the tray. "Be seeing you. I hope."

"You can bet on it."

When she had gone, he turned again to the window. The view was extraordinary as the plane angled out over the Caribbean. The clouds, which had been almost unbroken, had all but vanished. From this high in the air, the water looked almost smooth, like a gray-green slate that extended as far as the eye could see. It would be nice, he thought, to have a slate as clean as that. But he had come too far to consider the possibility as anything more than a dream. Too much had happened to him for things to be any different than they were. Amnesia couldn't wipe out half the things he'd seen and done. Now, once again, it was starting. As he'd told the flight attendant, with more truth than either of them realized, he had places to go and, most important, people to see.

And what people they were.

EL ALTO AIRPORT WAS as sleek and modern as most of Bolivia was backward. Unlike Venezuela and Mexico, more prosperous tourist meccas, Bolivia didn't get much of the carriage trade. It had no world-famous beaches, and its ruins did not enjoy the reputation of being a pre-Columbian Disneyland. If you were an American in Bolivia these days, chances were you were there to buy coke, or to get hold of someone else who bought it.

Bolan was at the luggage carousel when he felt a firm grip on the back of his neck. He turned quickly, ready to swing from the heels when he recognized Brian Callahan.

"Hello, Brian," Bolan said, gripping the younger man's hand. "You shouldn't do that. I have an itchy trigger finger."

"So I hear. But you aren't packing yet. That's why I wanted to get to you before you got your bags." There was a twinkle in the man's eye, and he laughed easily. Away from the bureaucratic juggernaut of D.C., the kid seemed more comfortable, less hostile. Bolan understood completely.

While they waited for the luggage, Bolan sized up the younger man. A big, solid-looking guy, he was nearly Bolan's height and outweighed him by fifteen pounds or so. Bolan recognized immediately that the extra beef wasn't fat.

Brian Callahan was a John Ford Irishman in the classic mold. His light brown hair, just long enough to turn up at the collar, was curly and windblown. An abundance of freckles covered his cheeks and forehead. The light sunburn that underlay them was a consequence of his Gaelic fairness.

Callahan looked like a rawboned farmboy from the Midwest, in town for a Saturday dance after wrestling with unruly spuds all week. Which was exactly what he would have been if he hadn't turned his back on the family occupation, a decision reached after three years of varsity football and very little soul-searching at the University of Iowa. He had been a walk-on his freshman year, but a full scholarship fullback after that.

When the bags popped through the waving rubber fingers and started their first circuit, Bolan grabbed one and Callahan its matching piece. He hefted the suitcase and grinned.

"Iron underwear?"

Bolan, who didn't smile easily, returned the grin. "Let's just say iron, okay?"

Callahan led the way. "We can bypass customs. I've already made the arrangements. I figured you might not want some drooling idiot pawing through your bags. Things tend to rust easily down here."

They slipped through a side door, nodding to the airport security guard who stood, in an approximation of parade rest, against the wall.

Outside, Callahan pointed out a three-year-old Ford Bronco at the end of a row of battered American cars, all belonging to airport workers. He reached for the keys, unlocked the back and laid the bag flat. He stepped aside and said, "You need anything in here, you might as well get it now."

Bolan rolled the combination wheels and snapped open the bag. Quickly he removed his gleaming .44 AutoMag and Beretta 93-R that were as close as he would get to faithful companions. He slipped off his jacket, slid into the AutoMag's harness and clipped the Beretta in place. When he shrugged back into his jacket, neither was noticeable. Unless you knew what to look for. Callahan, who did, nodded approvingly. "Nice tailoring." He laughed, and Bolan knew he was going to like working with Callahan, if only the kid could keep his hot temper under control.

"Where to?" Bolan asked, sliding into the passenger seat.

"Well, neither of us wants to jerk around down here, unless I miss my guess. So, I thought I'd take you out to beard the lion in his den. Figuratively speaking, of course. Cardona is quite the high-liver. You won't believe his crib."

"Sounds like a good idea."

Callahan cranked up the Bronco and backed away from the building. As the 4X4 nosed around the corner, Bolan caught a glimpse of his flight attendant, standing just outside a staff security door. Her head jerked as the car rolled past, and she seemed startled, as if she had recognized someone she hadn't expected to see. The reaction caught Callahan's eye.

"A friend of yours, Mr. Bolan?"

"Not really. She was a flight attendant on my plane."

"A fine-looking young woman. I'm jealous."

"No reason. We barely spoke."

"Yeah, maybe. But I'd say she's interested in you, regardless of your lack of interest in her."

"She gave me her address and phone number."

"That sounds like an invitation to me. Maybe you could introduce me as your young cousin from out of town."

"I may not know her, but I'm not sure I'd want to inflict you on her."

"I'm just a fun-loving young Yanqui, trying to make his way in the world."

"I wonder...."

"What?"

"Oh, nothing. Forget it."

Bolan lapsed into silence that was definite, though not impolite, and Callahan respected it without being asked. He turned his attention to the traffic, which was considerable and noisy. Many of the cars had long since seen better days, and the din was accompanied by generous clouds of oily smoke. There were few taxis, but the number of buses and trucks was surprising. People dangled from the buses at odd angles, and Bolan, who had seen such public transportation in all parts of the world, seemed bemused by it. He'd never been to La Paz, but somehow it wasn't what he'd expected. Not so far, anyway.

But it would be.

He knew that for sure.

CHAPTER SIX

Callahan handled the blocky 4X4 with casual skill. The traffic began to thin out as darkness approached. Hungry after the long flight from Dulles, Bolan told Callahan he wanted to check into his hotel and get something to eat before paying a visit to Casa Cardona. The younger man was more than willing to stoke his own fires and waited in the hotel coffee shop while Bolan freshened up.

Upstairs, Bolan tipped the porter a few pesos, despite having carried half the luggage himself. After a quick shower he felt awake, if not invigorated. La Paz was the highest city in the world. At more than thirteen thousand feet, its thin atmosphere was disinclined to go easy on foreigners, even one like Bolan, who was no stranger to the limits of human endurance.

The low oxygen level could cause a kind of lassitude approaching somnambulism, and Bolan was already feeling its effects. It was so pervasive it had a name of its own: *soroche*. The Aymara Indians who made up the bulk of the city's population, outnumbering mestizos and foreigners four to one, were about the only people immune to the condition. Like the Sherpas of the Himalayas, they seemed as if they respired nitrogen.

Bolan knew his endurance would be reduced, and his thinking, at least for a few hours, wouldn't be as sharp as usual. The reduced oxygen in the air meant less was available for the brain. An innocent effect for sightseers and vacationers, but Bolan was no tourist. His business was deadly enough without this added risk, but he had no choice. Cardona was the quarry, and La Paz was where he lived.

Back down in the lobby, he was nearly groggy and saw spots dancing before his eyes, just out of focus. Taking a seat in the booth opposite Callahan, he asked about the oxygen shortage.

"Well, I've been here off and on for two years, Mack. Even so, it still nails me for a few hours every time I've been down to more normal altitude for a few days and then have to come back. You'll be okay in a couple of hours."

"I think I want to wait a bit before paying a visit to Señor Cardona."

"Not a bad idea. If you want, we can take a look at the rest of the city first, kind of get you accustomed to the terrain, if not the atmosphere. You probably won't feel like eating much, either."

"I need some nourishment, though."

"Sure, but don't order too heavy. You won't finish, I guarantee. And if you haven't forgotten about that little air hostess of yours, I'd wait a few days before going to see her. Lust needs its oxygen, too."

"Thanks for the warning."

When a waitress appeared at their table, Callahan ordered for both of them, his Spanish perfect and nearly free of an American accent. The food came in short order, and Bolan found eating it more than he could handle. Pushing his own plate away, Callahan reached across to Bolan's with his fork, spearing the remaining chicken.

"You can have the rice and beans, too, Brian."

"Not hungry? Too bad." Callahan reached across the table a second time, this time grabbing Bolan's plate and putting it down on top of his own. The food vanished almost at once. Callahan not only looked like a fullback, he ate like one after a hard day in training camp. He paid and led the way back out to the street.

"First thing we ought to do, Mack, is go up top, toward that rim up there. We won't actually reach it, but we can come close. The view is incredible. And it's not just scenic, it's educational. You can get a good idea of the layout of La

Paz from up there. If we're gonna nail Cardona, a little geography lesson might come in handy.''

Bolan nodded, still tired.

Callahan cranked up the Bronco and jerked out into the traffic, which was even thinner than it had been a half hour before. The sky was almost dark now, the deep blue of it alive with glittering points of light. In the thin air, the stars didn't twinkle as much as Bolan was used to, and the color was unlike anything he had ever seen.

When they reached the outer limits of the city, Bolan looked down on a glittering bowl, alive with swarming fire. El Hueco—The Hole—was what *pacenos* called the city, and Bolan could see why. A depression in the altiplano had been filled in by the city, spreading upward toward the lip in every direction.

Callahan pulled over, killed the engine and jumped down from the Bronco. Bolan followed. The younger man climbed a flight of stairs made of flat slabs of rock. They seemed to have been fitted together without benefit of mortar, and led to the top of a wide stone wall, also unmortared, stretching off into the darkness on either side.

Like an emperor surveying his domain, Callahan grandly swept his hand across the breadth of the bowl. ''What do you think of our fair city?'' he asked.

''How fair can it be, when you have to look over shacks and shanties made out of scrap lumber, rusty tin and cardboard?''

''Well, now, do I smell a social reformer?''

''Not the kind you mean. But you have to wonder whether scum like Cardona isn't responsible for living conditions like this.''

''Look, Mack, I don't know how much you know about coke, but these Indians were chewing coca leaves for hundreds of years before the Spanish got here. It's part of the culture.''

''Maybe so, but they never sold it to kids in London and New York, did they? They didn't devise ways to make it accessible and more powerful, then turn girls out on the street to pay for their habits, did they?''

Callahan stepped back. The expression on his face was one of surprise. He looked for just a second as if he were going to explode. Bolan had intentionally hit a nerve.

''Look, I'm sorry if I—''

A soft scrape on the rock behind Bolan interrupted.

Callahan turned. He, too, had heard the sound.

Bolan dropped to one knee, angling for a better line of sight in the dim starlight. With the mountain rim behind him, he was staring into a deep purple well. He saw no one. But someone was there, had to be there.

Standing again, Bolan stepped toward Callahan, then turned his back. Callahan did the same. Now they could cover the wall in both directions. The gloom seemed to waver, like mist or smoke, before his eyes.

There was a soft puff and something slapped against his jacket.

''Down,'' Bolan yelled, pitching forward onto his stomach. He yanked the Beretta 93-R from its sling and stared hard into the blackness. There was something darker than the night, just below the rim of the wall about twenty yards away. He sighted in, uncertain whether it was just a shrub or a man's head. Before he could make up his mind, there was a rush of footsteps behind him. He heard Callahan shout, then three quick shots.

At the same instant, the dark shadow below the wall began to move toward him, gliding silently. It was now or never. Bolan squeezed the trigger and the Beretta spit its 9 mm parabellum slug. A soft thud and the sound of a heavy weight falling on broken stone told him he'd found his mark.

He rolled to his right, found the lip of the wall and dropped to the ground below.

''Callahan? You okay?''

''Yeah, you?''

''Yes. Slide off the wall.''

"Right."

Still trying to pierce the gloom, Bolan heard Callahan land heavily to his rear. Both men crouched against the cold face of the smooth rock.

"You hit anything?" Bolan asked.

"I don't know. I heard someone running, but that's all. I thought I saw a man in the muzzle-flash, but I didn't hear anything one way or another. How about you?"

"Yeah, I hit somebody, but I don't know how many there are. Or what they are."

"I can tell you that. We've just run into one of Mr. Cardona's more exotic hit teams. He—"

A scrape on the wall above cut him off. Bolan sprang back from the stone, whirling to face the point of origin. He aimed quickly and squeezed off three quick shots. A bundle of shadow fell heavily to the ground just to the right of where he'd been crouching.

Callahan sprinted into the night, running parallel to the wall. In an instant, he was gone from view. Bolan heard a shout in the darkness, coming from the base of the wall, but the voice was not Callahan's. Then a pistol cracked, and someone ran straight toward Bolan. The Executioner dropped to one knee, straining his eyes against the dark. He had to be sure it wasn't Callahan before he fired.

The steps came closer, and then the man was on him, a long tube clutched in one hand. The figure was vaguely outlined, but too small. It wasn't Callahan. Bolan fired and the man collapsed like a punctured balloon.

"You get him?" Callahan called.

"Yeah. You okay?"

Callahan materialized out of the darkness. He stopped alongside the fallen man, nudged him with the toe of one boot, then knelt. He reached into his coat for a small flashlight, and examined the body cursorily. Bolan joined Callahan as he turned the corpse on its back.

"You know him?"

"Not personally," Callahan said. "But he works for Señor Cardona. I'd bet the farm on it."

"Why?"

"As I was saying before we were so rudely reinterrupted, Cardona is fond of all sorts of exotic things—foreign cars, primitive art, Chinese women...Chinese boys. And these guys."

"Who the hell is he?"

"Jivaro. A headhunter. But not your run-of-the-mill corporate variety."

"You're joking."

"Uh-uh. I never joke. Not about headhunters, anyway. These guys are disappearing. Mostly Peruvian, they're losing out to twentieth-century progress. As the jungle gets more and more familiar, loggers, corporate farms, all that stuff, the native tribes are either getting assimilated or exterminated. This little rascal belongs to one of the least known and most feared. Cardona has—and don't ask me how—got a few of them on his payroll. That bamboo contraption is a blowgun. These bastards can shoot a dart a hundred yards. Accurately."

Callahan reached for a small leather pouch on a thin cord around the dead man's neck. He jerked hard, parting the cord, then flipped back the folding flap of the pouch. He pulled out what looked like a fistful of dark brown Pick-Up-Sticks, each with a puff of fiber, like a cotton ball, at one end.

"Yep, here they are," he said. He handed one to Bolan. "Be careful, don't stick yourself. It's poisoned. Curare, probably. You'd be dead in seconds."

Bolan looked at the small, slender reed. He was no stranger to the exotic packages in which death was delivered, but this had to be the most frail, least likely form imaginable.

"See," Callahan continued, "Cardona is a throwback, in some ways. More like a medieval baron, or a shogun. He has more money than the Bolivian government. Shit, you saw the file. Four *billion* dollars. Buying things nobody else can afford—guys like these—is something he can do that shows off his wealth and power. And that's real important to him.''

"I've seen his type before. We've got to take him down."
Callahan nodded. "It won't be easy."

"Let's see what else we've got here," Bolan said, moving back toward the wall. Callahan followed with the small torch. Another man, even smaller than the first, and like his companion dressed in rough black cotton, lay sprawled in a heap at the base of the wall. The blood on the black tunic was already clotting, as if trying to camouflage itself against the fabric. Three ragged holes marked the exit points of the three slugs Bolan had fired.

The two men moved quickly to the top of the wall, and Callahan shone the light down into the blackness on the other side. The third assassin lay on his back, a gaping hole where one temple should have been. Bolan's slug had taken him in the left cheek, then bored up and out, taking much of the left side of his face with it. Scraps of gray brain tissue clung to the shattered bone edges of the wound.

Callahan gagged slightly, then to cover his upset, laughed. "I'd say that was mighty fine shootin', pardner. I reckon these here fellers would be impressed."

"Yeah, well . . . It doesn't make much difference to them now, does it?"

"No." Callahan whispered his response. Under the swaggering cowboy fullback, Bolan knew, there was a different Brian Callahan, one with secrets he worked hard to keep. Bolan saw more than a little of himself in the young DEA man. He wasn't sure whether that was good or bad. Rather than try to decide, he chose the path of least resistance. He accepted it.

"I think I've had my fill of sightseeing tonight. Let's get out of here."

Bolan led the way back to the Bronco. He waited for the younger man to unlock the door and get in. Callahan then reached over to unlock Bolan's door. As he slid in, Callahan suddenly shouted, "Don't move!"

He pointed at Bolan's chest. There, dangling from the lapel of the tweed jacket, was a dart. Bolan gingerly pulled the shaft from his coat and examined it. Shaking his head, he snapped it in two, tossed the halves to the ground and opened his coat. There, a quarter inch from one edge of the Beretta harness, was a deep depression in the leather. The dart had narrowly missed punching through and killing him.

"That was a close one, buddy."

Before answering, Bolan bent and retrieved the pieces of the dart. "I think it's obvious Cardona knows we're here. I suppose it's about time we paid him a little visit."

CHAPTER SEVEN

Mack Bolan was angry. Not at the attempt on his life. He had come to expect that, part of him even relished it when he knew who wanted him dead, and why. But this was different. A high-priority, high-security operation had barely gotten off the ground, and already it had been compromised. If Cardona had sent someone after him and Callahan, it meant not only that Cardona knew of the operation itself, but also that he knew why he and Callahan were in La Paz. And that knowledge could mean only one thing: someone had told him.

Even Callahan couldn't be dismissed as a possible source of the leak. After all, he didn't know the kid, and although Cardona's bizarre hit team had failed, there was no way to know whether they were after Callahan, after him or after them both. Unless he knew that, Callahan had to be considered as a liability. Putting the very best face on things still meant someone on the inside was on Cardona's string. But Brognola had vouched for all the members of the team.

Great.

Now he had to wonder just how secure the operation might be. Over the years, Bolan had come to understand how public supposed secrets could become. Members of the clandestine communities had a tendency to unburden themselves to people they knew and trusted. It was only natural to want to share the weight.

You were constantly forced to do things you didn't like, sometimes couldn't stomach and often regretted. Do enough of them, and you wanted to let the steam off anyway you could.

Some agents drank themselves into oblivion or early retirement, others simply shared bits and pieces of their secret lives with family, the people with whom they were able to share so little that was normal. It was a way of including them, and preserving the illusion that what you did for a living was no different from a nine-to-five desk job at IBM. Everyone, except possibly the agent himself, knew this wasn't true, but families protect themselves from being torn apart. They do it any way they can. If it meant lying to themselves and to one another, so be it.

Bolan couldn't discount the possibility that someone had innocently told his wife or partner what was going on. But even if that was the cause of the problem, the consequences were no less deadly. No matter how, Cardona knew about the operation.

Then it wouldn't hurt to rattle his cage a little, right up front. If he was already nervous, so much the better. Let him lose a bit of sleep.

Callahan kept silent while he drove, as if he were in some other place. The roads were winding and treacherous enough, but there was more than concentration etched in the tight corners of his mouth. Bolan knew the look, had seen it on his own face often enough. Something had gone wrong, and somebody had to pay for the screwup.

But even that didn't let Callahan off the hook.

If Bolan was supposed to be taken out, then failure to accomplish that one little thing would itself be a screwup for the men who wanted it done. Cardona, certainly. Callahan? Who the hell knew?

The rusty tin roofs of the barrio shot by on either side. The Aymaras who lived in most of them were not large people, and the average roof was level with the line of sight afforded Bolan in the high-riding Bronco. He looked off over the huddled buildings into the night, broken here and there by a glimmer of light from a window only partially masked.

The sloping terraces gave every home a view of the terrain below, and it must have been hard to take for anyone who knew he didn't have the best of all possible worlds. The lavish homes of the Bolivian upper classes were spread out below them, impossible to ignore if you had eyes in your head.

And there was no point looking the other way, because all you could see was the base of the house above you on the slope and, if you craned your neck, the hard, unforgiving mountains beyond. Like a gargantuan saw blade, teeth to the heavens, the Andes cut off all hope in that direction. If you were poor and *paceno*, you aspired downward. The social ladder, like almost everything else in Bolivia, was upside down.

In La Paz, money showed its true weight and, incapable of ignoring gravity, it ran downhill to the bottom of the bowl. Somewhere in that bowl was Diego Cardona. Bolan wanted to get a look at the man, close up.

They passed into the heart of La Paz, and the change was abrupt. The cramped and winding streets of the barrio gave way to broad avenues. The tallest buildings, modest by North American standards, were still worlds apart from the residential area they had just left.

Even though nightlife in La Paz was limited, there was still some traffic. Those who could afford to party had a choice, but most often their preference was to entertain at home rather than bother with the discos that catered to the tourists, mostly American, who insisted on pub crawling wherever they happened to land.

In the heart of the city, almost at the bottom of the depression that contained it, the Plaza Murillo was lined with impressive government buildings. The presidential palace had seen more occupants than there had been years since its construction, but did its best to project a gravity suitable to the seat of government, no matter how restless that government might be.

The heart of the plaza was still busy, and well lit. Little groups of people clustered around the stray vendors who had something to offer, and a band of musicians was entertaining a small crowd. Bolan rolled down his window and listened to the plaintive sound that was older than the Incas.

The Bronco rolled smoothly over the well-paved Avenida Arce and shot out of the city center as quickly as it had entered. Ahead, Bolan could see trees and the placid gardens that could be cultivated only behind walls. This was where the wealthy and the foreigners lived. American businessmen, diplomats from all corners of the globe, Bolivians of influence and, more recently, the more successful of the *narcotraficantes*.

Not one to hide his light under a bushel, Diego Cardona had caused quite a stir when he acquired two adjoining estates. The stir became a scandal when he'd torn down the existing homes, lavish enough for most captains of industry, and the scandal an outcry when his new home had been erected. Flashy and outrageous, it had been designed by an American architect, who had been imported for six months at great expense to oversee its construction. Convention was something that bothered Cardona not at all, and it showed in the home he'd built for himself.

When they reached the edge of Cardona's property, Callahan slowed slightly and leaned over to point out the place to Bolan. He kept the Bronco moving to avoid calling attention to them, and said, "That's it. That's where the dragon lives."

Bolan said nothing.

They drifted past, Callahan falling back into the silence that had claimed him since they'd gotten into the car. Two blocks away, Callahan parked the Bronco on a pleasant, tree-lined avenue. When he turned off the engine, he sat with his arm extended, right hand on the ignition key, as if listening to something. Then, shaking himself, he opened the door and stepped out. Bolan joined him on the pavement, closing the car door carefully.

"Don't worry about the noise, Mack. There's enough money around here to absorb a Led Zeppelin concert. What we have to be careful of is the guards who patrol Cardona's place. If they know we're coming, and they obviously know we're in La Paz, you can bet they'll know what we look like."

"If they get close enough to see us, they're already in deep trouble."

Callahan shrugged and led the way down the street. The trees lining the avenue were so full, their branches interlaced, and the path ahead resembled a dark green tunnel. Callahan walked purposefully, his footfalls nearly silent on the broad, flat stones of the pavement.

After about a block, he stopped, signalling Bolan to come closer. "The next wall is the beginning of Cardona's place. What do you want to do?" he whispered.

"I want to see as much as I can. I'll be coming back here sooner or later. I want to know my way around."

"You can't see much from the street."

"Who says I'm staying on the street?"

"You don't plan to go inside, do you?"

"Hell, yes! How else am I going to get the layout of the place?" As much as he wanted to get inside the grounds, Bolan also wanted to see how Callahan reacted. If the kid had been turned, he'd never have a better chance to roll over on Bolan than he would with the big man in the belly of the beast. If he was going to work with the kid, he'd have to trust him. There was no better way to remove the uncertainty about that than by testing him.

Hard.

Bolan took the point, moving swiftly until he reached the bottom of the stone wall marking the edge of Cardona's estate. He knew from Brognola's papers that the twelve-foot wall was topped with broken glass and a ribbon of razor wire. These were hazards that could be avoided with a little caution. Not so easy to avoid, however, were the surveillance cameras. He couldn't take them out without alerting the security team, and he wasn't ready for a full-scale assault. Not yet.

But he had to get inside. Telling Callahan to wait, he walked along the base of the wall until he heard the soft whir of one of the cameras. It was sweeping back and forth in a semicircle, and paused at either end of the sweep. Each camera's range overlapped those on either side. Typical of its owner's arrogance, however, the home could be approached if you got over the wall. Cardona obviously assumed no one ever would, or he'd have been more discriminating in his choice of equipment.

That left only the electronic eyes to be avoided. They ranged directly along the wall, each beam paired with a sensor thirty feet away. As long as the beam was not interrupted, no alarm would sound. If he could clear that last obstacle, without being picked up by the surveillance camera, he would be home free.

Moving farther along the wall, Bolan found the next camera. He climbed the rough outcropping of the wall to a point just below the camera. Its lens barely peaked over the lip of the wall, and Bolan timed its oscillation four times, to make certain it wasn't random.

Keeping his stopwatch going, he moved back to the first camera and looked up. He sighed with relief when it poked its nose over the wall in perfect sync with the other one. He had the cycle down. Now all he needed was to find a tree he could use to get over the beam.

The only candidate stood almost midway between the two camera positions. With the oscillations synchronized, he'd have a narrow window every ten seconds when both cameras were pointing straight ahead, the tree falling just in the middle of the blind spot that shifted back and forth as they scanned the wall.

He moved back to Callahan's position and filled him in on his intentions. Callahan tried again to dissuade him, but Bolan shook off the warning. "There's no substitute for firsthand knowledge. I have to get inside. If I'm not back in sixty minutes, leave. I'll contact you when I get home."

"You mean if, don't you?"

"I said when, and I meant when."

Callahan was beginning to believe him.

"I'll be back," Bolan said, moving back in to the base of the wall. He sprinted to a spot directly opposite the tree. When his stopwatch signaled it was time, he raced across the pavement to the tree, slipping behind it. In successive moves, the black-clad warrior made his way up the tree, out on a limb and, in one final leap, over the wall. He landed heavily on the other side, holding his breath to listen.

Silence.

He didn't know whether he'd been seen, but at least he hadn't triggered the alarm. The lawn between the wall and the house was broad, but broken with clumps of shrubbery and trees. Moving from one to the next, Bolan approached the house swiftly. Security made no regular sweeps, so he didn't have to worry about patrols, as long as he made no sound.

The design of the building was anything but ideal, from the standpoint of an unwanted intruder who wished to gain entrance. Large flat faces of smooth stone or glass offered no handholds to reach the balconies that jutted out beneath several of the second-floor rooms.

Making his way along the foundation of the house, Bolan searched for a way in. An irregular polygon, the house was totally unpredictable. Along the third wall he'd examined, Bolan found an alcove where two walls met at an acute angle. In one face of flat polished stone was a pair of sliding glass doors. The room beyond was dark.

Bolan tried the door, but it was locked. He bent to examine the track and noticed only a narrow band of glass beneath the track rim. The door itself showed no sign of being wired. Placing both hands flat against the glass, he pressed inward. When no alarm sounded, he pressed upward.

The heavy glass gave and Bolan pushed harder. Glancing down, he saw he had the clearance he needed. Bracing the weight of the door on one toe, he slid one hand to the edge of the glass. He had just enough room for two fingers. Sliding the fingers in he tugged, still keeping his foot under the glass. The door gave slightly, and he could insert the rest of his hand. He tugged again. Still no alarm. One final yank, and the door was free.

He moved the heavy glass panel aside and leaned it against the stone. Once again, he paused to listen. Sounds from deep in the house drifted to his ear, but he hadn't been heard. The filmy curtain swung gently in the breeze. Taking a deep breath, Bolan stepped inside.

Diego Cardona had company.

CHAPTER EIGHT

Salvatore Maggadino was an imposing man by any measure. He was nearly six feet five inches tall, and at age sixty-three he weighed the same two hundred fifty pounds he'd weighed for almost forty years. Either hand would have justified his nickname of "The Hammer," and the arms to which they were attached were no less impressive. His hair was still coal-black, although somewhat thinning in recent years, and occasionally rumors circulated among some of the younger members of the family that he had been adding a bit of color.

His energy, legendary among the wise guys, hadn't flagged, but he was more tolerant, and less easily aroused to anger than he once had been. What some would have called wisdom, hotter heads were quick to categorize as approaching senility. For several years the underbosses—of which there were three—had been currying favor and, to cover their substantial bets, maneuvering among themselves, hoping for the honor of succeeding him.

Sally The Hammer was no fool. He recognized a threat when he saw one. When it came from outside the family, he knew what to do. When it came from inside, a little more caution was necessary. His business was not just business. He ran the family in Miami, had built it from scratch. Now he was threatened from outside and from within.

The greaseballs from South America wanted what he had, and the young turks wanted more. They wanted him out of the way, right now. And, more than anything, they wanted to fight the greaseballs on their own terms. To them, Sally was old news. The Hammer was a little rusty, a throwback to a more genteel era, when crime was more disciplined and criminals were honorable men. Gentility, to the firebrands, was indistinguishable from softness. Sally, they said, had gone soft, and they couldn't afford it.

Sally knew what they were saying about him, mostly behind his back, but loud enough for him to hear. Well, he'd show them a thing or two. He was still the man, and tonight he was going to show them. All of them.

And they were all there. Whatever they thought, they were still frightened enough to come when he hollered. Maybe they didn't ask how high anymore, but they still jumped. As long as that was true, he had a chance. Whether they knew it or not, he was looking out for them.

And God knew some of the bastards didn't deserve it. What they didn't seem to realize was that times had changed. In the old days, if you said anything negative about the boss, you were liable to fight for your last breath hanging on a meat hook someplace cold and dark. Those were the days when anything went.

But times had changed and the Mafia had changed with them. It was either that or go the way of the Indians. Any asshole could shoot it out to the last man. But that didn't solve anything. The way of the future had been to go corporate, be orderly, pay attention to business. Luciano knew that, and Lansky showed them how to do it.

Even the last of the cowboys, such as Genovese and Gambino, had learned to live with this new way of doing business. Some of them couldn't adjust, and they paid a high price for their inflexibility. Benny Siegel had paid it, and nobody but Charlie Lucky knew how much it hurt to lose a friend like that. But the organization was bigger than one man. The minute you forgot that, you were in trouble.

A student of politics, Sally knew the dangers in the cult of personality. He was the supreme organization man. And he knew how hard it was to subjugate your instincts. Hell, he had fought against the corporate way, too. But he learned. He wasn't just a wise guy, he was a wise man, not quite old and far from through.

Looking around the room, he saw the future, a seamless fabric rooted in the past. The faces were different, but the attitudes were still the same. These young hotheads were no different from himself and his friends forty years before. Sure, they wore better suits and had fancy haircuts. They didn't "dese" and "dose" you like the Mustache Petes, selling chickens from the backyard on Saturday afternoons.

But under the fancy veneer, they were still punks, some greedy, some just stupid. Some of them could be taught and some would never learn. Sally knew the day would come when he'd have to step aside, but there were still a few things on his personal agenda, things unattended to. As long as he was still running the show, there was a chance to attend to them. Tonight, he would begin.

Sitting in his high-backed leather chair, he wondered which of them wanted him out of the way the most. Johnny Carlucci, the weasel-faced fashion plate on the end, his hair razor cut and moussed, just brushing the collar of his Brooks Brothers suit, had been making the most noise. That probably meant he was the smallest threat. In this business, if you were going to whack the boss, you didn't tell anybody. You didn't even whisper it. Like any business, the family was full of guys you couldn't trust. Like General Motors, you never knew who they were. Until it was too late.

Peter DiMarzio, his studied visage a product of his Ivy League school and his social-climbing mother, was too intellectual for the rough stuff. He relied on the walnut-framed MBA from Harvard Business hanging in his office to get his way. It was less certain than muscle, but it was more businesslike. Peter would have been at home on Wall Street, but he was probably too honest to make a go of it. No, it wasn't Peter, either.

Next to the schoolboy was a slab of muscle. Frank Ianni, "Talking Mule," had the IQ of a newt. He was all balls and no common sense. When you wanted somebody to know you were serious, you had Frank deliver the message. He might follow somebody's lead, but Sally knew that Frank was loyal because he was too dumb not to be.

That left Joey Buccieri. Joey Boy. He had all the ingredients. Overweening pride, the pinched, ambitious face of Cassius, two mistresses and a wife. The pride and the ambition Sally could handle. The women cost money, lots of money. And Joey didn't know how to say no. If one of them wanted a fur coat, he bought them all a mink. A tootsie wanted a new car, they all got new convertibles. For Joey Buccieri, life was an expensive habit.

Seated around the large oak table in Maggadino's dining room, the men were growing restless. Finally Buccieri opened his mouth.

"Come on, Sally, time is money. What's this all about?"

"When I'm ready, Joey. When I'm ready. I don't want to say nothing reckless."

"Well say something, for Christ's sake," Buccieri snapped. "I got a date."

"That's your big problem, Joey. You got too many dates." Sal spoke almost fondly, smiling at the man seated directly across the table from him.

"No, Sal, he doesn't get enough ass, that's his problem," Ianni suggested.

The others laughed while Buccieri did a slow burn. He opened his mouth to reply, but Sal raised a hand, and Buccieri lit a cigarette, snapping two wooden matches before the third caught fire. He slammed the cigarettes down on the table, tossing the small foil-wrapped matchbox on top of the pack. Sal noticed it was from Maison Bonaparte, the priciest restaurant in Miami.

"What I want to know," Maggadino began, "is what is this business over on the Causeway the other night?"

"That was the greaseballs, Sally. You know, the Bolivians. They whacked four of our guys, and a couple of cops."

"That I know, Joey. Tell me something I don't know."

"Like?"

"Like what were these cops doing there in the first place?"

"How the hell should I know?"

"Do you have any idea how much I had invested in those two cops?" Sally yelled. One big fist pounded the table. "Three years, I spent, and I don't even know how much money. And what do I got now? What's a dead cop worth to me, Joey? How much?"

Buccieri looked stunned. "They were on the string for you?"

"That's right."

"I had no idea, Sally. I thought they—"

"An idea ain't all you don't got, Joey Boy."

"Sally, look, it was a sure thing, you know. Take down a couple of small-timers and roll over the nose candy. Cut down the competition and get a couple of free keys. There's real money in the snow. We can't walk away from that kind of score, let the greaseballs have it all to themselves. We've got to compete, Sal. You know, grow or die, like Petey says."

"What about what *I* say, Joey? You want to discuss the philosophy of business with Peter, fine. But ask him about business administration, while you're at it. Ask him who the CEO of this outfit is. And about this business of your working behind my back, we have to talk."

"Sally, I swear to God, I didn't mean—"

"Not now, Joey, not now. We'll talk some other time."

Buccieri inhaled sharply on the cigarette, then stubbed it out in a large glass ashtray. The butt bent in two and broke. It lay in the ashtray smoldering. Buccieri watched the tenuous strand of smoke coiling upward for a few moments before answering.

"Sally, I know you think we ought to go slow. We talked about it before. But you've also got to know the way things are. We let the greaseballs corner the market on this thing, we're never going to get 'em out. As it is, they're way ahead of us. Shit, the drug scene is changing. Every day there's something new. Read the papers, for God's sake, Sal, will you? I know all that shit about how you guys were there in the beginning, and how you built the heroin traffic from scratch. But heroin is old hat, Sally. So is coke. Crack is what's happening today. Tomorrow, God knows. But we've got to be there. At the beginning. Just like you were.''

"I know what you think, Joey Boy." Maggadino's controlled rage made the nickname sound like an insult. "And what I think is that you *don't* think. You don't think, Joey. All you know is money for your whores. I don't like that. It's no good, Joey Boy. No good.''

"You trying to tell me you never fooled around, Sal?''

"Number one, we're talking about you, not me. Number two, what I'm saying is be discreet. Stop thinking with your dick. It's not right, the way you treat Roseann. And it's not smart. Especially it's not smart to ignore what I'm telling you about this crack business.''

Buccieri stood up and began to pace back and forth behind his chair. He paused once to look at Maggadino, then resumed his restless movement. "Sally, why don't you ask the others what they think? Why are you reaming my ass, when you don't even know whether anybody agrees with me?''

"Joey, I don't give a rat's ass what the others think. I'm the boss. I'm in charge here, and when I say think what you're doing, I expect you to think." One hamlike fist slammed the table again. Buccieri's matchbox bounced off the cigarette pack and landed on its edge. The gold foil gleamed in the soft light from overhead.

Ianni reached out, placed the matches back where they'd been. "Sal's right, Joey. He's the boss. That's all I need to know.''

"Stay out of this, Frankie. You don't know shit.''

"Joey, sit down, will you?" DiMarzio asked. "We should talk about this from a business perspective. You're getting too wound up.''

"The hell with your perspective, and the hell with you, too. You guys are all chickenshit. The greaseballs will bury all of us if we don't do something."

"What would you like us to do, Joey?" Maggadino asked. His voice was unruffled, the very soul of reason, but there was an edge to the question, one he sharpened as he continued. "You want us to murder women and children, like the greaseballs? You want us to waste whole families, because somebody didn't bring the right amount of money with him? You want us to make widows, then orphans in the blink of an eye? We don't do business that way. That's no business for a man of honor."

"Honor? You want to talk about honor? I'll show you honor, Sal. I'll take you to St. Paul's Cemetery and show you Tony Lamonica's headstone. Would that be enough honor for you? Because you know what, Sal? It's too much honor for me. I don't need that kind of honor."

"And would Tony be in St. Paul's at all if you hadn't told him to go ahead?"

"*I* didn't tell Tony shit, Sal. Tony did what he had to do. I knew about it, sure. But so what? If you weren't such a goddamned pussy, we wouldn't have to be talking about it now."

"Hold on, Joey," Carlucci said. "You've got no business talking to Sal that way. Where's your respect?"

"Respect my ass. I've got no business talking that way? Well, I've got news for you, pally. If I keep listening to Sal, I've got no business, period. So, what's it going to be? You going to listen to this shit, or are you going to be a man? You going to let the greaseballs walk all over you, or are you going to take what's yours?"

"I think that's up to Sal, Joey." DiMarzio reached for the cigarettes. He took one and lit it inexpertly. Sal had seen him smoke only twice before, in twenty years.

"You nervous about something, Peter?" The old man's voice was genuinely concerned.

"No, Sal, no. I'm just a little upset, is all. I don't like all this dissension. It's counterproductive."

"Listen to the college boy," Buccieri snorted. "Why the hell don't you say what you mean, and quit hiding behind those big words?"

"I said what I meant." DiMarzio took a drag on the cigarette, then exhaled the smoke in a long thin stream. He resumed speaking before the smoke had cleared, and his words ruffled the small cloud hanging just in front of him. "But for the uninitiated—and the inarticulate—what I meant was that this discussion is not about business at all. It's about personalities, and there's no place for that in an efficiently run business. Cold, impersonal logic is more important than petty disagreements."

"I'm not petty," Buccieri countered. "And if anybody here is being illogical, it isn't me. It's not logical to walk away from millions of dollars in profits, month in and month out. It's even less logical to stand around and watch somebody else pick up your money and walk away with it. That's not logical. Maybe it is to Sal, but not to me."

Maggadino said nothing. DiMarzio had had his say. The others waited patiently. Finally the old man stood. "Joey, the one thing you don't want to understand—and this isn't logical to me—is that this is not a democracy. You can't run a business that way. You run a car dealership, you don't have some guy selling fish in the front office, just because he feels like it. Not as long as I'm alive. When somebody else is sitting in this chair, take it up with him. But I don't want to hear any more about it. And the next time any one of you feels like doing something like this, you make god-damned sure you talk to me first. Understood?"

Buccieri nodded. The others voiced their assent.

The difference was not lost on Salvatore Maggadino.

La Paz

CHAPTER NINE

The room was pitch-black. A door across the room was evident from the narrow band of light at its bottom. Bolan stepped inside, his feet sinking into a deep-pile carpet. With one hand extended in front of him, he made his way cautiously toward the door. As his eyes adjusted to the darkness, he could pick out dim shapes of furniture against one wall and the low bulk of a bed. He reached for his cigarette lighter, clicked it on to get his bearings, and then extinguished it. In the brief illumination, he noticed little other than the raw contours of the room, but he'd seen enough to make it to the door.

Pressing his ear to the door, he strained to hear what was going on deeper inside the house. He could hear at least three voices, one of which was markedly higher in pitch, probably a woman's. Bolan knew that Cardona, like most of the druglords, was a frequent entertainer. Even smugglers had their business lunches and working weekends.

The light under the door was bright, but he'd have to take a chance. He could learn nothing by staying where he was. He tried the knob. It felt cold to the touch, but turned smoothly and silently. He braced one arm against the doorframe and pulled gently, hoping the hinges were quiet and the clearance enough to permit a noiseless opening.

The sudden burst of light momentarily blinded him. When his pupils contracted he could see a long corridor extending straight ahead, two doors on either side of its length, evenly spaced between the doorway he stood in and the blank wall at the other end. He paused to listen. The same brilliant white carpet as that in the bedroom lined the long hallway. It must have been a hell of a vacuuming job.

The voices were louder, but still unintelligible. Venturing into the hall was risky. If anyone entered the other end or opened one of the four doors, he'd be hung out to dry. There was no place to hide. Paintings hung on both walls of the corridor, but it held nothing else, not even a table to hide behind. If he was discovered, and if his discoverers were armed, there'd be hell to pay.

He stepped into the hall, unholstering the .44 AutoMag and chambering a round, muffling the sound of the slide with one palm. Moving silently he approached the first door on the left. An ear to the polished wood panel told him nothing. He turned the knob and pushed. The door swung open on a dark room.

Stepping through the doorway, he closed the door and felt for the light. Its mercury switch glowed dimly in the dark wall. The switch was noiseless, and a soft glow bathed the room in response to his touch. Like the first room, this one was uninhabited. Furniture, identical to that of the other room, lined the walls, as if Cardona bought in bulk. It was as if the first room had been rotated ninety degrees. Satisfied that he had a safe haven if he had to duck out of the hallway in a hurry, Bolan turned off the light. The hall was still empty.

Bolan checked the remaining three rooms in quick succession. Each was a replica of the first two. Each was empty. As he approached the end of the hallway, the voices grew louder. Now he could catch an occasional fragment of conversation. Two men and a woman were talking, the men in Spanish, the woman in flawless English. Her accent placed her origin in the Chicago area. It was clear that she understood the men, but preferred to use her native language. From all he could hear, it was nothing more than casual conversation.

At the end of the corridor, Bolan had a choice. Another hallway intersected the first, each of its arms roughly twenty feet long. The same arctic-white carpet covered the floor, continuing the seamless expanse unbroken from the door through which he'd come. The voices were echoing along the right arm of the hall. Bolan turned left. He was here to see, not to be seen.

No doors broke the length of stark white wall. Two paintings hung on each wall, all four of them the formless graffiti smears that were vandalism in the subway and art in the gallery. Cardona was a happening kind of guy, trendy if tasteless. Bolan brushed past the first canvas, then paused at the next intersection. The hall bent to the right. Another hollow white tube, this one marked by a bright glow at its end.

The voices had faded to a background murmur. Bolan was moving away from the three people who seemed to be the only inhabitants of the capacious house. After the pinched hovels he'd just seen, it struck him as obscene that a man like Cardona could have room to burn. Moving cautiously, Bolan approached the bright wall. He stopped just before reaching the end of the hall. To his left, a flight of stairs led upward, while to the right, a scant ten feet away, he could see one end of a sunken living room. The stairs were inviting. He checked his watch. He still had a half hour before having to get back to Callahan.

Bolan nipped around the corner and took the steps two at a time. The second floor was more dimly lit, but the entire house seemed to be constantly aglow, as if the lights were meant to spend themselves. The stairs led to a long hallway that was open on its right side. The acute angle prevented Bolan from seeing much more than a waist-high banister of burnished mahogany. He slipped toward the opening. The voices below were growing louder again.

At the beginning of the banister, Bolan stopped. The open hall was more like a balcony. It overlooked a huge room nearly thirty feet high, which was like a central courtyard surrounded by the rest of the house. Its towering walls were adorned with a number of large canvases, paintings that were more ambitious versions of the spray-can specials he'd seen in the hall. Cardona might not know much about art, but he knew what he liked.

Leaning as close as he dared, Bolan tried to peer over the balustrade into the pit below. The room was generously furnished with sectional pieces that could be arranged in a variety of patterns. If anything, they were even whiter than the carpet. Like a hooker thumbing her nose at convention on her wedding day, Cardona had wrapped himself in the color of innocence.

The woman was facing away from Bolan. He could make out the top of her head, and one shoulder. She was blond, but that figured, given Cardona's obvious affection for things pale. Sitting across from the woman, a large man with a bushy head of jet-black hair was pouring a Dos Equis with half an eye. The beer foamed up and over the glass. With his free hand he gestured to the woman, who laughed, the sound brittle in the huge room.

Next to the large man was a less imposing figure. Slender, slightly effeminate, hands coiled loosely in his lap, his thoughts to be somewhere else. His head was angled toward the larger man, but his expression was listless. His eyes appeared, even at this distance, to be glazed. A vacant smile flitted across his features at regular intervals, regardless of the rhythm of the conversation.

Diego Cardona had his mind on other things.

And it was he, for sure. The photos in Brognola's dossier had been accurate, but had fallen short, the way photos often do. The camera can seldom—except in the hands of an artist—capture the essence, the soul of a person. A plain woman of intelligence and charm can be a ravishing beauty in the flesh, while seeming a dowdy frump in a family snapshot. And Bolan had never seen a photo of Hitler that captured the monster behind the mustache. Cardona, of course, wasn't in that league, but not for lack of trying.

While Bolan watched, trying to get a handle on the man, Cardona stood and stretched. He was dressed in a floor-length white caftan, its starkness broken only by a narrow band of scarlet piping and a scarlet sash. His feet were bare, and as he walked restlessly behind the sofa, he moved with almost elfin grace, the sinuous moves of a panther somehow transformed to heighten the impression of femininity.

It was so damned tempting to give Big Thunder free rein, but it would be self-defeating. An organization like Cardona's was like a hydra: you struck too soon, cut off one head, and two took its place. They wanted him firmly entrenched. Only another few days, the way he was moving. You had to snuff it out all at once, root and branch. Anything less was treating the symptom instead of the disease. They wanted Cardona, but not just the man. They wanted what he stood for. They wanted his mules and his muscle, his couriers and his chemists. Anything less would be nothing at all.

Bolan watched in fascination. He'd seen it all, been there and back. And yet it never ceased to amaze him in how many ways evil could be camouflaged. That a man of so little substance could be responsible for so much misery was either one of God's nastier jokes or a testimonial to the limitless span of human aspiration. Men like Cardona lived by one rule, and one rule only: Want? Take!

It was that simple.

Bolan checked his watch. He had less than fifteen minutes. Callahan wasn't supposed to wait, and he wasn't supposed to come after him. But Bolan knew enough about human nature—and had seen enough of the young DEA man—to know that Callahan would ignore his instructions if he failed to return. Bolan's law never failed. If you find yourself in a china shop, you can bet your ass there's a bull nearby.

The last thing they needed was to let it all hang out this early. There was too much to learn yet. It was only the top of the first inning, and the Executioner hadn't even left the dugout. This was a game they needed to win. A forfeit was unthinkable. It was bad enough that Cardona knew they were in La Paz. And that, too, was something Bolan wanted to know more about.

Inching away from the balustrade, Bolan saw the blonde stand and disappear from view. The big man on the sofa downed his Dos Equis in a single draft, placed the glass on the alabaster table with a sharp crack, then tilted the bottle for the last few drops. He stood and stretched, his arms extended over his head. The forearms were massive, the upper arms more massive still. Whatever his role in the Cardona organization, he wasn't there because of his intellectual capacity.

For a moment Bolan thought he'd been spotted. The big man was staring up at the balcony. His close-set eyes, reminiscent of a wild boar's, squinted as if he'd seen something. Bolan held his breath. For several seconds, the man continued to stare, then with a shake of his head he mumbled something and crossed the room, heading away from Bolan and out of sight at the far end of the central gallery.

Cardona wandered aimlessly, as if lost in a maze that no one but he could see. As Bolan drew the rest of the way back, Cardona raised both hands over his head, letting the loose sleeves of the caftan slide back toward his shoulders, to reveal frail, reedlike arms the color of toast. Like a high priest sermonizing to a multitude, he stood with arms upraised. He tilted his head back and began to laugh. The wheezy rasp was overwhelming, and Bolan wondered how such a sound could emanate from so diminutive a figure. Then Cardona, too, vanished, following the big man out of Bolan's line of sight.

Retracing his steps, Bolan reached the stairs and took them singly, taking care to make no noise. Winding back through the hallways, he reached the room through which he'd entered the house. Stepping in, he closed the door behind him and crossed to the sliding glass door.

Stepping through, he turned and hoisted the glass, trying to maneuver it back into place. As it fell into place, a shout erupted behind him. He turned to see a uniformed guard

sprinting toward him, an ugly automatic in his left hand.
The guard stopped no more than four feet away. He gestured with the gun, and Bolan raised his hands. Another
gesture, and Bolan turned back toward the house. He felt
the sharp prod of the gun and knew he had a chance. The
guard was reckless.

A quick frisk turned up the AutoMag, and the guard
yanked it from its holster. The thud of the .44 was muffled
by the thick grass when the guard tossed it aside. He
resumed the frisk, found the Beretta and tossed it after the
AutoMag. When he found no other weapons, the guard
stepped back. In crisp Spanish, he instructed his captive to
turn around. Bolan understood and did as he was told.

The guard stepped forward to poke Bolan in the ribs with
the pistol, then shoved him toward the front of the house.
Bolan fell to one knee, pivoting as he did so. Behind him, a
bright glare bathed the lawn. Someone had entered the room
and turned on the light. Bolan reached into his pocket as the
guard stepped back with a curse. He told Bolan to get up.

Leaning forward, the guard waved his pistol under Bolan's nose. Bolan began to stand, bringing his right hand up
in a swift arc, catching the guard under the chin. The glare
behind him grew still brighter as the curtains were swept
aside. The guard staggered back, his breath coming in short,
spasmodic gasps. Dropping his gun, he brought both hands
up under his chin and fell backward. Spasms racked his
body for a few seconds, then he lay still. Between his fingers, the bright light just picked out the broken shaft of the
curare dart.

The Executioner turned toward the wall, grabbed the
AutoMag and wheeled toward the doorway. There, in a
snow-white peignoir, stood the blonde he'd seen in the central gallery. One clenched fist was pressed against her open
mouth. Her eyes were huge, glazed with fear and with
something else . . . recognition. She stepped back from the
door and Bolan thought she was going to scream or to run,
or both. She ran to the doorway, and the light was gone.

Bolan waited, but the door never opened. She had extinguished the light, but stayed in the room.

Bolan, too, had had the shock of recognition.

The woman was Valerie Russell.

CHAPTER TEN

The phone wouldn't quit. Bolan rolled over and grabbed the receiver on the nightstand. He looked at the clock: 6:00 a.m. Whoever it was, it was too damn early.

"Hello?"

"Rise and shine, Bolan."

"Who's this?"

"Callahan, who else?"

"It's early."

"Didn't your mother tell you about the early bird and the worm? I'll be by in fifteen minutes. We got business." Callahan hung up without saying goodbye.

Fully awake, Bolan stared at the ceiling, wondering what business couldn't wait. He had tossed away half the night, trying to fit the pieces together. What was Valerie Russell doing at Cardona's? Was she on his string, or just a fun-loving girl who liked action, no matter where it came from? There were no answers, and he knew it. Not yet, anyway. But that didn't stop him from wondering about the connection.

Rousing himself, Bolan dressed hurriedly. When he reached the lobby of the hotel, Callahan was already there.

"What took you so long?" he asked.

"Funny. You called from the lobby, didn't you?"

"Hell, yes. No point running up the DEA's phone bill. We got enough budget problems."

"What's up?"

"One of our boys turned in an interesting little piece of intel. We got a lead on Cardona's biggest processing lab. At least it's his now. Used to belong to Ricardo Ribiero. The latest thing on wheels. Thought you might want to come along while we knock it over.''

"You better believe it."

"Let's roll, then."

Callahan's Bronco was out front, illegally parked. A policeman was just tearing a ticket from his book as they left the lobby. Callahan ran over to the cop. They exchanged angry words, Callahan gesticulating like an irate Italian shopkeeper, the cop moving nothing but his lips. The cop won. Callahan snatched the ticket, tore it up and threw the pieces into the back of the Bronco.

The cop smiled.

Bolan got into the Bronco, and Callahan, still muttering, walked around to the driver's side.

"What was that all about?" Bolan asked.

"Son of a bitch wanted a hundred pesos to tear up the ticket."

"So tell me why you didn't pay him."

"That's one of the big problems down here. Cops come plenty cheap. You can imagine how easy it is for the dealers to buy them. Hell, that guy probably makes fifty bucks a month tops, legit. On the side, he probably makes five times that. Gouging the tourists."

"Where we headed?"

"The woods, my friend. The forest."

"In this thing?"

"Nope. We got to stop off and pick up a jeep. And a few other goodies."

Callahan started the Bronco and peeled out into traffic, narrowly missing a bus that had as many people clinging to the outside as it had inside.

As if the ticket had freed him from all restraint, Callahan drove like a madman, or a Tokyo taxi driver. He pushed the Bronco through spaces that seemed too small, weaving in and out of the heavy traffic and alternately goosing the 4X4 and slamming on the brakes. The entire performance was accompanied by a steady stream of profanities, mostly local in origin and rendered in impeccable Spanish.

At the staging area, they were met by four other men who were already paired in jeeps. The engines were running. A third jeep was empty, but its engine, too, was running. Callahan hit the ground on the fly, Bolan right behind him. As the two men ran, the occupied jeeps began to roll.

They climbed into their vehicle and it lurched after the others, throwing Bolan back against the seat.

Over the roaring engine and grinding gears, Callahan shouted, "Check the back. Make sure we didn't forget anything."

Holding on to the side of the jouncing vehicle, Bolan looked over his shoulder. Two Uzi SMGs were bouncing madly on the rear seat. Several spare magazines rattled and bounced on the floor.

"Why Uzis?" Bolan shouted.

"You'll see," Callahan hollered back, smiling for the first time since getting the ticket.

The small convoy sped over the bumpy road. Neither Callahan nor Bolan spoke. The countryside was rocky and barren, but they were heading downhill toward a green line that couldn't have been more sharply etched if drawn with a ruler. Bolan knew the rain forest wasn't prime coca-leaf country. The scraggly plant thrived in the rocky wastes higher in the mountains, where it could get all the sunlight it needed. But the forest was better cover. The harvested leaves were taken there and processed in knocked-together sheds. Most of the drug czars were masters of cost effective processing. After all, they had better things to do with their money.

Any DEA man could tell dozens of stories about abortive raids on deserted plants. They hauled ass into the boonies only to find vacant sheds, sometimes with ashes still warm in the camp fires. The network of information that had grown up around the trade was an impressive thing. It was more efficient than most intelligent agencies, and sold its product to the highest bidder. Bolan wondered whether he was going to get a firsthand look at that kind of frustration.

The convoy's haste was spurred as much by the knowledge that they were probably already too late as by any eagerness to exchange fire with the smugglers. The success ratio was so low that the DEA was riddled with burnout cases, guys who had come up short once too often. Some of them just drifted away, catching on with another agency, some were rotated back for desk jobs and some, the worst, were turned around. Rusting away from the inside, tired of the endless struggle that seemed to do no good—and cost them so much nervous energy—they became part of the problem.

There were all kinds. Some just sold what they knew to anyone who would pay. Others simply switched sides. They took their knowledge and used it to advantage, slipping through the loopholes they knew only too well. One score was all they needed, but for some the energy high was addictive. They went full bore, setting up their own networks and sending kilo after kilo back home just for the thrill of getting away with it. For these guys, the money was secondary. It was nice, for once, to be the winner, to be able to stand in the hills and watch the DEA ants swarm around an empty camp, looking for something, anything at all to justify continuing the fight. Knowing how seldom anyone found it was all the comfort they needed.

The roadside was broken by splashes of color, as Aymaras in their woven ponchos and caps made their way up to La Paz. Many of them were accompanied by burros nearly hidden by the bundled coca leaves they were bringing to market. The coca farmers were legitimate in Bolivia, but much of their produce found its way into the export market, which paid better and didn't require them to haul the stuff into the cities and villages. The drug dealers could afford trucks. They picked up the crop. It was a good deal for everyone concerned.

After the boiling in kerosene and refining down, a ton of coca leaves yielded only fifteen or twenty pounds of paste. For such volume, technology put Stone Age techniques to shame.

The dry soil kicked up in small clouds, and the air was cold. It was getting easier to breathe, and Bolan knew they were getting close. Ahead, the road vanished into the green wall of the forest. The lead jeep seemed to accelerate, as if it sensed the nearness of their goal. Callahan, too, leaned on the gas. Time was their biggest enemy at this point.

The first trees exploded past, and the road began to level off. They were still miles from the nearest real jungle, but the air seemed warmer, and moist in comparison to the dry atmosphere of the mountains.

Callahan broke his silence for the first time. "Don't like this at all."

"What's wrong?"

"We were supposed to meet a detachment of the Bolivian army at the edge of the forest. Where the hell are they?"

"Do we need them?"

"Can't say. Some of these camps look like guerrilla bases. The pay is good, and they usually have more and better weapons than the good guys. It's not hard to understand why it's so easy to get recruits."

Bolan said nothing. The jeep continued its headlong plunge into the forest. Two miles farther in, the driver of the lead jeep held up a hand. They were getting close. From this point on, they had to move quietly. The jeeps slowed, their engines droning now rather than roaring. The lead driver set the pace, stopping every three or four hundred yards. After the fourth stop, he killed the engine and hopped down to the leafy mulch littering the forest floor.

When the two remaining jeeps drew up beside him, he said, "We have to go on foot the rest of the way. It's about a mile ahead, but sound travels out here. And they'll probably have lookouts posted."

He reached to the floor of his jeep and grabbed an Uzi. Handing it to his partner, he reached back for a second SMG, slung it over his shoulder and bent to retrieve the ammo clips. He gave four to his partner and kept four for himself.

"We're supposed to use M-16s," Callahan said. "You know, buy American and all that. But these babies are a lot more useful out here. Easier to maneuver when you're running through scrub."

"I never had any trouble with the 16 in Nam," Bolan said.

"Yeah! And we won that one, didn't we?"

Bolan said nothing. This was not the place for a political discussion. And from what he'd seen so far, there was little difference between the two situations. These guys, too, were fighting a war their superiors wouldn't let them win.

The driver of the lead jeep took the point. The remaining five men straggled along, strung out at intervals for safety. Bolan had a flash of déjà vu. This was all starting to feel familiar, too familiar.

Unlike real jungle, with its tangled undergrowth, the floor of the forest was relatively open. Dense clumps of scrub were scattered randomly, but the growth was sporadic, some places almost clear. It was a blessing and a curse. It would be easy to get to their target, but there wouldn't be much cover when they did.

They moved at a brisk pace. When they'd covered a thousand yards, the point man, Cowan, moved out ahead. One man had a better chance of getting in close unobserved. Once he'd scouted the encampment, he could fill the others in and they'd decide what to do next. The five men squatted and watched. Moving from bush to bush, the team leader was sprinting low, his feet making no sound on the soft cushion.

He disappeared, and the others stared at the ground. This was no time for conversation. At such times, Bolan knew, every man kept his own counsel. You did what you had to do to get ready, told yourself lies, mumbled pep talks under your breath, or you paced, trying to make your mind a perfect blank. The theory was that if you kept your head empty, you'd react better, faster. The sudden rush of information needed a clear route to your feet and your trigger finger. Quick was better than fast. There was no time for a head of steam.

Bolan looked overhead at the bright blue sky. Thin clouds, almost transparent in the midmorning sun, drifted by in a seamless film of gauze. The forest was silent. Even the small birds seemed hushed. An occasional insect dived in close, then with an angry buzz dashed off again.

Callahan was drawing aimlessly in the moldy litter, a thin stick in his hand tracing patterns of moisture where it uncovered the dry top layer of shredded leaves.

When it came, the noise was almost deafening. Gunfire, automatic.

The men leaped to their feet and sprinted toward the sound. It had been a single chatter, one long, stuttering burst, then nothing. As he ran, Bolan kept hoping for more shots. Return fire would mean that Cowan was still alive. The silence was ominous. Their feet rose and fell on the spongy surface, soft thuds of large men in rapid movement. That was all.

Bursting through a thick clump of shrubbery, Bolan spotted the camp directly ahead of him. Thin strands of smoke rose from several points, two camp fires and the distilling fires used to boil the coca leaves into mash. Cowan was nowhere in sight. The camp seemed deserted.

Bolan was the first man into the open. Keeping low, he raced toward a makeshift shed. It was the only substantial structure in the clearing. He noticed tire tracks on the ground, three vehicles at least. Bolan heard the others right behind him. He turned to signal them by hand, and waited until they'd spread out in a ragged line across one end of the clearing. With the men in place, he edged along the shed, the Uzi gripped tightly in one hand. Flattening himself against one corner, he peered around the side of the building. Nothing.

A door of raw lumber hung open in the middle of the shed. Bolan sprinted to the door, dived past it and came up on the other side. The interior of the shed was quiet. Bolan peeked into the darkness, which was broken by narrow bands of bright white light pouring through the hastily thatched roof. He waited for his eyes to adjust, then plunged forward.

He searched the interior, sweeping it with the muzzle of the Uzi at the same time. A dark mass in one corner caught his eye, and he was about to step toward it when he heard something behind him, in the doorway. He turned, ready to let off a burst from the Uzi. It was Callahan.

"You see anything?" Callahan whispered.

"Yeah, over here." Bolan moved toward the shadowy clump and dropped to one knee. It was a man lying on his stomach, very still. And very dead. He grabbed one shoulder of the dead man, feeling the sticky wetness he knew so well. He didn't have to turn the man over to know it was Cowan.

Callahan stood over him for a moment, then wheeled and, with a bellow, lashed out at the corrugated-tin wall of the shed. It fell away with an angry rumble as light poured in through the gaping hole. Cowan had been riddled with bullets. His camou shirt was a solid, dark red, broken only by ragged tears where the bullets had struck him.

Another burst of gunfire exploded behind them. Both men tumbled through the hole in the shed wall in time to see a group of Bolivian soldiers open fire on the four DEA men.

Callahan called to the Bolivians in Spanish, but they ignored him. Their fire was murderous. It poured into the bushes where the other three agents had sought cover. Bolan watched as the bushes were torn to shreds under the barrage. There was no return fire after the first few seconds, and Bolan could only hope they'd gotten away.

Callahan ran at the lieutenant commanding the patrol, calling again for them to cease-fire. As Callahan drew near, the lieutenant turned and fired once with his side arm. The .45 slug slammed into the agent's shoulder, spinning him around before he fell to the ground. A dark pool of blood began to seep from under the fallen man.

Bolan knew, too late, that this was not a simple case of mistaken identity. He turned to run and found himself staring into a semicircle of M-16s.

CHAPTER ELEVEN

The police station was a caricature out of a thirties movie. Instead of taking Bolan back to La Paz, the lieutenant had taken him to the nearest village with a police presence. The Bolivian army jeep screeched to a halt on the hard-packed dirt, scattering chickens in every direction. The town was little more than a collection of shabby buildings, leaning against one another to stave off gravity and decay.

Large shutters, with several slats missing from each, and so long unpainted they had turned the dark gray of twilight, dangled perilously from rusted hinges. A rickety hitching post stood to one side of the entrance, and on the other a watering trough. Bolan felt as if he'd been transported back in time to the days of Butch Cassidy.

He had tried to convince the lieutenant that there was no reason to arrest him, but the man was single-minded. After the first few sentences met with stony silence, Bolan gave up. He had asked for Callahan to be given medical attention and received assurances that "We know what to do with your friend, *señor*." Bolan's last glimpse of the DEA man was of his prostrate form beginning to stir. At least he was still alive. Bolan had no idea what happened to the others. Only one thing was clear: they had been set up.

The lieutenant, continuing to brandish his side arm, hopped down from the jeep and swaggered toward the open door of the police station. Bolan felt the prod of a pistol barrel between his shoulder blades and stepped from the jeep. The two enlisted men riding in the back got out and the smaller of the two gave Bolan a shove, sending him reeling through the door. The interior was no more prepossessing, and no more modern, than the outside.

To the left of the entrance, a chest-high counter ran the length of the room. Behind it, two desks, which were littered with paper, faced each other. An ancient telephone stood at one end of the counter under a bulletin board liberally cluttered with Wanted posters, fliers and public notices. Apparently the police station was also the social center of the village. The cork on the bulletin board was the newest thing in the room.

When Bolan regained his balance, he noticed the lieutenant in whispered conversation with the local lawman. The two men were standing in a second doorway leading to the cell block. Even in the dim light, Bolan could see the place was not sanitary. It stood to reason that underdeveloped South American countries could hardly be expected to have an enlightened attitude toward prisons. In Bolivia, a guard was still a guard, not a corrections officer or a penal sociologist.

Bolan's entrance brought the conversation to a momentary halt. The lawman gave him a once-over, then said something that tickled the lieutenant's funny bone. That seemed to put an end to the discussion, and the lieutenant swaggered back toward the front. He stopped in front of Bolan, spreading his feet and cupping his hands behind his back. For a moment he said nothing. He looked thoughtful, absently stroking both ends of his bandito mustache. His black eyes glittered like two shiny marbles.

"*Adios, señor,*" he said, stepping around Bolan and walking toward the door. Then, as if he had forgotten something, he turned back. "Your friend will be okay. I am not so sure about you. Sleep with one eye open, but only if you can't stay awake. *Señor*, there are some things a man has to do that he doesn't like. A soldier has to follow orders. I think you know what I mean." His features softened just for a second, then he was gone.

The lawman stepped into the office. He had a face like old leather, nearly hidden under a week-old growth of scraggly whiskers. His eyes were bloodshot and yellowed. He moved in close, and Bolan got a whiff of days-old sweat and stale tobacco. His features were vaguely Oriental, and Bolan realized he must be a mestizo. The man was tall and hard looking, running slightly to fat, a paunch bulging over his gun belt. The cowboy in him was evident from the Colt Peacemaker he wore low on his hip. He folded his arms and walked in a circle around Bolan, sizing up the new prisoner.

Satisfied with the results of his survey, he moved to a table and chair in one corner of the room and sat down. He pulled a second chair over to prop his feet on, then motioned to a deputy, who pushed Bolan toward the remaining vacant chair. The lawman nodded for Bolan to be seated. With his hands cuffed behind his back, Bolan had to perch precariously on the forward edge of the frail-looking chair.

"*Señor*, you are in big trouble," he began. "Big trouble." He nodded slowly, as if someone else had spoken and he was simply expressing agreement.

"I haven't done anything," Bolan said. He kept his voice low and even, despite his anger.

"I never yet met a criminal, especially a *traficante*, most especially a gringo *traficante*, who wasn't innocent, *señor*. And you have done worse than smuggle drugs, *señor*. I know this."

Bolan shrugged. "You know what you want to know, don't you?"

"Of course, my friend. I don't want to know what I don't want to know, so why should I bother to know it, eh?"

"You're adept at wordplay, aren't you?"

"No jokes, please. You are in most serious trouble. You gringos come down here all the time for the coca. I know this. And I also know that mostly you get away with it. Maybe that's not so bad. Or maybe it's not my business. But murder, *señor*, murder I don't like. And to turn on one's friend, that is the worst thing a man can do."

"I haven't murdered anyone."

"This I do not believe. I can smell it on you, *señor*. Death is in your eyes. And in your heart. You can't disguise it. Not enough to fool me."

"Then tell me who I am supposed to have killed."

"Why, Señor Cowan, of course. Your *traficante compadre*. Don't try to tell me you didn't know him."

"I knew him, but I didn't kill him."

"Of course not. He shot himself, no? It happens all the time. Coca makes men do strange things." He reached into his pocket and took out a couple of flat, dry leaves, rolled them into a ball and placed them in his mouth, like sticks of chewing gum. He began to knead the leaves with his mouth open. "We are very fond of coca here. But it is not for gringos. The *norteamericanos* have taken everything else. Surely they don't need coca, too?"

"You're right about that."

"Then why are you smuggling the coca, *señor*?"

"I'd like to talk to an attorney."

The request seemed to amuse the sheriff. He called in a loud voice, "The gringo wants his lawyer, amigos. What do you think of that?" He smiled broadly while the others in the room laughed. Then he turned to the corner of the room behind him and spat the pasty ball of chewed leaf onto the floor, where it came to rest with several others.

He stood up, the smile gone. "*Señor*, this is not Los Estados Unidos, eh? Here, we have laws to protect the people from the criminals. Something you might not have done before you got involved in this dirty business. This, I think, is how the newspapers will see it, anyway. We will, of course, provide them with all the information they might need."

Bolan stared at him impassively.

"Maybe you need to spend a few days with us, eh? Learn our ways a little, learn to have some respect for Bolivia. We are a poor country, yes, but we have pride, *señor*, dignity. *Dignidad*. It is all a man needs, *señor*. *Comprende?*" He gestured to the deputy, who grabbed Bolan by the shoulder as he began to rise.

Bolan was hustled through the door to the cell block. He heard a jangle of keys, then one grated heavily in a lock. The deputy yanked him by the cuffed hands, then shoved, and Bolan went sprawling. Before he could get to his feet, the heavy door clanged behind him. The cell was small and foul smelling. One window high on the wall cast a small block of sunlight on the floor.

Once on his feet, Bolan examined the cell. It was no more than ten feet wide, and a little deeper. The back wall, under the window, held two bunks, one on top of the other. Both were of heavy metal bolted securely into the wall, their outer edges supported by thick chain. The bunks and the chain had been painted and repainted. The chipped surfaces showed six or seven different layers, and several colors. Instead of a mattress, each bunk had a thin pallet, probably straw, covered with frayed, striped ticking.

The floor was gritty beneath his feet, the walls damp and covered, floor to ceiling, with undecipherable scrawl. Bolan was reminded of the artwork in Cardona's mansion, but this stuff was better. At least it gave the sense of having been done for a purpose, even if only to pass the time.

The cuffs were tight, the cold metal chafing his wrists. He thought for a moment about asking to have them removed, but realized at once that if they were willing to take them off, they would already have done so. He decided to get them off by himself.

If he could.

The cuffs were old, but the steel was hard. The first order of business was to get them where he could see them. He lowered his arms until the cuffs were behind his thighs, then sat on the edge of the lower bunk. Bending forward, he just managed to get one leg through his circled arms. The other was too tight a fit. In frustration, he picked at the laces on his shoe, then slipped it off. With the heel out of the way, he could get the other leg through. Now, at least, his hands were of some use.

Examination showed the weakest spot to be the short chain that held the cuffs together. The metal was too hard for him to tug them apart, but there was a slight separation in one link, where the weld had failed. If he could find something thin enough to slip into the opening—and strong enough not to break—he'd have a shot.

On hands and knees, he scrutinized the littered floor under the bunk. Bits of paper, straw and long desiccated food scraps but no metal. The edges of the bunk were too thick to be of any use. Frustrated, he lay back on the lower pallet.

The walls of the cell were bare, except for the scribble. The old stone and masonry were peeling here and there, but that didn't help. Idly examining the wall stone by stone, he noticed some graffiti that had been scratched rather than written on the thick paint.

With a glimmer of hope, he got up off the bunk and walked to the wall. Bending down directly beneath the chiseled graffiti, he sifted through the drifted dust and litter. If someone had been able to work his message into the paint that way, maybe there was a nail or something he could use. He smoothed out the refuse with his hands, then rubbed his fingertips carefully and slowly through the layer of dirt. He found some chips of paint, a few small chunks of stone, but no nail. Nothing he could use.

He kept one ear on the noise from beyond the cell-block door while he worked. Ready to pack it in, he looked more closely at the writing chipped into the paint. The letters were smooth edged and even, as if their outlines had been cut before the paint was flaked off. He ran his fingers over the letters, then over the rough joint between two stones that formed the lower margin of the writing.

He'd found it.

Wedged between the two blocks of stone was a snapped-off blade of a pocketknife. No more than two inches long, it wasn't much, but it was all he had. The broken blade had been inserted with its cutting edge in. With a fingernail, he found the groove cut into the blade used to open the knife and tugged. At first, it refused to budge. The blade had been tightly wedged in. He tugged again, but his fingernail broke. He used another finger and tried again. This time he was rewarded with a slight rasping sound. The blade was beginning to move.

It pulled free after one more yank and fell to the floor with a jingle. It took him a moment to find it in the garbage. He picked the blade up and stepped into the block of light coming through the window. It seemed like good steel. It was a bit rusted on its outer edge, but it might work. He had his tool, but he was far from home free. The chain was too short to permit him access to it with the fingers of either hand. He'd have to find some other way to use the blade.

Where the chain met the outer edge of the upper bunk was a thick washer that didn't quite meet the metal below it. Working quickly now, fearful of losing the slight advantage of the fragmented blade, Bolan tried to wedge the blade under the washer. It wouldn't quite fit. He scratched at the paint with the blade point, managing to scrape away enough to get the blade in place. It was precarious, but it might stay long enough for him to do what he had to.

Twisting his wrists around, he brought the chain of the cuffs up against the blade edge, taking care not to dislodge it. The opening between the links was just large enough to get the edge of the blade in. The next step was crucial. He had to exert direct pressure—and straight in—or the blade might snap, perhaps even leaving a piece in the gap. Slowly he pressed inward. The blade started to bend, and he adjusted his angle. The blade began to slide in place. He pressed harder and the blade went in deeper. The link was giving way grudgingly.

A sudden snap and the blade passed all the way into the gap. It still wasn't wide enough to disengage the links, but now Bolan had some options. He tapped the blade against the bunk, and it fell to the floor. The under edge of the upper bunk was thicker than the blade, but it had a sharp edge. He pressed the partially open link against the bunk metal and felt the edge slip into the opening. But the angle was all wrong. He had no leverage.

Lying on the lower bunk, he could reach the edge comfortably, with a little room to spare. He refitted the opening and pressed upward, with arms extended. The strain was tearing at his wrists. The edge shot through with a snap, spreading the link even wider. He yanked the cuffs free of the bunk, and twisted the chain. The next link caught for a second, then pulled loose. He still wore the cuffs, but now they were no more than exotic bracelets.

His hands were free.

The voices in the outer room grew louder. The deputy was back, pushing another prisoner ahead of him. Bolan clasped his hands together to conceal their freedom and feigned sleep. The three other cells in the small block were empty, but the deputy stopped in front of Bolan's door. The lock grated, and Bolan stirred as if dimly aware of the noise.

"Wake up, gringo. You got company. For a little while." The guard chuckled as he shoved the newcomer through the door and relocked it. Then he stepped back and closed the door to the outer office. He shuffled his feet nervously, like a kid at his first movie.

Opening his eyes, Bolan saw the biggest man he'd ever seen. His clothes were unmistakably Aymara. Everything about him was.

Even the knife dangling from his belt.

CHAPTER TWELVE

The deputy stepped back from the bars, folded his arms across his chest and stood grinning. Bolan smiled back. The Indian seemed disoriented. His eyes blinked spasmodically. Bolan noted the size of his arms. The Indian's faded work shirt was rolled up to just below the elbow, then pushed up over the biceps. The rolled fabric was lighter than the rest of the shirt, as if stretched nearly to the point of tearing.

The man's black eyes danced from corner to corner of the cell, lightly flicking over Bolan in transit. If he noticed his cellmate, he made no sign. Bolan kept his gaze steady, waiting for the first hint of the confrontation that would surely come. A grating noise in the corridor indicated the deputy was getting restless. He shifted his feet, scraping them on the rough flooring.

Still the huge newcomer made no move. His hands hung limply, dangling away from his sides as if the massive upper arms permitted them no closer to his body. He shuffled his feet, blinked twice in rapid succession, then fixed his gaze on Bolan. The Executioner glanced once at the sheathed knife, calculated the odds on making the first move. They were long.

Weary of the standoff, the deputy turned to go, glancing once over his shoulder before closing the door behind him. The wry smile had faded, the mouth turned down now, as if angry at Bolan or the Indian, or both. The situation was deteriorating as Bolan assessed it. It looked as though he'd get no sleep. It was something he couldn't afford. If he took the lower bunk, the Indian would have the drop on him from above, any time he cared to make his move. If Bolan took the upper, he was an easy target for the knife thrust up through the skimpy pallet.

Sleep was sooner or later going to be necessary. Bolan had no idea what the man would do. Rather than sit and wait for it to happen, he realized he had nothing to lose by starting things on his own. At least he wouldn't be surprised. The advantages of acting rather than reacting were sometimes marginal. This was the textbook proof of that proposition. Still, if you were locked in with a bull, you had nothing to lose by grabbing the horns.

Bolan stood slowly, looking off to one side. The Indian took no notice. His eyes had become vacant, as if he were asleep on his feet. Bolan knew he was in better shape, and sure as hell had better training. But the whole point of combat training is to prepare you to counter the other guy's training. A free swinging brawler, not to mention a back-woods assassin, just might get lucky. There was nothing you could do but hope. And pray if you knew anybody who might listen. Bolan shrugged, then let go with a round-house right. It caught the big Indian in the stomach, just below the sternum. The blow should have knocked the wind out of him, at least.

If the Indian was surprised, he didn't show it. He blinked again and shook his head, his thoughts obviously else-where. He ignored both the punch and its author. He brushed past Bolan to vault into the upper bunk with the ease of a big cat. Watching the maneuver, Bolan increased the odds a notch or two. The springs of the upper bunk groaned under the sudden weight. It was the only noise in the cellblock. The split second took an eternity to pass. Bolan backed up until he felt the bars behind him. The Indian closed his eyes. That he would even try to sleep seemed un-likely. A moment later, he was snoring.

Bolan's muscles ached with tension. He couldn't turn his back, and he couldn't sit down. The grace and agility the Indian had demonstrated were an impressive combination. Throw in the knife, and it was deadly.

There had to be an explanation. If the Indian was not an assassin who was put in the same cell to dispose of him, why was he armed? If he wasn't an assassin, why was he there at all?

Bolan knew that the sheriff's story of his being suspected of drug trafficking was garbage. A quick check with the DEA would have cleared that up in a second. But they had showed no interest in who he was. They didn't have to; they already knew who he was. They took no statement and asked few questions, discounting the answers even before they were given. The sheriff was on somebody's string. Bolan was sure of that, less so about the lieutenant. Who knew what he had been told, and by whom?

He prayed Callahan was all right. The lieutenant said he would be taken care of. Bolan hoped like hell that wasn't a lie. Callahan was his ticket out of here. Maybe his only one. If the kid bought it, there'd be no one left to tell his side of the story.

His cellmate started to moan. It started as a low rumble and rose to a steady thunder. He moved restlessly, the straw of the pallet rustling as his weight shifted. In the dim light, Bolan could see that he was prostrate, but awake. The nightmare noise from his throat was a conscious sound. That wasn't reassuring.

The Aymara sat up with a sudden movement, the strap springs of the cot groaning under his concentrated weight. There was little warning—a slight tension in the air, perhaps, or some sixth sense. Whatever it was, it saved Bolan's life. He dived to one side, landing roughly on his right shoulder. The metallic clang still echoed in the cell block as he got to his feet. A dull gleam at the base of the wall told Bolan where the Indian's knife had landed.

Bolan debated whether to try for the knife. The Indian sat motionless, as if in meditation. The dim light was enough for Bolan to see the big man's eyes were wide open, unblinking. He seemed to be in some kind of a trance. Bolan passed on the knife. He knew his adversary expected him to try for it; it was what he was concentrating all his attention on.

Bolan had other ideas.

Gathering himself into a tight coil, Bolan feinted toward the knife. The Aymara barely moved, a slight smile flickering on his lips. Bolan sprang. He went straight for the Indian.

The larger man sat on the upper cot with knees crossed, approximating the lotus position, like a Latin Buddha. The Indian bent away from the impact of Bolan's lunge. Like a child's punching bag, he sprang back effortlessly. Bolan reached for the man's long hair and found it. A glancing blow caught him over the left eye, but did no damage. Tangling the man's hair in his fist, Bolan fell backward, yanking with all his strength.

The man bent forward, but didn't utter a sound. Faster than Bolan thought possible, a hand flashed out from under the Indian's torso. The sudden pressure on Bolan's wrist was enormous. The Indian had the superior position. Whether he understood physics was doubtful. That he knew how to take advantage of leverage was beyond question. He began to twist, at the same time thrusting his weight forward. Bolan's arm began to go numb.

With his free hand, he chopped at the Indian's neck, but his reach was short. The blows slammed into the back of his enemy's shoulder, with no discernible effect. Forced to take the defensive, Bolan grabbed the Indian's arm with his one hand, twisting the other as he did. The sudden shift caught the man by surprise, and his grip loosened enough for Bolan to pivot his captive arm. Now he could grab the Indian's arm with both hands.

The prisoner was now the jailer. Bolan turned his back to the Indian and dropped to one knee, yanking on the guy's arm. He had two choices: he could try to stay where he was and let Bolan break his arm, or he could give up the advantage of the high ground.

The man was no fool. He needed his arm. His legs un-coiled and he tumbled forward, somersaulting over Bolan to land on his feet. The men were locked back to back. The Indian's strength was awesome. He curled his imprisoned arm in toward Bolan's throat, closing around it with a grunt of satisfaction. Bolan let go of the big man's wrist long enough to drive an elbow into his kidneys. The Indian grunted again, but held on. Bolan twisted to the side, re-leasing the pressure on his throat.

The headlock was beginning to have its effect: the tre-mendous pressure began to blur Bolan's vision. The Indian leaned forward to get his body into it. As Bolan began to lose consciousness the Indian shuffled his feet. Off balance for an instant, he'd given Bolan the opening he needed. Driving forward with all his strength, Bolan forced his ad-versary headfirst into the stone wall.

The blow stunned him long enough for Bolan to break free. He turned, shaking his head from side to side, and seemed more surprised than angry. Bolan backed into a corner, trying to recover his own faculties. The Aymara was a powerful man, but he seemed to rely on brute strength rather than cunning. As long as Bolan could stay out of his reach, he'd have a chance.

Bolan's eyes flicked toward the knife then away. The In-dian seemed to have forgotten about it. Or he was now so confident of his own abilities that he disdained its use. Moving parallel to one wall, Bolan angled toward his huge adversary. The Indian moved along the opposite wall, as Bolan had hoped. He was halfway to the Indian's knife when he feinted forward, then stepped back. The Indian remained impassive. His close-set eyes were unwavering, and if he blinked at all, it was too fast for Bolan to notice.

Bolan started along the next wall, cautiously feeling his way along the rough stone with his left hand. The Indian continued mirroring Bolan's movement. So far, neither man had said a word to the other. Halfway across the wall, Bolan stopped. The knife was just to his left. The Indian gave no sign he knew what Bolan was up to.

Bolan bent low and made as if to charge. The Indian anticipated his rush, sending his weight backward. Bolan bent and grabbed the knife before the big man could regain his balance. Hefting it, Bolan was impressed. It was a masterpiece of cutlery. Its weight was perfectly balanced in his hand, giving the impression of solidity without feeling cumbersome.

The Indian smiled. He spoke for the first time, in a guttural growl, *"Bueno, bueno."* He reached into his shirt and withdrew a second knife, identical to the one in Bolan's hand.

Bolan backed flat against the wall, keeping his weight on dead center. The Indian was unorthodox, unpredictable. More of a barroom brawler than a trained killer, he might try the obvious just because it was something you weren't supposed to do. It would be gut instinct rather than sophisticated reasoning, but Bolan had to be prepared.

Neither man moved.

The Indian seemed to be pondering his next move.

Bolan had no option but to wait for it.

He didn't have to wait long. With a bellow, the man charged straight across the cell. He held the knife low, swept it upward in a vicious arc and caught Bolan with the point of the blade. He stepped back to survey the damage. Bolan felt a sharp pain, then cold, in his left forearm, halfway between wrist and elbow. The warm sticky flow told him he'd been cut badly. He flexed the arm gingerly. Everything still worked. It was a deep gash, but nothing had been severed.

The Indian's face was impassive, almost contemplative. He seemed to be waiting for Bolan to respond. It was a curious chivalry. Bolan shook his injured arm, trying to restore feeling. Pain shot up along the arm and exploded in his elbow.

Bolan glanced at the arm. He was losing a lot of blood. He'd have to take the man quickly, before his strength faded. He feinted toward him, stepped to one side and whirled, the knife extended in his good arm. He felt contact and halted. The Indian held his left bicep, blood seeping through his clenched fingers. His face remained stoic. Still holding his injured arm, he began to circle the cell. Bolan mirrored his movement.

The Aymara held the knife against his wound, trapped against the upper arm by his splayed fingers. Bolan watched, waiting for a misstep, an eye blink, a moment of vulnerability. After three circuits of the small area, nothing had changed.

Bolan felt himself getting sleepy. The bleeding had slowed to a trickle, but the arm was almost useless. The Indian was as patient as the stone walls that constrained them. It was now or never.

Bolan lunged.

The Indian had been waiting. But he'd waited too long. His sound arm moved swiftly in an arc. He never noticed the knife spinning away on a path of its own. Slippery with blood, it had spun free of his fingers and windmilled to the stone floor with a clatter.

Bolan speared through the crossed forearms and struck home. The razor-sharp blade clanked against the man's thorax, paused, then slipped free and down, sliding in all the way to the hilt. The big man grabbed Bolan's arm in both hands before he could twist the knife or slice downward. Holding Bolan rigid, he backed away from the blade, then stared at the bloody hilt in Bolan's fist. As if mesmerized, he stepped to one side, still holding Bolan at arm's length. Blood spurted in great gouts, to the beat of his giant heart. Another step, then another. The floor was getting slick. With a sigh, the Indian fell to one knee, still refusing to let go of Bolan's arm.

The Executioner felt the Indian's grip slackening, then the man lay crumpled on the floor.

Bolan dropped to one knee, felt for a pulse and, finding none, laid the blade flat on the ground next to the Indian's hand. He searched the cell for the other knife. Finding it, he arranged himself on the floor near the Indian, then smeared blood on the front of his shirt. Ready for act two, he gave an agonizing shout. The awful noise seemed to rattle the bars and echoed off the stone.

As if on cue, the deputy stepped through the steel door. Bolan hooded his eyes and lay still. The deputy hollered something unintelligible over his shoulder, then walked to the cell door. He stood quietly, his hands on the bars. Bolan felt the deputy's gaze lingering on him. A jangle of keys announced the man's satisfaction. The lock grated and the heavy door swung open. The deputy entered, stopping beside the Indian. He kicked the massive body once with his heavy boot and was rewarded by the sound of fetid gas belching into the confined quarters.

The deputy bent to retrieve the knife that lay beside the dead Aymara. He wiped the bloody weapon on the man's shirtfront, then stuck the blade in his belt. Stepping across the prostrate form, he knelt beside Bolan and poked him in the ribs once, then again. He sensed something wrong, but it was too late.

Bolan moved like lightning, grabbing the man by his hair and yanking him down hard. At the same time, he put the blade of the second knife under the deputy's chin and pressed in until the soft throat resisted the razor edge.

"Not a sound, *compadre*," Bolan hissed. *"¿Comprende"*

The deputy's eyes bulged in their sockets as he nodded, trying to keep his throat away from the blade.

Bolan grabbed the man's side arm, then got to one knee. The weapon was an old Webley Army Express .45 caliber. It had seen more than a few years' use, but felt solid in his hand. He stood up. The deputy, one arm bent behind his back, rose with him.

"How many men out there?" Bolan asked.

"Two, *señor*."

"Don't lie to me, friend. Your life depends on it."

"I'm not lying, *señor*. Two only."

Pushing the man forward, Bolan guided him through the cell door, keeping the knife at his throat. In his left hand he held the captured revolver. At the door out of the cell block, they halted. Bolan looked over the deputy's shoulder. Two men were seated at desks. The nearer of the two, sensing that something was wrong, started to get up. Bolan shot him twice, the revolver sounding like thunder in the confines of the small office. The first slug struck him just below the heart, hurling the rising man backward over his chair. The second slammed into the man as he fell, breaking his right wrist and cracking three ribs as it bored into the spinning body.

The second man raised his hands over his head, pushing away from the desk. Bolan walked his captive halfway around the office to a wall rack near the door. He snatched a pair of handcuffs from the rack. Indicating the radiator steam pipe behind the desk, he tossed the cuffs. "Put them on. Fast."

The deputy said, "He doesn't speak English, *señor*."

"He knows what I mean."

The man turned, saw the pipe and picked up the cuffs. With shaking hands, he snapped one bracelet around his wrist, then secured the other to the pipe. Bolan, forcing the deputy ahead of him, walked over and dropped the chained man with a swift blow of the pistol butt. The crack sounded like wood breaking, and the man fell to the floor.

Bolan pressed the knife a little harder into the deputy's throat. "Now, you are going to give me some information, *compadre*."

The frightened man gulped audibly and nodded.

"*Sí, señor*. As you wish."

CHAPTER THIRTEEN

Mack Bolan was on the move. After searching the small police station for first-aid supplies to bind his wounded arm, he'd turned his attention to getting information. The deputy hadn't known much, but it was enough. Callahan was back in La Paz, in the hospital. The others were dead.

Yes, the sheriff was on somebody's payroll. No, he didn't know who. Not for sure. Yes, he'd heard the name Diego Cardona, but that's all he knew. A *traficante*, maybe the biggest, certainly the meanest. He could be paying the sheriff. Yes, he knew the lieutenant. An honest man, his wife's cousin. He could not be bribed.

The deputy had been too frightened to lie. He'd been shaking like a leaf the whole time Bolan interrogated him. He hadn't talked willingly; he was as afraid of someone else as he was of Bolan. Maybe the sheriff. But the honcho wasn't the problem. He took his orders from higher up, and whoever was giving them had weight.

Bolan had to get to Callahan, but his arm needed tending. He had to find somebody he could trust, or at least somebody they wouldn't be watching. It hit him then. Valerie Russell. He still had her address. Nobody but Callahan knew that he knew her. He probably couldn't trust her, but he didn't have a choice.

He stole a jeep. The deputy drove part of the way into La Paz, then Bolan cuffed him to a tree some distance from the road. It would be hours before anybody found him.

The road back to La Paz seemed longer than it had that morning. The darkness was complete. No lights along the road, and no white line to follow. Pushing the jeep as fast as he dared, Bolan strained his eyes to see into the green tunnel ahead. When the forest thinned, and the jeep began to climb, the night didn't seem to be so dark.

He strained his ears, half expecting to hear someone behind him. Once in a while, he'd pull over and kill the engine, but there wasn't a sound, not even the jungle night noises Hollywood was so fond of.

After the third stop, he decided to forgo checking for a tail. If anyone was on his trail, he was already at a disadvantage. The terrain was alien, he was weak from losing blood and he was exhausted. As the vehicle climbed toward La Paz, it would be easier to be seen than to see. Suddenly he stopped the jeep again, but left it running this time. He hopped out and went to the rear. With the butt of his captured pistol, he broke the taillights. It wasn't much, but it was something.

Once again in the jeep, he placed the pistol on the seat beside him. His own weapons were back where they belonged, their weight comforting against his aching ribs.

The road climbed still higher, and La Paz loomed ahead of him, a glowing line where its taller buildings rose above the stony bowl that contained the capital. Entering the city in the jeep was risky, but he had to get to Valerie Russell's before dawn.

The moon was already sinking toward the mountain rim. Soon, the sun would start its daily crawl over the ragged edge of the Andes. Scattered buildings announced the city limits. There was little traffic, but he stuck out like a sore thumb in the early dawn. He stopped for a moment to pull on his jacket. He was disheveled, and his face was battered, but at least the jacket hid his bloody shirt.

Bolan ditched the jeep two blocks from Valerie's apartment. The first buzz of commerce was beginning. Farmers were rolling into the markets on anything with wheels. Burros groaned under the weight of woven baskets, their hooves clip-clopping on the cobbled pavements. No one took any notice of him. The people were too busy scratching out a living to worry about an unkempt foreigner wandering around at first light.

At the corner of Avenida Santa Cruz—where Russell's apartment building was located—Bolan stopped. Here in this quiet residential neighborhood, he could be more easily spotted. He towered over most of the people in the streets. His clothing alone wasn't enough to set him apart, but as a stranger, he would catch a stray eye or two. Stopping in front of a closed shop, he checked the street behind him. Nothing seemed out of place. He quickened his pace toward the apartment building, reached it, then walked past without looking at it. Continuing on to the next corner, he checked again. Nothing had moved. The few cars parked on the street were all empty.

The street was a quiet block that was lined with modern apartment buildings. Inca motifs were the only evidence he wasn't in Chicago or San Francisco. Whatever its functional merits, modern architecture had nearly obliterated local character. You could drug someone in Berlin and fly him to Bangkok, and he might not realize the difference for a few hours, as long as he didn't leave the building.

Bolan headed back toward Valerie's building, then ducked down an alley to the service entrance. The rear of the building was as nondescript as its facade. The obligatory steel door next to the obligatory pile of aluminum garbage cans and green plastic bags announced the building as a bastion of the middle class. The poor didn't have cans, and the rich didn't have garbage.

Bolan tried the door, but it was locked from the inside. It rattled a bit when he yanked the knob. He sifted through the heap of refuse for something he could use to pry open the door. He needed something metal, stronger than a curtain rod, but not as thick. A coat hanger would do the trick, if he could find one rigid enough. He spotted a black wire poking through one of the green bags, ripped the plastic away and was rewarded by a half-dozen hangers. Four of them were too flimsy. He took the fifth, fashioned a double loop and stepped back to the door.

Working quietly, he forced the loop between the door and its frame, then wiggled the wire. It slipped in farther, then with a click, pushed the latch bolt out of its recess. He pulled and the door swung outward.

The long hallway before him was covered with vinyl tile. The walls were painted egg-shell white and a soft blue. He stepped softly down the hall. The freight elevator, its door open, lay just ahead. If it was running, he was home free. He stepped in and examined the control panel. The light switch clicked, filling the car with a harsh white light. He pressed Door Close and the motor hummed softly. The door hissed shut.

He pressed the button for the fourth floor and felt the car lurch. The cables creaked as the car rose grudgingly. At the fourth floor, it bumped to a halt, and the door opened a moment later. He stepped out into a carpeted hallway.

Valerie Russell lived in 410. He started to the left, noticed the numbers rising from 421, and doubled back. He found 410 near the end of the hall. He rapped softly on the door. When no one responded, he pressed the bell. A tinny arpeggio chimed twice.

After a minute, he pressed the button again. She had to be home. She'd told him she was on a two-week layover. That was only two days ago. Unless she was still at Cardona's. He was about to ring the bell a third time, when he heard someone mumble, "I'm coming. Hold your horses."

The peephole rasped, and Bolan saw a large, bright blue eye peering at him through the fisheye lens. The doorknob rattled, and the door opened. Valerie, her hair mussed, but otherwise unruffled, smiled.

She caught him as he fell.

THE ROOM WAS UNFAMILIAR. Dull blocks of light marked the three windows. Bolan struggled to sit upright, the weight of the covers almost enough to restrain him. A shadowy figure sat in a wicker chair in one corner. Bolan blinked, trying to shake off the darkness. His arm throbbed dully. He felt it tentatively, his fingers almost caressing the thick bandages.

"Valerie?"

"Good, you're awake. How do you feel?"

"I've been better."

"I shouldn't wonder. You lost a lot of blood. What in heaven's name happened to you?"

"How long have I been out?"

"Me first. Tell me what happened." Her voice was firm, almost harsh, echoing eerily from one corner of the high-ceilinged room.

"I'd rather not."

"All right then." Her jaw fairly snapped shut. Bolan felt as if he'd been chastised by a stern teacher. All he needed now was detention. In a softer voice, as if she regretted her brusqueness, she continued, "You don't have to trust me, if you don't want to."

"Should I?"

"You came here on your own, remember? I didn't invite you."

Bolan nodded. He remembered knocking on the door. Reaching back a little further, he remembered deciding to come here. What he couldn't remember was why.

Softening still more, she said, "Is there someone I should call?"

"No!" His own voice startled him. It was coming back into focus now. Still groggy, he felt uneasy without quite knowing why. But he was sure of one thing: no one must know where he was. Not for a while. Not until he felt stronger. He'd had a near miss, and his present condition was too precarious for a repeat performance. He remembered the Indian. And the knife. And Callahan. He had to get in touch with Callahan. The deputy had said he was in the hospital.

A sitting duck.

"Did you bandage my arm?" he asked.

"Do I look that much like Clara Barton?"

"Well, no. She was rather chunky, as I recall."

"Thank you." She breathed a mock sigh of relief. "Actually, Dr. Gonsalves did it."

"Who is he?"

"A friend. You needn't worry. He knows a secret when it bleeds all over him."

Bolan nodded again. This was some woman. More than he'd expected. Despite his uneasiness, he sensed that somehow he'd made the right move in coming here.

"You're tougher than you look, aren't you, Valerie?"

"For someone of my frail constitution, you mean?"

"Not exactly. But then there's nothing very exact about you, is there?"

"What is that supposed to mean?"

"You're not just a flight attendant, are you?"

"What makes you think that?"

"The company you keep, for one thing."

"Cardona?"

"Uh-huh."

"That's a long story."

"I'll bet it is. I have time, though, and I'm all ears."

"Not now. I'm already late for an appointment."

Bolan struggled to get out of bed. Valerie left her chair to press him back firmly into bed. "I'm late, but you're not going anywhere. Not until you're ready."

"I'm ready."

"The hell you are. I don't need to know who cut you up to know you're not ready for round two."

"But I have to see a sick friend."

"Mr. Callahan isn't going anywhere for a few days, either."

"How did you know that's who I meant?" Bolan was genuinely startled.

"I told you. It's a long story. Don't worry, Señor Cardona won't know you're here. And I'm sure that's what you're concerned about. Isn't it, Mr. Bolan?"

Bolan said nothing. He lay back and closed his eyes. He believed her, for reasons he didn't understand. There was something about her that commanded his trust. In retrospect, even seeing her at Cardona's hadn't surprised him as much as it should have. Her presence there had some purpose he couldn't know, he was certain of that. What it was, for the moment, was her secret. And he knew, without having to ask, that Cardona had no more of an idea than he did of what it might be. Valerie Russell was more than a thrill seeker, and more than a flight attendant. How much more than either would have to wait awhile.

"There's food in the refrigerator, but I don't think you ought to get out of bed for a while." She stated that with confidence that he wouldn't argue.

Without opening his eyes, he agreed. The throbbing in his arm was insistent. He wanted—needed—to sleep. He heard her approach the bed and felt her hand on his brow. It was cool and soft but strong in the way only delicate things can be strong. He heard rustling beside him, then a straw was forced between his lips. He drew on it, eagerly taking the cool water. Only then did he realize how thirsty he was.

"I'll leave this on the nightstand. With some painkillers."

Before he could thank her, Bolan heard the door close. A jangle of keys was followed by the closing of another door.

He was alone.

The puzzle had so many pieces. More than Brognola knew. Valerie Russell was somehow connected, but whether she was the key or just one of the pieces he didn't know. She had known Callahan's name. And his. In itself, it was significant...and puzzling. Her knowledge suggested some dark connections, a tangled web that led to who knew where.

But he was going to find out.

Yeah. And soon. He couldn't afford loose ends. There were too many already. And loose ends meant dead ends.

He was determined none of them would be his.

Chicago

CHAPTER FOURTEEN

The hawk was out. Lake Michigan was a natural funnel for the worst of Canadian weather. It roared out of Ontario, picked up steam over the water, and by the time it hit Chicago, it was in no mood to be argued with. Everybody knew about the Windy City. You had to live there to know how cold it could get.

Albert Richards knew all about it. Seventeen years of scuffling on the streets of the South Side had taught him a lot, more than a kid should have to know. Winter was still weeks away, but Albert was already cold. There wasn't much he could do about it, and it made him mad. He had two choices, neither one of them good. He could do nothing, or he could look for a job that didn't exist, and for which he wouldn't be hired if it did. A seventeen-year-old dropout wasn't prime employment timber.

One of six kids, three of whom were still alive, Albert didn't much give a damn anyway. Getting by was all there was, so it had to be enough. Getting by meant getting high, and getting high meant getting his hands on some bread. There was only one way to do that. He was still thinking about it, standing in a doorway and rubbing his hands against the early cold when he heard somebody call his name.

It was only six-thirty in the morning, too early for any of the friends he'd managed not to alienate. He poked his head out of the doorway, but saw nobody. Maybe he'd been imagining things. He shrugged and stepped out into the wind to get a better look. He heard it again, this time closer.

Shit, it was his brother. Lee was always on his ass. When he was around, that is. "Albert, man, you got to get it together." "Albert, man, don't be screwing around with no drugs.'' ''Albert, get you an education.'' The son of a bitch talked a good game, but what the hell did he do with his own life? He had money sometimes, but nobody knew where it came from. Albert didn't need a map to know what that meant. Now here he was again; that's the way it was with Lee. He'd be there one day, hammering on him, and the next day he was gone, like he'd never been there at all. Six months later he was back, talking like he'd never been away. Well, screw that, Albert thought. He was through listening to that jive.

Setting his jaw, he waved to his older brother.

''Albert, man, where the hell you been? I been lookin' for you for two days.''

''Yeah, well, I been around.''

''Mama's worried.''

''She always worried, man, you know that.''

''You don't have to make it worse, do you?''

''It don't make no difference what I do. Half the time, she too drunk to know whether I'm there or not. The other half, she just as soon I not be there. What the hell you care, anyway?''

''You my brother, Albert. I care.''

''Uh-huh. I hear it, but I don't see no proof, man. You never here, so why don't you just go away and not come back, this time? Get out of my face, Lee. I take care of my own self. Been doin' it a long time, man. You know?''

''Yeah, well...'' Lee looked away, staring down the street. He took it all in: the garbage in the gutters, the peeling window frames, broken glass and vacant buildings, sheet metal and plywood ripped away by somebody who wanted to get inside. Some did it for shelter, others to hide what they'd rather not do in plain sight. Even the sky was grayer on the South Side. Everything was.

He turned back to his younger brother, the pain on his face too real to hide. Albert noticed and taunted him.

''Man, you look like you about to cry. How come, Lee? You worried about your little brother? That it?''

Lee understood the frustration, wondered whether he could get past it. He wasn't sure, but he had to try. "Nothing wrong with crying, Albert. Not about somebody means something to you."

"Yeah? What I mean to you, man? I don't hardly see you. What right you got to say you care about me?"

"We got the same blood, Albert. That counts for something. And I can do something about things, now. Make it better for you and Mama and Lurleen."

"Shit, Lurleen got less use for you than I do, man. Sides, she home less than you. She *never* home, man."

"But I got the money to do something about it, man. You can't blame somebody not bein' home, when they got no home worth bein' in. But that's all gonna change. I scored the big one, just like I always said I would."

"Oh yeah? I didn't read about no bank robbery, man. Where'd you get it? Find it?"

"That don't matter. I got it, that's all. We can get a house now, get the hell out of Chicago."

"Right, man, I hear you. I can see it all now, man. Mama in her apron, just like on *The Brady Bunch*, right? You got enough, maybe we even adopt a white kid, you know. Some white Gary Coleman. Just like on TV. Huh, can we do that?"

Albert didn't see the blow coming. At the harsh sound of flesh on flesh, Lee jumped, as if he, too, had been surprised. Albert staggered back against the door, its rusty hinges squealing with the pressure. He slid down to the chipped concrete step, his face in his hands.

"Hey, man, I'm sorry, Albert. I didn't mean that. I—"

"Fuck you, man. That's your problem. You don't mean nothing. Why the hell you come back, man? Why?" Albert took his hands away from his face and looked up at his brother. Tears ran freely down his cheeks, but Albert seemed not to notice. The streetwise punk who had been so scornful of his brother's watery eyes a moment before bawled like a baby. And he didn't give a damn.

Lee knelt beside him, reaching out to take him by the shoulders. Albert slapped the hands away. "Get away from me, man. Leave me alone."

Lee stood and looked at the sky again, helpless. He had known it would be hard, but even in his worst scenario it hadn't been this hard. Maybe the kid was right. Maybe it was too late for all of them. He didn't want to believe that. The hope that things could change had kept him going, building a reputation as the best. And the best made the most. That was the way the world worked. And he'd been lucky. He'd got the big one earlier than he ever dreamed. He had the bankroll and the will. The only question was whether he still had the family he'd done it all for.

Albert got up, his face still wet. He wiped a small trickle of blood away from a corner of his mouth. He looked absently at the bloody smear on his fingers, as if it were a newspaper clipping, or an empty book of matches. It meant nothing to him. Blood was common enough. This wasn't nothing at all. He started walking.

"Where you goin', man?" Lee hollered after him.

Albert didn't bother to answer.

THREE BLOCKS AWAY, two men were getting ready for business. The heavy steel door was locked, the steel bar in place. One man, a heavyset Hispanic in Army fatigues, lifted a cardboard carton onto a makeshift table, placing it beside two others. He took an x-acto knife and slit the filament tape sealing the top, then with the deftness of an old fisherman gutting a trout, he slit sidewise, freeing the flaps at both ends. He opened all three cartons, then turned to his companion.

"We got some good stuff, here, Juanito."

His diminutive companion frowned. "Maybe," he said. "But I tell you something, amigo. I don't like it."

"What's not to like? We got the stuff. Who cares if it comes from somebody new? The money will be just as green."

"Where was Carlos? Why didn't he tell us he was sending somebody else?"

"Carlos was busy, man. The guy told us that, didn't he?"

"Yeah, man, he told us that. Carlos didn't tell us. *He* did."

"Look, amigo, it's just business. We got the goods. What do we care where it comes from? You want to make money, don't you?"

"Sure. Sure I do, but something funny's going on, Victor. I don't like it. It smells funny."

"We ain't got nothing to worry about. We're too far down the ladder, man. It happens all the time. I say we just go about our business. Long as we got something to sell, we got nothing to worry about. That's the bottom line."

Juan shrugged. He walked to the heavy door and opened the padlock that held the sliding panel closed. He put the keys into his pocket and slid the panel aside. The hallway outside was dimly lit, a single bare bulb dangling loosely from the crumbling plaster ceiling. Nothing in the hall betrayed their presence. The outer surface of the door was the same dark, peeling varnish as all the others. If you looked closely, you might notice the countersunk bolts, spackled over and tinted to match the original surface. But nobody looked closely. If you were in the hall, you were there to do business, or you didn't care. There were no other options.

The building was almost abandoned. Two other apartments on the floor below were still occupied, but the tenants knew better than to climb one flight up, or to say anything to those who did.

Victor went back to his cartons, unpacking dozens of small plastic vials, their friction caps bright splashes of red, blue and yellow under the harsh glare of two fluorescent lights suspended above the worktable. Their contents were small, off-white clumps, shoved in place by someone Victor had never met. The vials were full of crack. And for Victor, it was as good as gold.

"You know, man," he said, turning to Juan, "you got to admit this is better than standing on the corner pushing grass or nickel bags."

"Maybe . . . maybe not."

"Fuck you, man. If you don't like it, I can always get somebody else. We're supposed to be partners, man. This is a business enterprise. The American dream ready to come true. Why don't you relax and enjoy it, man? Why you have to always piss and moan?"

Juan said nothing. He couldn't shake the uneasy feeling. Victor, as he usually did, missed the point. He had no qualms about selling the drugs. That wasn't what bothered him. But their regular supplier had failed to show for a drop. Somebody else was there. He had the order, just as Carlos would have. But something was wrong. It probably wasn't a setup for a bust. The narcs wouldn't have let them walk off with the stuff.

Most of the shit came from Colombia and Bolivia. Those bastards were crazy. If there was a drug war going on, guys like him and Victor would be chewed up and spit out. Mexicans like them were far too civilized. They were fair game. With the cowboys on one side and the black mobs on the other, it was a tight squeeze. Either side might kill them for working with the other.

Hell, some of the big guys might kill them just because it was a rainy day and they were feeling a little grumpy. Most of them were users, and coke paranoia was notoriously unpredictable. It went with the territory, but only a fool would ignore the only warning he was likely to get.

And that was just what it had been, a warning. Why a guy you've worked with for six months didn't show, and somebody you've never seen did, you damn well better pay attention.

Victor had his mind on other things. Each of the three cartons contained a thousand vials. At ten bucks a pop, that was thirty thousand dollars' worth. It would be gone in less than a week. In less than an hour, people would start streaming upstairs, like ants to a sugar bowl, then filing back out, two or three of the vials in their pockets.

The traffic could get heavy, but nobody seemed to give a damn. The cops looked the other way, some because they'd been paid, some because they didn't give a damn one way or the other and some because they knew it was a losing battle, and it hurt too much to think about it. It was this last bunch that troubled Victor.

Every once in a while, somebody would snap, decide he didn't care whether it made a difference. He'd go on the warpath and start busting chops, maybe even moonlight, like some deranged version of Dirty Harry, prowling the midnight streets with a gun on his hip. These assholes didn't understand that Dirty Harry was in the movies. He didn't belong in the real world. But people got killed that way. Victor knew that. It bothered him a little, but not too much. It was as close as he ever came to worrying about anything.

The loud banging on the door surprised them. It was too early for any of the regulars. This was a business, after all. They had hours. You came when the store was open. When it wasn't, you didn't. Juan went to the peephole. Some skinny kid he'd never seen was pounding on the door again.

"What you want, man?" Juan shouted.

"You know what I want."

"Go away, man."

"Not till I get what I came for."

Victor joined Juan at the door. He pulled a .45 automatic out of his fatigue pants and chambered a round.

"I told you, go away."

"Listen," the kid persisted, "I got money." The shadowy figure waved something in his left hand. Bringing it up to the peephole, he slid it back and forth. It was a fifty-dollar bill.

"What do we do?" Juan whispered.

"Shit, give him what he wants, man. It's the only way to shut him up."

Juan shrugged, then shouted, "Okay, wait a minute." He walked to the table, took five vials from one of the trays and went back to the door.

"Listen, man, you put the money in the slot when I open it. When I get the money, I put the stuff in. Just like a bank, man."

"I know how it works, man. Open the damn slot."

Juan turned a crank, opening the small slot like that on a New York taxi. He heard the crunch of a bill being stuffed in, then cranked it back. The fifty was brand-new, but balled and crinkled. He held it up to the light. It looked okay. He tilted his palm, listening to the small plastic vials drop in, then cranked again. The eager scrabbling to remove the vials sounded more like rats in a wall than human fingers.

"I be back later, man, if this shit is any good."

"You'll be back, then," Victor hollered. "That's good shit, man."

Albert Richards smiled grimly as he walked down the stairs. He had everything he needed right in his pocket. He didn't need no Lee, no goddamn brother. He was his own man.

He could take care of himself.

La Paz

CHAPTER FIFTEEN

It was dark again when Bolan awoke. He knew where he was this time. He sat up carefully, but the dizziness was gone. He still felt weak. The water pitcher Valerie had left was half-empty, but the water was still cool. He poured a glass, took two of the painkillers and popped them in his mouth. He stood after washing the pills down with water. His arm hurt, but not as much, more a dull ache than a constant throb.

He opened the door and walked out to the living room. It was nicely, but sparsely, furnished. Although Valerie's taste was expensive, it was something she evidently indulged infrequently. He called her name, but there was no answer. The gnawing hunger in his gut told him he'd been out for quite a while. He wasn't sure what day it was, so he had no idea when he'd last eaten.

The kitchen was softly lit by a small lamp over the stove. The refrigerator in the corner caught his eye. As he was about to open the door, he noticed the small note tacked to the fridge with a magnet shaped like a pear. In a delicate, lean script the note encouraged him to eat and to wait for her return. He opened the refrigerator, grabbed a handful of sandwich materials, then looked for the bread.

A loaf of rye, unopened, lay in the oak breadbox on a counter next to the sink. He made a couple of sandwiches, then ate them ravenously. He washed them down with cold tap water. He was beginning to feel better already. Bolan took a glass of water into the bedroom and found his clothes draped over the back of a chair. The pants and jacket were neatly pressed, the shoes, under the chair, had been shined. His shirt was gone. In its place was one nearly identical, the same color, but with thinner stripes than his had. It was a perfect fit. Whatever else Valerie Russell was, she was a careful nurse.

When he bent to put on his shoes, his arm throbbed a bit. He ignored the pain, but tucked the small plastic bottle of painkillers into his jacket pocket. His guns were neatly laid on a high-topped bureau in one corner. He strapped on the harnesses, then checked the weapons. Each had been cleaned and oiled, the magazines fully loaded. The sharp tang of the gun oil made him smile. She *was* thorough.

Despite her hospitality, however, Bolan had no intention of heeding her command to wait for her. It was obvious he could trust her, but he didn't know how completely. Nor did he know what he could afford to let her know. She obviously already knew more about him than he did about her. In this business, that was too much of a risk. He had to get Brognola on the horn, ask him to find out more about her. As it was, it would be a tall order. He knew her name, where she worked and the address of her La Paz residence. Other than that, all he really knew was that she knew Diego Cardona, and that she had access to information about Mack Bolan. And about Brian Callahan. She had said he was in the hospital. All of which required some explanation. Rather than wait to confront her, he wanted to have some surprise ammunition of his own.

The first thing he needed was a secure phone. Valerie Russell had too many connections. He wasn't going to risk using her line. It could get him killed, and the young woman as well, depending on who she was and who was listening. He shut off the light and stepped out of the bedroom, jacket in hand. He closed the door behind him and crossed the living room to the front door. Another note, this one held with Scotch tape, said, "I knew you wouldn't wait. If you can't listen, at least be careful. V."

Bolan smiled as he opened the door.

He was nearly to the elevator, when he heard a noise at the other end of the hall. He turned in time to see the fire door closing, but nothing else. On a hunch he decided to pass on the elevator and ran back to the fire door. He turned the knob and kicked it open. The door banged back against the cinder-block wall, the noise reverberating in the stairwell like overhead thunder.

Cautiously he peered into the dimly lit stairway. He heard nothing and saw nothing unusual. Stepping into the stairwell, he closed the fire door behind him, then tiptoed up one flight. As racing footsteps sounded on the landing above, he bounded up the stairs two at a time.

The person above retreated, no longer trying to be silent. Rounding the corner to the next level, Bolan saw one high-topped black sneaker vanish upward. He ran faster now, gaining on his quarry. His arm throbbed painfully, the elevated blood pressure asserting itself in no uncertain terms.

As Bolan turned the corner to the next landing, a sharp pop sounded above, ahead of the fleeing man. In rapid succession, he heard three more pops, then a door banging closed. Rounding the next bend, Bolan nearly tripped over the prostrate form on the stairs. A small hole in one temple told why the man had stopped running, but not who'd put it there.

Ducking low, Bolan stepped over the dead man and bounded up the stairs. There were two more flights, and the killer had to have gone through one of three doors. If he wasn't on one of the top two floors, he was on the roof. Bolan opened the door to the eleventh floor, stood back away from the frame. The hallway inside was silent. He took a quick look, saw nothing and skipped ahead to the twelfth, and last, floor.

The twelfth-floor hallway, too, was empty. That left the roof. The fire door to the roof was heavy steel plate. Before opening it, Bolan reached up to unscrew the bulb in the ceiling. Backlit in the doorway, he would be a sitting duck for anyone on the roof. With the light out, he pushed the door with his foot—it refused to budge. He pushed harder, but it still wouldn't yield.

It shouldn't have been locked from the outside, and the slide bolt on the inside was open. Either it had been jammed, or the fugitive was holding the door closed with his own body. Bolan put his shoulder to the cold steel and put his weight into it. His shoes slipped on the painted concrete landing. He was too weak to do anything more than try again, knowing it was useless.

Bolan went back down the stairs to the body. He had thought at first it was a young boy, but a closer examination surprised him. It was a young woman, perhaps nineteen or twenty years old. Her hair was closely cropped and partially hidden under a cloth cap. Her loose clothes obscured her figure, which was slender enough to have been a boy's in any case, and she wore no makeup. Her face was colorless—except for the dark red hole in the side of her head.

Checking her pockets, he came up empty. She carried no purse or wallet, wore no jewelry. Nothing on the body would identify who she once had been. There was no point in lingering. Bolan stepped carefully over the body and pushed open the door to the hallway. Inside, it was the same quiet, the same soft light.

The elevator came quickly, and Bolan stepped in. He pressed Lobby and felt the slight surge in his stomach as the car began its descent. It stopped once, on the third floor, but no one got on. When the doors closed, Bolan wondered whether the stop was significant, or if someone had simply gotten impatient and chosen to walk. Like so much else about this assignment, he would probably never know.

He closed his eyes as the car lurched back into its descent to the lobby. Against the red background of his closed eyes, Bolan saw the body of the young woman again, clearly. Too clearly. Who she had been seemed less important than why she had been killed. The tangled web grew more snarled the harder he yanked on it. Instead of coming apart, it had begun to collapse inward, like an imploding star, growing more dense and less comprehensible with every tug.

The lobby was quiet and empty. The doorman's podium stood to one side of the stylish bronze double doors, set in a marble arch. The small brass lamp over the podium glowed wanly in the overhead fluorescent light. It seemed odd that so upscale a building would not be attended this early. Bolan approached the podium and stood for a moment. Perhaps the doorman was simply taking care of some other business.

After several minutes, Bolan grew suspicious. Behind the podium, a small alcove contained the service room where packages and laundry were kept and mail sorted. Bolan stepped around the podium and stuck his head into the alcove. He called hello, but received no answer. He was about to leave, when something caught his eye. He noticed a narrow band of light on the floor of the alcove, against the bottom of a door he took to be the broom closet.

Stepping to the door, Bolan turned the knob. He unholstered his Beretta, then pushed the door slowly open. It swung back about halfway, then stopped, as if jammed. He pushed harder, and the obstruction gave a bit. The door was open wide enough to admit him. Sliding through the partially open door, gun hand first, Bolan found himself in the custodial area.

A glance at the floor explained the door's reluctance to open. The doorman lay on his back, eyes glazed. The stench of death filled the small room, covering the sickly-sweet odor given off by the pool of blood beneath the doorman's head. He had been shot twice at close range. Bolan stooped to examine the body more closely, and noted the singed hair and charring of powder burns around two small holes in the left side of the dead man's skull. Probably a small caliber, .22 or .25, Bolan thought.

Could whoever had killed the girl on the stairs also have killed the doorman? Or had she killed the doorman and in turn been taken out by someone else? Whose side was she on? For that matter, whose side was *he* on? Too many questions for an already overcrowded hopper.

Bolan stepped outside, just as an overdressed elderly couple were leaving a taxi. He slipped in and told the driver he wanted Holy Trinity Hospital. The cabbie nodded and squealed into a tight U-turn, leaving the old folks to gape at a small cloud of rubber smoke as he roared down the block.

Valerie had assured him that Callahan was all right, and being well-cared-for. Things being as fluid as they were, he wanted to see for himself. And if Brian Callahan was, indeed, out of danger, a few questions were in order.

The cab squealed to a halt in front of the hospital's modern glass doors. Bolan paid in a hurry, then disappeared into the lobby before the cabdriver could repeat his drag-strip departure. The polished marble floor echoed the hard slap of his feet as he rushed to the admitting desk. The nun on duty directed him to the third floor.

Waiting impatiently for the elevator, Bolan ran down the list of his options. It wasn't a long one. Right now, it contained two items: work with Callahan through channels and work on his own. At the moment, the latter seemed the wiser course.

He stepped into the elevator, making room for an orderly pushing an empty gurney. As the door closed, the orderly smiled at him. Bolan nodded to be polite, but said nothing. At the third floor, the orderly struggled to get the gurney through before the automatic doors could close. As he leaned forward, the pants of his greens rode up, revealing rather unorthodox footgear: black, high-top sneakers. It was not the first pair Bolan had seen that day.

Something didn't seem right. Bolan watched the man with the gurney move down the hall. He pretended to go in the other direction, then slipped into an alcove for a moment. The sneaker-clad orderly abandoned the gurney in the middle of the hallway and proceeded on. Bolan stepped back into the hall just as the orderly entered a room. A sign suspended over the doorway identified the room as 339. Callahan's room.

Bolan ran past the gurney, drawing his Beretta. He skidded to a halt, dropped into a crouch and entered the room. It contained two beds. The first, just in front of the door, was empty. Brian Callahan lay sleeping in the second. The orderly stood poised at the foot of the bed, a large hypodermic syringe in his hand.

"Drop it," Bolan shouted.

Startled, the orderly hesitated. Then, turning toward Bolan as if in compliance, he stabbed downward with the syringe. Bolan fired twice. One slug shattered the man's arm, striking just above the elbow. Blood spurted from the gaping wound, splattering the sheet and bedspread beneath it. The second bored in through the chest wall, cracking a rib and driving bone fragments through lung and heart.

The bogus orderly drooped forward, then spun to the side, falling to the floor with one hand full of blanket as he tried to keep himself erect. Bolan stood as if paralyzed. The syringe, its plunger fully depressed, still quivered where it projected up over the blanket.

Bolan could not tell whether the needle had struck Callahan. He rushed to the bed, reaching in under the blanket, carefully probing to find the shaft of the hypodermic. As his fingers closed over the slender metal, which was embedded in the mattress just a fraction of an inch from Callahan's left foot, Bolan heard a rustle.

He looked up into the face of a smiling Brian Callahan.

"You trying to tickle me, or what?" The blanket rustled again as Callahan swept it aside to reveal the small Smith & Wesson .25-caliber automatic in his hamlike fist. "I appreciate the gesture, Mack, but I never could sleep worth a damn."

Bolan sighed. "Where'd you get the gun?"

"Your lovely flight attendant. Quite a resourceful gal. Come on, tell me, she's not really a flight attendant, is she?"

"I asked her the same thing the last time I saw her."

"What'd she say?"

"She didn't."

"Now, why am I not surprised?"

"How you feeling?" Bolan asked.

"I've been better." Callahan smiled weakly, his skin pallid under a smattering of ordinarily unnoticeable freckles.

Steering the conversation to more urgent matters, Bolan indicated the would-be assassin on the floor, and continued, "Listen, our friend here is just one more link in the chain. We have a lot to talk about. Then I have a phone call to make. And a couple of errands to run."

CHAPTER SIXTEEN

The time for delicacy had passed. The post-Miranda pas de deux was never Bolan's favorite dance. Getting back in the government's good graces meant a lot, but he'd be damned if he was going to walk away from the purpose of his life. To be sanctioned was one thing; to stand around waiting for things to happen was another. To his surprise, Brognola had been candid on the phone. He didn't like what was happening, and he agreed there was a serious leak. "Sure, Mack, do what you think best," he'd said. "That's what you do best."

So, where to go from here?

Guess.

Diego Cardona's house was dark. The wall was a piece of cake. He'd done it before. This time, though, he was taking no prisoners. He went straight to the glass door he'd penetrated last time.

Once the door was out of the way, the Executioner checked his Ingram MAC-10, reslung it, then slipped inside. The silenced Beretta 93-R was within easy reach. He wanted as little noise as possible, to get as much done as he could without discovery.

The hallway door swung open silently, perfectly balanced on its high-tech hinges. The hall was dimly lit, the white decor as spotless as before.

He'd been watching the place for three hours, waiting for darkness. Cardona had company. As the sun set, the grounds were lit by discreetly placed security lights, a barrier against the night.

But only Mack Bolan knew just how dark it was going to get.

Bolan went directly to the security station. His last visit had told him most of what he had wanted to know about the place. There were still problem areas, but he'd deal with them. Standing in the upper gallery overlooking the huge living room, Bolan strained his ears. Nothing. Dead silence.

He peered cautiously over the balustrade, but the room was empty. He crossed to the other end, keeping low in case someone was to walk in. Once past the open wall, he straightened. The security control room was buried in the center of the mazelike house. Cardona's bunker mentality had learned more than a little from the German army.

Bolan reached the stairs leading to the control room. Unlike the rest of the house, this staircase was purely utilitarian. Steel stairs, steel banister, straight out of the Occupational Safety and Health Administration handbook for industrial safety. The metal rungs vibrated with his steps, seemed to hum as he placed one foot silently before the other.

At the bottom of the staircase, a steel door was set in the wall, rivet heads the size of grapes studding its perimeter. Finding it again had been easy. Getting inside would take a little ingenuity, and some luck. Typical of the arrogance of Cardona, the hallway outside the control room was itself surveillance free. Either he had thought no one would get that far, or he believed that, if someone managed, it would already be too late.

Before Bolan could decide what to do, he heard voices approaching. Someone was near the top of the stairs. Bolan stepped away from the door, looked for someplace to hide. A few feet beyond the steel door was an elaborate wooden door. He walked over and tried the knob, which turned easily. Holding his breath, Bolan pulled. The oiled walnut panel swung open to reveal a broom closet—with a two-thousand-dollar door.

Bolan slipped inside, pulling the door almost closed. There wasn't much room, but it would have to do. Peering through the crack, he watched the stairs. He could still hear the voices, but couldn't make out what they were saying. Then a black sneaker appeared on the top step. A white sneaker appeared beside it.

Two men, both armed with submachine guns, descended. They were arguing heatedly. As they drew nearer, Bolan could catch their drift. *Futbol*. They were arguing about a soccer game. Not unusual. Stadiums full of people had come to blows in South America, in riots to make Watts look like a block party, all because someone had disparaged someone else's favorite team. Why should Cardona's muscle be any different?

The two men stopped outside the security door. They continued to argue. Bolan waited patiently. If he timed it right, they would save him a lot of trouble. Finally, one man reached into his pocket and withdrew a large roll of American bills. He peeled several from the thick wad and slapped them contemptuously into his companion's outstretched hand.

"Thanks. Next time, bet on a winner, eh?" The recipient laughed.

The second man shook his head, still angry. Replacing the bankroll in his pocket, he brandished a key. It scratched on the lock plate, then with a solid thunk slid home. Bolan bunched his muscles. Before the door could swing back, Bolan opened his own and stepped out.

The Beretta was extended and Bolan crouched in a combat stance. His weapon spit once, then again. Without a whisper, the winner fell back against the stairs. A large bloodstain blossomed over his heart, obscuring the Miami Dolphins logo on his T-shirt. The second man, no more fortunate, caught a 9 mm parabellum slug in the temple. The impact hurled him sideways, a spray of blood and tissue painting the wall red and gray.

Bolan hauled the dead men to the broom closet one at a time. He couldn't do anything about the mess, but it might take someone a while to notice. The key to the steel door was still in the lock. Bolan turned it, tugging the heavy door open by the sturdy handle mounted just below the lock.

Inside, two men sat before an elaborate console. Beyond them, an array of TV monitors filled a wall. One man glanced up as the door opened. Bolan placed a finger to his lips, gesturing with the Beretta. The man stood, raising his hands. His movement caught the eye of his companion, who turned to him, then noticing the raised hands, to the doorway. He reached for an automatic on the console in front of him. Bolan fired once.

The slug tore through his forehead, blowing out the back of the skull. He slumped in his chair. One screen imploded, shattered by fragments of bone and bullet. Blood streaked several others, fine crimson stripes slowly growing toward the floor. The standing man flinched. If he had been thinking of going for his own weapon, he changed his mind.

Bolan pulled the door closed, keeping his gun trained on the captive. "I want a quick course in security."

The man nodded. He wore a bushy, Fu Manchu-style mustache, which twitched nervously. Bolan stepped closer, yanked the man's side arm from its holster and stuck it in his own belt. At Bolan's gesture, the man turned his back and was patted down. A gravity knife in his back pocket was the only other weapon. Bolan opened the knife, slid the blade into a crevice between two desks and snapped it off. He tossed the handle into a corner.

The man was big and well muscled. His tan forearms bulged, biceps stretching the sleeves of his pullover. His jeans were neatly pressed, an intricate design ornately stitched over their back pockets. Bolan tapped him on the shoulder with his left hand. "Okay, sit down."

The big man sat in one of two identical vacant chairs. Bolan sat in the other rolling it backward to get a little distance between them.

"Now, I'm going to ask you some questions, and I want answers. I already know some of them, but you won't know which. I don't have much time. So, whatever you do, don't lie to me. Understood?"

"Yes, understood."

"How many security men are in the house?"

"Ten, *señor*." He glanced at the dead man in the chair. "I mean, nine."

Bolan nodded. With the two in the closet, that meant seven were left. "What about staff...maids, butlers?"

"Six or seven. It changes all the time. Diego, Señor Cardona, he can't make up his mind, you know?"

"How many guests?"

"Four that I know of. I only came on an hour ago. They came after I went on duty. I don't know of anybody else."

"Can you check? Is there a list anywhere?"

"No. No list."

Bolan leaned forward.

"I'm not lying, I swear. No list. We're not that organized. Besides, people are always coming and going. Diego knows a lot of people, you know, has a lot of friends. Big wheels, politicians, you know."

The man seemed to be regaining some of his courage, now that the surprise had worn off. Just thinking about Cardona's connections seemed to lift his spirits.

"I know what you're thinking," Bolan said. "You're thinking Cardona knows too many people for me to get away with this. But I've got news for you. Before I'm finished with Señor Cardona, he won't have any friends."

The muscle man sneered. "You think so?"

"Yes, I do," Bolan stated. His soft voice puzzled the guard, unused to such quiet assurance. Bluster and macho swaggering were more his style. He didn't know what to make of the soft-spoken gringo.

"Where is the alarm?"

"*Señor?*"

"The alarm, where is it? Show me."

Annoyed, Bolan stood up. He could find it himself, but it would take time. He'd rather not waste it. The guard denied there was an alarm, but his eyes betrayed him. They kept flickering toward a bank of green toggles on the console.

Bolan crossed to the control board. Nothing was labeled. His attention diverted, he dropped his guard. Not much, but enough for the hardman to make a move . . . and a mistake.

The chair creak alerted Bolan. He turned just as the guard launched himself into the air. Bolan flashed the Beretta in a vicious arc, catching the man on the side of the head. It was a glancing blow, and only slowed him down. The collision pitched Bolan backward. He lost his balance and slid to the floor. The hardman was reaching for his partner's automatic. His fingers closed on the butt.

Bolan kicked, but couldn't reach the outstretched arm. He had no choice. An unsilenced gunshot might alert the entire household. He squeezed the Beretta's trigger twice and heard the impact of the two slugs. The hardman groaned, reaching for his ribs. The first slug had caught him in the upper arm, but the other had found a more critical mark. Bolan fired a third time, taking the guard in the chest as he rolled over.

The guard sighed once, then again. A small trickle of blood rolled from the corner of his mouth, then bubbled as he coughed once. And died.

Bolan would have to figure it out on his own. He got up, clutching his wounded forearm, still sore from the knife wound. It had slammed into the edge of the console and was only partially protected by its gauze wrapping. Bolan glanced at the bandage. There was no blood.

Just pain.

He turned his attention to the console again. A quick survey convinced him the green toggles were for the alarm. One of them, larger than the others, might be a master switch. A small red diode, which was mounted on the panel next to it, glowed. Above it, a small embossed plaque said Power On. Bolan grabbed the large green toggle, took a deep breath and yanked. The red light went out. Nothing else seemed to happen.

Bolan stepped to the monitors. Nine were still functional, six of them showing portions of the wall around the estate. They didn't concern him. The others showed various rooms, all uninhabited. One screen, larger than the others, seemed to be some kind of master monitor. The control panel contained an array of thirty-one buttons. One of them, marked Scan, was depressed. Bolan watched the screen. Every ten seconds, the picture jumped, and a new location appeared. With each change of picture, a red light next to one of the buttons blinked off and another winked on.

Bolan pushed number one. The Scan button popped out. The picture on the screen jumped once and remained steady. It showed the main gallery. Pushing another button, he found himself looking at another room. Bolan pulled up a chair and started to work his way through all the rooms in the house.

In quick succession, several bedrooms, a large library and a dining room flashed onto the screen. The latter held a table large enough to seat King Arthur's knights. The color monitor blazed with flashes of color, stark blotches against the universally white walls. Cardona seemed to have a thing for white.

The next three buttons showed outdoor views of the house, the next zeroed in on the front gate. Bolan was getting impatient. Punching the buttons more rapidly, he almost missed what he was looking for.

He backed up in time to catch a graceful arc of water on the screen: the indoor swimming pool, a kidney-shaped sweep, surrounded by glass walls and a jungle of potted plants. Three men sat on white wicker chaise lounges. A ripple broke the surface of the water. A head popped up, long brown hair streaming water. A woman swam gracefully to a ladder and pulled herself out of the pool. Narrow white lines across her back and hips showed where her bikini would have been . . . if she'd been wearing one.

The woman was slender, but generously proportioned. She moved like a dancer as she walked to an empty lounge alongside one of the men. As she wrapped herself in a large white towel, Bolan shifted his attention to the three men. He punched a button marked Zoom, and the four figures leaped to one side of the screen, then disappeared altogether. Bolan depressed the Pan button and found them again. When he punched Hold they stayed center screen. He punched Zoom again, and the figures jumped straight toward him. He punched it once more and found himself staring into the eyes of Diego Cardona.

For a moment, Bolan thought Cardona was looking right at him.

"Soon," Bolan whispered. "Soon."

CHAPTER SEVENTEEN

Joey Buccieri didn't listen too well. He didn't give a damn what Sally Maggadino wanted. He knew a good buck when he saw it. No greaseballs were going to take down somebody bought and paid for, and laugh all the way to the bank. Sitting in the Sons of Napoli Social Club, he sucked on a loose filling, drawing circles on the table with a wet finger.

Frank Ianni watched him, his slack jaw partly open. He wanted to know what he was supposed to do, but he wouldn't ask. That was the one thing about him that Joey liked most. He hated to be asked questions when he didn't have the answers. Frank was too dumb to know what the questions were supposed to be.

Finally, lighting a cigarette, Joey asked a few questions of his own.

"So, Frank, what'd you find out?"

"You know, Joey. It ain't easy getting a straight answer."

"You got it too?"

"Got what?"

"You don't get straight answers, you can't give one either?"

"Sure, Joey, sure. I just meant—"

Joey cut him off. "I know what you meant, Frankie. Just tell me what you found out, all right? Then we can figure out what we're going to do about it."

"Well, like you told me, I grabbed one of them Bolivian dealers, a little fish, you know? And he told me where he got his stuff."

"And . . . ?"

"It wasn't easy. We had to persuade him. Over at the Fish and Game Club. The back room. It's nice and quiet out there."

"I know all about how nice the Fish and Game Club is, Frankie. What I don't know is what the guy told you."

Ianni sighed. "I'm getting to that. We took him there, like I said. A little juice, a little smacking around, he don't say nothing. I figure we got to make him understand we're serious." Ianni mimed the swing of a butcher's cleaver. "After a couple of fingers, he got the point."

"And what'd he tell you?"

"Gave me the name of his supplier." Frank smiled with pride at his accomplishment.

"That's it? That's all he told you? What's wrong with you, Frankie? I swear to—"

"Naw, Joey. That ain't all. It's all I got from him, but it ain't all I got."

Buccieri exhaled loudly, lit a new cigarette from the butt of the old and flicked ashes into a Cinzano ashtray on the table. "Will you get to the goddamn point?"

"Well, it worked once, see, so I figured why not do it again. We grabbed the supplier and sweated him a little. That's the good part."

"Would you mind telling me the good part, Frankie? I'm going to be an old man, here, for Chrissakes, before I know what the hell you're talking about."

"All right, all right, Joey. Jeez. I'm trying, all right? Give me a chance." Ianni lit a cigarette of his own, borrowing the stick matches from a little box in front of Buccieri. "It worked better this time. The guy we grabbed, he didn't want to lose no fingers. Not that he needs any now." Ianni laughed.

"He tipped us to a some street punk, a small-time hustler named Pablo something. Anyway, Pablo is a snitch for Vice, you know. He's plugged in. They tell him stuff, ask him to nose around a little. He figures, what the fuck? It's extra coin, and he gets his ass in trouble, the fix is in. Makes sense, I guess. But it don't make him too secure.''

Ianni paused to look at Buccieri, as if to see if anything he'd said was making sense. When Buccieri gave no indication one way or the other, Ianni shrugged and continued.

"So anyway, Pablo is just full of interesting information. It seems some Bolivian guy is making a move on the whole coke business.''

Buccieri perked up. "What kind of move?''

"Nobody knows for sure. Looks like he's trying to corner the market. He's been hassling the other Bolivians, mostly. But the Feds think that's just the first step. Pablo will let me know more.''

"What? What did you say?''

"Pablo. He'll let me know more when he finds out.''

"For God's sake, Frankie . . . The guy's plugged into the Feds and he'll let you know more? What'd you do, give him your phone number?''

"C'mon, Joey. I ain't that stupid. No, I'm going back to see him tomorrow. Besides, there's nothing to worry about. I told you, he's a snitch. He talks to everybody for money. I paid him plenty on account, with more later, if he delivers.''

"You fucking idiot." Buccieri stubbed out the cigarette. Ashes spewed out of the ashtray, and the butt snapped in two. "This guy can roll over on you, like that." Buccieri snapped his fingers. "Why the hell did you let him walk?''

"I told you, so he could find out more. What's the big deal?''

"I'll tell you what the big deal is. For all you know, this guy is undercover. That's all I need. How the hell am I going to tell Sally about this? He'll have my nuts in a jar.''

"No problem, Joey. I see the guy, find out what he knows, then I whack him. What's the big deal?''

"You better whack him, Frankie. You better go see him tonight, you understand me? That guy is a time bomb. Find out what he knows, then lose him. I want him buried so deep, they got a better chance of digging him up in China. You know what I mean?''

"Sure, Joey, no problem. Besides, don't worry about Sally. I'll tell him it was me who screwed up. Don't worry about it, all right?''

"Yeah, Frankie, you do that. You tell Sally, all right. And Sally won't think it was me, right. He won't blame me for this colossal screwup. In a pig's eye, he won't. You heard him the other night. I'm not supposed to do anything unless he knows about it. You better hope he doesn't find out about it, Frankie. I mean it. If he does, we'll both be dead. Pick me up here at eleven o'clock, alone. And whatever you do, don't use your own car.''

Ianni nodded, properly contrite.

Buccieri stood up, pushing away from the table. He reached for the cigarettes and matches, dumped them in his pocket and left the social club.

He cursed himself. He never should have let Ianni do anything on his own. The guy was too dumb to be believed. But maybe it wasn't too late. Maybe the snitch had something worthwhile. Maybe.

"We'll see," he mumbled, handing a five to the parking valet. "We'll see.''

He got into his car, leaving the valet to wonder what he was talking about.

IANNI WAS NOTHING, if not prompt. At eleven on the button he stepped into the social club. He had changed out of his suit, and now wore a Hawaiian shirt loose over his belt. A wave of after-shave preceded him across the floor to Buccieri's table.

"You ready, Joey?''

"Does it look like I'm not?'' Buccieri stood up, grabbed a Windbreaker from the back of his chair. He was dressed casually in jeans and a red-and-white softball shirt. A matching cap sat on his head, perched cockily.

"So, where's this guy live?''

"In Little Havana, Joey. With the spics and such. I don't know how he stands it."

"You asshole, the guy's a spic himself. What kind of name you think Pablo is, Irish? It's a spic name, and he's a spic, Frankie. Jesus!"

"I know that, Joey. I just meant—"

"Never mind. Where's your car?"

"Around the corner."

"What is it?"

"A Camaro, all white. Man, it's beautiful, wait'll you see it."

"Yeah, I can't wait."

Buccieri led the way out the side door, stepped into the alley and waited for Ianni. The two men walked around the corner, neither speaking. Buccieri was still annoyed with Frankie, and reluctant to show it. Ianni, on the other hand, knew he'd made a mistake. All he could think about was making it right. He knew better than to say anything to Buccieri until he had done so.

When they were in the car, Ianni said, "What do you think, Joey? Nice wheels, huh?"

Buccieri grunted.

The drive to Little Havana wouldn't take long. In ten minutes, they were already on the fringes of the section of Miami long since taken over by Cuban refugees. People had been pouring into the section since Castro's ascension to power. Spanish became the dominant language, and the area continued to grow as more and more escapees poured into Miami.

Eventually, Latins from other Spanish-speaking countries added to the explosion. It was a melting pot of sorts, but the prevalence of Spanish kept the pot on simmer. For all practical purposes, it was an independent city-state within a city, as self-contained as the Vatican or any major North American Chinatown.

Every other store seemed to be a *bodega* or *botica*. Buccieri, for all his bravado, was uneasy. He never cared for

Latins, or anybody else who could speak a language he
didn't understand. Distrustful by nature, made more so by
his chosen profession, he was inclined to assume he was the
subject of any conversation he couldn't comprehend.

"You know exactly where this guy's place is, Frankie?"

"Sure, Joey. What do you think?"

"You don't want to know, Frankie. Trust me, you don't
want to know."

"You still pissed?"

"Is your buddy Pablo still breathing?"

When Ianni didn't answer, Buccieri reached into his
pocket for a cigarette.

"You're smoking a lot these days, Joey."

"I'm nervous, that's all. Mind your own business."

"What are you nervous about?"

"Like you don't know, right?"

Ianni lapsed into silence. Turning onto West Flagler, he
hung the next right at SW 29th and then a left on SW 8th,
now called Calle Ocho.

At the corner of SW 27th, Buccieri stared at the Orange
Bowl, a few blocks to the north, while they waited for the
light to change. On SW 17th, Frankie slowed, searching the
storefronts for a familiar sign.

Finally spotting the sign he was looking for, he grunted,
gunned the engine and drifted a block past the side street he
wanted. He pulled over to the curb, gunned the engine then
shut it down. He was out of the car a moment later, waiting
for Buccieri on the sidewalk.

Buccieri sucked the last smoke out of his cigarette, tossed
the butt out the window—narrowly missing Frankie—and
rolled the window up. He slammed the door so hard the
Camaro rocked for several seconds before settling back on
its springs.

"All right, Frankie, where we going?"

"Not far. Back that way a block and down 23rd Terrace."

"This son of a bitch better be there."

"Don't worry about it."

"Look, I'll worry, all right? Nobody else worries, that means I got to."

Ianni shook his head and marched off. Buccieri followed a couple of paces behind him. It was late, but the night was warm. People lounged in windows or sat in doorways. Here and there, men played noisy games of dominoes and drank beer, flirting at women strolling by in pairs and threes.

If you forgot about who they really were, Buccieri thought, they could have been his childhood neighbors back in New York. Little Havana and Little Italy weren't that far apart. Even the garlic in the air was the same. If he closed his eyes, he could have been on Carmine Street. Thank God he wasn't. He was so absorbed in his reflection, he almost slammed into Frankie when he stopped in front of a narrow doorway.

"This is it, huh?" Buccieri wrinkled his nose to show his distaste. The place was too damn much like Carmine Street. Even the same dreadful paint, a red-brown mixed from a half dozen nearly empty cans, flaked off the doorframe. Lead-green glass, with wire embedded in it, made up the upper half of the chipped door.

Ianni led the way into the dark vestibule. Inside, the smell of garlic was almost overpowering. Like most poor people, the residents of this building tried to cover the inadequacy of their diets with their favorite spices. It was a practice all too vividly memorable to Joey Buccieri. One low-wattage bulb from the top of the narrow staircase threw Ianni's shadow on the steps. A dank hallway led off to the left.

Ianni stopped at the last of three doors. He knocked once, lightly. A low voice asked him to wait a minute. Several seconds later the peephole rasped, the lock rattled, then the knob. The door opened slowly.

A short, swarthy man in a faded green T-shirt stepped aside, waving them in.

"Hey, Pablo. How you doin'?"

"I been better, man. But I been worse, you know what I'm saying?"

"Yeah, man, yeah. I do."

Ianni seemed to ease, genuinely glad to see the little man. Buccieri said nothing. Better to let Frankie do all the talking.

"Oh, hey. This is my friend, Tony," Frankie said, indicating Buccieri.

Pablo stuck out his hand. Buccieri gave it a quick squeeze, then dropped it, like a wet fish.

"You guys want a beer?" Pablo asked.

"No, thanks, man. We gotta be someplace. Listen, did you get any more on what we were talkin' about?"

"Oh, hey, man. Not much, no. I mean, I got the name of the Bolivian guy, the one I told you about. Cardona. But that's all, man. And it don't mean nothing to me, man. I mean, I heard of the guy, but that's all. I asked around, you know. But nobody had nothing to say." Pablo sat down at a rickety table in one corner.

"You guys sure you don't want no beer? It's cold."

"No, thanks. We got to go. And remember what I told you. Keep your ears open. You hear anything else, there's gonna be some bread in it for you."

"You couldn't let me have no more now, could you, man? I could use it."

Ianni looked at Buccieri before answering. "Yeah, I guess I could let you have a few bucks. On account, you might say."

"Okay, man, that's great. I really appreciate it, you know?"

"Don't mention it." Ianni reached into his jacket. He shot Pablo twice through the head. The little man sprawled backward into the corner, then slid off his chair to the floor. Ianni crossed to the corner and bent down to feel for a pulse.

There was none. He shot Pablo again, this time through the temple. Just to be sure.

Then Buccieri shot Frankie through the head. Twice. And, just to be sure, he shot him once more.

CHAPTER EIGHTEEN

Diego Cardona seemed to be in an expansive mood. Bolan watched him on the monitor for a minute. He didn't recognize the other two men, and he'd never seen the woman before. Chances were Cardona hadn't, either. Coke profits could buy more than fancy houses and underpaid cops.

Finding them was only part of the problem. Getting to them, through a bunch of hired guns, was going to be tougher. Bolan's cursory reconnaissance on his previous visit had been useful, but far from comprehensive. He needed a guide, or a map. Scanning the control, he spotted several pairs of buttons marked Grid. Shrugging, he punched the first button. Instantly, a map of the main floor flashed on a small black-and-white monitor next to the main color screen.

He punched the companion button, and small dots of white light appeared. One light was flashing. On a hunch, Bolan changed the camera selection, and a different light began to flash. That could only mean the flashing light indicated the room whose surveillance camera was fed to the main monitor. Reversing his selection, the first light began to flash again. Now he knew where the swimming pool was located.

He knew where they were, and where he was. The last step would be to find the heavy hitters. Quickly skimming through the huge house, room by room, he located the house staff and all but two of the remaining guards. Cross-checking locations on the grids, he figured the first floor might be easy. The staff was buried in the rear kitchen area. Only two guards were on that floor, the others concentrated in a suite of rooms adjacent to the staff quarters.

After running through the floor plans one more time,
Bolan was ready. He hoped to grab Cardona alive. Killing
him would be a last, desperate resort. Brognola's mandate
was to roll up the network, bottom to top. Going after Cardona now was starting at the wrong end. It might feel good
to nail the big honcho, but, as Bolan knew only too well,
organizations often had lives of their own. Kill one boss and
two others were right there, ready to take his place.

In some respects, being the boss meant you had to watch
your back. Too many guys were ready to stick a knife in it,
wanting what you had. They fancied themselves just as ca-
pable, and more deserving, than the man above them. Often
they were right.

Taking Cardona alive would at least give Bolan a chance
to work backward, skim off the top couple of management
layers. It might not be perfect, but something was wrong,
the leak too damaging. Hal had been checking and re-
checking credentials. So far, he'd come up empty. Tacitly,
he'd agreed to Bolan's suggestion that he be allowed to wing
it, at least until the leak was plugged.

All those years in the cold Bolan had worked alone, half
hoping one day to be sanctioned again. He'd forgotten what
a straitjacket it could be. With a shrug, he turned off the
unpleasant reminder. He was still his own man, couldn't be
anything less. But he still had the spooky sensation of
invisible strings tugging at his wrists and ankles.

He walked to the door then glanced around the control
room once more. Hedging his bets, he concealed the MAC-
10 in the closet. It just might be useful to have some hidden
backup. For now, he had the Python in his belt. With the
Beretta and Big Thunder, it would have to be enough. If he
needed more hardware, he needed more help than he could
get. He pushed the door open and stepped into the hall.

He knew from the floor plan that he was in the basement. He took the steel stairs quietly, two at a time. The
longer he waited, the greater likelihood that one or more of
the people he'd spotted would change location.

At the top of the stairs, he began working westward along an outer wall. The corridor made a detour about two-thirds of the way toward the swimming pool. Along the same wall, something labeled Game Room had appeared on the grid. Two guards were inside. That would be his first and, if all went well, his only stop. Keeping close to the wall, Bolan sprinted along the hallway.

The leftward jig in the corridor was just ahead. If he'd read the floor plan correctly, the game room would be on the right, just around the corner. Bolan paused after he made the turn, hearing voices that came from an open door. Listening for a moment, he heard the telltale clack of ivory on ivory. The hardmen were playing pool.

Pressing flat against the wall, Bolan inched along the hallway and stopped just outside the door. He glanced across the hall and leaped back, startled. A full-length mirror occupied a floor-to-ceiling alcove directly across from the door. He realized he could see the two men, both absorbed in their game. But if he could see them, they could also see him.

Bolan inched forward again, just far enough to get both men in view, sharply etched on the near edge of the glass. One man was bent over the table, stretching out over the white felt, trying to line up a bridge shot. The balls were sharp spots of color on the snowy surface. The table must have been custom made.

The second man stood to one end of the table, leaning on his cue. He was too busy trying to rattle his opponent to notice anything else.

Both men wore side arms. If they had any heavy artillery, game room etiquette had consigned it to the sidelines.

Bolan moved.

He burst through the doorway, the Beretta in his fist. The guy leaning on his cue saw him first. He opened his mouth to mutter something, then dropped the cue, diving for a leather bench on the wall opposite the door.

Bolan saw the move and squeezed off a 3-round burst. Three bright red splotches blossomed on the first gunner's blue oxford shirt.

Bolan turned his attention to the second hardguy, who still straddled the edge of the table. He was staring, mouth open, as if he didn't believe what he was seeing. He dropped the bridge, raised one hand to ward off what he knew was coming.

Bolan's first shot tore through the upraised palm, slamming it back into the guy's face. Too late. The bullet had gotten there first. The second and third slugs followed in quick succession. The man fell off the table edge, leaving bridge and cue behind.

The Executioner stepped around the table. Both men lay dead on the floor.

Bolan's eye leaped to the table, caught a bright smear of blood near the side pocket. The white felt was ruined.

The weapons on the bench were Uzi submachine guns. Compact and deadly, the *traficante*'s friend. Bolan grabbed one and took the magazine from the second. He draped the SMG over one shoulder and walked back to the door.

The swimming pool was down the short hall and around the next corner. Its walls were all glass, probably bulletproof. Cardona wasn't going to trust his safety to a room anyone with a scope could penetrate from five hundred yards.

Bolan juked across the opening to the short hall leading into the swimming area. Flat against the wall, Bolan inched forward. Not knowing where the surveillance camera was located meant he had no idea where Cardona was sitting.

The doorway into the area was stained glass. The bright lights beyond it cast colorful shadows on the white wall, smears of misty red and foggy blue. A bright yellow overlapped both, adding orange and green to the rainbow. Bolan's skin turned a ghastly, jaundiced shade of chartreuse as he approached.

He paused with his hand on the door, then shoved. The door swung open.

The woman noticed him first. She was lying on a chaise lounge, squirming under Cardona's ministering hands. The two other men were watching and laughing. She had opened her eyes to say something to Cardona, and saw Bolan. A scream echoed against the hard glass of the walls.

Bolan raced around the edge of the pool, keeping the Beretta trained on the fat boys with Cardona. The woman continued to scream. Her high-pitched shriek must have made dogs uncomfortable for a couple of miles, but nobody seemed to hear it.

One man reached for a gun that lay on a chaise, the sheet of fat on his chest quivering like tan Jell-O. Bolan fired once, then again. The big man fell backward over his lounge, landing on a cluster of African violets in a stone planter.

"Everybody freeze," Bolan yelled. His voice echoed eerily in the high-ceilinged room. The humidity was oppressive. It felt more like a sauna than a swimming pool. The greenhouse effect. Thin rivulets of condensed moisture ran shimmering down the pale green-tinted glass. They caught light from a series of sunlamps tracked discreetly overhead, fern-drenched and shrouded in creeping moss.

Cardona was apoplectic.

"Who are you? How did you get in here? What do you want?"

The rapid-fire interrogation ricocheted off the glass. Cardona struggled to get to his feet, but the woman clung to his arms, unintentionally holding him down. Roberto Cabeza, perhaps the wisest of the surviving trio, raised his hands over his head. That wisdom was not lost on Bolan.

"Shut up, you banshee," Cardona yelled. He wrenched one hand free and struck the woman a sharp blow across the face. She stopped screaming. The room seemed suddenly quiet.

Bolan edged around the room, keeping one eye on the three prisoners, and one on the slippery edge of the irregularly shaped pool. Cardona seemed preoccupied, as if he were debating with himself. No fool, he had to know any move was potentially hazardous. But Bolan grew uneasy.

He turned to look over one shoulder, thinking he might have missed a guard when he scanned the room by camera. He saw nothing. Moving more deliberately, he stole quick looks at the other three walls of the enormous room. Still, nothing. He had reached one end of the pool, now, and would soon be face-to-face with Diego Cardona.

The druglord made a sudden move, and Bolan countered. He lost his footing and fell to the concrete, landing on his shoulder. The woman screamed again. The impact jarred the Beretta loose. It skittered across the stone slabs embedded in the floor, landing with a clack against a stone trough full of gardenias.

Struggling to regain his feet, he swung the Uzi up into position, just as a figure emerged from the tangled greenery at the base of one wall. Without aiming, Bolan squeezed the Uzi's trigger, sweeping the muzzle in a shallow arc. The rain of slugs snipped and pruned the bushes, throwing bits and pieces of bark, leaves and branches everywhere. His target shuddered and began to fall, trying to support himself with a slender rod.

A blowgun.

Cardona's Jivaro hit men always worked in teams. That meant there was at least a second, somewhere in the bushes. Bolan unleashed another swarm of lead hornets. They hummed and buzzed through the domesticated rain forest along a second wall. The clip ran dry, and Bolan jammed the other in.

Backing toward his captives, Bolan swept the Uzi back and forth, his finger trembling on the trigger, waiting for a target. He saw nothing. The woman's shrieks coiled and twined among the branches, echoing off the glass.

Another rustle in the bushes caught his ear. He wheeled, the Uzi ready, and saw trembling leaves. A small black circle seemed ready to swallow him. Bolan dived to his left, rolled over and squeezed in one continuous motion. The second blowgunner pitched forward. He lay half out of the foliage. His legs, still buried in the bushes, kicked spasmodically, shaking the miniature jungle like an angry jaguar on the prowl.

The shrieks turned to a strangled cry. Bolan got to his feet and ran toward the clustered furniture. The first thing that caught his eye was the woman, twitching on the lounge. A small, dark shaft protruding from between perfectly formed, pale white breasts. The Jivaro had found the wrong target. Cabeza knelt by her side. The look on his face said it all. It was hopeless, and he knew it. The woman struggled for breath, twitched once and lay still.

A sudden rush of footsteps echoed on the pavement. Bolan turned in time to see Cardona sprinting for an opening in the shrubbery at the far end of the pool room. He loosed a burst over Cardona's head, the bullets impacting against the sturdy glass.

Cardona skidded, then kept running. He must have known Bolan wasn't trying to kill him. It was all the edge he needed. The *traficante* disappeared into the green curtain. A brief glint betrayed a glass door opening, then it was gone.

And so was Diego Cardona.

CHAPTER NINETEEN

Lee Richards sat up all night. He was waiting for his brother to come home. Albert had been acting more and more like a stranger. He didn't blame the kid, in a way. He hadn't been much of a brother, and their father had been gone so long that neither of them rightly knew what he looked like. The few dog-eared snapshots in a shoe box showed a man like thousands of others: hair styled in the fashion of the times, a woman on his hip looking up at the man of her dreams. Dreams, hell, the man of her nightmares. But she didn't know that when the pictures were taken. She didn't know it when Lee was born. And by the time she was pregnant with Albert, it was way too late.

Now, maybe to forget him, and maybe to punish herself for having known him at all, Loretta Richards spent much of each day in an alcoholic fog. Albert, too frightened and too confused to do anything else, took it out on her. He was too young to understand how it was for her. What scared Lee, though, was that his younger brother just might be too angry to live long enough to understand.

That had been what his life was about. He didn't much like what his mother had become. Sure as hell, he didn't like remembering the fractured dreams and broken bones that had been the stuff of his childhood. But he knew it could be different, not just for him, but for all of them—Albert and, most of all, his mama.

Learning how to kill had been easy. The streets offered college and graduate school on a walk around the block. Learning how to shoot had taken longer, and shooting well was something he was still learning. He had mastered the technique, explored the science. Now he was polishing the art.

And it had paid him handsomely at times. Never better than putting the hit on Yanez. In the dark room, early sun still just a hint at the edge of the window shade, Lee thought about it again. It had been on his mind every day since it happened. He didn't like it. For the first time since he'd made the big leagues, he'd been unable to resist looking past the target, at the man.

He had a cool million on tap, and it didn't mean a damn thing. It all turned to dust in his hands, crumbling like an old newspaper. The rosy future he had painted faded to a rusty sepia, a memory before it had become a fact. If he couldn't talk some sense into Albert, it wouldn't make a difference how much money he had.

For his mother, it was simple. She couldn't be saved, but she could be comfortable. But Albert was different. He was smart and he was strong. As rough as the white world could be, if you had those tools, you could get over. That was what life, and its taking, had taught Lee. Not an easy lesson, but a necessary one. If only he had enough time to teach his little brother.

He heard a scrape in the hallway, then the doorknob rattled. Albert? Whoever it was seemed to be having some difficulty with the locked door. A muffled curse was followed by an angry kick. The door rattled in its frame as Lee got up to open it. Before he reached it, the door swung inward, its knob banging into the raw wound in the ancient plaster wall. Chips of paint and a fine cascade of plaster dust hissed down to the small pile on the floor.

It was Albert.

"Where in the hell you been all night?" Lee demanded.

"That's none of your business."

"Well, it ain't yours, Albert. You ain't got no business."

"Get out of my face, man. I told you once, why don't you just leave, man. Let me alone."

"Because you're my brother. That's all the reason I need."

"Uh-huh. What you want? You want to take me into the family business, man? That what you want? 'Cause I'm too old to learn a trade, man. And I don't need to bust my butt passing ammo to no hit man."

"I'm through with that. I told you. I got enough bread, Albert. We don't have to live here no more."

"We. Man, what 'we' you talkin' about? You ain't lived here in years."

"We. That's right, you, me, Lurleen and Mama."

"Mama ain't got no more use for you than I got. She too far gone to give a damn about either one of us, man."

Lee stepped around his brother to close the door. "Keep your voice down, Albert. This is personal."

Albert said nothing. He walked past his brother, opened the refrigerator and took out a beer. The can was almost pretty. A light blue, it said "From the Land of Sky-blue Waters" across the bottom. Albert pulled the tab and tossed it into the sink where it rattled on the dirty dishes.

He looked at the sink for a second, then turned back to his older brother with an artificial smile. "Since you so determined to make us a happy family, why don't you start with the dishes. Then you vacuum, throw some paint on the walls. You know, man. Tidy up some. This place looks like shit."

"You got a smart mouth on you, Albert."

"Yeah, well..."

"Don't 'well' me, man. I'm serious about this."

"You got any money you can give me, man?"

"What do you need it for?"

"Just answer the question. You got it or not?"

The younger man was starting to fidget. A thin glaze of sweat made his upper lip shiny in the pale light from a table lamp. Lee stared at him, wondering what was wrong with the kid.

"What you looking at, man? Don't look at me like that, damn it. Just don't, okay?"

"What's the matter with you, Albert. Are you sick?"

"Naw, man. I'm okay. I just need some, you know...some money. Just a couple of yards, you know. One, maybe will do it."

"What are you on?"

"Nothing, I'm not on nothing."

"Like hell you're not. Tell me."

"Nothing, man. Just nothing, all right? Okay? Nothing."

"Who do you think you're kidding?"

Albert's eyes narrowed. "Mama tell you to ask me that?"

"No."

"She did. She told you, didn't she? That bitch, I told her—"

The smack caught him by surprise. Lee, stunned by the blow he'd delivered, stared at his own hand in amazement. The palm stung, and his wrist throbbed. It felt as though he might have sprained something.

"What you do that for, man?" Albert started pacing. He was no longer looking at Lee. His angry pace became a constrained sprint. Back and forth across the small room. One hand was still glued to his cheek.

The question slid into an angry monologue, barely audible. He was mumbling and railing at somebody or something. Without knowing what Albert was saying, Lee knew why. The paranoid rambling, just hinted at the day before, had become more pronounced. As Albert grew more agitated, his sentences, fragmentary at best, deteriorated still further.

"I'm sorry, Albert. I didn't mean that."

Albert kept pacing.

"Albert? Listen, man, I'm sorry."

The younger man stopped in his tracks. He turned slowly, deliberately, to stare at Lee. "You say something, man? You talking to me? You still here, even?"

"You okay?"

"Yeah man, I'm okay. I got my medicine right here." He reached under his shirt. He fumbled around for a few seconds, the shirt rippling comically over the lost hand. Then it was back, wrapped around a .25-caliber automatic. His knuckles paled under the strenuous grip.

"I asked you before, man. You got any money? You remember? Remember I asked you that?"

"Yeah, I remember."

"You didn't say nothing then. Did you?"

"No. No, I didn't say nothing."

"You gonna say something now?"

"No."

"You gonna give me the money?"

"No, I'm not."

"Lucky I got this gun, huh? I can take it, if I want. The money, not the gun. I already got the gun. You shouldn't have left it in your suitcase, man. You supposed to be a professional, ain't you? Now, lemme ask you, what kind of jiveass turkey leaves something this dangerous lying around where his little brother can find it?"

Lee said nothing. Albert was close to the edge, walking a fine line. He was so close to going over, the slightest movement might tip him.

"Guns don't kill people, Lee. People kill people. I seen that on a car. That true? This gun ever kill anybody? Or did you do it?"

"Put it down, Albert."

"No, man, I ain't putting nothing down."

"You don't know how to use that thing. It's dangerous."

"Damn right, man. It's so dangerous, I don't *have* to know how to use it. Long as I got it. Ain't that right?"

He pointed the weapon at Lee's midsection. Lee couldn't tell whether the safety was on or off. He had left it on, but Albert might have taken it off.

Albert looked up at the ceiling. "You hear anything?"

"No."

"I do. Man, I hear something. I hear rats. I swear to God, right up there in the damn ceiling. They have rats where you work?" Albert laughed. It was soft, almost genuine. The lunatic edge just audible, more in the tension than anything else.

He looked at Lee again. Two quick steps and he was right in front of his older brother. Prepared for anything, Lee wasn't expecting anything in particular. The blow caught him just over the left eye. A second swipe of the pistol and he went down to one knee. He saw the butt descending, but was powerless to stop it.

The gun glanced off his forehead, and he crumpled to the floor. He tried to rise, but rubber arms made it impossible. He saw the floor coming as if from a great distance, slowly approaching. His nose slammed into the scratched linoleum. He heard his head hit the floor. He didn't see Albert stand over him, point the gun down and pop his lips, once, then again.

"Blam! Pow! Hot damn, a piece!"

La Paz

CHAPTER TWENTY

Roberto Cabeza looked blankly at the big man in black. He shook his head from side to side. Getting to his feet, he turned to face the uninvited guest.

"It's no use, *señor*. She's dead. Curare."

"Meant for me."

"Of course."

"Who is she?"

"No one, now. Who are you?"

"Let's say an interested party. Where would Cardona go?"

"It would not be in my best interest to tell you, even if I knew."

Bolan waved the Uzi impatiently. "It's not in your best interest not to. And you do know."

"You won't shoot me, *señor*. You think I can help you. If I knew anything, and if I told you, I could help you no longer. *Then* you would shoot me."

"You have my word."

"What value am I to place on the word of a man I do not know, who wears the clothes of a burglar and carries a machine gun? Those are not credentials to inspire trust, *señor*."

"And I suppose Señor Cardona is a trustworthy man?"

"That used to be true. Now, I don't know. He is a changed man. Not the Diego I grew up with. Not even the Diego I went into business with. He is as much a stranger as you."

"Do you know where he went?" Sensing a subtle shift in Cabeza's attitude, Bolan lowered the muzzle of the Uzi. He suspected the man might still have a conscience. If he was right, he might use it to his advantage. "Things got out of control, didn't they?"

"Things? What things?"

Cabeza backed toward a chaise lounge, a white terry-cloth robe draped over its back. He reached into the pocket for a pack of cigarettes. With one stubby finger, he poked around in the open pack and removed the one remaining cigarette. Then he crumpled the pack into a ball and tossed it into the swimming pool, where it landed with a soft splash, spinning slowly to a halt.

"Perhaps you want to tell me what you know," Bolan coaxed. "You're in over your head, you know."

Cabeza nodded. "*Sí*. We all are. I wish we... Do you mind? I feel uneasy talking to a man whose name I don't know."

"Belasko."

"Señor Belasko, Roberto Cabeza."

"I don't have much time. Cardona could be on his way to the airport. If he gets out of the country, it will take me weeks to find him."

"No, *señor*, not weeks. You will never find him." He lit the cigarette, puffing noisily. "Unless you know where to look. We will talk, and perhaps I will tell you. It is not a bad gamble, Señor Belasko."

Bolan nodded. He walked to one of the vacant lounges, took a robe identical to Cabeza's and draped it over the dead woman.

"A small gesture, *señor*, but eloquent. I, too, used to be as meticulous. Now..." He shrugged, exhaling a long plume of smoke. "I want to ask you a few questions. If the answers are acceptable, I will help you. If not, you have lost five minutes only."

"Agreed..."

"You work for the American Mafia, do you not?"

"No."

"Then for whom?"

"The U.S. government."

Cabeza stepped back, sweeping his hand vertically before him. "And the U.S. government sent you here to do what?"

"You already know the answer to that."

"Indulge me, *señor*."

Bolan sighed impatiently. "All right. They sent me here to dismantle Diego Cardona's coke operation."

"You are DEA?"

"No."

"What agency?"

"None."

"I see. So, Diego has overstepped his bounds, just as I feared. I warned him. He had such grand ideas, Señor Belasko. A king, he wanted to be, the king of coca." Cabeza shook his head.

"You sound like more than just a friend. Are you ... ?"

"No, *señor*, I know what you are thinking. I am not his brother. More like ... we are, were, very close. Those were desperate times, Señor Belasko. Growing up in La Paz fifteen years ago was difficult at best. People do strange things. I make no apologies now. If I was wrong, I will know it one day."

"You and Diego Cardona were lovers."

"If you wish."

"And you still care about him."

"*Sí*, I care. But not like that. More as a brother, or a good friend. We wanted much the same thing out of life, Diego and I. We came close, but for Diego, enough was no longer enough. He wanted everything." Cabeza paused. He looked at Bolan for the first time since his colloquy began. His voice took on a new vigor, a new firmness. He tapped his temple with one pudgy finger. "He is loco now, a little, I think. El Perro Demente, they call him. The Mad Dog. Too much coca. I warned him, but he is very stubborn. He could have been a great man, Diego." Cabeza shook his head sadly.

"Will you help me find him?"

"On one condition, *señor*. I don't know why I trust you, but I do. You are a man of honor, I can see that."

"I'm not in a position to make deals, grant immunity, none of that."

"I don't want that. Promise me that you will try to take him alive."

"I can't guarantee anything like that. You know him better than I do."

"No guarantee, Señor Belasko. A promise only. If you have to kill him, then so be it. I understand it may be necessary."

"Not may, Señor Cabeza, probably will."

"*Sí*, probably will. I have your word?"

"You do." Bolan extended his hand. The two men, strange allies, shook, and it was done.

"Good. Diego has three other places. Follow me, I'll get some paper and a pencil. You will need a map for one of them."

ARMED WITH THE INFORMATION, Bolan made his way back to the sliding door. Guards were still present, and probably had no idea Cardona was gone. Cabeza had accompanied him partway, then returned to Cardona's office.

As Bolan reached the doorway to the bedroom through which he'd entered the house, he heard a single, sharp crack. Then nothing. He knew a gunshot when he heard one.

Sprinting back down the hallway, he careered into the office. Cabeza was seated in the large leather chair, tilted back from the desk. He looked almost contented, even with the obscene smear of red that dripped down the wall behind him.

The pistol was still in his mouth.

Bolan sighed deeply, wondering what kind of man Cabeza could have been in other circumstances. No matter, it was too late for might-have-beens and if-onlys. Cabeza had made his last bid for his oldest friend. Now, it was up to someone else to carry the ball. Thinking of the promise he had made, Bolan wondered just how hard it would be to deliver.

And if he would even try.

Retracing his steps, he closed the bedroom door behind him. This time he didn't bother about replacing the sliding door. Cabeza hadn't known for sure where Cardona would go, but he knew the drug czar better than anyone. His best guess was better than none at all. It had to be.

Bolan raced to the wall and was over in one swift movement. He didn't worry about the cameras. As his feet hit the pavement on the outside, he heard the shrill bleating of an alarm. Like so much else in Cardona's world, it was too little and too late.

Cabeza had bet on Mexico City. Cardona had a house there, and he had a small plane at the airport. Its range was too short for Miami, and the third place was the safest, but the least likely. A fortress high in the mountains, it was where Cardona would go when there was no place left to run.

Cardona had contacts in Mexico City and bank accounts. According to Cabeza, he would concentrate on getting even. To do that, he needed firepower, readily available in Mexico.

Bolan jumped into his rented car, kicked it over and raced to his hotel. He wanted to talk to Callahan, but that would have to wait. He had a shot at Cardona that was too good to pass. Once the man got into Mexico City's netherworld, they might never find him.

Bolan careered through the night streets, left the car in the underground parking garage and went upstairs to his room. The elevator was too slow, and he didn't feel the need to slow up for lobby traffic.

Once in his room, he threw several things into the bag, clicked it shut and prepared to leave. He debated calling Brognola, letting him know where he was going. Things were in a state of flux, and secure phones were nonexistent.

He left the room. He could always call from the airport, time permitting.

Bolan hailed a cab in the street. The driver, used to the impatience of gringos, didn't bat an eye as the Executioner shouted his destination as he got in. The cab lurched, throwing the passenger back against the rear seat. They were moving into the traffic before Bolan regained his balance.

Armed with the address of Cardona's Mexican home, he had a point of departure. Beyond that was anybody's guess. He'd improvise, depending on what he found there. The sooner he got to Cardona, the easier it would be to take him down. If Cabeza was right, Cardona would try to hire an army.

The druglord had all the resources he needed in Bolivia, but he was growing more and more suspicious. Every shadow became an assassin, every sneeze a laugh at his expense. He wanted a clean sweep, a new army, new friends. He had the money...and he had the motive. Unforgiving fell short of the mark. Cardona was bound and determined to implement his plan, Bolan or no.

The cab screeched to a halt at the Aeromexico terminal, and Bolan dashed into the airport. He found the airline's desk and bought his ticket, the flight scheduled to depart in fifteen minutes. He had time to talk to Brognola.

Bolan checked in his bag, then looked for a phone. The bank of booths lining one wall was less than private. Bolan raised the long-distance operator and placed the collect call. While he waited, he leaned against the wall, scanning the waiting area of the terminal. Few travelers were about this early, and half the people in the large hall were asleep, college students waiting for cheap flights or street people crashing until the next cop came along to chase them back into the night.

Two men, who pretended they weren't together, lounging less than casually on the long plastic benches that were the one universal of modern transportation, caught his eye. One man wore an expensive suit, cut in a late-sixties style.

He sat facing the phone bank, one leg crossed over the other knee. His black leather, ankle-length boot dangled out of a bell-bottomed trouser cuff, exposing a scrawny shinbone.

The other man sat at the opposite end of the bench. He wore a T-shirt, jeans and sneakers, the scruffy ensemble topped off by an expensive, thigh-length leather jacket. He held a newspaper in his lap, but glanced at it less often than he turned its pages.

Bolan turned back to the phone as a crackle signaled the arrival of Brognola. Quickly, he filled in the big Fed on the night's events, pointedly omitting any reference to his promise to Cabeza. The arrangement troubled him. He had never intentionally broken his word before, and knew that the first time would be the hardest step in a trip that would end in a downhill slide. Circumstances aside, he wasn't sure it was a journey he was prepared to make.

Brognola tried to get more information out of him, partly, Bolan guessed, because he'd had no luck trying to plug the leak. He was about to put the question point-blank when he noticed the two men on the bench huddle for an instant. The Carnaby Street refugee stood up and stretched, then made a beeline to the phones.

"Gotta go, Hal. Call you from Mexico City."

He hung up the phone without waiting for an acknowledgment. Carnaby Street was only fifteen feet away when Bolan wheeled. He stared him in the eye for a second, then brushed past him and crossed the open waiting room to the rest rooms. Inside, he checked the stalls. They were empty.

Bolan grabbed the air-conditioning duct overhead and swung himself up to lie in the space between duct and ceiling. A moment later the man in the leather jacket walked in, his newspaper held across his stomach.

Bolan could see him through a narrow gap against the wall. He seemed puzzled. Dropping to one knee, he looked along the row of stalls. Realizing they were all empty, he cursed. As he climbed to his feet, Bolan dropped down behind him, grabbing the off-balance tail by his long hair and wrapping his left forearm around the man's throat.

"You looking for something?"

"Fuck you."

Bolan hauled the guy's wallet out of his pocket. Awkwardly flipping through it, he glanced at the contents. An eagle caught his eye.

"DEA?"

"What of it?" the guy choked out, squirming against the pressure of Bolan's forearm.

CHAPTER TWENTY-ONE

Joey Buccieri had a bad night. Frankie Ianni wasn't exactly
a friend, but he was at the very least a business associate. He
might have been a screwup, but he was a straight shooter.
Sally Maggadino was going to want to know what happened to him. Giving the devil his due, Joey knew that
Maggadino looked after his own. He might smack you down
if you stepped out of line, but it was his prerogative. You
didn't mess with one of Sally's boys. He would want to get
even with whoever whacked Frankie. Joey couldn't tell him.
Not unless he wanted to end up as stiff as Frankie.

Joey knew he was a lousy liar. No way could he bluff his
way through a meeting with Sally. Telling him the truth was
asking for a one-way ticket to hell. That left going head to
head with the old man. Talk about slim to none, those were
good odds from where Joey sat.

But they were the only odds he had.

Sitting at his desk, which was a tacky chrome-and-glass
number from a chichi place that specialized in overpricing
its goods, in cahoots with purported decorators of dubious
gender, Joey tallied the debits and credits. The balance sheet
didn't look good. Like most overreachers, Joey owed more
than he was owed. There were some chips he could call in,
returns for past favors, help due for help given, but not
much.

The current situation was the best argument he could
think of for charity. If only he had done unto others, there
might be a few people ready to do unto him. Right now, a
bullet in the head might be the best thing anybody could do
for him. As a lesson to the others, Sally would take him
apart joint by joint, like a butcher breaking in an appren-
tice.

No matter how he cut it, the deck was stacked against him. His only hope was to charge straight at the old man. If he could whack Sally before the rest of the underbosses knew what was happening, the general dissatisfaction of the younger made men just might translate into a collective amnesia. If they were willing to forget about Sally Maggadino in exchange for a shot at defining their own futures, he just might swing it. An elephant clinging to a straw in a flash flood probably had a better chance, but desperation was notoriously optimistic.

And Joey Buccieri was nothing if not optimistic. It gave him a bad case of mixed emotions. He had loved the old man like a second father, once. And Sally had looked after him, taught him the ropes, patted him on the back when he did good, kicked him in the butt when he screwed up.

But times change. And no matter what, the old just kept getting older. When a man had more of a past than he had a future, maybe he should have some dignity and step aside. That was Sally's problem. He didn't know when to retire.

Joey turned the scratch pad facedown on the desk. He leaned back and looked at the framed, autographed photos on the wall. F. Sinatra. Joe D. J. Vale. Sally Maggadino. Joe D. had class. He knew when to step down. He didn't dig in his nails and hang on to the ladder, slipping down to Triple A, Double A, finally ending up shagging flies in some weedy Texas League outfield. He went out with style.

Sally should have taken a hint from the Clipper, hung up his spikes and lived off the memories and goodwill. Hell, better men than he had done it. But if you kept on kidding yourself, there came a time when those around you tired of the joke. They stopped laughing and started looking away because nobody bothered to mix his pitches anymore, preferring three smokers down the pike and next case. When that happened, dignity was something somebody else had.

Sure, Sally had been good to him. But, hey, he'd been good to Sally. Saved his ass more than once. Did a nickel at Raiford. Didn't screw Maria Maggadino, even when she

threw herself at him. More than once. Shit, the boss's
daughter was supposed to be the yellow brick road to success. And Joey Buccieri passed it up out of respect for the
old man. Well, there it was. That and a buck would get him
a ride on the subway. He and Sally went way back. Nobody
could say he wasn't properly respectful.

Until now.

But that was okay. You did what you had to to get over.
And Joey Buccieri was damned if he wouldn't try to get over
just this one more time. And deep inside, he knew he was
also damned if he would. And when all was said and done,
wasn't it better to be hanged for a thief?

THE YELLOW VAN MOVED too cautiously, driven, one would
suspect, by a driver who wanted to keep a low profile: hes-
itant at yellow lights, keeping a good five miles under the
limit. Pete Thomasino hadn't seen that much courtesy since
Driver Ed. The department-issue Montego had no trouble
keeping up with the van. Thomasino decided this was one
of those nights when a muscle car was a waste of horse-
power.

Working Vice wasn't all it was cracked up to be. Dope
dealers weren't a classy bunch. But thanks to TV, everybody thought a Vice cop drove a Ferrari and drank with
people whose principal flaws were imperfect teeth and fading tans.

And TV hookers were a joke. Clear skins and forty-inch
D cups were about as rare on the street as tits on a bull. The
blond hair was courtesy of E.I. DuPont de Nemours. You
never saw the track marks and razor scars, let alone the
dozen species of fauna, some still awaiting classification,
that hung around looking for new blood.

So, with all that sordid entertainment wearing a little thin
after six weeks on the night shift, tailing a properly obser-
vant van was welcome diversion, a *TV Guide* crossword
puzzle after three years of the Sunday *Times* of London.

In other words, Pete could live with it.

The van continued on its way, stopping at anything that even looked like a red-and-white octagon. Heading south on SW 57th, the van hit the South Dixie Highway and sped up, keeping an even fifty under the needle. Pete hung back, letting a couple of strays drift in between. He dropped back a little farther, hit the left lane and came on strong. Passing two Audis and a Buick, he had a green Ciera between himself and the van. He pegged the plate number, dropped back and got on the radio. He knew the Z meant a rental, but a check of the hot sheet might be useful.

Dispatch got back to him with a negative. If the van was stolen, nobody knew about it yet, except the thieves.

Pete was a study in contradictions. Not long on curiosity, he was still a sucker for the extraordinary. And this paragon of highway rectitude was definitely offbeat. On a hunch, Pete got back into the left lane, gunned the Montego and blew by the van.

Falling to the right, he pulled ahead, checking the lights in his rearview. All the lamps were lit. No reason to pull it over, no probable cause. They could have a ton of high grade in the back and anybody with a law degree from Woolworth's would have them on the street in thirty minutes, never to be seen in court again. The city could keep the dope, of course, and that was a small blessing. But they'd be back with another van and another load in two weeks.

In South Miami, the van turned off Dixie and began to move a little faster. The traffic was thinning as the city fell away behind it. The comforting glow of the streetlights disappeared. Pete felt the ocean breeze, and he rolled his window down all the way. A few drops of rain spattered the windshield, making red spiders of the van's taillights.

He had to hang back even farther because of the light traffic. As it was, the men in the van might already have made him. He had only limited authority outside Miami proper, none at all outside the county. But in for a penny, in for a pound. He was along for the ride.

The rain started to pick up, and he was forced to turn on the wipers. Three days of dirt and road oil made the windshield a mess as the first few strokes of the wiper blades splashed across the glass. Pete hit the wash button, spewing foamy blue water over the windshield. The sudsy smear washed off in the quickening rain, and the glass was finally clear.

A quarter mile ahead, the van turned off. Its taillights disappeared. Pete resisted the urge to speed up, in case they were waiting to see what he would do. Keeping a steady speed, he reached the turnoff in fifteen seconds. The van lights were small specks down the narrow side road.

Pete killed his lights and made the turn. He drove by instinct, following the white line just visible in the darkness. As long as he could keep the red lights in view, he'd keep following. If they lost him, what the hell. Maybe they were just going fishing.

The red lights winked out.

Pete goosed the engine. He didn't know the road that well, and they might just have rounded a bend. After a half mile, he knew they hadn't. He'd seen only one narrow, rutted road off the pavement. Kicking the Montego into reverse, he rocked the car back to the turn-off. The car rolled from side to side in the rutted, overgrown lane.

He had gone less than a mile when he saw bright lights ahead. At first he thought it was just a porch light. But the color was all wrong. The reddish orange seemed to quiver and grow like a living thing. Fire! Something was on fire. Pete threw on his headlights and dropped down a gear.

The Montego roared as its wheels slipped on the rain-slick weeds. They caught with a high-pitched whisper, and the Montego shot forward. Tree limbs and stringy shrubs grabbed at the sides of the car. The radio antenna spronged and whipped in an angry circle.

The lane blew out into a clearing. Ahead was a broad marshy meadow, a band of trees at its far edge. A narrow strip of weeds ran straight through the meadow. At its far end, he saw the van starkly outlined against the trees. Three low buildings, black bones within the skin of flame, were to the left. Even at this distance, Pete could make out the figures of several men.

The figures danced and weaved, a football play with avant-garde choreography. Pete floored the Montego, feeling the traction come and go as the car slipped and slid toward the fiery tableau. The van was fifty yards away when the first spray of bullets took out his headlights. They pinged and whined off the hood, fragments starring his windshield. Instinctively, Pete ducked and hit the brakes.

The car spun wildly left, its rear wheel sinking into the mucky weeds off the narrow road. He grabbed the door handle and shoved, hitting the wet ground with one shoulder, then rolling into the marsh. He yanked his service revolver free of its sling just as a second burst of automatic fire found the Montego's radiator. A hiss of steam gave sound effects to the silent inferno ahead of him.

Rolling farther left, Pete knew they couldn't actually see him. He crept forward, hoping like hell he didn't run into a cottonmouth. He was close enough now to see the three sheds clearly. The outer wall of one fell away like a theater curtain, ripping down the middle and peeling toward both ends. An instant later the first explosion arced debris into the air. Until then, he had wondered what was going on.

Now he knew.

A processing lab had been hit. A damned sophisticated one, too, from the size of it. The location was as out of the way as you could get and still be within shouting distance of Miami. The question was not what was being burned to cinders, but who lit the match. It wasn't DEA's style, and Vice would have clued him in. That left only one possibility: a drug war.

He'd heard of getting burned, but this was classic. The flames, fed by kerosene, ether and other raw chemicals, were taller than the trees, thick black smoke coiling like dark rope into the air, dancing to some invisible fakir's music.

The gunfire was intermittent now. All the standing figures seemed concentrated near the van. It looked like the home team had lost. And he had no wheels. As it dawned on him, the men clustered near the van returned their interest to the helpless Montego. Several submachine guns started yammering simultaneously. Every last shard of glass in the car was blown away. That meant only one thing.

Now they were coming for him.

Pete slid sideways in the tall weeks. Left and rearward, a clump of shrubbery stood on an elevated hummock. He crept behind it, getting it between him and his pursuers.

Then he ran like hell.

When he reached the trees, he turned to watch. One figure detached itself from the search party. He saw the Montego's dome light go on, then off. The figure moved to the rear of the Montego. A small flash, probably a cigarette lighter, was followed by a small blister of flame on the rear fender. The shadow ran. The car was blown to pieces. A ball of flame rolled up into the rain and disappeared.

A moment later, the van's headlights flashed on, it backed into a K, wheeled around and sped toward the ruined hulk of the Montego. The shadowy figure climbed in. The van lurched forward, shoving the remains of the Montego into the muck a little farther, eased around the blackened shell and skidded back the way it had come.

Thirty seconds later, Pete Thomasino was alone. He waited while the flames died, slowly making his way toward solid earth. He climbed out of the marsh as the skeleton of the last shed collapsed with a brittle sigh.

This one was going to turn some heads.

CHAPTER TWENTY-TWO

The air smelled of bad food and human waste. Diego Cardona wrinkled his nose, sniffing at the array of foul odors assaulting his delicate sensibilities. It was a long time since he'd been forced to endure such unpleasant sensations. But not long enough.

He knew he was a hunted man. How could it happen, so soon after the initiation of his grand scheme? Someone must have betrayed him. No other explanation was possible. A beautiful, economical scheme like his was a rare thing. So simple, and yet so elegant, he had worked on it for months.

Now he would have to make a few minor adjustments. That was the first order of business. Revenge on the traitor would have to wait. The sweet slow vengeance he dreamed of would require time. Leisurely indulgence would make it all the sweeter. The quick stroke would make him feel better now, but later, when he had reestablished order, he wanted to have something to savor, something to amuse his memory on lonely nights. That meant patience.

In the meantime, there was work to do. The Mercedes limousine should have been out of place in the squalor of Cuauhtémoc. The houses leaned against one another, threatening to topple like dominoes. Most of them were built by the people who lived in them, recognizing no construction standards but the whim of the builders. If it looked good, it would work was the only rule—that and the limits on what looked good imposed by restricted capital. It was hard to build well and truly when you had no money, harder still to make something strong enough to resist the trembling of the earth, and the incessant shifting of the entire city, built on a lake bottom six hundred years ago.

Cardona watched a trash picker work her way from pile to pile, an infant slung on her hip. How familiar it all seemed. It was not as long ago as he wished to think that he himself had been scratching a living in the same way.

Revolted by the recognition of his own roots, he rolled down the window of the Mercedes and called to the woman.

At first she ignored him. No one could have anything good to say to her. Cardona persisted. Finally, fearful of the attention being called to her, she relented. Turning, she saw the luxurious car. Warily she approached it. The man would offer her money for sex, she thought. She stopped to look at herself in the dusty glass of a ratty shop window. She was still pretty, almost, but no *puta*, no whore. She would listen and then, when he had made his offer, she would scream, maybe get a few dollars to stay off the street for a week.

She drew alongside the car, and Cardona leaned out of the window. *"Buenas días, señora."*

"Señorita," she corrected.

Cardona looked at her carefully. The dark good looks were familiar. Her long hair was unkempt, but clean. Her clothes had seen better days, but it was the look in her eyes that held him. A fire, so like his own. She could have been his sister. He had a sister, he knew, though he hadn't seen her in ten years. Maybe, when this was all over, he could look for her. He had the money. He could still find her. If she was still alive, and if he could recognize her. He would try. It would be a good thing to do.

The woman, puzzled by his silence, turned to go. Perhaps he had mistaken her for someone else. She had started to move away when Cardona called to her again.

"Señorita?"

She turned back to the car and moved closer. The tinted glass of the window was already rising when she reached for the extended paper. Her hand, streaked with the dirt of a morning's salvaging, closed over the crisp paper. It crinkled in her fingers. It was money, she knew that. There must have been some mistake. The window had been raised all the way. She could see nothing through the dark glass. Turning, she ran past the car, the baby still on her hip, still sleeping. Turning into an alley, she stopped to look again. The bills were American. Five of them, still smelling pungently of ink. Brand-new one-thousand-dollar bills, for her.

Back in the car, Cardona imagined the look on her face when she realized what he had given her. He was right on the money. If only the rest of life were that easy, he thought.

He was startled by a tap on the other window. Through the tinted glass he recognized the man bending to peer in. Cardona mumbled to his driver, "You ready?"

"*Sí.*"

"Watch him, like I told you." The tenderness was gone. Cardona's voice was razor sharp, almost brittle.

He leaned over to unlock the rear door, then straightened as the newcomer slid in and closed the door behind him.

"You're late," Cardona snapped.

The man made an elaborate show of looking at his naked wrist. "Not by my watch."

"Why did you insist on meeting here?"

"Does the mountain come to Mohammed?"

"You can be replaced," Cardona said. His voice lacked conviction, and he knew it. He didn't like the feeling.

"If that is so, you wouldn't have come, would you. Beggars can't be choosers. Besides, it is good for you to remember where you came from. Most of us stop there again on the way down." The man laughed. He was outrageously dressed, affecting a subdued Pancho Villa look. A considerable mustache nearly obscured his mouth, its wild ends drooping past his chin.

"We'll see."

"I guess so. Now, what can I do for you? I am a busy man."

"Twenty-four men. Good ones."

"I thought you had your own army."

"I bought an army, now I want to buy another one. It's none of your business why. Can you do·it?"

"How much?"

"How much will it cost?"

"A lot."

"Do it."

"Do you want to talk about the price?"

"I don't care what it costs. Do it."

"Will you be providing the weapons?"

"No."

"The price has just gone up."

"Do it!"

The man shrugged his shoulders, then opened the door. He pressed the electric window control, waited until the window was all the way down, then stepped out of the car. He closed the door carefully, leaned in through the open window and smiled. "I'll call you."

"Tomorrow morning."

"First thing. Adios. Mohammed."

The man was gone. Cardona leaned forward to his driver. "Close the window."

The electric motor whirred, and the glass struck home with a thud.

"Let's go," Cardona said.

The driver started the Mercedes, and its engine throbbed evenly. Cardona could feel the power through the floorboard. It felt as if the earth was shifting again.

The car picked its way through the crowded streets. Vendors were already opening their carts, shop windows were open and their doors swung wide. Easing its way through the spillover crowds milling around in the gutters, the sleek black automobile looked like a cruising shark, ignoring small fry, searching for the perfect meal, one worthy of its reputation.

Working toward the heart of the city, the car was soon surrounded by others. It began to lose its identity, blending in with the morning bustle. Cardona was getting back on his home turf and his mood improved.

Nudging into Paseo de la Reforma, the Mercedes joined the flood of traffic. Ahead, through the tinted windshield, El Ángel, newly gilded, glistened in the morning light. Nearly as tall as the buildings surrounding the plaza, the monument slipped by, its shadow painting the car a darker black for a moment, then it was gone from view as the Mercedes entered the circle. A few moments later, the golden angel was visible out the rear window.

Cardona didn't bother to turn around.

IN THE BASEMENT of a lavish colonial hacienda, Cardona looked at the three men who sat before him. Wearing a white caftan and leather sandals, he looked more like a guru than a *traficante*, but his audience knew better. Against the dark green walls of the reinforced bunker, his slender figure seemed almost ephemeral.

"Alphonso," Cardona began, "you have to go to La Paz and run things for me there for a few days."

"What about Roberto?"

"Roberto is dead. So is Alberto."

"What happened?"

Speaking softly, Cardona walked in small circles, the silk of his caftan swishing quietly as he moved. "Somebody betrayed me."

"Not Roberto?"

"Maybe. I don't know."

"But I thought—"

"Look. We all thought we had bought enough protection. Now I know better. We have lots of enemies. Not only the DEA and the National Guard. Those we can handle. But others, like ourselves, are a threat. Especially now that we have begun to move. And there are still others. The Mafia in Miami and someone I don't know. I saw him. He came to my house in La Paz. I want him out of the way."

"What about the Mafia?"

"Later. I want to consolidate our forces first. Until that is accomplished, it would be too risky to take them on. We can't wage a war on two fronts. When we get control of the production, then we can worry about the distribution. I moved too soon in Miami. But the damage has been controlled."

"So what do we do now?"

"I am making arrangements here. I need some assistance, but I have already taken steps. They will be flown to Bolivia in two days. Then we can hit Salazar, Quinones and the others. If we take out their labs, they'll have nothing to sell. Everyone will have to come to us. Then we can cut our own deal on the distribution side. If we corner the market, the Mafia will have to deal with us. There is no point in waging a war if we can get what we want without it."

"The Italians will never work with us."

"Then we can move them aside. If they have nothing to sell, they're out of business. It's that simple."

"When do you want me to leave?"

"Tonight. Arrangements have been made."

"What about me?" A man so fat he was almost a ball asked the question. "What do you want me to do?"

"You will have to go to Miami. I want everything there halted temporarily. This plan can work. I don't want to see it fall apart because I was overanxious. Get in touch with Morales. Tell him you're in charge. Make sure he doesn't do anything without my approval."

"He won't like it."

"Jorge, he works for me. So do you. Do what I tell you, all right?"

Jorge said nothing. Cardona stopped pacing and went to sit at the table. His eyes were glassy. He sniffed, then reached into the caftan, withdrawing a scarlet silk handkerchief. His nose was running. He wiped it with the delicacy of a finishing-school senior. He looked at the handkerchief a second before returning it to the folds of his robe. The others noticed the darker red stain.

Cardona bent to the table, sniffed twice, and two lines were gone. He did another. The fourth lay there, slightly crooked. Cardona took the razor blade and tried to straighten the line. His hand shook. The line became more crooked. In disgust, he threw the blade across the room.

The remaining coke lay there on the table, its delicate whorl a question mark in the silent room. Cardona stared at it, as if trying to decipher the answer.

The third man coughed nervously. Cardona looked up, as if seeing him for the first time.

"You want me to do anything?"

Cardona stared at him blankly. "What?"

"You want me to do anything?" the man repeated.

"Why?"

"I just wanted to know. I thought you—"

"Why do you want to know? So you can betray me, like Roberto and Alberto? Is that what you want?"

"No, I just, you know, I thought that . . ."

Cardona reached into his caftan again. The others waited patiently, expecting to see the handkerchief again. Cardona smiled. His hand rose slowly, still below the table. Then, like a hawk pouncing, it moved swiftly. He fired once, then again. At point-blank range, the .25-caliber Iver Johnson automatic was deadly.

Jorge and Alphonso sat in stunned silence.

"I warned him," Cardona muttered. "You know that. I warned him. But he couldn't help himself. He had to be the big man. He had to betray me. So, there you have it. That is what happens to traitors."

Cardona stood.

Then he was gone.

The dead man lay back in his chair, his head thrown to one side, eyes open. He stared at the ceiling, wondering what was wrong. His companions already knew.

Cardona had gone over the edge.

Chicago

CHAPTER TWENTY-THREE

A band of light lay across his face. His cheek felt hot where the strip of sun struck him. It was this, rather than the brightness, that woke him. Sitting up, he felt dizzy. The room swirled, its dull colors blurred by double vision, and he shook his head to regain focus. Hot sparks danced in his skull. He felt his jaw, the welt where he'd been hit, and wondered if his jaw was broken.

Forcing his eyes to open wide, he yawned to relieve the stiffness of his jaw. It had swollen, and the muscles felt tight. Getting to his knees, Lee willed the room to be still. Like a blurry news photo, everything he saw had blurred edges. Dropping back on his haunches, he waited for the sharper vision he knew would come.

Only then did he wonder where Albert had gone. Lee Richards felt like a sap. His own brother had taken him down. The brother who was more mysterious to him than any stranger could ever be.

As his eyes cleared, his memory grew more lucid. He remembered looking up at the pistol, saw Albert's lips move, his cheeks puff up. The curious soft explosions must have been sound effects, Albert playing cowboys and Indians. Lee had been certain he was going to die, for reasons he only dimly understood.

Still wondering whether he was, in fact, dead, Lee stood. He groaned, thought for a moment he had been too loud, then remembered there was no one to wake up. Albert was gone and his mother had never come home. Or had it all been a dream?

Shaking his head again, Lee walked into his brother's bedroom. It was empty. The tangled sheets lay in a heap at the bottom of the bed, and the threadbare blanket lay on the floor in a ball.

Lee sat on the edge of the bed. Its springs squeaked like alarmed rats as he shifted his weight. He had a few things to sort out, and sitting in the ruins of his brother's life might be the best place to do it. Everything in the room spoke of either poverty or its frustrations. A poster of Michael Jackson hung by a pair of pushpins on the wall over the bed. The famous glove had been crudely altered to a fielder's mitt, "Michael" overscrawled in black marker with "Reggie."

Chaka Khan, in a seductive pose, watched Lee over one bare shoulder. Like a reluctant guardian angel, she stood watch over Albert while he slept, and more than likely figured in not a few dreams.

A cheap stereo supported a stack of records and sleeves. Lee got up to sift through them. Most of them were well worn, whether from hard play or carelessness, he couldn't tell. Hard funk and MOR crap, mostly, he thought, searching in vain for some Miles or Bird. No blues, either. Finally, at the bottom of the pile, still in its sleeve with the plastic shrink wrap still intact, was a copy of *Kind of Blue*, the classic Miles Davis album. Lee had sent it to Albert on his twelfth birthday, five years before. Albert hadn't even bothered to open it. The small card was still in its envelope, stuck to the jacket with Scotch tape.

Lee opened the flap and tugged the card from the envelope. He unfolded the plain white paper and read the inscription: "Al— This is as good as it gets. Happy birthday. Lee." The unintentional irony of that greeting came home to him now. How could he blame the kid for being bitter?

Lee stood and walked to the window. He tugged at the shade pull, and the shade shot up, flapping like a wounded eagle as it wound itself into a tight coil. The window looked out on an air shaft. Years of grime clung to the glass. He took a moistened finger to see whether it was inside or outside. The cloudy smear under his fingertip solved the problem. It was both. No matter which way you looked at it, the window was dirty.

Peering down into the shaft, the bottom four stories below, he realized why it didn't matter. The litter there would someday be an archaeological windfall. Everything that no longer worked or mattered lay in a pyramidal mound. If you got burned on shoddy merchandise, chuck it out the window. A bill came you couldn't pay. Kite it. TV set bite the dust? Bounce it.

The memories came flooding back. Mr. Wilcox on the top floor, steamed when the Cubs dropped a close one, dropping his radio out the window and, for good measure, bombing it with his wife's iron.

Once Lee had contributed, an act shrouded in all the mystery of an initiation rite. Darlene McLemore had given him back his pin. To prove how little she and it mattered, he had gone to the roof and tossed the pin backward over his shoulder, standing stock-still until he heard the tinny plink as it struck some nameless thing at the top of the pile.

He had expected to feel better. He didn't. And that was his first and final contribution to the midden. Whatever cathartic power it held for others, for him it did nothing. He opened the window now, brittle putty chipping away from the ancient wood. Slowly, deliberately, he picked up the Davis album, slit the plastic with a thumbnail and slid the disk from its sleeve. He bent to look at the label. The title of one tune said it all: "So What."

Lee read the title aloud, rolling it bitterly on his tongue, then incanted it and finally roared it out defiantly, the words reverberating in the tomblike air shaft. Casually he flicked his wrist and watched the disk skate on the air, spinning like a UFO for a few seconds then slipping sideways and, edge first, plummeting with the finality of a guillotine into the shadows below.

He had to find Albert, and he had no idea where to look. The street was the obvious place to start. Lee grabbed a heavy jacket from the back of a chair and started for the door. He hesitated, then walked back to yank a suitcase from behind the couch. He rolled the combination wheels and opened the lid. He clipped the automatic in its holster to the back of his belt. It was time to go.

He closed the door quietly, as if someone were home.

The street was nearly deserted. A bitter late-fall wind blew down off the lake whipping scraps of paper into vicious spirals. As in most inbred neighborhoods, everybody knew everybody else around here. If he could find a kid Albert's age, he could find out where Albert was likely to go.

Lee circled the block, but saw no one likely to know where Albert might be. Back in front of the tenement, he started a larger circuit, walking two blocks to the east. Rounding the corner at the end of his first leg, he saw a knot of teenagers clustered around a barrel full of burning wood. Half a dozen kids circled the steel drum, rubbing their hands and jiving.

They glared at him as he approached. One of the older boys stared hard for a few seconds, then burst into a smile. "Lee, man. That you? What's happening, bro?"

"Charlie Johnson? Man, it must be six, seven years. How are you?"

"I been better and I been worse. And it's eight years, man. Graduation night. That was the last time I seen you, man."

"You know my brother, Albert?"

"Know who he is, yeah. Why?"

"Can I talk to you in private a minute?"

Johnson hesitated. Private conversation with somebody he hadn't seen in eight years couldn't be good news. The only question was who it was bad news for. "Yeah, I guess." He walked around the steel drum, clapped Lee on the back, then draped his arm around his old friend's shoulders. He looked back at the others. "I be back in a minute. Me and my man Lee got some business to discuss."

Once away from the others, he dropped the cool stance. "What's up? Albert in trouble again, man?"

"Again? What do you mean 'again'?"

"Oh, nothing. You know how it is, man. Them kids, they don't know no better. Sometimes it comes home, 's all."

"You know where I can find him? Look, I got to find him quick. He's got a gun."

"Ain't the first time, bro. Shit, half the dudes around here suck on a pistol 'stead of a pacifier. You know that."

"Yeah, I know that. But this is different. He's—"

"I know what he's like, man. That's crack for you. Makes mothers eat their young, case they don't already have a reason."

"How long he been into crack?"

"Since it hit the street, man. Albert's a pioneer, man. He ain't got a wagon, but he don't need it. Do enough crack, you thinks you *is* a wagon, man."

"Where would he go to score?"

"Don't know, Lee. Don't know."

"Your ass."

"You callin' me a liar, man?" Johnson dropped his arm and backed off a step.

"No, man, I'm tellin' you to cut the crap. I got to find Albert, and I got to do it now. You know where he might be at, then tell me. You don't, quit wastin' my time."

"Look, I don't want no trouble, man. Not with you, and not with Albert. And especially not with them."

"Uh-uh, C.J. Wrong. You especially don't want no trouble with me. Look it up, man. See my picture under *T* in the dictionary. I ain't got time to play no games with you, man. You know, you better say something now. Anything happen to him, I get there too late, I be coming back this way."

Johnson thought it over. He knew the stories about Lee. His occupation was as much a point of neighborhood pride as it was an open secret. Everybody knew something, and nobody ever discussed it. By osmosis, it passed from person to person.

"All right, Lee. But don't tell nobody I told you. Even if you kill them bastards, somebody be takin' their place. That shit is gold around here."

"Where, man?" Lee grabbed him by the lapels. In an elaborate show of bravado, Johnson brushed the hands away and stroked the lapels back into a smooth crease. Lee recognized the move as a prelude to capitulation and let it go unchallenged.

"Three blocks over, on Indiana. 329. Next to last floor. In the back. You don't know me, man." Johnson backed away. He raised a finger to point at Lee, then waved it like a scolding teacher. "You don't know me, and I ain't seen you in years. Graduation night."

Lee nodded. When Johnson rejoined the others, he walked to the corner, struggling against the impulse to run as fast as he could. Once he'd rounded the corner, he broke into a sprint.

CHAPTER TWENTY-FOUR

The building looked as if it shouldn't be standing. Bricks had fallen from the masonry walls that served as banisters. The front door had only one pane of glass remaining out of nine. All of the other windows on the front of the five-story building were covered with sheet tin, rust spots showing where it had been nailed to the underlying wooden frames.

Lee watched the building for several minutes as he sat casually on a stoop across the street. Most crack houses worked like the old heroin shooting galleries. A steerer or two would stand on the street, directing addicts to the place to make a buy. Surveillance was constant, assistants to the dealer keeping an eye out for trouble. In the drug trade, trouble was more likely to be competitors than the law.

The cops, if they cared at all, and if they weren't on someone's payroll, were mostly too demoralized to bother. Any bust usually meant the dealer was on the street an hour later. Three hours after that, they were just finishing their paperwork. By that time, the dealer had made another several thousand dollars. And the ones the cops did nail were usually small fry. They were expendable to the heavyweights, were paid extremely well and knew better than to talk. If you've been bought, one thing nobody had to tell you was that everybody else had his price. For anything.

After fifteen minutes, Lee saw what he was waiting for. On the roof of the building, two men were peering over the edge of the crumbling facade. He had too many years in not to take all the necessary precautions. When he went upstairs, he knew he'd be facing a door tough to get through. He could handle that. But he wanted to know who else

would be there, what kind of support the dealers had in re-
serve. Now he knew.

Lee stood and pulled his jacket more snugly around him,
looking for all the world like somebody who had nothing
better to do than sit on a cold Chicago doorstep. He moved
down the block, falling almost instinctively into the ghetto
shuffle he'd have sworn he'd long since forgotten.

He crossed the street at the corner and walked a block,
then made a left. Now he was on the block behind the crack
house. His intention was to sit and wait for Albert to show.
No way would they let him watch from the stoop all day
long. And once he made his move, he'd have to take them
out anyway. Might as well get some of the heavy work done
now.

The building directly behind the crack house was a car-
bon copy. It seemed to be abandoned, but appearances were
more than deceiving in a place like this. Potentially, they
were deadly. Shuffling up the stairs, like a wino looking for
a place to flop, Lee slipped through the building's dilapi-
dated door. Once inside, all pretense of uncertainty and in-
capacity were gone.

Lee was back in business. Mechanics fix things. And he
was going to fix the bastards who had been selling dope to
his brother. The dark stairs smelled of urine and days-old
vomit. He couldn't see anything in the dark.

Taking a small, powerful pocket flashlight from his
jacket, Lee began to make his way up the first flight. The
krypton bulb threw an intense, sharply etched beam. Just
outside the moving circle of light, Lee sensed the presence
of things that were uncomfortable in the light. They skittered and scratched along, trying to avoid the beam.

The smell seemed to grow stronger as he climbed. Nearing the second-floor landing, he noticed a sudden change in
the nature of the stench. Less that of ancient decay, more
that of something newly dead. The fecal odor was strong,
and squeals and skittering feet seemed to come from the
same direction. Gaining the landing, Lee cast the beam

down the hall, slowly scanning the floor and walls. Several doors were set in one wall, the building seemed to have five or six apartments to a floor. The corridor itself was heavily littered, but otherwise empty.

One of the doors was open a crack. Lee moved close to the wall, sliding along its peeling wallpaper, holding the light out in front of him. One of the two guns he'd brought along was in his other hand. He reached the partly open door. There could be no question; the apartment behind it was the source of the odor. He kicked the door wide, throwing the beam into the middle of the room.

To one edge of the circle of light, Lee saw a shoe. He moved the beam toward it, and a heaving gray mass, sprinkled with dozens of fiery yellow points, like small stars, froze in midpulsation. Rats, dozens of them, were devouring what was left of the shoe's owner. Nearly retching, Lee stumbled toward the door. He aimed his silenced automatic into the squirming mass and emptied the magazine. Several of the rodents were hit and immediately set upon by the others. They were too hungry to be frightened off.

Lee backed into the hallway, pulling the door closed behind him. He leaned over the banister and heaved. He thought it would never stop. When his guts stopped churning, he spit, trying to wash the awful taste out of his mouth. It wouldn't leave. Neither would the image of the awful sight that precipitated it.

Lee wiped away the cold sweat that beaded his forehead. He looked for the next stairway, spotting it at the opposite end of the hall. He ran past the room he'd just vacated, sprinting to the third floor in a panic. As he climbed higher, the litter seemed to thin out, almost as if litterers came in degrees of hardiness. Most were too easily satisfied, unwilling to climb five flights of stairs when one or two would do.

He continued his climb, turning now to the final flight leading to the roof. The skylight over the stairwell was so dirty that it only faintly called attention to its existence. Lee took the last steps cautiously. At their head was a steel door, which had been tarred over, but much of the tar now peeled away from the rusty metal underneath it.

He approached the door, pushing it open a crack to peer out onto the roof. The sun was brighter than he expected. The door was open just far enough to give him a partial view of the crack house roof, which was marked by a low stone parapet. A narrow alleyway separated the two buildings. A second parapet, many of its bricks missing, formed the rear edge of the crack house roof. To get across, Lee was going to have to jump both walls and the alley between them.

He pushed the door open wider, flattening himself against the wall at the top of the stairwell. The opening was now wide enough for him to see the entire roof. It was deserted. Lee stepped into the open.

Overhead, the sun was bright, the sky a hazy blue. Scattered clouds drifted toward the sun. In a few minutes, it would get dark as they passed in front of it. Not for long, but long enough for him to make his leap.

He approached the parapet, keeping a rusted ventilator shaft between him and the other building. The shaft was only five feet from the parapet. He crouched behind it, waiting for the clouds. While he waited, he scanned the opposite roof. A shiny new brass bolt and bracket were all the proof he needed he had the right building. The logical escape route for the dealers was through the door and over the roofs. Throwing the bolt would buy them all the extra time they needed. Unless trouble came from above. But they hadn't seen trouble yet.

Not until they met Lee Richards.

And it wouldn't be long now.

While he waited for the clouds to pass overhead, Lee watched the roof door of the crack house. A brief shadow came and went. Lee held his ground. A large dark cloud was a minute away. With ten seconds to go, he crept from behind the ventilator. Suddenly the door burst open, and the two men he had seen from the street burst through. A small-caliber automatic barked behind them.

Lee jumped and landed in a crouch. The two men heard the thud of his landing and turned. He fired twice, his silenced Coonan .357 Magnum automatic bucking just a bit. The first shot nailed his target just below the breastbone. The second struck the same man higher in the chest, to the left of the heart. He fell like an empty canvas sack.

Hitting the roof on his shoulder and rolling to the left, Lee came up firing. The second man had yanked the door wide and crouched behind its heavy steel plate. Lee tossed a pair of shots his way, which glanced harmlessly off the steel plate, whining away over the rooftops.

The second gunman peeked out from behind his shield, his .375's slugs chewing at the graveled tar to Lee's left. The hardman fired three shots in quick succession, each hitting closer than the last.

Lee dived behind a chimney, realizing that the last thing he needed was a standoff. Shots fired from a roof would bring the cops and a SWAT team, even in this neighborhood. Taking a quick peek at his opponent, Lee realized his best chance was unorthodox. He aimed carefully. Firing twice, he nailed the concealed shooter in the left ankle, exposed just below the bottom edge of the door.

A snarl of pain rewarded the marksman. The gunner's pistol clattered to the roof as he slumped to the tar, reaching for his shattered ankle. As he lay there moaning, Lee rushed him. Letting go of his ankle, the wounded man reached both hands back over his head.

Lee fired twice, the slugs crushing the man's forehead. He convulsed briefly, rolled to the right and twitched. Blood oozed from the shattered skull, flowing sluggishly toward the twin depressions. Lee was through the door before it reached its goal.

Inside the crack house, a single, low-wattage bulb glowed overhead. It was barely discernible in the glare pouring through the open doorway as the sun reappeared from behind the clouds. Lee heard a shout on the stairs below.

He started down the steps as a rapid series of shots reverberated in the stairwell. Lee paused. A long moment of silence was broken by an angry shout.

"You better open up, you bastards."

Lee was startled. There was no mistaking the voice: it was Albert.

Two more shots rang out, followed by a groan, and silence returned. Lee started down the steps again. As he reached the fifth floor, he heard the clack of a heavy lock being opened. A door banged back against a wall. Then he heard voices.

"Where is that little fuck? Did you get him?"

"I think so."

"Check it out. I'll cover you. I don't want this door open too long."

"Right."

The floor below was suddenly flooded with light. Lee leaned around the corner. A shadow fell across the floorboards, which were relatively free of litter, as if the inhabitants of the drug store were cleanliness conscious.

The first voice spoke again "Can you imagine that little shit, trying to take us off? You find him?"

"Not yet. He's hit, though. There's blood on the wall over here."

Albert was somewhere below, and he was wounded. Lee started to descend, the shadow becoming a bulky figure. He drew a bead on the man, but held his fire. He wanted them all. The door had to be open.

The shadow moved away, keeping low against one wall. Lee took another step, one more, and the hallway was visible. Albert was nowhere to be seen. Almost to the fourth floor, Lee stopped and waited.

The coiled figure suddenly bolted, crossing the hall and kicking at a door. The door swung back. Two shots sounded from inside the room, then the tell-tale click of an empty gun. The bulky man laughed and stepped toward the open door to the room. Lee had no choice. He aimed quickly and fired twice, his automatic silent under the hammering of the bulky man's gun. The man spun sideways and fell heavily to the floor.

In seconds, another man bounded down the hall, racing past the foot of the stairway. Lee aimed but held his fire, deciding, instead, to turn the corner, and rush the guy. He slugged him hard behind the right ear, and the man slumped forward. Lee placed a foot in the small of the hardguy's back and shoved. The man sprawled into the room, landing in a heap on the floor.

Lee clicked on his flashlight. The unconscious man lay in a pile of litter against one wall. To his left, Albert sat on the floor, leaning against another wall. He was bleeding heavily from a bullet wound in his shoulder. A small trickle of blood ran down his chin. His brother dropped to his knees.

"Albert? Can you hear me? Say something, man. It's me, Lee."

Albert smiled weakly. "Hey, man. What you doing here?"

"What are *you* doing here? What the hell were you trying to do?"

Albert coughed. Blood bubbled from his open lips. He tried to talk, but could only manage a whispery rasp. Another cough, and the smile faded. "When you got to have something, man, you got to have it. You know that." Albert laughed, then coughed again. "I had to have something, man, and this is where I got it."

"Drugs? You got your ass in this mess for some goddamn drugs?"

"You don't know what it's like, man. It rides you and won't get off."

"How long you been on?"

Albert shook his head. He coughed again. "Forever, man. Forever." He sighed. His eyes closed.

Lee shook him by the lapels. "Look at me, man. You look at me, Albert. Albert?" he shouted, his voice echoing in the empty room. "Albert?" This time a whisper. It was useless.

Albert was dead.

Lee smashed his fist into the wall over his brother's head. A scraping sound emanated from the hall. He got to his feet, instinct taking over. There was no time for grief. He ran to the doorway, listening intently. A shadow moved slowly along the floorboards.

When he judged the man to be no more than two feet from the doorway, he fired twice. A third man fell to the floor. Lee charged the drug store, its door yawning open. As he drew close, a hand reached out for the handle, tugging at the door to close it. Lee fired again, his shot taking the unseen man just above the elbow.

He rushed through, diving to the floor and rolling in time to nail the man with a shot to the throat. Blood spurted across the room, drenching Lee and the floor around him. He fired again at the slumping figure beside the door, the bullet striking him in the head.

He rushed back down the hall to the single survivor. Stepping into the room again, he grabbed the unconscious man by the hair and shook him roughly.

"Wake up you son of a bitch." Lee jerked the man's head from side to side, slapping his cheeks with his free hand. The man groaned and tried to rise. Twisting the handful of hair, Lee waved his gun in front of the groggy man's eyes.

"See this, motherfucker? You see this? You tell me what I want to know, and maybe I won't blow your worthless brains all over the wall."

Wide awake now, the man stammered, never taking his eyes from the wavering muzzle of the gun. "Wh-what do you want to know? Don't shoot, man, I'll tell you anything you want."

Methodically, Lee questioned his captive, keeping one ear open for approaching sirens.

When he had learned everything he wanted to know, he stood up and looked at the man for a long moment. Then, casually, as if he were brushing a bug from his shoe, he brought the muzzle of the gun against the seated man's left eye and squeezed the trigger. A second shot echoed through the deserted room, and the dead man lay gaping at the ceiling through two bloody tunnels. In the distance, a siren keened.

Lee climbed the stairs to the roof.

CHAPTER TWENTY-FIVE

The warehouse stood all by itself, wrapped in fog. The sound of waves lapping against the pilings was all Bolan could hear. Through the high wire fence, he saw the halos thrown by night-lights mounted high over the loading docks. For all practical purposes, the place looked as innocent as its sign would suggest: Salvatore Imports Fine Furniture Objets d'Art. But the highest art represented by its contents was that of refining. The place was full of coke and grass.

Bolan snipped the heavy cyclone fence, making a hole large enough for him to slip through unimpeded. The guard dogs would find him sooner or later, but he'd deal with them when he had to. Right now he was more concerned with getting inside.

The main receiving depot for the Mob's Miami drug operation, the place was operated as a legitimate business. It turned a modest profit on its own, just enough to justify continuing in business. The dollar volume of illicit traffic was anybody's guess.

Taking the warehouse out was Bolan's primary purpose, but he had an ulterior motive. Everything he'd been able to learn suggested a novel approach to smashing Cardona's operation. Legitimate means hadn't worked for the DEA. Brognola had intimated that Cardona had too many people on his payroll, both in Bolivia and the U.S. But there were other ways to skin this particular cat.

He'd just missed Cardona in Mexico City. The DEA agent who tailed him to El Alto had given him a bum steer. Things were out of control and, as far as Bolan was concerned, the DEA was a rusting sieve. He could trust Callahan, maybe. He wasn't sure about that. What he did know was that a new approach, anything new, had to be better

than anything they'd tried so far. And here he was, back to
square one. He'd lost ground, but the race wasn't over.

Not by a long shot.

If he could get the various factions fighting among themselves, they'd get careless. Too busy with one another, they
wouldn't notice him until it was too late. Any incidental
damage they inflicted on one another was a plus. The
smuggling operations were his ultimate goal, but cutting into
the available supply would cramp their style and hurt their
pocketbooks in the short run. The more they worried about
one another, the easier they'd make it for him.

Tonight was the first step. He knew the Bolivians and
Colombians weren't particular about civilians. Some even
made it a point of pride to take out whole families, even infants, in their vendettas. For that, Bolan was sorry. But he
didn't make the rules. He simply had to play by them.

Dressed in black, he moved like a shadow through the
fog. He carried a small satchel full of C-4 plastique. The
warehouse was ideally located for a drastic surgical removal. He could blow the place into atoms and nobody who
didn't deserve it would get so much as a scratch.

The sounds of the Miami waterfront were typical.
Through the heavy fog, he could hear the deep basso pro-
fundo of freighters warning all and sundry to get out of the
way. The creak of cables straining against the tidal surge cut
through the thick air. Half a mile away, a night crew unloaded a recent arrival, their shouts nearly as loud as the
heavy equipment. They posed no threat, unable to see the
warehouse through the pea soup.

Bolan reached the warehouse in short order. Behind him,
a small fleet of trucks sat in two rows, sitting ducks. He'd
take them out as well, time permitting. Money was the name
of the game. The more he could make them bleed, the more
it cost them, the madder they'd get.

And the better he liked it.

The warehouse doors were locked. A heavy padlock at
either edge secured each of the rolling gates. Security was

light, but Bolan wanted as much time as he could buy. He could have blown off the locks in short order, but the guards would hear the racket. Slow and quiet was what he needed.

Like most busy warehouses, the place was loaded with tools. Walking along the loading dock, he found what he was looking for on a pile of wooden crates. A long, heavy crowbar lay where it had fallen at the afternoon whistle. Longshoremen, no matter who they worked for, followed the rules to a tee. Quitting time was time to leave. The boss paid for the tools. If he didn't give you time to put them away, that was his problem.

Bolan walked back to the central loading bay, the heavy bar in his hand. He forced the prongs of its curved end under the mounting plate of the first lock. Putting all his weight behind it, he felt the bolts groan. The plate began to give, then with a sharp squeal it gave way. He repeated the procedure on the second lock, stuck the crowbar through his belt and bent to open the door.

Its creaky rollers squeaked in their tracks as the articulated door slid up and back, striking home with a boom. The sound echoed in the cavernous interior, as though a dozen other doors were opening. Bolan stepped inside to darkness of another kind. The fog had been dense, cutting off his vision several yards away. Here, he could see dim shapes, stacks of crates and skids of smaller cartons. Long aisles threaded through the towering inventory.

Somewhere inside this huge building was a fortune in illicit narcotics. Exactly where didn't matter. Before he was done, it would all be reduced to ashes and rubble. The legitimate business was simply a front, so its loss was no concern of his. Every penny he took out of the Mob's pocket was a plus.

The guardhouse was at the other end of the building, near the parking lot and front gate. The guards themselves might be innocent; Bolan wasn't interested in them and would ignore them as long as they left him alone. The Dobermans were something else again. Three of them roamed the warehouse after closing time, then were coaxed back into their pens in the morning by their handler.

Bolan made his way down one of the long aisles. Dim light from the security lamps filtered through long rows of windows high on each wall. The dull squares enabled him to gauge his location with some accuracy, but gave no light to work by. He was nearly at the very center of the warehouse when he heard the first dog.

Padding silently, the click of its nails on the concrete floor the only sound it made, the Doberman was nearly on him before Bolan could react. He turned just as the big dog, fangs bared, leaped at him. Bolan snatched the crowbar from his belt, swinging it in a tight arc and catching the dog in midflight. The bar struck home, cracking on the dog's skull. The animal lay on the floor, twitching. Bolan regretted injuring the dog, which had only done what it had been trained to do. But it was on him before Bolan could use the tranquilizer gun.

Bolan climbed onto a stack of crates to wait for the other two dogs. Drawn by the same sharp senses, they were certain to be close by. Bolan slipped the CO_2-driven tranquilizer gun from its holster and waited patiently. He didn't have to wait long.

The second dog skidded around a corner and raced toward him. Waiting until it reached the foot of his tower, Bolan fitted a dart into the gun and drew a bead on the animal's black shoulder. He squeezed the trigger and the dog whimpered at the pain as the dart struck home. Drawn by the commotion, the remaining dog trotted into the open, teeth bared and mouth slavering. Bolan waited until the animal was just below him, beside its tranquilized companion, who was now coming under the influence of the drug. Bolan fired another dart, then waited a good five minutes for the dogs to become immobilized.

Now he could get down to business.

Bolan located the four huge pillars that supported the roof. Taking a brick of C-4 from the satchel, he attached it

to the first pillar with duct tape. He inserted a detonating
cap, then moved to the next pillar, repeating the process
three times. It took less than ten minutes.

Bolan began to prowl the aisles of the deserted warehouse. He walked the length of three aisles, one by one,
checking crates and cartons, before he found what he was
looking for. The crate, four feet by four feet by eight, was
marked Fabric. Its point of origin was Guatemala.

Like most smuggling operations, this one consisted of
several carefully thought-out steps. Each had its own veneer of legitimacy. Most of the material shipped was precisely what it pretended to be. And it had to appear to be as
ordinary as possible in order not to attract more than passing interest.

Once customs agents got used to a particular business,
they tended to be casual in their examinations. The new
business was the one they looked at most closely, that and
the unusual. But nothing could be more ordinary than native fabrics shipped into the States from Guatemala.

The coke trade was particularly lucrative because the
substance itself was cash intensive. It took tons of marijuana to equal the cash value of a five-kilo bag of pure coke.
If you had to get something into the country illegally, there
was no question which one was easier, and which paid the
most for your trouble.

Bolan took the crowbar from his belt and jimmied the lid
of the crate, then played the light over the contents. Several
bolts of brightly dyed cloth were on top and beneath them,
at a right angle, was another layer, then a third.

Bolan laid the flashlight on an adjacent crate and dug in
with both hands. Under the fourth layer, he found what he
knew would be in the crate: an ordinary plastic garbage bag,
taped shut with shiny silver tape. He rapped the bag sharply
with the crowbar. It thumped, and he jabbed again, this
time point first. The cardboard box inside gave way, releas-
ing a cloud of fine white dust.

202 TROPIC HEAT

Bolan moistened a finger and inserted it through the tear in the package. It came out white. Tasting the fine glaze on his finger, Bolan smiled grimly. Pay dirt. The package was fairly large, occupying much of the center of the crate, so it could weigh somewhere in the neighborhood of two hundred pounds. Depending on its purity and how it was cut, the coke in this one package might be worth twenty million dollars or more.

Bolan left the drug cache and went to retrieve the five-gallon cans of solvent he had seen earlier. He lugged several of the cans to aisle intersections and removed their caps. When they had all been opened, he worked his way back along the aisles, kicking each can onto its side. The solvent splashed and gurgled as the cans emptied, small rivers of the highly explosive chemicals running under skids and mingling with one another. The center of the warehouse was awash in flammable liquid.

Bolan ran back to the door, pulled it closed behind him and sprinted for the fence. The fog was lifting now, and the loading area was much brighter. He'd have to forget about the trucks. He slipped through the fence and dashed to his car, started the engine.

Pulling onto the potholed asphalt of a side street, he gunned the engine and cornered into the broad avenue fronting the warehouse district. He cruised slowly past Salvatore Imports, then slowed in the middle of the next block. Reaching into the console beside the gearshift, he depressed a small red button on a radio detonator. The roar that followed shattered the windows of several warehouses around him.

The roof collapsed and, as the solvent ignited, a huge fireball mushroomed up through the ruined structure, turning the lingering fog a muddy orange. The fireball disappeared, and columns of smoke took its place. Bright yellow flames licked at the shattered windows high on the wall. Bolan didn't know how much more coke was in the warehouse, but a twenty-million-dollar loss was bound to get somebody's attention.

Welcome to Miami.

SALLY MAGGADINO WAS LIVID.

"I'm telling you, I know that son of a bitch. I've seen him before. I know it. Run that tape again."

The three men sat staring at the large-screen TV. The blank screen flickered, then a shattered picture congealed into wavy lines. The picture locked, and through a hazy fog they could see the loading area of a warehouse. Their warehouse. One loading bay door was darker than the others, obviously open. Suddenly a small black figure appeared in the doorway. It paused long enough to close the door, then leaped from the pier onto the asphalt parking lot, sprinting right toward the security camera. The figure passed out of view as he ran under the camera. The wide-angle image was less than perfect, but the man's features were discernible, even in the dim light.

And Sal Maggadino knew who it was. He kept silent while the picture remained still. For three or four minutes, the warehouse looked as silent and deserted as it should have been. Then the screen caught fire. The roof collapsed and broken windows flew in every direction.

"Sally," Buccieri said, breaking the subdued silence, "no way you could tell who that guy was. I say he works for one of the Bolivian bastards."

"And I'm telling you, Joey...and you better shut up and listen. I know that guy. He's been on our case for years. Vegas, New York, Chicago, you name it. Including right here in Miami. Once you see him, you don't forget him. And I want him. I want him now, and I want him alive. I'm going to take that son of a bitch apart with my bare hands. You understand me, Joey?"

"Yeah, Sal, yeah. I understand."

Maggadino stood and stalked out of the room. The television screen continued its silent replay of the raging fire of the night before. Buccieri looked at Carlucci and DiMarzio and shook his head.

"The old man's losing it," he said.

He took their silence for consent.

CHAPTER TWENTY-SIX

The Lincoln Town Car was a stately gray in color. It left the garage and its tires crunched on the white gravel of the semicircular driveway. The chauffeur, uncomfortable in a uniform two sizes too big, piloted the big car to a halt before the sweeping marble staircase ascending to the columned portico. He left the car running while he lit a cigarette. Glancing in the rearview mirror, he canted the cap a little more forward over his brow.

The man in the back seat shifted nervously. The chauffeur could hear his clothes rustling on the leather seat. Both men watched the doorway of the large white house. It was taking longer than they had expected.

Finally the broad glass door swung open. A tall, heavy-set man in a gray pin-striped suit and shiny black oxfords bent to kiss a slender birdlike woman on the top of her head. She wore a tasteful evening dress, off the shoulder, and her white hair was cut short and swept back along either side of her face. It could have been an ad right out of *Town and Country*, style for the gracious senior.

The big man waited until the door closed, then turned to walk down the steps. He seemed surprised for a second, stopping to adjust his dark blue tie, snugging the knot a little tighter under his chin. The only false note the passenger saw was the open collar of the shirt. The man's neck, still pink from the razor, was larger than normal, almost sloping directly from his shoulders to his jawline, like that of a defensive tackle. It wasn't fat.

Recovering from the momentary hesitation, the big man reached the bottom step, crunched across a narrow strip of the white crushed stone and opened the rear door of the

Lincoln. He slid in gracefully for a man his size, and pulled the door closed. He had started to turn to the left when his massive jaw felt the cold prod of the gun muzzle.

"Don't even think about moving," the other passenger whispered. "Just don't."

The big man nodded.

"Let's go."

The driver took a final drag on his cigarette, flicked the ash one more time, then flipped the butt out onto the white gravel. The brown filter was noticeable against the impeccably tended driveway. Closing the power window, the driver put the car in gear and drove slowly away from the house.

The big man heard the tires crunching on the gravel—just as he had a thousand times before—but without knowing quite how or why, knew this time was different from all those others. When he started to look back toward the house, the gun nudged him under the left ear.

"Don't turn around. Please, just face front and keep your hands in your lap, where I can see them."

The big car purred effortlessly out into the broad avenue, which was lined with dozens of homes no more or less elegant than the one whose driveway the vehicle had just left. Most were set well back from the street, partially screened by stately palms. Broad lawns, largely free of the tacky plaster flamingos northerners envisioned when they thought about Southern wealth, stretched away from low stone or brick walls, flowing around the large houses like a green sea.

The big man looked through his window, wondering how he had managed to come so far. True, it had taken him a long time. But he'd had it for a long time now, and was comfortable with his money. There were worse things.

Never easy with strangers, he knew better than most that people who had nothing wanted something from those who had everything. He'd been on the other side himself a long time ago. But not so long ago that he had forgotten.

This unease had kept him apart from his neighbors. He was regarded as something of a recluse by those who knew him slightly, and as a mystery by those who had never met him. That was all right. He liked it that way.

As the big Lincoln cruised sedately through the community, he realized that he had never been invited to most of the homes that shared the quiet seclusion of the neighborhood, and had been inside fewer still.

The car was easing out of the quiet residential area, entering one of the teeming boulevards leaning to the edge of the city. More traffic rushed past, easily outdistancing the Lincoln's leisurely pace. So much seemed new to him, as if he were seeing the city for the first time. It had changed so much from his first visit, nearly thirty years before. The twenty-five years he'd lived in Miami had been busy ones.

They were moving faster now, out on the Dixie Highway, heading south. The big man turned to his companion, forgetting the injunction to keep his eyes forward.

He spoke quietly, his rich baritone resonant, even in the confines of the limousine's back seat. "I know where we're going," he said. "I was just wondering who you were."

"Does it make a difference?"

"No. But I'd like to know."

"I bet."

"You're not going to tell me, are you?"

"No."

"All right."

The big man turned back to the window, a tourist exploring his own home. The cityscape dwindled away to scattered buildings, then was gone altogether. Rolling country, waist high in saw grass, stretched away on either side. In some respects it was not that different from the marshes of New Jersey he had seen so long ago, from his companion's perspective.

"What goes around, comes around," he said, thinking of his youngest daughter, now a sophomore in college. He had first heard the phrase from her, and liked the ring of it. It had that cynical tolerance of the inevitable that passed these days for genuine stoicism. She had laughed when he first said it and teased him still, on those rare occasions when he saw her.

"You got that right," the passenger said, intruding on his reverie.

Turning to him, the big man asked, "Where is Fred?"

"Who?"

"My chauffeur."

"In the garage. Taking a nap."

"You didn't hurt him, did you?"

"Naw."

"Thank you."

"He didn't feel a thing." The passenger laughed grimly.

They hadn't passed or been passed by another car in several miles.

The passenger leaned forward and spoke to the driver through the open panel between the front seat and the rear compartment. The driver nodded, and the car slowed.

A weedy side road yawned suddenly, crisp white sand sparkling where it met the main highway. The car braked, and the driver negotiated the turn with some difficulty. Fifty yards from the highway, the vehicle was no longer visible to a passing car. The limo rocked slowly ahead until the passenger leaned forward again. The driver braked, killing the engine.

The hit man gestured with his pistol. His target nodded, sighed once and opened his door. The passenger slid across the leather seat and joined him on the sandy margin of the marsh.

For a moment, the two men stared at each other in silence. Neither had ever met the other. It was business, but it was more than that. They had as much in common as any two men ever did. Each had made a living in the same way, though the big man had left it behind, in favor of more pressing responsibilities. Still, it was a bond the younger man could not help but notice.

He raised his pistol, threaded a silencer snugly in place and aimed. He fired three times, taking the top of the big man's head off. Fragments of skull rained into the marsh grass.

The hit man lowered his pistol and stared at the body, now sprawled indecently in the muddy water at the edge of the swamp.

"Like shooting fish in a barrel," the driver said laughing.

The assassin stiffened. He turned, a frown tightening his features. He fired twice, punching both slugs through the driver's forehead.

"Asshole. Shouldn't make fun of real class. Didn't your mama teach you nothin'?"

Sally Maggadino was dead. That didn't mean he should be laughed at. The driver should have known better than to mock his betters.

He threw the gun as far into the grass as he could, watching its graceful arc in the orange light of late afternoon. He hated to part with a good weapon, but there were more where that one came from. In his business, you had to know that.

And no one knew it any better than Lee Richards.

JOEY BUCCIERI STEPPED OUT of the shadows. He shifted nervously from foot to foot, looking up and down the deserted street. Strange neighborhoods made him nervous, and being alone was worse. The two hundred thousand dollars in a briefcase at his side was the last straw. The price had been steep, but he wanted the best, and he wanted him on short notice.

In a way, he was lucky. The hitter agreed to a price that was less than half what he would have paid, and throwing the Bolivian into the package had been the mechanic's idea. The whole thing made him nervous. He didn't like using out-of-town talent, but if he was going to hold things together—and keep his own head on his shoulders—he had no choice. You don't use a known quantity to take out the head of your family.

Now, he could blame Sal's murder on the mysterious visitor to the warehouse and the Bolivian, and bring the mechanic into the open, the man he hired to get Cardona to even things up for Sally. It was simple, and that was the only reason Joey thought it had a prayer. The only hitch was that the hit man could finger him as the man behind Sally's hit, but once the Bolivian was out of the way, he could take care of that. And two hundred thou in old bills would make anybody careless, especially with the promise of another three when the job was finished. All he had to do was keep his cool with Carlucci and DiMarzio. That would be a cinch.

He heard footsteps up the block, and he ducked back into the shadows of the alley. The gun in his back was a complete surprise.

"You bring the money?"

"Yeah, yeah. What the hell is this?"

"Where is it?"

"In the briefcase. What the hell is the matter with you? I thought we had a deal?"

"We do. I did my part. Now it's payday."

"What about the other half of the job?"

"Don't worry about it. When it's done, you'll get a bill. Dig?"

"I don't like doing business with a gun in my back."

"Huh." It was a laugh, but it sent a chill through Buccieri. He felt his short hairs standing on end. "Never knew a wop to worry about professional courtesy before. You a piece of work, man."

"Who are you calling a wop?" Buccieri snarled, turning halfway around until the gun rapped him sharply on the spine.

"Man, I been called everything from boot to spade by Eye-talians. What you so touchy about? You nervous? Nobody here but us chickens."

The laugh again. Buccieri stood in the dark, his hands rigid at shoulder height. He no longer felt the gun, but didn't want to chance another rap on his already aching spine. "I'm not nervous. Why should I be?"

He waited a few seconds and repeated his question. "I said, why should I be nervous?" The silence was deafening. Slowly, steeling himself for another rap with the muzzle, he turned. The blow never came.

The alley was empty.

CHAPTER TWENTY-SEVEN

The garage looked innocent enough, but Mack Bolan knew better. Nestled in a small industrial suburb of Miami, at the end of a dead-end street, it did a token body-and-fender business as a cover. At night it did another, much more lucrative, kind of business.

Bolan waited in the sparse woods behind the garage, waiting for the transformation. The metalworkers, three of them, stood outside, talking and joking, knocking down a cold beer. It had been a hot day, and the bugs had been unmerciful. Bolan was irritable and impatient. The warehouse had been easy. Where to go from there was more problematic. Getting intelligence in bits and pieces, scrounging for leads, he was nearing the boiling point. Tommy Calabrese had finally come up with the body shop as a good place to start.

The lab was going to be the first in a series of quick strikes. He wanted the Mob and he wanted Cardona. If he could set them at each other's throat, they'd be less likely to watch their backs. In essence, Brognola's game plan had gone by the boards. But there was more than one way to skin a cat.

And the Executioner was ready.

Finally, the beer bottles empty and consigned to the overfull Dumpster in the alley alongside, the men said goodnight. Two of them jumped into their cars and pulled out, lake pipes roaring, primered, vented hoods vibrating over supercharged engines.

The third man walked back to the garage door. He snapped a heavy padlock in place, then stepped into the open office door. Through the open window, Bolan could see him moving around. The lights on the sign went out, then the office itself went dark. A moment later the man reappeared on the street. He slammed the glass-paneled door closed, locked it and walked to his own car.

Before the engine turned over, Bolan was gliding toward the office. The engine rumbled and rubber peeled. Bolan pressed himself against the side of the building and watched the car's taillights recede. In an hour, he knew, the shop would change gears. But tonight there'd be a new man on the crew, waiting.

Bolan rapped sharply on the glass of the side window. With a quiet tinkle, the glass broke inward, shards smashing on the floor. He reached up and undid the latch, opened the glassless frame and hauled himself through. Once inside, he opened the door to the garage and entered.

He closed the office door to block the beam from his flashlight. A quick circuit of the interior revealed the false wall to the rear of the garage. A doorway, its seams visible only on close scrutiny, stood to the left of a chest-high tool cabinet. Bolan found the spring latch, depressed it and pushed. As the camouflaged door swung inward, a sweet odor rushed out of the darkness.

Bolan stepped into the dark room and closed the door behind him. He played the torch beam around the inner chamber. Large containers of ether, hydrochloric acid and kerosene lined one wall. Three huge vats sat in the middle of the floor, industrial gas burners under each of them. A green garden hose lay coiled on the floor next to one of the vats. In one corner, a stack of plastic-wrapped packages reached almost to the corrugated-tin roof.

Bolan checked his watch. He had less than thirty minutes to wait. The processing lab was a basic operation, but everything was there. Hundreds of pounds of sugar, Epsom salts and low-grade amphetamines—to step on the coke and cut it down to street-level percentage—were piled in boxes against the opposite wall.

Bolan slid in behind the mound of cartons. He had just enough room to conceal himself without cutting off his freedom of movement. The next twenty minutes would seem like an eternity. Bolan clicked off his flashlight. In the darkness he checked his weapons, chambering a round in Big Thunder and snicking off its safety. The night crew was small, either four or six men, depending on the volume of the drug to be processed. Judging by the quantity in the corner, tonight would see the larger figure.

While Bolan waited, he considered his options. They weren't attractive, and they weren't many. The warehouse hit had provoked an outcry in the press, but nothing had surfaced. The police had dismissed the explosion as the work of rival drug factions. So far, neither Cardona nor the Mob had taken the bait.

A car door slammed shut in the alley adjacent to the garage. Bolan steeled himself. The rasp of a sliding door was followed by voices in subdued conversation. Men reporting for work, whatever it might be, were usually more boisterous. Something was wrong.

The weight of Big Thunder calmed him. His mind seemed suddenly sharper. A hand rattled the latch. Bolan shifted lightly on his feet, angling his body toward the sound.

A block of light appeared in the wall, then flooded the inner chamber as overhead lamps went on. A dark figure flashed past the opening, one arm extended, then disappeared. A small *crump* sounded in one corner of the room. Out of the corner of his eye, Bolan noticed a small cloud beginning to blossom, a pungent aroma filling the room.

Tear gas.

They knew he was here. All right. Let them try to cash it in. Glassware began to shatter on the steel shelving to his left. Several jars of acid ruptured, the sharp sting of its fumes rising as cloudy streams of the corrosive chemical spilled over painted metal. Under the cascade of breaking glass, Bolan recognized the familiar sound of a suppressed Ingram. The spitting sound, like that of an angry lynx, snarled through the doorway. There were two of them. That widened the odds a little.

Bolan scanned the room, a large sink in one corner catching his eye. The tear-gas canister was just to its left. Bolan fired twice, taking out the overhead fluorescents. As the room went dark, the Ingrams poured a deadly hail through the open doorway. Easing out from behind the cartons, Bolan dropped to the floor and rolled.

Slamming into the wall, he reached out for the sink, its outline dimly visible in the light from the doorway. Groping with his free hand, he grabbed the tear-gas canister and tossed it into the sink. Getting to his knees, he turned on the water. It wouldn't kill the gas entirely, but it would keep it down. The rushing water would also cover the sound of his movements.

Bolan crouched and rushed toward the door, diving behind a pile of boxes. The gunners paused, uncertain what to do next. Bolan heard new magazines being inserted with the slap of a palm, the old ones clattering to the concrete floor. It was a standoff. They couldn't come through the door, and he couldn't get out. One tentative burst clanged against the metal sink, the ricocheting slugs whining at random, slamming into boxes, breaking more glass.

Bolan was sliding off at an angle, and as he moved, his field of vision changed. Peeking out from behind the barrier of cartons, he caught a glimpse of a shoulder. He drew a bead with Big Thunder. The shot was too tight. He needed something to nudge the guy into a mistake.

The lab was loaded with chemicals. A chance spark might ignite a holocaust. Being burned alive held no appeal for Bolan. He had to make a move. Bolan hefted his flashlight in his left hand, then tossed it in a high arc. It shot through the doorway and slammed into the floor about halfway across the garage. The shoulder moved as its owner turned to look behind him. Bolan squeezed off a shot.

The shoulder burst into a bright red flower before it disappeared. Bolan raised his head. The wounded man lay sprawled on the concrete. Bolan fired again, hitting the prostrate form in the back of the head.

One down.

But how many to go?

Inching closer to the doorway, Bolan spotted two more men, crouching behind the garage air compressor. Against the wall behind him, Bolan felt another bank of steel shelves. He reached back and grabbed a can from one of the shelves. Linseed oil. Another can of the same. The third can was more promising—benzene, but it was almost empty. The fourth was also benzene, but this one was full. The can was cylindrical, two-quart capacity. The screw top mounted in the center of the lid was tight.

Twisting it free, Bolan was stymied by the crimped tin inner seal. He rapped it sharply once, then again, with the butt of the AutoMag. The seal bent inward, one lip rising. He placed the lip against the shelf and yanked. The seal came free, benzene sloshing out of the open lid.

Bolan fired two shots through the open doorway, buying time. One Ingram returned fire, the second lying useless under the corpse of the dead gunner.

Bolan tore the pocket from his shirt, stuffed one end in the benzene can and shook it. He felt the volatile liquid soak the end of his makeshift fuse. Setting the can of solvent back on its shelf, Bolan fired again, his shot pinging off the air compressor.

His pocket lighter clicked, the wheel sparking in the dark. The flame vanished immediately. He clicked it again, this time using two hands. The flame caught and held. Holding the lighter carefully, he turned his body to the side. He knew he'd only get one throw, and it had to be good.

He grabbed the benzene can, lit the fuse and hurled. As if in slow motion, the can tumbled through the air, the small flame of the fuse suddenly dimming as the can flew into the lighted garage. A small trail of black smoke curled behind it.

One of the concealed men realized what was happening. He darted out, hitting the floor and rolling, but he wasn't fast enough. Big Thunder exploded. He slammed into the front of a Buick that was up on blocks. He didn't move again.

Two down.

The benzene bomb slammed into the top of the compressor. A dull thud was followed by a river of flame coursing down the side of the machine. The hidden man screamed, then burst into the open, his clothes drenched in flaming liquid. Bolan fired twice into the moving fireball. Like a tinder scarecrow, the flaming figure collapsed, crumpling to a crackling ball on the concrete. The benzene quickly burned itself out, leaving a charred hulk on the floor. Tendrils of smoke rose uncertainly, tossed by the currents, then dissipated altogether.

The odds were looking better all the time.

The garage was silent. Bolan calculated his next move. At least one man still remained. One of the guys with an Ingram. Bolan dived past the open door, expecting a hail of fire from the SMG, but nothing happened.

Bolan hauled himself to his feet, trying to get a look through the doorway. He felt hampered by the narrow field of vision. It worked to his own advantage as well, but he didn't like not knowing what his opponents were up to.

The acid fumes were stronger now, spreading through the confined space. He noticed a ventilating fan in the center of the roof, a chain dangling from its motor. Bolan gave it a yank and the fan groaned into motion. It would take out some of the coruscating fumes. Still, he couldn't stay where he was. Not for long.

Before he could decide what to do, an engine roared in the garage. With a peel of rubber, the unseen vehicle began to move. With a shudder, the wall before him began to give way. They were trying to force their way in.

Bolan slammed a new clip into the AutoMag and stepped to the doorway. Two men sat in the cab of a fenderless pickup truck. Its front bumper strained against the wall, the engine whining as the rear wheels squealed on the concrete floor. The smell of burning rubber warred with the stench of charred flesh.

Bolan stepped through the door and emptied the AutoMag into the truck's cab. The windshield and side window shattered. The horn began to blow. The din was deafening. Then the wall gave way. Bolan dived behind a tool cabinet.

The truck shot forward, grinding metal and cracking timber drowning the sound of the racing engine. A deafening crash jarred the rear wall. The engine died; the horn continued to howl. Bolan yanked his Beretta free and waited. Nothing moved. He began to creep out from behind his cover.

The roar of the chemicals in the lab catching fire sounded like napalm going up, the hot, sucking wind rushing past into the raging inferno. The shelving collapsed, cascading fire over the cab of the truck. The horn stopped.

It was over.

All he had to do was figure out how they knew he was going to be there. And there was only one answer to that question. Tommy Calabrese of the Drug Enforcement Administration was going to give it to him.

And there was no time like the present.

CHAPTER TWENTY-EIGHT

Lee Richards sat in the Corvette, admiring his new shades in the rearview mirror. The customized '63 Stingray, candy-apple red, cost a bundle, but, hey, it was only money. He remembered the old radio show, *The Shadow*. He was too young to have heard it on the air, but Freddy Johnson collected tapes of old shows. He liked that one the best. The guy, Lamont Cranston, used to talk in a creepy voice at the beginning of the show. He always said something like "The weed of crime bears bitter fruit." Then the creepy mother would laugh.

Well, now Lee knew what he meant. But this time, he was going to bring in the crop. Some son of a bitch had made it possible for his brother to die. Albert was just a kid, he deserved a chance. Lee had tried to buy him the chance, but he had to be the big man. Instead of staying in touch, letting the kid know, giving him something to hang on to, he wanted to spring it on him all at once. The kid was smart. He could have gone to college. Now he was dead.

And Lee was going to get even.

The Italian was even going to pay him for the pleasure. But he had to get to him, first. Grabbing on to the tail of the kite, Lee was going to climb all the way up. Then he was going to cut the damn string.

The Vette was a class act, just the kind of thing to get him noticed by the right people. He had the money to make a big buy. But the Vette told everybody in a way that nothing else could. Flash, that was the ticket. Having bread was nothing, man. Shit, a dentist had money. But flash, that was something else. That was a big spender putting his money where his mouth was.

Hanging out in the right clubs was the next step. Knowing which ones they were was easy. Getting to the man with the goods was a little tougher. But Easy Street was the best place to do it. Lee climbed out of the Vette without opening the door. He put on his best strut and crossed the street.

The loud music was just a subliminal throb as he reached the sidewalk. A six-four slab of beef in a muscle shirt fisheyed him as he strutted under the glittering marquee. He reached for the glass door, but it slid to one side before he made contact. The music blared, guitar and electric piano submerging the pulsing drums and bass he'd heard from the street. He lost his cool for a second, and the slab of beef chuckled.

"Hey, my man, you might look cool, but..." Lee turned to see the bouncer shaking his head. Lee stepped back.

"You talking to me, white man?"

The bouncer glared. "So?"

"So, you want to see cool, you just keep an eye peeled, my man. I gonna freeze your eyeballs."

Lee stuck a twenty in the guy's belt and sidled through the open glass panel. He chuckled over his shoulder. "Save that smoke comin' out your ears, my man. You goin' to need it."

The club was dark and full of colored laser beams splattering on the mirrored walls. A fine mist of cigarette and marijuana smoke turned the air gray-blue.

A bandstand was raised high above a contorting mass of dancers. Its cables hummed with the energetic gyrations of the lead singer. Rail thin and shirtless, he couldn't have weighed more than a speed freak on his last legs. Long blond hair, damp with sweat, hung in soggy coils, sticking to his glistening shoulders.

Behind the singer, two black women shared a microphone. Their costumes were shiny plastic minidresses, translucent and brilliantly reflective by turns. Chosen more for their bodies than their talent, they spent most of their time dancing to and from the microphone. Lee reconsidered who he'd like to give what.

He turned sideways to wriggle through the gyrating patrons. It wasn't possible to get to a table without considerable contact. Lee was apologetic, until he realized most of the dancers didn't notice him, and those few who did didn't care. As he reached a vacant table, the band finished its set, and the lighting changed from laser display to revolving mirrored balls.

Lee's taste ran more to blues or jazz, and the raucous music, techno pop heavy on the synthesizers, that began blaring over the sound system left him cold. The waitress who suddenly loomed over him made a Playboy bunny look overdressed.

"What's your pleasure, handsome?"

"A good book and some Mozart," Lee said, smiling with his lips alone.

"You got the wrong place, honey."

"Tell me 'bout it."

"You want a drink, or what?" She shifted her weight from one foot to the other. The half moons of flesh over her narrow halter jiggled. Flashes of white showed where her courage under the sun ended. "I got a job, here, you know? You drinking or leaving?"

"Sorry, baby. Bad day, you know? Bring me something with ice, anything you want." He peeled a twenty off a thick roll and stuck it in her halter. "For you, darlin'."

"Hey. What are you doing? What do you think I am?"

Flashing a genuine smile, Lee laughed. "That's my secret. What I *know* you are is a fine-looking fox gonna bring me a drink. I ain't trying to buy you, babe. Not even rent you. Just my way of apologizing."

"No problem," she said, tucking the bill more securely between her breasts. She smiled back, but Lee had already turned to watch the floor. He had business.

Watching the earnest attempts at having a good time, he wondered why anybody should have to work so hard to have fun. But then, for most of the club's patrons, having fun was a job, not a reward for one well done. They came here to see and be seen, to cut deals and hustle anything from guns to butter. If you wanted something illicit, Easy Street was where it was at.

His initial contact told him to be here at nine. Buster Rodriguez would find him. Some name, Buster. Sounded more like a cartoon character, but word was Buster had the juice. He was plugged in to all the right circuits. Only partway up the kite tail, but closer, always closer. Lee could feel the wind rising, and he wasn't anxious to look down.

The waitress was back. She plunked a frosted glass on the table. "You running a tab, sweetie?"

"Cash money, babe. Don't never owe nobody nothing. That's my one rule in life."

"It's a good rule," she said. Tearing off the check, she fluttered it in front of him. "Right now you owe me five big ones."

"For this?" Lee asked, indicating the drink.

"Two for the juice and three for the little plastic umbrella, honey."

"S'pose I don't want the umbrella?"

"Then it's five for the juice."

"Figgers."

He gave her a ten. "Keep the change."

"You've never been here before, have you?"

"Nope, and at these prices, babe, be a while before I come back."

She left without thanking him for the tip. Her cheeks winked from the tight bottom edge of her plastic shorts. There was no white showing.

He leaned back in the chair and surveyed the dance floor. The mechanized pulse of the sound system had people feigning automated frenzy, their movements jerky, like cartoon robots. The whole damn place was like some giant comic book.

To cover his distaste, he picked a long blonde out of the crowd. Her limbs seemed more fluid, even in the robotic mime. She was good looking, but not a knockout. Her virtue was that she still seemed human. That and a nice set of jugs. He was considering whether to cut in on her oblivious partner, when a shadow fell across the table.

A man in a silver-filigreed sombrero sat down without being asked. Lee stared for a minute.

"How's Pancho?"

"What?" The man jiggled his Villa mustache.

"You the Cisco Kid, right?"

"Even if I am, you ain't Richard Pryor, amigo."

"You want something?"

"I'm supposed to ask you that."

"So, ask."

"Buster wants to see some green up front."

"No white, babe, no green, dig?"

"You want white, I got white." The Cisco Kid unfolded his hands to push a small envelope across the table. "Snow white."

"Shit, anybody can score a little. I'm talking heavy coin, and you waltz in here with a street bag? You a comedian, or an idiot?"

"Eh, *señor*, what kind of choice is that, and what kind of talk for business partners?"

Lee stood up. "Later, chump." He started to walk away from the table. The black sombrero grabbed his arm. Lee reached down and squeezed the other man's wrist until he cried out. "I don't have partners, my man. See you around."

"Buster thought you wanted to deal."

"Deal, yes. Buy, yes. Help, I don't need."

"Okay, okay. So, we talk business, okay?"

"I'm through talking, a-mee-go. Right now, I'm walking."

"You make Buster unhappy."

"I don't give a damn. Tell him that for me, will you?"

"No way, amigo. I like my *cojónes*."

"You fond of miniatures, or what?"

"You talk big, my friend."

"I don't just talk . . . and I ain't your friend."

"Why are you so hostile?" The voice was suddenly unctuous.

"Hostile? Me? Why should I be hostile? Man supposed to sell me four keys, he sends a Mexican cowboy to play games. No reason for me to be hostile, is there?"

"Buster don't know you."

"I don't know him, either. I bring the money, he supposed to bring the goods. Bring it, you dig, not send it."

"You could be a narc."

"If I had tits, I could be Pam Grier, but I don't so I ain't."

The sombrero stood up. "Let's go, amigo."

"Forget it."

"I thought you wanted to buy. Four keys, you said. Big money, you said. Long green, no? I take you to Buster now."

Lee sat down. He appeared to think it over. He swirled the ice in his glass and took a long swallow. The empty cracked down on the plastic table. "I ain't in the mood no more."

"Cold feet? Buster make them nice and warm . . . if he doesn't cut them off, amigo. He went to a great deal of trouble to get your order filled."

"Let him tell me about it."

"If you don't come with me, he surely will."

"And if I do?"

"Why, then, the first step of a long and profitable business relationship has been taken."

"Uh-huh." Lee started threading his way through the crowd to the front door. Halfway across the floor he turned and mouthed the words "Let's go, amigo."

The sombrero followed obediently. As the door slid shut behind him, two men in the corner rose, tossed a sheaf of bills on their table.

Lee waited in the Vette, the engine idling roughly, its racing cam restless. Sombrero climbed into the passenger seat, then glanced over his shoulder, a casual gesture Lee noticed without comment. He also noticed the two men getting into a gray Ferrari.

"Where to?" Lee asked.

"Straight ahead. I'll tell you when to turn."

He peeled into the traffic. It was late, and the traffic light. The street was slick with a light rain that had fallen while he was inside. The pavement glowed with reflected headlights from oncoming cars, obscuring the white lane markers. Lee drove fast and easily. From time to time, he drifted into the fast lane, checking on the Ferrari, which was hanging back a few cars.

Making what Sombrero described as the last turn, Lee spotted a classy marina dead ahead. Even at some distance, he was impressed with the size and number of boats at anchor. All but one of them were dark. The exception showed dim red lights in its cabin. The marina was fronted by a deserted parking lot the size of a football field. Coasting through the gate in the cyclone fence, he braked and threw the Vette into neutral. The big engine throbbed.

"Now what?" he asked.

Sombrero waved his hands dismissively. "Have patience."

A moment later, a stretch Cadillac cruised into the parking lot, drifted past the Vette and stopped down near the water. The rear door opened and two men in Hawaiian shirts got out, each armed with an Uzi. They stood one on either side of the open car door.

"Buster?" Lee asked.

"Sí, maricón."

Lee opened the Vette's door and walked toward the Cadillac. Sombrero dawdled, but Lee kept drifting at an angle, keeping the gaucho in sight. At the Cadillac, one of the Hawaiian shirts stepped forward, shifting the Uzi to frisk Lee.

"Back off, chump."

The man hesitated for a second, then resumed his approach. Lee waited until he was in close, then shot his left arm straight out, fingers together and stiffened. The blow sliced under the big man's chin, and slammed into his Adam's apple, not enough to crush it, but more than enough to draw a cough. The man gagged and struggled to breathe. The second hardguy raised the Uzi, its muzzle drifting lazily across Lee's knees and back.

A voice from the Cadillac barked in Spanish, and the second man lowered his weapon. Without leaving the car, Rodriguez inquired whether Lee had brought the money.

"Depends on whether you got my stuff," he replied.

A woman slid out of the car, legs first. Her electric-blue silk skirt was slit to one hip. She was barefoot, and stepped gingerly over the broken stone. Planting herself directly in front of Lee, she reached into her bodice. The gesture momentarily tightened the wispy cloth across her chest. Evidently, she was excited about something. Her hand reappeared with a small golden pillbox. One bloodred nail clicked it open, revealing a small mound of white powder.

She scooped some of the powder on an inverted fingernail and held it under Lee's nose. He stabbed his tongue into the powder. The numbing sensation and bitter bite were a good sign. "Taste is all right. Now, let's see."

Taking the delicate arm by its fragile wrist, he guided the powder to his nose. Lee snorted, snapping his head back and exhaling contentedly.

"Good shit. How I know it's all this righteous?"

Fingers snapped and the Caddy's trunk lid popped open. Lee circled the blonde, facing the Hawaiian shirts as he walked to the rear of the car. The man he had nailed was still coughing and rubbing his tender throat. Two gym bags lay in the trunk. Lee unzipped one and pulled it open. Two solid packages in clear plastic lay inside. He pulled a switchblade—seemingly out of the air—and slit one package. He scooped a bit of white powder on the knife blade and sniffed. It was the same high grade as the previous sample.

"Okay, I believe you."

The disembodied voice asked again, "Did you bring the money?"

"In the car. I'll get it." Before Lee could move, one Hawaiian shirt raised his Uzi and leveled it at him. The other sprinted to the Vette, racing back with a brand-new briefcase.

Lee snarled at Sombrero. "What is this shit, man? You trying to burn me? I'll cut your balls off, man."

Sombrero grinned, snatching the briefcase from the Hawaiian shirt. Still grinning, he held the case in front of him, flat on one arm, while he clicked the latches. Lee bunched his muscles. Sombrero opened the case. He was still grinning when the nail bomb went off. Two hundred ten penny finishing nails pinwheeled in every direction.

Lee hit the deck, flicking the switchblade at the same instant, catching Hawaiian shirt number two in the throat. He dropped the Uzi and fell backward, gagging on his own blood. Lee skittered on the ground, grabbing the Uzi just as the driver's door opened. He raked the front of the car with 9 mm slugs, cutting the driver in two as he emerged. Swinging the SMG's muzzle farther back, he emptied the magazine into the rear of the car.

He stood up and grabbed the two gym bags from the Caddy's trunk. On the way back to his car, he passed Hawaiian shirt number one. He lay on his back, his chest and face ripped and pitted. Several nails protruded from his trunk and skull. He looked as if he'd just lost an argument with a steel porcupine.

Sombrero fared less well. The whirling nails had made mincemeat of him, pulping his eyes and shattering his skull. One arm lay ten feet away, still oozing where it had been joined to the shoulder.

It was too bad about the blonde. She had been one good-looking woman. Now, even the coroner wouldn't be sure. It was no way to die, but then hers had been no way to live, either.

Lee didn't bother to check on Buster. He wouldn't recognize him anyway. And it wasn't Buster he wanted. He wanted Buster's boss, and he'd just sent him a message. It wasn't subtle, but it was sure as hell hard to ignore.

And it was cheaper than a telegram.

Stepping around Sombrero's corpse, Lee waved. "Adios, a-mee-go."

CHAPTER TWENTY-NINE

It looked more like a flower show than a funeral. The altar was awash in sprays and wreaths. They spilled over into the aisles and halfway back to the confessionals on either side of St. Anthony's Church. Joey Buccieri sat in the second pew. He felt eyes on his back and a chill in his spine. To quiet the queasiness in his stomach, he counted the floral offerings, looking for his own at the same time.

Finally, he found it, the fifty-first, to the left of the altar. The silver banner was coiled among gladioli from another spray, but he didn't have to read it to know what it said. It had taken him four hours to get the wording down: To Sal, with deep respect. Rest in peace.

The eulogy was dragging on. The priest was one of those effusive types who had to mention every wonderful thing the deceased did, and if he didn't do it, it was mentioned anyway, and everyone was expected to pretend he had done it.

So far, nobody had said anything to Joey. Two funerals in a week was making them all jittery. And this one drew heavyweight mourners from out of town. Frankie Ianni was neither missed nor mourned. Nobody had expected him to live as long as he had. There was even more than a little relief that he had died without dragging them all down with him. But Sally Maggadino was a man of some substance. His death was different.

The commission was well represented. Representatives from most of the major families were present. They had flown in from Las Vegas, Chicago, Detroit, Milwaukee and Philly. The New York contingent alone numbered six, including a boss from each of the Five Families, as well as Johnny Poggi, who had been a close personal friend.

It was Poggi who scared Buccieri. Business associates were inclined to pragmatism. Sal had been a good man. He made enemies. He was getting old, slowing down a little. He made a mistake. It happens. It was the Mob version of a pension. But for Poggi, it was different. Sally had been like an uncle to him. And Johnny had a hot temper.

He was not entirely trusted by the others. His fuse was short, and according to some, always lit. If he took it into his head to find out what happened to Sal, the conventions would be swept aside. And if he got onto Joey's case, Joey would turn up missing, in parts of three states.

He was sorry now that he'd been so pushy on the Bolivian thing. Word of that would get around. Johnny was smart. He could put two and two together, and that added up to trouble. As the priest droned on, Joey struggled against the urge to turn in his pew and look for him. He was certainly there.

Joey should have felt happy. He'd solved a giant problem. With Sal out of the way, he could expand the drug trade, rake in the millions Sal had been too damned stubborn to go after. Shit, there were literally billions at stake.

Back in 1982, one bust alone had netted two tons of coke, with a street value of one billion, three hundred million dollars. The numbers were staggering, and this greaseball Cardona was trying to sweep it all into his own pocket. But Sally Maggadino just didn't see it.

Every buck Cardona made could have been theirs. And every buck made him stronger. Holding their own didn't make it, not when you were going against a guy who wanted it all. If you didn't get in his face, he was halfway home. Joey was going to make sure he missed the boat.

If Johnny Poggi didn't get in his way.

Finally the priest concluded his eulogy and walked slowly to the foot of the altar. The rest of the mass went quickly. The pallbearers, sitting on the center aisle, began to shift in their seats. The familiar gray gloves with black piping on the backs of the fingers began to wave, then were donned.

Father Domenici intoned the dismissal, in Latin as Sally had requested. *"Ite missa est,"* he said, raising his hands over the heads of the altar boys. He descended the altar steps slowly, his cassock sweeping the gleaming marble. He stepped through the gate in the altar rail, the one Sally had donated on the occasion of his daughter's wedding, and led the procession out of the church.

Joey was in the first group behind the pallbearers. Descending the stairs, he felt a hand on his arm. He turned and was startled to see Johnny Poggi.

"I was sorry to hear about it, Joey."

"Yeah, thanks, Johnny."

"Who did it?"

"I dunno. I got the word out, you know?"

"You hear anything, you let me know."

"Sure, Johnny, sure. First thing."

Buccieri hurried down the steps, splitting from the crowd and heading to his car. His Cadillac was well down the line. Even a funeral was built on priorities. Power, and the respect it demanded, were paramount. Buccieri had been close to Maggadino, but he wasn't the logical successor. Not even Joey thought of himself that way. But unlike the realists who would ultimately make the decision, Joey had plans for himself that would significantly enhance his standing.

If there was one single thing that got you noticed, it was making money for the organization. DiMarzio had a better grasp of business. The standing joke was that Peter had a head for numbers, while Joey had an eye for figures. It was probably true.

Carlucci had a smoother style, and everybody, including the media, were conscious of the Mob's desire to enhance its image. The corporate style was eagerly cultivated; three-piece suits and MBAs were more important than knowing how to break a man's spirit . . . or his knees. Carlucci could have worked for IBM. It was rumored that even his underwear was pin-striped. He had a normal neck and only had to shave once a day. It was a joke that such things should be so persuasive, but it was a reality Joey had come to terms with.

Money could solve most of his problems, and he was determined to make some heavy bread. Once he routed the greaseballs and took over the coke distribution in Miami, he'd open a few eyes. Sitting in the Caddy, staring out at the crowd of sightseers, his head throbbed with plans, and with the anxiety implicit in their implementation.

He grew nervous, waiting for the funeral procession to get rolling. It crossed his mind that he could put his time to better use. Standing there at the graveside, kissing the widow and saying a few words wasn't going to get him anywhere. But he had to go, had to do it. Poggi would be watching for anything out of the ordinary.

The last thing Buccieri needed was Poggi breathing down his neck. He'd almost jumped out of his skin when he'd looked up and found himself staring into Johnny's face. Poggi's eyes were flat and quiet. They looked right through him and a thousand miles beyond. Joey thought they might even be able to see things he hadn't even dreamed of yet, as though he knew not only what you were thinking, but what you were going to think.

Buccieri was starting to sweat. He leaned forward and told his driver to crank up the air-conditioning. Wiping his brow with a damp handkerchief he tapped his feet nervously on the car's thick carpet.

But what ate at him most wasn't the fear of discovery. He was terrified that Sal had been right about the mysterious figure emerging from the warehouse. Sal knew him. That was for sure. But he whispered the name, as though the guy was a legend or something. But that had to be horseshit. The Indians could have all the legends they wanted about avenging angels and winds of death. Fairy tales were for kids. But sitting in that room, watching the tape, then watching the look on Sal's face when he talked about the guy, you had to wonder. If only he'd managed to catch the man's name.

Sal had broken a few bones in his time. He might have been getting old, but scared he wasn't. Joey wanted to ask around, but there were more important things to take care of first.

Finally the cars began to move. Up ahead he could see the motorcycle escort. There was a gentle irony in the police leading the way. Death was the great equalizer, maybe, but Sal must have been smiling at the thought of one of Miami's finest clearing traffic so the boss of its underworld wouldn't be late for his final appointment.

Buccieri hoped the ceremony would be short. His hands were sweating, even with the air-conditioning full blast. He wanted to get home and take a shower. He felt sticky and uncomfortable. And there was still the matter of Cardona to be dealt with. The high-priced mechanic was supposed to be getting in touch with him any day. As soon as the greaseball was out of the way, he could make his move.

Cardona had softened up the opposition for him, and that was an advantage he couldn't have bought at any price. But in Miami things had grown suddenly quiet, as if Cardona had changed his mind or something. After the greaseballs lost the garage lab, it was just like the way the air got still and quiet before a hurricane. He wanted to move, but wasn't sure, yet, where or how.

And timing was crucial. Let Cardona get too much control, and he'd be impossible to move out of the way. Shit was still flying in Bolivia, though, so there was a chance. As long as he was busy with the other greaseballs, there was time.

BUCCIERI LEFT HIS CAR and watched it disappear around the corner of the house. When the taillights vanished, he turned and headed toward the stone patio. He brushed past the tall yew trees at one corner, kicking gravel with the toe of his expensive loafers. Something shiny caught his eye in the stones, and he bent to pick it up. As he straightened, he felt the pistol barrel rammed into his back.

"Shh. Say nothing, *señor*." The heavy Spanish accent crooned in his ear. Rough hands grabbed his shoulders, and a blindfold was whipped across his eyes. Tied roughly, its pressure on his eyes was painful. Both hands were yanked behind his back. Sticky tape was lashed around his wrists, pinning his arms tightly. It happened so quickly that he never uttered a sound. Another strip of tape was bound across his mouth and strapped behind his head.

He felt the rope slip over his head and for a second thought he was going to be hanged in his own front yard. He began to panic, struggling against the bonds. A yank of the rope pulled him forward and he stumbled, unable to see where he was going. The pressure of the rope remained steady, and he had no choice but to follow where it led him.

They walked quickly, covering several hundred feet in a matter of minutes. Hands grabbed his shoulders and pressed him downward. He was shoved forward and landed on something soft, which had been laid over something very hard. It felt like a carpet, probably in the back of a van. Despite the blindfold, he was aware of a greater darkness than the night. Doors slammed behind him.

He lurched with sudden motion and knew he was in a vehicle of some kind. He wanted to cry out, but the gag limited him to a mumble. He wanted to keep track of the turns and twists as the van sped through the night, but soon lost track.

Eventually, the van stopped. He heard the rear doors open, and hands helped him out. He stumbled and fell, unable to gauge the distance to the ground. His unseen captors hauled him to his feet, then shoved him forward. He walked rapidly, trying to avoid another prod of the pistol.

He felt pavement under his feet, sensed a door opening, then closing behind him. Now he was walking on thick carpet. His feet began to click on a hardwood floor. He was guided through several turns, which he guessed to be doorways. Shoved again, this time from the front, his legs were taken out from under him by a sofa or chair. He landed on soft cushion, his pinned shoulders wrenched by the impact.

A sharp prick stabbed into the back of his neck. The feel of cold steel on his skin made his flesh crawl. Suddenly, the tape was slit free and yanked away from his eyes and mouth. His vision was blurred by the pressure, his eyes watering at the sudden blaze of light.

He became aware of someone staring at him. He shook his head to clear his vision. A slender, almost effeminate man, lightly tanned and impeccably dressed in white, sat behind a large mahogany desk. He smiled.

"You are surprised to see me, I think, Mr. Buccieri."

Getting his sight back calmed his nerves. "I'm always surprised to see people I don't know in places I've never been invited."

"Oh, but you do know me. In fact, you have been thinking, one might even be so bold as to suggest dreaming, about me."

"I'm no fruit."

"Why so defensive?" The man smiled, curling his lips back in a seductive grin. "I suggested no such thing. Perhaps you are hiding some secret, even from yourself, eh?"

"No way. Who the hell are you? What am I doing here?"

The man stood and glided around the end of his desk. He bent over Buccieri to remove the rope, still looped around his neck. Then he slid his slender hands inside Buccieri's jacket. He removed a small automatic from its holster, then opened the lapels wide to read the label.

"A very fine tailor, Mr. Buccieri. You have good taste. In some things."

He took Buccieri by one shoulder, bending him forward at the waist. He removed a switchblade from his pocket, clicked it open and slit the tape binding Buccieri's arms. He stripped the tape free, rolled it into a ball and extended one hand.

"My name is Diego Cardona. I believe we have a few things to discuss."

Buccieri saw his life flash before his eyes. He decided to tough it out. "What do we have to talk about?"

"I understand you are . . . shall we say . . . resentful of my recent business success."

"I don't know what you're talking about."

"Señor Buccieri, please, believe me, I know a great deal more about you than you know about me. I think it would be best if we were honest with each other. After all, you have nothing to lose. If I wanted you eliminated, I think your presence here under these circumstances should persuade you that it can be done rather handily."

"All right, let's say I agree with that. So what?"

"I would like to propose that we pool our considerable resources. I think we would make a rather formidable team."

"I'm listening . . ."

CHAPTER THIRTY

Tommy Calabrese looked at the carpet. The sofa rustled as he lifted one foot and checked the sole of his shoe. It made no sense to have a white rug. The sole looked clean, but he wasn't convinced. He wondered what kind of guy would waste money on a rug he'd have to have shampooed once a week. Leaning back on the white sofa, he surveyed the room. After the once-over, he knew it didn't matter. The kind of bread this guy had, he could buy a new rug every day and pay for it out of petty cash. Tommy smiled. That new car might not be too long in coming, after all.

It was spooky, sitting in the room alone. He raised his glass and tilted it back. The ice rattled, a drop of dew fell onto the front of his shirt. His eye lit on a black smear on the wall. It looked like him and moved when he moved. It took a minute before it registered. It was his shadow. He turned his head a little, admiring his profile in silhouette, sharply etched by the stylish halogen floor lamp. He straightened his tie, shaking his head from side to side to snug it up under his collar.

He tossed off the rest of the drink, placing the glass carefully on the marble coaster. He felt the glass slide on the wet ring it had left behind, stopping only at the raised marble lip. The place was quiet. He noticed the filmy white draperies moving gently and realized the place was air-conditioned.

Where the hell was everybody? The phone call had politely requested his presence on a matter of urgency. The caller had declined to be specific, but assured him it would be worth his while to show. He had nothing better to do. Life in Miami was pretty boring. Brognola's crusade was dead in the water. Why not have a look?

The room was starkly furnished, all chrome and sharp angles. The high ceilings were bathed in indirect light. The sterility of the walls was broken by wide, colorful canvases. He didn't know anything about art, but this was the kind of stuff they had in museums. He stood up to stretch and relieve his tension. He crossed the room to look at a painting more closely. It was all flat planes of color with black squiggles, the kind of stuff his younger daughter did with her crayons. He didn't like it at all. Shrugging, he figured that probably meant it was worth a bundle. The kind of thing he would buy if he had some loose change.

"It's a Basquiat. Do you like it?"

Calabrese spun around. The voice seemed to come from nowhere. It was soft, almost like a woman's. Kind of husky, sort of like Brenda Vaccaro sounded. Finally he placed the speaker. The man was standing stock-still in one corner under an arched doorway. At first Tommy had thought he was a statue.

The man continued. "I paid fifty thousand dollars for it. It will be worth several times that in a year or two."

"Actually I was just thinking how my kid does the same kind of stuff. Maybe you want to buy a couple of hers."

The man looked offended for a moment, then suppressed the irritation. Only a pout lingered, like that on a petulant child's face after a reprimand by Grandma. "Perhaps your child is more talented than you know."

"Yeah, maybe so."

The voice changed, took on a harder edge. "But we're not here to talk about art, are we?"

"I don't know why I'm here. I guess you probably live here."

"I do."

"Then since it's your party, why don't you tell me your name, and why I was invited."

"I am Diego Cardona. We will get to the rest of your question momentarily. Would you like another drink?"

"Yeah, sure. Same as before." He should have recognized the guy, Tommy realized. But he didn't look at all like his pictures. Or maybe he did. Maybe it was just the clothes. And the setting.

Cardona clapped his hands. Calabrese walked back to the sofa. He was expecting the same muscle-bound butler. His jaw fell when he saw the woman. Dressed like a French maid, she teetered into the room on spike heels. Her costume and shoes were as black as the carpet was white. She must have been five nine or five ten without the shoes. With them, she towered over both men. She looked familiar, somehow, but Calabrese knew he'd never seen her before. You didn't forget a woman like her. Not with a body that spectacular and a face to match. Not ever.

She carried a small tray. Cardona spoke softly to her, then she walked to the table and bent to retrieve Tommy's glass. Her shoulders were draped in hair as black as night. The costume was cut low, and her cleavage generous. Instinctively Calabrese reached out when she bent over, certain she was going to fall out of her stiff décolletage. She noticed the gesture and smiled. "Thanks anyway, but they never fall out."

"Too bad." Calabrese smiled. His face felt like putty. He knew he was pinker than he'd been in years.

The woman turned, her exaggerated swagger metronomic as she left the room.

"She is attractive, isn't she?"

Calabrese noticed his host's accent for the first time. It was almost undetectable. He didn't answer the question. It was obviously unnecessary.

"So, you were about to tell me why you invited me here."

"Of course. Business before pleasure, isn't that the saying?"

"Yeah, it is."

"All right, then. I have reason to believe that you are in a position to do me a very great favor. I wish to discuss the matter with you, as well as your compensation."

"Compensation. You mean, like money?"

"That is one possibility."

"If you pay me for it, it ain't a favor, is it?"

"It is if I choose to think so. And compensation need not be limited to money."

"What else is there?"

"Madeleine can deliver more than a drink."

"Madeleine?"

"She'll be back in a minute. With your drink."

"Are you telling me what I think you're telling me?"

"Yes. Provided we can come to terms, and provided, of course, that such a quid pro quo is agreeable to you."

"What's that, Latin?"

"The language, yes. The concept is universal. I think you understand what I mean. Tit for tat."

"And just what is that tat I gotta deliver to earn the tit?"

"Nicely put, if a little crude."

Calabrese laughed. He kept watching the doorway.

Cardona continued. "You are acquainted with a man named Mack Bolan, are you not?"

"I know who he is, if that's what you mean."

"Come, come, Mr. Calabrese. You know considerably more than that. I have already been the beneficiary of your knowledge, and you of my largesse."

"Why don't you drop the highfalutin horseshit and say what you mean?"

"Very well. I've already bought some information from you, in Mexico City and in La Paz."

"Bullshit. I've never seen you before in my life."

"Look, you want me to cut the horseshit, I'll cut it. I can buy you for pocket change, Calabrese. You've been taking money in exchange for information for more than two years now. Who do you think was paying you? I don't have to waste my time meeting two-bit informers in cheap dives. I pay people to do it for me."

Cardona's voice crackled with contempt. The man was like a chameleon. Challenged to meet Calabrese on more comfortable terrain, he seemed more at home there than Calabrese himself. For a moment Calabrese was stymied. Shifting gears, he got more belligerent, trying to keep Cardona off balance.

"Then why are you dealing direct this time? If you're such a big man, why the hell don't you send somebody to meet me in some cheap dive?"

"Because this time, I'm not just buying information, Calabrese. This time, I'm buying your soul. And don't tell me it's not for sale. All we're discussing is the price."

"Pretty sure of yourself, aren't you?"

"I can afford to be. What can you afford, Mr. Calabrese? A week in Atlantic City, if you're lucky. A second car, used. Maybe an occasional woman on the side. And for that, you have to shake down nickel bag street hustlers. Oh, yes, Mr. Calabrese, your soul is very much negotiable. And I have already ordered a bill of sale."

"You assholes are all alike. You think money makes the world go around. You think because you have it, you can do what you want."

"Your righteous indignation is amusing, Mr. Calabrese. And your perspective all wrong. I don't think money makes the world go around, I *know* it does. And I don't do what I want because I have money, but quite the opposite. I have money because I am not afraid to do what I want. You, on the other hand will have money only because you will do what *I* want. We are very different, you and I. That you don't recognize the distinction only proves my argument."

Before Calabrese could muster a response, Madeleine returned. Some things money couldn't buy, not the kind of money he'd have, anyway. Cardona smiled and said nothing. Madeleine's walk argued his position more eloquently than words ever could. The look on Calabrese's face spoke volumes. The deal was settled. Everybody in the room knew it.

When Madeleine placed the drink on the table, Cardona said, "Madeleine, Mr. Calabrese will be staying the night. Please make his room ready."

She smiled at Calabrese but answered Cardona. "I've already taken the liberty, Señor Cardona." She winked at Calabrese.

When she had gone, Cardona crossed the room, finally taking a seat on a second sofa under the painting. "Here is what I want you to do."

THE SUN WOKE CALABRESE EARLY. He stirred, feeling its heat on his naked back. The sheets still felt cool, and he yawned, stretching his arms over his head. It wasn't until he opened his eyes that he realized he wasn't in his motel room. He sat up abruptly, his hip bumping the woman beside him. His head ached, and he groaned, closing his eyes against the brightness. When his head cleared, he looked at the woman. Madeleine was curled in a ball, the sheet drawn over one hip. She was facing away from him. Her hair was spread over the pillowcase, impossibly black against the white satin.

Calabrese slid a hand under the sheet, stroking the soft flesh below the hip. Her skin felt cool to the touch. He remembered the night before, how muscular her body had been, despite its lushness. He slid his hand back along the hip, circling her waist and cupping one breast. Even in sleep, the nipple felt hard, as if she were waiting for him. He bent to nuzzle her neck.

She stirred, mumbling something he couldn't quite hear. Rolling on her back, she opened her eyes. With one hand, she casually swept stray wisps of hair away from her forehead. Her breasts were more voluptuous than he remembered.

"Was it as good as you expected?" she asked.

"Better."

She smiled, but there was no warmth in it. The expression stopped at her lips. Her eyes were hard and cold. She tossed the sheet off, bending one leg at the knee, tucking her foot under the back of her extended leg. "I hope so. A condemned man is supposed to enjoy his last request."

"What do you mean, condemned man? This is just the beginning of a long partnership."

"Not on your life. Nobody sleeps with me and lives. Diego won't stand for it. You're dead, pal. As soon as he gets what he wants from you."

"We'll see about that." Calabrese knew that his voice was quavering, but he kept on. "That fruity son of a bitch better think again if he thinks I'm afraid of him."

"That fruity son of a bitch will have your balls in a jar."

"No way."

"You want my advice, find the deepest hole you can and crawl in. When you get to the bottom, dig it a little deeper. Maybe he won't find you."

"Why didn't you say something last night?"

"Because the cameras were on. And he'd kill me if I said anything."

"What cameras?"

"This place is wired, and everything that goes on is filmed. Diego likes to watch as much as he likes to do."

"And you let him? Film you? Like that?"

"The pay's good. Besides, I don't have any choice."

Madeleine stretched again, scissored her long-legs, then stood up. She walked to the mirror on one wall, turned sideways, and stretched her arms over her head. Cupping her breasts in her hands, she sucked in her stomach and smiled at Calabrese. "Nice, huh?"

"You better believe it."

"Take a good look. It's the last time you'll see me naked."

"That's not what Cardona said."

"Diego is many things. Trustworthy, however, is not one of them." She blew a kiss to Calabrese and was gone.

He showered in the half-bath off the bedroom, dressed hurriedly and went downstairs. The house seemed deserted. Calabrese left through the side door. His car was parked outside the garage, where he'd left it. He got in and started the engine. He was about to pull away when he noticed the envelope on the passenger seat. It was letter-size, made of heavy, brilliant-white paper. The envelope bulged heavily in his hand. He ripped it open.

Quickly he counted the sheaf of bills. Fifty crisp, new one-thousand-dollar bills. Calabrese smiled, almost forgetting about Madeleine's warning.

Then he read the note.

"Mr. Calabrese: Don't even think about reneging on our agreement. Diego."

He looked around, half expecting to see the bizarre white-robed figure in the bushes alongside the garage. But he saw no one. He drove down the long, winding lane to the street. Still he saw no one.

Not even the slender young black man in the red Corvette parked across from the gate.

CHAPTER THIRTY-ONE

The phone call from Calabrese caught Bolan by surprise. Three in the morning wasn't his favorite time to go to work, but Calabrese had been insistent. Cardona was orchestrating a major deal, and here was the chance to nail him with his hands in the cookie jar. If they moved quickly, Calabrese insisted, they could send him up for life. It would be the big score, the biggest bust in history with the biggest dealer on record going down for the count. It was too good a chance to pass up.

Something made Bolan uneasy—something about Calabrese. The guy seemed like a straight arrow, but the leak was still dripping, and Calabrese had to be considered at least as likely a source as anyone else. He seemed to know about things that no one else did. Like the body shop.

Bolan had seen the type before. An eager beaver with aspirations far beyond the reasonable expectations of a reasonable narcotics agent. They did strange things when those expectations weren't realized. Some of them flipped over, and some of them flipped out altogether. Some became the dark side of the enemy they once had fought. Giving the devil more than his due, they became dealers on a grand scale. When illusions died, so did morality. They tried to outdo the men they had been unable to defeat.

Others simply sold out. Envious of the life-style readily available to the dealers, they bought in. Selling advance information on scams and pending busts, they bought a small piece of the good life. The price was more than they realized, but they found enough comfort in booze, women and fast cars, so they seldom looked back.

Bolan didn't know which, if any, of these types Calabrese was, but something didn't ring true. So he carried extra caution as he left his room.

The meet was set for an amusement park on the Miami River. The place was closed for repairs, and would be deserted at this time of night. It was an ideal place for a drug buy—or for a setup. Bolan parked two blocks away and approached the park from the river side, making his way around the chain link fence that stretched down to the waterline.

Calabrese had said to meet him under the Ferris wheel. There was no way to miss it. The giant ride loomed over the park like a futuristic nightmare, its spindly tower seeming too flimsy to support the gigantic wheel itself. It looked as if a few rotations would be all that was necessary to set the wheel rolling free, a runaway steel skeleton that might not stop until it sank into the Gulf of Mexico.

Bolan approached the Ferris wheel cautiously. He slipped into the shadows outside a Byzantine fun house and waited for the DEA man to show. Calabrese was supposed to be there at 4:00 a.m., a half hour before the meet. It was 3:50, and Bolan was already in the shadows.

He took a position that enabled him to watch the main gate without being seen. The gate was closed, and the guardhouse empty. A light rain had been falling all night, and small puddles collected in depressions in the asphalt paving covering most of the park.

At 3:55, Bolan stepped out of the shadows of the fun house and walked to the Ferris wheel ticket booth, which was unlocked. He stepped inside, ducked down. He left the door open a crack to keep an eye on the gate. Calabrese had said he'd be driving a black Buick. At 3:59, a black Buick stopped outside the gate. The driver got out, but he was too far away to be seen clearly.

The gate rolled aside and the Buick shot forward. If it was Calabrese, he wasn't alone. The figure at the gate walked on through, not bothering to close the gate behind him. That was strange. If you wanted to queer a bust, all you had to do was make the pigeon suspicious. Most dealers were skittish enough, as often as not turning on one another or their customers for a raised eyebrow or a slow answer.

The man on foot tagged along behind the Buick, now cruising just a little above walking speed. Man and car reminded Bolan of the symbiotic relationship between infantryman and tank. People who didn't know better thought the tank was there to protect the foot soldier. In fact, the grunt was there to make sure nobody got close enough to blow the tank. Bolan filed the thought in the back of his mind.

The Buick finally halted about fifty yards from the Ferris wheel. The man on foot drifted off to the side, Bolan losing sight of him through the narrow opening. The Buick was still running. He couldn't hear the engine, but a small spiral of exhaust swirled in the humid air before dissipating a foot away from the tail pipe.

The car door opened, and the driver got out. He was close enough for Bolan to see him clearly. It was Tommy Calabrese all right, but he looked nervous. And he hadn't come alone.

Slipping the safety off Big Thunder, Bolan stepped out of the ticket booth. Calabrese had his back to the ride and was staring toward the main gate. Bolan approached him quietly, clamping a hand over his shoulder. Calabrese jumped a foot off the ground.

When he realized who it was, he sighed. Bolan thought it was exaggerated for his benefit. "Man, you scared the hell out of me. I didn't think you were here yet."

Bolan said nothing about the other man. "We still have more than half an hour to wait. Why don't you fill me in? You didn't say much on the phone."

"There, uh, there wasn't really time. Besides, I don't know very much. Just that Cardona is supposed to be here for some kind of big buy, or something."

"That's a little uncharacteristic of him, isn't it?"

"I guess so. That's why I think it must be really big."
Calabrese still seemed nervous. He repeatedly checked his
watch, and his gaze kept drifting off to one side, as if he
were waiting for some kind of sign.

At 4:10 he raised one arm in the air, as if he were trying
to nab a fly on the wing. Suddenly the sky caught fire. Every
light in the park went on at once. The wet pavement seemed
to burst into flame as the bright lights fragmented in the
puddles and rainbowed in the oily slick filming the water.

Calabrese dived for the Buick, ducking behind it. Bolan
hit the deck as the sound system exploded into life. Carnival calliope music roared from every speaker. Bolan hauled
Big Thunder off his hip and fired a round toward the Buick.
It struck the rear fender at a sharp angle and glanced off into
the night.

Bolan rolled through the oily water, getting to his feet
behind the ticket booth. The second man was nowhere to be
seen. The Ferris wheel began to rock, then churned to life,
its seats squeaking as they swung back and forth. Bolan
looked up, then realized it was meant to distract him. He
dropped to the pavement just ahead of a burst of submachine gun fire. The wooden booth was chewed up, its
window blown out.

Bolan ran for the fun house. The SMG chattered again,
chipping at the asphalt as Bolan zigzagged into the shadow
of the building. He dropped to his stomach and wormed his
way across its front beneath the proscenium facade. As he
passed the center, a ghoulish cackle roared behind him.

He whirled around, firing at the sound. The proscenium
was ablaze with light. An enormous woman's head fragmented and disappeared. The ungodly cackle continued. It
took him several seconds to realize he had blown the head
off the fun house fat lady. Her huge form continued to rock
with laughter, the folds of her dress rippling with the mechanical motion of her stomach. The headless neck jutted
above the gargantuan dress like an obscene gesture.

A door was set back under a shallow arch at the far end of the stage front. Bolan crawled over to it and reached for the knob, which rattled in his grasp, then slipped from his fingers. It was damp from drifting rain. He tried again, and this time the knob turned.

Bolan threw his shoulder into the door, and it burst free, slamming back against the inner wall with a hollow boom. From the bowels of the fun house stage, the park looked like a scene from hell. Spinning lights, blazing pinwheels of red, green and blue cast garish colored shadows on the slick pavement, glittering in the rippling puddles.

Footsteps echoed on the stage overhead. At least one of the gunmen had gotten to the fun house. Bolan tried to guess where the man was standing, and fired twice up through the floor. The plywood shattered, and Bolan heard a groan. One of the slugs had found its mark. More footsteps pounded on the planking, but Bolan couldn't count the number of men.

He backed deeper under the stage, groping in the dark until he found the rear wall. The footsteps above him had stopped. Suddenly a shadow loomed in the open doorway, framed against the rainbow fire. Bolan aimed and squeezed. The figure in the doorway sprawled backward, landing with a splash in one of the deeper puddles. For good measure, he pumped a second slug into the prostrate bulk, saw it buck with the impact of the AutoMag's heavy projectile.

His fingers found a vertical slab, which felt like a doorframe. Groping past the ridge of wood, he felt a panel. He'd found a door, but would it open?

There was no knob. Holstering Big Thunder, he felt along both edges of the panel working from top to bottom. Halfway down he found a slide bolt on each side. He eased the bolts toward the panel's center, felt them slide free, then yanked. The panel gave, showering dust over his face and hands. Something large and hairy crawled along one cheek. He brushed it away, feeling the spider crumble under his fingers.

A dark room greeted him. Without a light, he debated whether to risk entering. He remembered the flurry of footsteps and knew it was no decision. He stepped into the room, the AutoMag in one hand, the other extended before him, feeling for a wall, a door, anything that might loom up in front of him.

Bolan's steps splashed softly as he crossed the floor. He judged the water to be two inches or so deep, probably run-off from the asphalt outside. It was difficult to gauge distance in darkness. He'd gone about twenty feet when his extended hand struck another wall, which was covered with paper and seemed to be hollow. On a hunch, he pressed his ear to the wall. He heard nothing.

Stepping back for leverage, he aimed a kick about waist high and was rewarded with a burst of light. A flap of the barrier hung inward, hanging by its paper cover. The wall was only Sheetrock. He kicked again, this time knocking a larger chunk of the brittle wall through into the room beyond. One more kick and he had a hole he could fit through.

The room wasn't as brightly lit as he'd first thought. It was about twenty feet square, and contained a maze of waist-high barriers, like hitching posts. The floor was made of angles and inclines, the whole crazy quilt a puzzle. Bolan leaped over the rails, making his way quickly toward a door in the opposite wall.

This chamber was bathed in orange light and a huge barrel slowly turned in its center. Like a funnel, the walls closed in toward the mouth of the barrel, leaving him no choice but to go through. As he stepped in, the barrel began to spin faster, nearly throwing him off balance. He reached instinctively for the wall to brace himself, but it spun up and away, leaving him prey to gravity and inertia. He stumbled through the whirling barrel into a second, spinning in the opposite direction.

The walls then widened out, leaving him a choice of three doors in the wall beyond. He chose the one on the left and was startled as an earsplitting howl greeted him. He almost smiled at the irony. Locked in a life-and-death gun battle, pursued by an unknown number of men who would blast him to smithereens, he jumped like a schoolboy when a simple amusement park trick caught him off guard. He was so focused on his immediate problem that the surprise element implicit in the amusement was even more effective.

A bright strobe began to flash. In its glow, a skeleton swung toward him, its articulated joints swinging awkwardly. He ducked under Mr. Bones and pressed forward. A second skeleton appeared in a far corner, advanced rapidly, then abruptly jerked upward, where it dangled from a noose. He pushed past the hanged man, sweeping it aside with his free hand. A third figure loomed ahead of him in a darkened doorway.

He ran toward it, realizing in midstride it was no illusion. The gunner seemed just as startled. He was slow to raise his Uzi. Bolan drilled him a third eye just as the gun reached his waist. The splatter of blood and bone was weirdly beautiful under the pulsing strobe. The dead men fell backward, crumpled in the doorway.

Bolan grabbed the Uzi, then nicked a pair of ammo clips from the dead man's camouflage jacket. He stepped over the corpse into a dark room with glowing green walls. The phosphorescent paint cast a dim green pall over the laboring witches at the center of the room. A smoky haze drifted over their caldron, collecting against the ceiling. The sound of furious bubbling echoed from the cavernous utensil, only an occasional burst of static revealing its electronic origin.

Bolan sprinted past the caldron, heard a hiss overhead, like venting steam, and then a flurry of sound he couldn't place. He looked up in time to see an enormous snake, its tongue flicking, as if licking at the descending cloud. It undulated, then dropped like a stone, its huge head sliding from side to side on the floor. Bolan leaped to one side, falling to his knees and fired a quick burst from the Uzi. Two spare clips flew from his pocket as he landed hard.

The snake's head burst open with a flash. Through the shattered wreckage, Bolan saw the splintered green of a circuit board, bright flashes of copper and colored wires. The ruined animatron began to smoke, its length quivering as the electrical impulses randomly triggered those few motors still functioning.

Regaining his feet, Bolan bent to retrieve one of the magazines. The caldron tolled like a bell, nearly obscuring the hammering of another SMG. Bolan turned to the wall behind him. In a gaping window high on the wall of what must have been Macbeth's castle, a man jerked his head back out of sight. A second man was just popping into view in another window. Bolan was about to loose a second burst from the Uzi when he heard his name behind him.

"Having fun, Mr. Bolan?"

CHAPTER THIRTY-TWO

Bolan wheeled. The two men in the doorway behind him were dressed in combat fatigues and carrying AK-47s. The taller of the two stood in front. In the ghostly green glow, Bolan noticed a gold tooth. The faint sparkle must have been from a diamond inlay.

The tall man was grinning. He stepped forward with a casualness that was almost contempt. The second man stepped to one side, trying to divide Bolan's attention. That was their mistake. The movement triggered a horrendous squeal. Bolan thought the loudspeakers would burst. A fluttering flap off to the left distracted both men.

The tall man wheeled, his AK-47 hammering in the enclosed space. The huge mechanical bat, its wings flapping spastically, careened to one side, knocking the shorter man to the floor. Bolan swept the Uzi in a tight figure eight. Red flowers exploded above the knees, then again on the reverse pass, this time just above belt level.

The guy on the floor struggled to get his rifle out from under him. This was no time for chivalry. Bolan didn't wait. He let go a burst of 9 mm hornets, stitching the prostrate gunner from hip to throat. A luminescent purple geyser spouted from a neck wound.

Bolan dived behind the caldron, just ahead of a parabellum rainstorm from the windows. One slug slammed into the heel of his shoe, chipping rubber and leather. The impact spun Bolan's foot out of harm's way as the withering fire shredded the black rubber floor beneath him.

Remembering how he'd gotten through into the fun house, Bolan jammed a fresh clip into the Uzi. Rolling once to peer out from the other side of the caldron, he zeroed in on the first window. He squeezed the trigger, a tight coil of 9 mm slugs punched through the slime-green Sheetrock. Small puffs of gypsum powder gusted out and down. The clatter of a dropped gun confirmed the kill.

The second window was empty now. Busy with his first target, Bolan guessed the second window man had fallen flat. He aimed low, slicing halfway across the wall. The uneven row of holes wavered six inches above and below the center line. The second clip was empty.

Ejecting the spent magazine, Bolan paused to listen. Silence on both sides of the flimsy wall. He clicked the third and last clip into the breech. Waiting was deadly. He had to move. Taking a chance, he got to his knees, then to a crouch. He peeked out and ducked back, hoping the quick glimpse might draw fire. Silence.

Bolan sprinted straight toward the wall, slamming it hard with his shoulder. The impact shook somebody loose. Footsteps, above and to his left, were all the help he needed. The Uzi hammered in a vicious sweep, cutting free an entire slab of the Sheetrock. It crashed forward, propelled by the dead man who fell through, hitting the floor headfirst. The guy's neck bent at an awkward angle on impact, a sickening crack finishing him as his spinal cord severed just above the shoulders.

The fun house was a sieve. All cover was illusory, real danger too hard to tell from mechanical thrills. Bolan ran through the doorway into another room. Stumbling, he banged his head, shook it and found himself staring into a face six inches in front of him. It was his own. He'd found the hall of mirrors.

He'd be all right as long as the only man he saw was himself. If somebody else got in the hall before he got out, they'd both be in trouble. There was no way to tell flesh from reflected light. His opponent would have the same problem, of course. But there were no odds in this wilderness of mirrors. Luck was not something the Executioner cared to rely on.

He walked slowly, feeling his way. The light was bright. Glare assaulted him from every angle. To left and right a dozen Bolans crept along, locked in step, each as baffled as he.

Yard by yard he made his way. Every angle gave way to still another. Dead end followed cul-de-sac. The insistent light flooded his eyes, burned them until they teared.

And suddenly, space exploded in front of him. Open air and a hundred Bolans stared at one another. The heart of the maze was an intricate configuration of mirrors. Each stood at an angle to a half dozen more. He diminished in size in every one, trailing off into infinity like a visual echo, finally vanishing in points of darkness, a black hole at the heart of every glass.

Bolan stood as if mesmerized by his multitude. Every glass face hid an exit into another section of the maze. Reflective niches and mirrored alcoves promised escape and delivered deception. Bolan made a random choice. He ducked into a cavern, reducing his number to five, turned a corner and found himself stranded. Backing out, he tried again, this time winding his way through several turns before hitting a blank wall. He stared at his frustrated image in the dead end. It was so tempting to lash out, release his fury on the helpless planes of silvered glass. But every panel was a deadly threat. Shards of the thick, razor-sharp glass could cut him to ribbons. He was not interested in watching himself bleed to death.

Retracing his steps, he entered the main hall and froze in his tracks. He had company. Lots of it. Two men, their images fractured in hundreds of replicas, stared at him from every panel. Two of them were real. But which? He could only guess and, if he guessed wrong, give himself away.

Backing into the alcove again, he watched and wondered. And watched them wonder. The only certain thing was that they were not together. Each looked at the other in the angled glass, wanting to talk and afraid to speak to a lifeless image. They were confused, and judging by their expressions, frightened. It wasn't much of an edge, but it was all he had.

Bolan jumped out and back. A sharp flash jumped a hundred times and glass rained to the hard floor like a crystal palace torn apart. Peeking out again, Bolan saw a gaping hole where their mirrors had been.

The black edge of the shattered mirrors doubled and redoubled in the undamaged glass. Bolan jumped again, drawing another burst of fire. Another panel shattered, and the gunner winced. A fragment caught him in the shoulder, striking deeply into the muscle. He dropped his gun. Even the sound was fractured, bouncing off the hard surface of the mirrors and glancing around the room. The guy sat back on his haunches, staring at the razor-sharp spear of crystal protruding from his shoulder. Shadowed by his bent head, the glass was dark.

Bolan watched, waiting for the clue, the single wedge he needed. He didn't even know what to look for, but he knew he had to have it.

The second man rushed to his companion only to slam headlong into one of the mirrors. He cursed and wheeled, a drove of dervishes in an angry whirl. The injured man and his silent companions rubbed their battered noses.

Bolan reached down and grabbed a shiny spike. He broke it against the glass wall, tossing fragments into the open hall. A single piece skittered to crash into another mirror. Another struck home, provoking a cry of pain from the prostrate man.

And Bolan had his edge. He knew where he'd thrown the glass. Drawing a bead, he squeezed the Uzi gently, coaxing a short burst. The tight spiral ripped into the seated man, stitching his chest from rib to throat. He fell backward, the shining silver catching fire as it fell back into the light.

With only one man to watch, Bolan could take a chance. He swept the Uzi in a broad arc. Glass shattered, wedges flying in every direction. The flying fragments crashed and rattled, beating themselves to pieces on the unbroken planes.

A fine glaze of glass particles collected at the foot of several panels, glittering like diamond dust.

The gap had narrowed, but the fire had given away his location. Backpedaling into the maze, he waited for the return. It wasn't long in coming. The roar of the SMG was drowned out by the rasping clatter of breaking glass, panel after panel shattering, scattering hunks of lethal crystal in every direction.

The hammering stopped, and Bolan inched forward. The room was a shambles. Firing blindly, the remaining gunner had reduced the place nearly to rubble. Few panels remained intact. Like a crazy man, the gunner kicked at the ruins in a frenzy. The heavy fragments chipped and nicked his shoes and he stood raging, starkly outlined against a flat black wall where a mirror once had been.

Bolan squeezed off a burst. The noise seemed somehow diminished, swallowed by the growing darkness that had replaced the glittering puzzle. The man fell, turning toward the sound of the weapon. The look on his face was one of amazement, then almost relief. He grinned lopsidedly, blood oozing from a dozen holes in his back and side. He laughed once, blood bubbling through his lips, staining the cracks between his teeth.

He closed his tired eyes, finally released from the mocking prison. He seemed almost happy.

A door yawned open in the ruined wall. Bolan stepped over a knee-high fragment of glass and through the door. He found himself in an unholy parody of the mirrored hall. Three wavy panels of silver Mylar bent and twisted him into grotesque permutations.

A short, squat Bolan waddled past, then transformed itself into an ungainly Ichabod Bolan, an anorexic nightmare out of Washington Irving. Its spindly, sticklike legs stilt-walked into the last panel, where an hourglass-shaped Bolan wore a six-inch belt over gargantuan hips.

And then he was outside.

The rain had picked up, the driving downpour splashing and splintering the whirling wheels of fire reflected in the wet pavement. Bolan looked for the Buick, and beyond it saw a man run up the rails of a roller coaster. A rifle strapped over one shoulder, the guy was struggling as the slope got steeper. Stepping from tie to tie, leaning forward to keep his balance, he had nearly reached the top of the steepest rise.

He was too far away for Bolan to see him clearly, but it looked as if he were the only one not wearing camou gear. Before the significance of that hit home, Bolan spotted two shadows beyond the still-idling Buick.

Ducking down, keeping the car between him and them, the Executioner rushed forward. Leaning over the warm hood of the car, he shoved a new clip into the AutoMag. A slug caromed off the roof of the car, scattering chips of paint that clung to the wet windshield.

A second shot blew out the rear window, and Bolan dropped down behind the engine compartment. Sliding along the front fender, he looked into the shadows. The figures had gone.

Turning back, he saw the fun house burst into flames. The shimmering lights and twirling movement of attendantless rides was too much to take in all at once, let alone examine. He hadn't seen Calabrese since he'd first disappeared.

Finding the leak was worth the trouble. Plugging it was going to be a pleasure. But where the hell was he?

Bolan walked past the Buick, still trying to decide where to look next. The sharp, faraway crack of a high-powered rifle drove him to the wet pavement, a thud behind him making him roll and wheel. Another of the fatigue-clad hitters lay in the puddle where he'd fallen. The shot echoed from high up, back toward the roller coaster.

The climbing man was either no marksman, or he was on Bolan's side. A second rifle shot rang out. Bolan turned in time to see the next victim of the hidden rifleman tumble through the ticket booth of the Ferris wheel.

That shot was no accident. But who the hell was doing the firing?

Before he could answer that question, a car sped out of the shadows, its lights snapped on, and roared directly at him. Bolan dived over the hood of the Buick. Barely discernible behind the wheel of the onrushing car, Tommy Calabrese looked as if he were running for his life.

And Calabrese had no idea just how true that was.

He couldn't run fast enough.

Or far enough.

CHAPTER THIRTY-THREE

The airplane touched down roughly, jolting Callahan's tender shoulder. The slug had been dug out, and the bone chips removed. The muscle tear would take longer to heal. He was still weak from the loss of blood, and a mild infection had been raising hell with his weakened system.

Leaving the plane through the long corrugated tunnel, he fancied himself one more particle of refuse sucked into a giant vacuum cleaner. The mechanical smiles and "have a nice day" were not calculated to make him feel any less insignificant. That old Irish melancholy had him by the throat and wouldn't let go.

He had been laid up for several days. During the recuperation—and the fever that intermittently retarded his recovery—he'd had plenty of time to think. For one of his temper and temperament, this was not a good thing. It was not for nothing that the law of inevitable foul-up is named for an Irishman. Callahan's Law would have been as apt a title as Murphy's.

He wasn't dying to see Bolan again. He'd come too close to that the last two times he'd seen the big man. At the hospital in La Paz, he'd wanted to talk, but Bolan wouldn't let him. There wasn't time. And he blamed himself for the idiotic rush into the wrong end of a blender that had gotten him shot and four other men killed. He needed to talk about it, to purge himself.

He hadn't wondered too much when Brognola was noncommittal when asked where Bolan was. You didn't have to be a genius to know when a life raft had sprung a leak. In his own high-pressure business, you had to be downright dense not to hear the explosive leak of a security seal gone bad.

Touching base with others on the team, he'd gotten the cold shoulder. Andrews, the CIA geek, he could understand. They hadn't hit it off right from the start. But Bob Levine should have understood. Or maybe he did. Maybe that was exactly why Bob hadn't been willing to talk. Callahan had been turned away when he really needed help. Not once, but every time.

Except by Tommy Calabrese. He hadn't been able to reach him at all. At times he wondered whether Calabrese might be the leak, and at others it seemed so ludicrous a notion he laughed out loud. Logic played tricks when you thought your partner might have rolled over on you.

Well, he knew he'd have to pay the piper. He'd called the tune in Bolivia and the tab was his. First things first, though, and the first thing was to apologize to Bolan. Straight out, man to man, he'd look him in the eye and swear he hadn't known what was going to happen.

About Bolan, he couldn't make up his mind. The guy was like a well, the deeper you looked, the darker it got. He knew enough about the big guy to know that it never went down easy when a good man bought the farm. Four was four farms too many. He wouldn't blame Bolan if he slapped him silly, then broke his neck. In Bolan's shoes, he half suspected that's exactly what he would have done.

But that need to wipe the slate clean, to set things right again, was paramount. He didn't give a damn about black marks on his record. You didn't work at his trade without getting a few, not if you were doing your job. The old saying about pain and gain could have been coined just for the DEA.

And the fact that he had a few personal scores to settle along the way just made it that much more likely that he'd overreach once in a while. Anxious for a justice that more enlightened but less realistic souls would characterize as vengeance, Callahan had been plodding along for four years. Sometimes he guessed. That wasn't a crime. There wasn't a great hitter alive who didn't guess more than occasionally, except maybe for Ted Williams. But hell, there was only one of those.

The airport terminal was crowded. Threading his way through the throng to the luggage carousel, he juked and zigzagged, trying to protect his injured shoulder. It always seemed as though faceless mobs sensed weakness, planting an elbow in tender ribs, stepping on broken toes.

The carousel area was roped off. He slipped through the turnstile, waiting for the American Tourister special. It seemed like real suitcases had gone the way of the Volkswagen Beetle. Everything was canvas and nylon. If there was one virtue to soft luggage, it was that there was no place to put decals. Callahan grabbed his bag and slipped gingerly through the waiting passengers. He showed his claim ticket to the bored attendant, stepped through a second turnstile and walked to the cabstand.

The ride to the Marriott's hotel took fifteen minutes, the driver using New York language and New York moves. Callahan didn't have to ask the driver where he was from. After checking in, he ordered room service and lay back on the bed, spent by the travel.

He wasn't sure how long he'd been asleep—at least a half hour, since room service seldom took less than that. It was the insistent knocking that woke him.

"Just a minute," Callahan hollered, reaching for his jacket. He got a bill ready to slip to the waiter and opened the door. The waiter's back was to him. When the door swung open, he immediately stepped aside to let the waiter haul his cart into the room.

Callahan wondered what the local room service staple was. In California he could never get anything that didn't have avocado or potato chips, usually both.

"Where would you like this, sir?" the waiter asked, reaching forward to close the door. Callahan got a flash. Room service never closed the door.

He started to answer as the waiter turned. He was staring into the biggest pistol muzzle he'd ever seen. Mack Bolan gestured to the nearest chair.

"Sit down, Mr. Callahan. You have a little explaining to do."

"What the hell is going on here, Bolan?" Callahan took a step toward the big guy, remembered the gun and stopped.

"I told you to sit down."

Callahan did as he was told. He slumped in the over-stuffed chair. "I don't understand . . . what?"

"What do you know about Tommy Calabrese?"

"Everything there is to know, I guess. I mean, we were partners for more than a year in La Paz. Why?"

"How long has he been working for Diego Cardona?"

"He's not! Are you nuts? I mean—"

"He almost got me killed last night. And not by accident. He set me up. Just like you did at Santa Rosa. Remember that? Remember the hot lead that we couldn't pass up? And the hot lead that killed four men, supposedly friends of yours?"

"Are you trying to say that I set you up? That it was a setup and that I knew it? What the hell is wrong with you? Why would I do that? Why would I let myself get shot? That's crazy."

"Look, Callahan. You know as well as I do that DEA guys on the take are like Kleenex. If you have Cardona's kind of money, you buy them by the box, use them and throw them away. If he got me, he wouldn't need you anymore. You were expendable. He wouldn't tell you that, of course. You're not a complete fool. But it happens, more often than guys like you care to think."

Callahan struggled to his feet. "Look, Bolan, I've had about enough of this shit. Guys like me? What do you know about guys like me? Fucking glamour boy, you are, flying around the world. Big guns. Special connections. When was the last time you had to bust your ass for six goddamned months setting up one of these jerks? You? You never do that. Oh, no, you're too big a deal. You know what you are? You're like a goddamned placekicker. You come in once or twice, never get your uniform dirty and you get headlines. Nobody gives a shit about guys like me and Tommy, guys in the trenches for the first seventy yards, busting our humps. Give me a break and get out of here. Weak as I am, I'll take you apart, pal. And tell Brognola he can shove his tac squad. I'm walking.''

Bolan stared at the kid. Nobody had talked to him like that in a long, long time. Not since his old man, really. There was something about it, something real. Bolan responded to the passion, and the hurt. Callahan was genuinely hurt that Bolan suspected him, the kind of hurt that comes from the heart.

He put his gun away and sat in another chair.

''Look, Brian. I'm sorry. But I had to know. Calabrese is dirty. He told me a big buy was going down at an amusement park, and that the man himself was going to be there. I showed up early, and so did Calabrese. When I went to meet him, all hell broke loose. And your friend Tommy didn't bat an eye when the shooting started. He knew about it. He set it up.''

''I don't believe it.''

''Who told you about the factory in Santa Rosa?''

''It wasn't Tommy.''

''Then who?''

''Somebody else. A Bolivian guy, one of our snitches.''

''Who told him?''

''I don't know. There wasn't time to check it out. We had to move on it right away. Then, well you know what happened then.''

''Yeah, I do. But I don't know why it happened. You must realize it was orchestrated. They were waiting for us. It was too pat.''

''Of course I realize that! How stupid do you think I am? But that still doesn't mean Tommy had anything to do with it. He was here in Miami. How could he have set us up?''

"I intend to ask him about that very thing."

"No."

"Why not?"

"Because it's not true. It can't be."

Bolan lowered his voice. He didn't know how to persuade Callahan. The kid's loyalty was everything it was supposed to be. It was misdirected, but that was something no argument could persuade him of. He'd have to learn for himself. Bolan didn't envy that education. It was going to be a painful lesson.

"Look, I'll make a deal with you. You handle it any way you want, but you have to handle it. All right?"

"Handle what? I don't know what you're getting at."

"As far as Calabrese is concerned, I'm a dead man. The last thing he knew, I was still in the amusement park. The morning papers haven't IDed anybody, and they won't. Not until Brognola gives the okay."

"So?"

"So, talk to him. See what you learn. See what he says. If he's as clean as you say, fine. You be the judge. But if not, if he's as dirty as I say he is, I'll be the jury."

"And the executioner?" Callahan smiled grimly. He stared at Bolan hard, daring him to deny it.

Bolan didn't.

After a long pause, Callahan sighed. "All right," he said, "but I want your word that if I say he's clean, he's clean."

Bolan thought it over. He was beginning to be convinced Callahan was okay. He wasn't sure, though, that the kid's heart would let him see clearly enough. It was risky, but Callahan was right. Calabrese was his partner. That wasn't something you walked away from, not unless you were sure. The kid was too good to let Bolan talk him into anything. And too good to let Calabrese talk him out of anything.

"Deal," Bolan said.

The kid looked at the aluminum serving cart. "You want this sandwich?" he asked. "I kind of lost my appetite."

CHAPTER THIRTY-FOUR

In Miami, Calabrese always stayed at the Laguna Motel in Coral Gables. It was one of those places that couldn't decide whether it wanted to be classy or seedy. As a result, it was a little of both and not much of either. Favored by vacationing secretaries because of its moderate rates, and by traveling salesmen because of the secretaries, it lay south of Miami along a stretch of Biscayne Bay not blessed with perfect beaches. The sand was adequate, and the swimming was decent, but not much more.

But the Laguna was perfect for meetings that required privacy and discretion. The mingling salesmen and secretries were too valuable a source of income for the owner to bother much who saw whom at what time. The ledger had more than its share of Smiths and Joneses. Neither name caused so much as a raised eyebrow.

Tommy Calabrese was—and looked—too Italian to get away with either Smith or Jones. When he wanted to use another name, he was confined to something larded with vowels. Carmine Infante was one of his favorites. Brian Callahan checked in under his own name and stole a look at the ledger while he did. There was Infante for the previous few days. That meant either Tommy wasn't there, or he was using another name.

Brian unpacked his light travel bag, turned down the bed and lay back to watch TV—and to wait. If Tommy was in trouble, and if he wanted to get to Brian, this was the first place he'd look. With the remote control, Brian flipped casually through the channels, skipping quickly past the usual mix of black-and-white reruns.

He checked out a skin flick for a couple of minutes, a concession to the salesmen, but the two women were hard looking and the guy was carrying about twenty extra pounds. Brian figured maybe they were so popular with the double-knit and seersucker crowd because it wasn't much different from looking in a mirror.

The sun was getting ready to disappear. The glare around the drawn curtains began to fade. The flickering TV screen threw a shimmering blue light over the walls and sheets. The dark green carpet, more like AstroTurf than a rug, looked pale, its worn spots exaggerated by the harsh illumination.

While he waited, Callahan wondered about Bolan. He hadn't even thought when he blew up. He had said some things he didn't believe, and some things that he'd never thought about but that were probably true. On balance, he couldn't believe he'd reacted that way. But he and Tommy had been through too much, too many heavy times.

He didn't want to believe Bolan was telling the truth, but deep in his gut, he knew it was all true. Tommy had been coming unglued for months. There had been comments about how easy it would have been to skim a little off the top, or resell a take. Once he'd even suggested they set up a buy with agency funds, that then, instead of making the bust, they take the money and the goods and split for Venezuela.

They had all been jokes. Or at least that's how Brian had taken them at the time. Now he wondered. Jokes all too often thinly veiled a deeper truth. They were a way of saying the unspeakable and getting away with it.

But maybe the most significant thing, in retrospect, had been Tommy's deteriorating marriage. There had been women, two or three of them, and Tommy had been paying a little too much attention to them and not enough to business. It was easy to overlook when you knew the family situation. Brian didn't approve, but he refused to be judgmental. He wouldn't lie to Susan for Tommy, but he wouldn't tell her anything, either. It was a bitch, caught in the middle between people you liked a lot. But Susan had never adjusted to the pressures Tommy had to face every day. Tommy resented it, blamed her for not trying hard enough to accept the hazards of his job.

On the fringes of the drug world, beautiful women were no novelty. If you had a flashy car, easy access to coke and a thick roll in your pocket, cherry picking could have been a full-time occupation. One of the perks, was how most of the agents looked at it. Why kick her out of bed if nobody really gave a damn? For Brian it was different. It was a personal thing he rarely thought about anymore, and still more rarely spoke about. Not even Tommy knew the whole story.

But the bottom line was that Tommy Calabrese was his partner, and partners were family. Even closer than family. You seldom had to depend on your brother to watch your back. In this business it was a daily thing. If he wasn't any good, your life expectancy would make an actuary cringe. And coming full circle, that was exactly what Bolan was saying about Tommy Calabrese. He had rolled over and sold out the agency, himself . . . and his partner.

Callahan looked at the clock on the night table. Its greenish glow read 9:30. He tried to get comfortable, rolling on his side and turning the TV volume down. His shoulder was beginning to ache again. Getting up, he took a couple of painkillers with a glass of water, then lay back down on the bed. The droning laugh track of an *I Love Lucy* rerun lulled him.

He grimaced as he shifted his weight on the bed. Rolling to his back, he watched Lucy press grapes with her feet. He couldn't remember how many times he'd seen that particular episode. It seemed as if it was a fixture in every motel, as if it were on tape instead of cable. He wondered whether he could get a cut-rate room if he passed up the chance to see it again. Making a mental note to ask about it the next time, he turned off the TV and closed his eyes.

He slept for nearly two hours. Groggy from the painkillers, he shook his head to clear it and got up for another drink of water. He clicked the TV back on, keeping the volume low, just in time to hear Ed McMahon announce *The Best of Carson*. The whole world was in rerun tonight.

The phone didn't ring, it buzzed. For a second he thought he'd imagined it. The second buzz disabused him. He grabbed the receiver, wincing as he flexed his wounded shoulder a little too much.

"Hello?"

"Brian? It's me, Tommy."

"Where are you? Are you okay?"

"Yeah, yeah, I'm fine. I was hoping you'd be there. Listen, I gotta see you."

"Where are you?"

Calabrese sounded as if he were whispering, and cupping the mouthpiece to avoid being overheard. "A couple miles down the coast. Sunshine Motor Lodge. That yellow place with the big neon flamingo."

"I remember it."

"How soon can you get here?"

"What's going on? Are you okay?"

"I got into a little jam, that's all. I'm okay, but I need a little help."

"What kind of jam?"

"I'll tell you all about it when you get here."

"I'll be there in twenty minutes. What room are you in?"

"Two twenty-nine. On the back balcony, over the ocean."

"Okay, sit tight. Do I need to bring anything? Money? A gun for you?"

"No, no, nothing like that. Everything's cool. Or it will be, anyway."

Callahan hung up and scrambled into his shoulder holster. He hadn't worn it earlier because the bandages made the fit a little too snug. The straps pressed on the wound and he was afraid he might pop the stitches.

He had rented a Pontiac Firebird, and the spiffy red number sat at the curb outside his room. He stepped out into the night, the flashing green neon sign of the motel the only light other than small yellow insect bulbs in front of each motel door.

Callahan keyed the ignition and gravel spewed from beneath the wheels as he backed away from his parking place. Cutting the wheel sharply hurt his shoulder, and he hoped he wouldn't have any heavy work to do. It was no better than fifty-fifty he'd be able to handle anything more than conversation.

He pulled out onto Old Cutler Road, cutting in front of a convertible full of teenagers. They leaned on the horn and cursed at him. Callahan flipped them the bird, then leaned on the gas. The Firebird began to pull away. The driver of the convertible took it as a challenge and roared up alongside. Two couples, all four of them slightly tipsy, yelled and waved. The guy in the rear seat was nearest to Callahan. He tossed a beer bottle at the vehicle, which clanged off the rear fender. The convertible pulled in close, its rear seat abreast of Callahan. The kid yelled something and raised another dead soldier over his head.

Fed up and in no mood for an argument, Callahan unholstered his .38 and pointed it straight at the rowdy punk. He looked the kid square in the eye, mouthing the words "Bang! You're dead." The kid threw up his hands and screamed something to the driver, who stood on the brakes. The convertible squealed and fishtailed, rapidly disappearing from Callahan's sideview mirror. Looking back over his shoulder, he saw the convertible swerve off the shoulder of the road, rocking to a halt in the grassy margin.

The Sunshine Motor Lodge was a couple notches down the scale from the Laguna. Callahan spotted the garish sign a half mile away. He stepped on the gas, as if he feared the motel might drive off and leave him. The Firebird slid through the sandy driveway, its back end bumping over its potholed edge. He parked in a small corner of the lot marked Visitors, then hit the asphalt on the run, rounding the corner just as another car pulled into the driveway.

The rear of the Sunshine overlooked the bay, separated from the waves by seventy yards of indifferent sand. A narrow boardwalk ran the length of the building, but Callahan ignored it in favor of the sand. The going was tougher, but quieter. He stepped back to read the number on the door above, the first one on the balcony. It was 201. Calabrese must be at the other end.

As Callahan slogged through the sand, he realized just how weak he was. The sprint had winded him, and his legs felt rubbery in the loose sand. He was puffing by the time he reached the other end of the building, where a set of weathered wooden stairs climbed to the balcony level. Callahan grabbed the banister and stopped on the first step to catch his breath.

As he reached the balcony level, he spotted a man rounding the far end of the building, on the sand below. Probably a guest of the motel. Brian rapped on the door of 229, but there was no answer. He rapped louder, his knuckles stinging from the blows.

He stepped past the door to look through the room's wide picture window. A dim light burned in the bathroom. The TV was on, but the picture was turned down, only dull shadows flickering on the wall. The sound was off. He heard nothing.

Callahan stepped back to the door and tried the knob. It rattled loosely in his hand, turning easily. The door was open—not too likely, if Tommy was in a jam.

Leaning back against the wall, he shoved the door open with his foot. He unholstered the .38 and cocked it, holding it at shoulder height. He heard running footsteps approaching from behind him as he stepped into the gloomy interior of the room.

"Tommy? You here? Tommy, where are you?" Callahan whispered.

He got no answer. He stepped away from the open doorway, losing himself in the darkness of the wall behind him, and reached for the light switch. He clicked it on, flooding the room with harsh light from the overhead fixture and the two table lamps that were plugged into the same line.

He saw the two men at the same instant. Calabrese stood in the bathroom doorway, his .38 Special in his hand. But it was the man to his left, behind a chair, who got his full attention. A heavyset Hispanic man in jeans and a work shirt leveled an Uzi at his gut.

Everything seemed to go into slow motion. He opened his mouth to speak, but the words didn't come, or if they did, they were drowned out by the shattering glass of the picture window to his right. A large hole appeared in the center of the butterball's forehead. Blood, bone chips and brain flew in a gory corona against the wall behind him. The man slid slowly to the floor, the third bloody eye vacant, the original pair wide in amazement.

Calabrese lost it for an instant. He looked at his ally, then seemed stunned by the ring of gore on the wall above the chair. He shook his head and raised the .38 toward Callahan, who instinctively raised his own gun, squeezing off two quick rounds. The first shot slammed into Calabrese just below the left shoulder, breaking the collarbone and shredding arteries before it smacked into his shoulder blade.

The second shot was cleaner. It chewed through the heart. Calabrese sprawled backward into the bathroom, his gun sliding across the tiles and skidding to a stop against the wall.

Callahan ran to the doorway of the bathroom, kneeling beside Calabrese. He raised his partner's head, but the glazed eyes told him he couldn't deny what he'd done. The man was dead. Callahan looked at the ceiling, and for the second time that night his lips formed words he didn't speak. The silent "Why?" had no answer, and he knew it.

Suddenly remembering the shattered window, he turned to the doorway. Mack Bolan lowered his AutoMag. He didn't say a thing to Callahan.

He didn't have to.

CHAPTER THIRTY-FIVE

The wooden plank creaked. Bolan wheeled, raising Big Thunder. The shadowy figure on the balcony advanced with raised hands. They were empty.

"There's nothing here that concerns you, guy. You'd better move on."

"That ain't how I see it," Lee Richards said.

"Who are you?" Callahan asked. His voice was subdued. He was still reeling from the shock.

"Might ask you the same thing," Richards responded. He indicated Bolan with a shrug of his shoulder. "Him, I don't have to ask. I *know* who this dude is. Saw him last night. At the fun house."

Bolan looked quizzically at him. Then he flashed on it. "The roller coaster. You were the guy on the roller coaster."

"You win a teddy bear, Jack."

"What were you doing there?"

"I had some business needed taking care of, you know?"

"What kind of business?"

"Don't matter. It got done."

Bolan nodded. "Why? That's what I want to know."

"That don't matter neither. See, the thing is, we got the same set of problems. You got your reasons, I got mine." Nodding in Callahan's direction, he continued, "Him, I guess he got his own reasons. We got to talk, I think."

"About what?"

"Business, my man, business. But we best haul ass out of here. This place may be one down, but somebody's sure to call the cops."

"Where to?"

"His place," Richards said. "Laguna Motel. That be all right?"

Callahan shrugged.

"Let's go, Jim."

"The name's Brian," Callahan snapped.

Richards stuck out his hand. "Lee Richards. See you at the Laguna." He turned and left.

When Richards's steps sounded on the boardwalk below, Callahan laughed. "What in the hell was that all about? And why'd you let him leave?"

Bolan said, "He told us where he was going. Besides, whoever he is, he saved my life last night. Twice."

"I can live with that."

"Then let's go. Jim."

Callahan shook his head. "I should stay here. For the police."

"Like hell. Brian, this thing is so complicated, you can't trust anybody." He looked into the bathroom at Calabrese. Callahan understood.

"Then why do we trust Mr. Richards?"

"We don't. But we don't have to. Not yet. All we have to do is listen to what he has to say."

Bolan led the way down the stairs.

RICHARDS WAS WAITING in Brian's room. The TV was on, the sound turned down. He indicated a six-pack of beer on the night table. "Talking makes me thirsty."

Callahan grabbed a beer and popped the lid. He offered one to Bolan, who declined.

The big guy sat down and Callahan stretched out on the bed. He reached for his shoulder, then pulled the pain pills out of his coat. He spilled a pair into his hand, then washed them down with a long pull on the beer.

Bolan unconsciously rubbed his bandaged arm through his shirt sleeve. It was better than it had been, but still tender. Richards noticed the gesture.

"You guys been tore up pretty good, so far. You need me."

"Tell me why," Bolan said.

"You after Cardona, right?"

"Go on."

"So am I."

"Can I ask why?"

"Sure, you can ask."

Bolan waited. When it was obvious Richards would say no more on the subject, he waved him on.

"You ever hear of Joey Buccieri?"

Bolan nodded. "Maggadino's underboss, right?"

"Not anymore."

"You took out Maggadino, didn't you." Bolan's voice was soft. Richards knew it was a statement, not a question.

"That's right. And he wanted me to take out Cardona, too."

"So why didn't you?"

"Cardona had other ideas. He snatched Buccieri, and they cut a deal. It was either that or pal Joey took a long walk on a short pier."

"How do you know all this?"

"'Cause I was there, man. I was waiting for the chance to drop the hammer on Señor Cardona. Dude has more security than the President, man. Couple of weird-looking little guys as well as the usual muscle."

"Jivaro," Bolan said.

"What? Who's that?"

"Not who, what. Headhunters. Cardona's got a bunch of them on his payroll."

"No shit! That's a bunch of grins, man. Headhunters. And I thought I seen it all."

"So, about this deal?"

"Yeah. A truce, you know, a sit-down, like in *The Untouchables*."

"What's the arrangement?"

"As near as I can piece it together, it's like this. Cardona wants the whole cheese, but he ain't ready. He didn't realize it at first, bit off more than he could chew. When you guys started rattling his cage, he backed off to regroup. He tells Buccieri he can handle distribution on this end. He'll be the sole supplier. That way he can move on the competition in South America. Then, when he gets that end under control, I figure he wastes Buccieri."

"A tall order."

"That dude thinks he's Wilt Chamberlain, man. Nothing too tall for him. And you know what? He's got the bread, and he's got the balls. If he has a little luck, he's going do it for sure. Mean mother. The eyes on the man are unbelievable."

"If you got that close to him, why didn't you waste him?" Callahan demanded.

"Look, Bro. I'm a professional, you dig? You don't last as long as I have without you cover your bets . . . and your butt. Don't believe me, ask this badass *ninja* mother here."

Bolan almost smiled.

"So what's your proposition? I still don't know what you want, and why you're here."

"Chill out, man. I was getting to that. Dig, I want Cardona. Why don't matter. But he's back in La Paz. I need some help on that end. You want Cardona, too. My proposition is we pool our resources. We all get what we want, and everybody's happy. What could be simpler?"

"I still want to know why, Richards." Bolan left no doubt, either that he was seriously considering the proposal or that it hadn't a prayer unless Richards told them what his interest was.

Lee sighed. Standing up, he flipped the empty beer can into the wastebasket and grabbed another from the night table. "All right, I'll tell you, but not all of it. I'll tell you the truth as far as you need to know it. Then, either we deal or we walk. No arguments, no bullshit. Okay?"

Bolan's nod was enough.

"My brother, man, Albert. Cardona killed him, see. I mean he didn't pull the trigger, but he's responsible. I loved that kid. Never did nothing right for him, but I was always trying, man. Making plans, you know? But when the time came, it was too late. He was into crack. He took me off for a piece and tried to burn somebody for a score. I got there a little too late. Couldn't even stay for the funeral on account of who I am and what I do for a living."

Richards looked at Bolan. The big guy nodded.

"So, I did some work for Cardona. In Bolivia. Then, when Albert died and I start pulling on the string, damn if he ain't at the other end. Sitting there in his big cushy house. And Albert laying on the floor in that crummy hallway. Rats in the goddamn building next door eating an OD. I like to puke. I *did* puke. You ever see that? Maybe they got Albert, too. I don't know." Richards's voice choked. He looked at Bolan, tears in his eyes that couldn't fall, because he wouldn't let them. Not yet.

"I want that bastard's ass, man. And I'm going to have it, with you or without you."

"Get in line," Callahan said.

Richards held out his hands, palms up. "I'll choose you for him, man."

Bolan cut in. "Look, this isn't a game. We got a tough row to hoe, here. Now, we better figure out what we're going to do, and do it."

"Fine by me, man."

"You said Cardona has gone back to La Paz. You sure?"

"Yeah, I'm sure. He's planning something. I don't know what, but it's plenty big. He bought himself an army of Mexicans. They already there."

"How do you know?"

"Business contacts, my man, business contacts. Ain't nothing happens in this line I can't find out about if I turn over enough rocks."

Bolan looked at Richards. The other men became aware of the sudden cold silence.

Richards looked him straight in the eye. "Something you want to ask me?"

"You assassinated President Yanez, didn't you?"

He nodded slowly.

"For Cardona..."

"Yeah. I never dealt with him directly, it was that butterball he had with him, Roberto Cabeza. Strange dude, Roberto."

"Why?"

"I don't have to answer that."

"No, you don't."

"All right, then, I will. Money, man. Plain and simple. It's what I do. For a living."

Bolan stared at him. Richards seemed flustered for a second. Then he said, "Look, man, it ain't no different from what you do. You get paid, man. You got bills, somebody gives you cash. They ain't doing it out of charity, man. You know that. Shit, don't go getting on no high-and-mighty moral horse, man. Morality just depends on who picks up the tab. The man on the inside pays, you done a moral thing. The man on the outside pays, you be a sinner. Remember that song 'Sympathy for the Devil'? That line about making all the sinners saints? That's you and me, man. Right now, you just be a saint and I a sinner. Next week, who knows?"

Bolan sighed. "There is a difference, Lee."

"Yeah? And what's that, man?"

"I believe in what I'm doing."

"You think I don't? You think Cardona don't believe in what *he* doing? Think about it."

"Oh, I have. And I will. And no matter how you slice it, a man who kills for money alone is no man at all."

"Man, I need some air," Richards said in response, getting to his feet. "It's too damned noble in here for this jive-ass nigger. I be back."

He walked to the door, turned once to look over his shoulder, and then was gone.

"Why didn't you stop him, Mack?"

"No need to. He'll be back."

"I'm not so sure."

"He didn't believe all that garbage. That was his way to rationalize. I don't think he realized it until he said it just now. But now...now he knows."

Lee walked down to the waves. The night was warm, but he felt a cold sweat on his neck and shoulders. The big guy gave him the willies, looking right through you. Got a bullshit detector built right in.

He sat on the sand, kicked off his shoes and peeled off his socks. The tide was coming in. Wet sand, darker than the rest of the beach, bubbled as each wave ran in, then out. Lee stood up, stripped off his shirt and his pants. Wearing only Jockey shorts, he walked toward the waves, the water slapping at him gently. He hadn't felt like this in a long, long time. A wave ran up on him suddenly, the chill water splashing his stomach and chest.

Lee dived in and started swimming. The cold water felt good. His skin tingled and the steady rhythm of his stroke relieved a tension in his body he hadn't even known was there. After several minutes, he stopped swimming, turned over on his back and floated, looking up at the stars. Behind him, a channel buoy clanged irregularly, rising and falling on the surge.

He hadn't known the sea could be so cleansing, so invigorating. But then there was so much he hadn't known. It was only now coming into focus.

Filling his lungs with air, Lee flipped, dived straight down and felt the gritty bottom with his fingers. Pushing off with flattened palms he rose straight up, bursting through the surface like a breeching whale. He expelled the stale air from his lungs with an exultant shout.

Settling back into the water, he floated a while on his back, watching the lights of the shoreline. He drifted down the beach, sixty yards or so away from the motel. Rolling onto his stomach, he settled into a steady crawl, digging against the tidal drift. He didn't look up until he felt the sand at the waterline.

He stood up, knee-deep in water, then walked up the beach to where his clothes lay in a neatly folded pile.

"I wondered how long it would take you," Bolan said.

"How'd you know, man?"

"Because you were right in what you said back there. We are very much alike, you and I. But not the way you think. You're more like me than you ever dreamed."

"Got a long way to go, man. A long way."

"Not nearly as long as you think." He stuck out his hand. Lee grasped it firmly and helped him to his feet. "You better get dressed. We got a lot to do."

CHAPTER THIRTY-SIX

The delicate balance was about to come apart. Mack Bolan was going to give it a little shove. The *Sicilian Princess* was ablaze with light. Chinese lanterns were strung from mast to mooring and back. From the small dinghy on the seaward side, Bolan was able to watch the preparations. It looked as if one hell of a party was planned for the night.

The dinghy tugged at its light anchor. The muck and sand below were none too secure to begin with, and the anchor was little more than a couple of pipes screwed together. The plan wasn't particularly complicated, but it depended on split-second timing.

Richards was going to clear the yacht with a phone call. Bomb scares were a dime a dozen, but this one was to good purpose. Unwilling to jeopardize people whose only crime was bad judgment in their choice of company, Bolan wanted the boat cleared. Then he was going to show them a real party.

As soon as the phone call had been made, Lee would send up a small flare. Lying in the bottom of the boat, just peeking over the gunwale, Bolan checked his hardware, then his watch. Ten minutes to go. Everything checked out. All he had to do was wait.

On the button, a small orange ball of fire appeared in the sky, off to the left of the yacht. It was time. Reaching over the stern, Bolan cut the anchor line. The boat was powered by a small electric outboard in order to keep the noise to a minimum. As soon as the line parted, he started the engine. The tinny hum was soft, and sounded more like an angry insect than a source of power.

Looking over the bow of his dinghy, Bolan saw people running around on the deck. The cabin lights were still on below deck, but the Chinese lanterns had been extinguished. The dock was full of scurrying people. Given the nature of the gathering, Bolan was counting on the fact that there would be no police.

Joey Buccieri didn't need anything less than he needed the attention of law enforcement. It wasn't his way, and it most definitely wasn't the Mafia way. If you couldn't handle a little problem like this, you couldn't handle anything.

Buccieri was already on shaky ground as the acting boss of the Miami family. The commission would make its final decision in a few weeks. Until then, Joey Boy was supposed to keep things in running order. If he did well, maybe he'd get the nod. Otherwise, he'd get the shaft, and he knew it.

The party was supposed to be a confidence builder, for Joey as well as for the rest of the family. Acting the part was half the job. The rap on him had always been that he was too hot-tempered and that he lacked the aura of dignity necessary to inspire respect and confidence. You could run the family with fear, of course. But it wasn't the best way.

Image was everything. Despite the gradual transition into legitimate businesses and the desperate currying of respectable favor, media attention was never very far away. What the commission wanted was somebody who would look respectable and could handle the pressure of public scrutiny. In the age of public relations, it was important to have a front man who made good copy if he couldn't avoid making any at all.

The country was used to invisible men of influence. Daniel Ludwig and Howard Hughes were billionaires, and not one person in a million could honestly say he'd shaken hands with either of them. But when you had the reputation of Gambino or Genovese, it was assumed you were hiding something. When you were Howard Hughes, you were simply eccentric.

With that in mind, the commission had already let it be known that a change was in the wind. Joey was only a custodian until further notice. But if he could establish reasonable connections with those closest to Sally, and if he could convince the commission that he was the best man for the job, his custody could be made permanent. And that was where the real bucks were.

Right now, he was no better than a Kelly Girl. He didn't have the key to the front door, let alone the safe. Everything he did would be dissected and analyzed. The big cheese never got audited. They trusted you until they had reason not to. Everybody knew that skimming went on. It was one of the perks. Lining your own pocket was expected. It was also expected that the pocket would not be unreasonably large. The blind eye was the next best thing to an incentive plan. And Joey Buccieri, if he had anything, had incentive.

Now this nutso had to call up and say there was a bomb on the boat. Fifty G's to a caterer ready to go down the tubes, fifty G's he didn't have yet. If he found out who was responsible, he'd roast him in a pizza oven. It crossed his mind that maybe it was some kind of test. They might be wondering how well he could handle pressure. He was determined not to lose his cool.

Besides, he had the taco eater from Bolivia to worry about. The son of a bitch had already kidnapped him and threatened him. He'd agreed to the lunatic proposal because he had no choice. But he had no intention of honoring it. He'd just bide his time. When he had the bastard where he wanted him, he was going to tighten the screws, watch the bastard squirm before putting out his lights.

The whole thing had been tricky. Presenting it to the family as a positive, a brilliant scheme that required patience, had been touch and go. DiMarzio, for one, hadn't bought it. But he went along with it. The damned yuppie was a gutless pencil pusher, anyway. If the numbers worked, what was he going to do? The closest the wimp ever came to danger was when his adding machine tape got into the blue zone.

Well, the hell with him. And the hell with whoever set up this little fire drill.

Buccieri stood at the top of the gangway, the very picture of confidence. DiMarzio was already on the dock, standing in the back. God forbid there might be a little loud noise. Johnny Poggi stood a few feet away, one foot on the rail. Buccieri waved him closer.

"Listen, Johnny. If you want to go ahead ashore, don't worry about it. I can handle things here all right."

"Joey, Joey," Poggi said, pinching Buccieri's cheeks in a five-fingered vise, "I'm supposed to keep an eye on you. You know that. How can I do that, if I ain't with you, Joey boy? Besides, you might need me here. You never know."

Buccieri grinned. It wasn't sincere and Poggi knew it. And Joey, swallowing hard, knew that Poggi knew. Most of the others had already gone ashore. Vince Clemenza was checking the engine compartment. Danny Cavalieri was checking out the main cabin.

If they didn't find anything, Joey wanted the party back in gear. If he got it going again quickly enough, he'd be one up. If not, hell, he could still pull it out. He had to be the front-runner. No way in hell they wanted a gutless wonder like DiMarzio to run a town the size of Miami.

"Johnny," Buccieri said, "I'm going to go see Vince, see if he found anything. If the place is clean, let's get everybody back on board in a hurry."

"You're the boss, Joey." Poggi grinned, wriggling his nose like a cartoon character. Buccieri held his temper and walked to the head of the companionway that led down to the main cabin. He climbed down until his head was just above deck level. He turned back to see Poggi, still grinning, his arms crossed and big butt comfortably perched on the deck rail. The bastard.

Bolan was a hundred fifty yards away and closing. The LAWS rocket rattled on the bottom of the dinghy. He wanted to get a little closer. He hadn't used one of the feisty things in quite a while. With the pitching of the small boat adding an element of uncertainty, closer was better.

At one hundred twenty yards he reached back for the LAWS and steadied it against the side of the small boat. It was still humming forward, but the ebbing tide was pushing it relentlessly sideways. Bolan reached one arm into the water, using it as a rudder to control the small craft.

The cool water felt good on his injured arm. It no longer stung to get it wet, a good sign that healing was well under way. Flattening his palm against the sea, he managed to turn the dinghy enough to confront the yacht head-on. Sighting it on the stern, Bolan fired.

The small rocket trailed smoke and pale flame across the dark water. It slammed into the yacht about fifteen feet forward of the fantail. A ball of fire erupted, fragments of the hull skidding across the waves, white spears in the orange glow. On deck, Poggi was hurled off the rail and hit his head hard on the polished mahogany. He struggled to rise, then slipped into unconsciousness.

Joey Buccieri had just ducked into the main cabin. A gout of orange flame spurted through the bulkhead leading to the engine compartment. He heard a horrific scream as he fell backward, slammed into the iron stairs by the concussion. Sharp pain shot up along his spine.

In the engine compartment, Vince Clemenza rolled in the oily water sloshing through a gaping hole in the hull. Fragments of the projectile shattered the fuel tank and ripped the fuel lines to copper ribbons. The high-octane fuel blew in a second, larger, fireball. Greasy smoke filled the compartment as water continued to rush through the torn hull. Burning fuel coated the water and lapped ever closer to Clemenza, momentarily stunned by the blast.

Clemenza reached for his right arm, trying to stop the blood gushing from a horrendous gash from wrist to elbow. The severed arteries spouted in continuous spurts as his heart struggled to compensate for the loss of blood pressure.

He struck his head on the engine mounting. Fighting to keep his eyes open, he squirmed back away from the advancing tide of burning fuel. Thick oil slopped onto his legs and clothing. With a soft whoosh, it caught fire like a barbecue overdosed in lighter fluid. Clemenza whirled and flailed in the water, trying to extinguish the flames.

Danny Cavalieri lay unconscious just outside the engine compartment. The concussion had flattened him. Buccieri stared at him, unable to decide what to do. He heard Poggi yelling on deck, then a flurry of gunshots. He started toward Cavalieri, then turned back to the companionway.

Danny was going to have to look out for himself. It was more important for Johnny to see him take command. He struggled up the companionway, falling prostrate on the deck. The yacht was beginning to list badly. She was shipping water rapidly, and the broken hull slipped farther and farther under water. As she slipped lower in the waves, she took on more and more water. Poggi lay on the deck, a pistol pointed out to sea.

As Buccieri climbed to his knees, Poggi fired twice and then a third time. He kept squeezing the trigger, but his magazine was empty. Poggi reached into his pocket for another clip, tossing the empty one overboard. Buccieri crab-walked to a point just behind Poggi and to his left. He strained his eyes into the seaward dark, but could see nothing.

"What the hell is going on, Johnny?" Buccieri shouted.

The prostrate hardman snarled back, "You tell me. This is your party."

The gunner's pistol was reloaded, and he turned away from Buccieri. The latter looked again at the dark water. A small dinghy was less than thirty yards away. It appeared to be abandoned. He couldn't believe there was a connection between this harmless flotsam and the blast that had threatened to sink Maggadino's yacht. It wasn't possible.

Poggi began firing, spacing his shots and systematically chewing at the waterline of the dinghy. Two spouts indicated shots that had been wide. The others slapped into the old wood of the rowboat, sounding like strange, solitary, wooden applause for a performance no one else appreciated.

The dinghy began to sit lower in the water. Its drift had slowed, indicating it was taking on water. Not knowing what else to do, Buccieri threw several slugs from his own gun. Suddenly, with a noise halfway between a burp and a sigh, the dinghy was gone.

Buccieri stood and raced to the seaward rail of the yacht. It was a downhill race, with the larger craft listing still more heavily.

"We got the son of a bitch, Johnny," Buccieri shouted. "He's gone."

"Guess again, *señor*."

The words sent a cold chill up Buccieri's spine. He started to turn toward the speaker.

The arctic voice stopped him dead. "Don't."

He heard Poggi's voice, the snarl all but unintelligible. A shot sounded from where Johnny lay on the deck. Two quick shots from the general direction of the uninvited guest, and Joey heard no more from Poggi.

"*Señor*," the heavily accented voice intoned, "I have a message for your friends in New York. Tell them they are not welcome in Bolivia. Tell them Bolivian business is for Bolivians. Tell them Diego Cardona wishes no interference in affairs that, as of this moment, no longer concern them."

Buccieri said nothing.

A sudden, cold prod at the base of his skull made him shiver.

"Nod your head if you understand me, *señor*."

Buccieri did as he was told, cringing from the cold steel on the back of his neck.

Then the lights went out.

CHAPTER THIRTY-SEVEN

"You sure these are Cardona's men, Lee?"

"Bet on it, Jack."

"It's Mack," Bolan said.

"Not to me, Jim."

They sat in Richards's Corvette, watching a black panel truck, its tinted windows blacker than the paint, cruise into an abandoned warehouse.

Two men left the van and drifted beyond the reach of Bolan's binoculars.

"How many?"

"The two guys who got out, they're backup. Got to be a driver and probably two more men in the back. That's five. Plus however many come for the pickup. Got to be at least three. These dudes are all paranoid. They don't really trust nobody."

"Would you?"

"I ain't a dope dealer."

Lee reached for the glasses. He swept the inside of the warehouse, getting a feel for the layout. The huge floor was almost unoccupied. A few crates of heavy machinery sat in one corner, their sides long since ripped open to reveal a generator and a couple of turbines. Too heavy to move, and worth too little to bother stripping down.

"One of them boys is behind that pile of junk in the corner. Can just make him out. I can't see the other one at all. Light's no good."

"We'll be okay as long as we remember he's there. What time's the buy going down?"

"S'posed to be three, but it's almost that now."

"Who's making the pickup?"

"Point men for Buccieri. They are supposed to take the van and all, the whole shooting match. Then they make a couple of drops. Like a goddamned newspaper truck, dropping bundles for the paperboy. Unbelievable."

"Not so very unbelievable," Bolan said. "More like history repeating itself. The story I heard was that magazines got distributed by Mob trucks after prohibition was repealed. They had all this rolling stock, when the bottom fell out of the bootleg market. They already knew how to apply muscle. All they needed was a little market research, and they were back in business."

"I was a paperboy, once. Lasted two weeks. Had to meet the man at 6:00 a.m. to get my consignment. Two weeks of that shit in the middle of January, and I didn't give a damn whether anybody got the paper. The third week, I just burned the suckers in a barrel for some winos. Ripped off a grocery store to get the receipts. The fourth week, I didn't even bother to show up." Richards laughed quietly. "The beginning of a life of crime."

Bolan took the glasses back. As he focused on the open warehouse door, a dark blue Oldsmobile rounded the corner and doused its lights. It paused at the entrance to the warehouse, then rolled on in, braking to a stop at the center of the building. It was dwarfed by the high ceilings, and looked more like a child's toy than a real car.

"How we gonna handle this, Jack?"

"Easy. We take the drugs *and* the money. Nail the whole bunch. Cardona will blame Buccieri, and vice versa."

"It'll never fly."

"Sure it will. Cardona's already paranoid. Buccieri will be so enraged after what we did to his party that he won't be able to think straight. Each of them is just looking for an excuse to ice the other. I'm not worried it'll work. I'm worried we won't be able to find Cardona when we get back to Bolivia."

"You're the boss. Let's go."

Richards slipped easily out of the Vette. He opened the trunk and removed two Ingram MAC-10s. Bolan joined him at the rear bumper, taking a handful of magazines from the trunk. He slid one into each SMG and tossed the rest into the front seat of the car. They got back in and Lee started the engine. He didn't bother with the lights. The engine screamed as the car bore down on the open door of the warehouse.

Bolan looked at the needle in the dim light. It read 80 mph as they roared into the cavernous building. Lee handled the car well. Heading straight for the van, he braked in a tight arc, bringing the car to a rocking rest between Olds and van. Two men had already left the car. They looked confused for a moment, then dived for the open doors. The driver panicked. His tires squealed, tight spirals of burning rubber gusting out behind him. The oiled concrete floor gave little traction, and the car didn't move.

"Whatever you do," Bolan shouted, "make sure the van is still usable. That's how we're getting out of here."

"And leave my red beauty here? You crazy?"

Before Bolan could answer, a burst of gunfire came from the rear of the van. Its doors had swung wide, and at least two men leaned out, spraying fire wildly from their handguns.

Bolan ignored them. He raked the Olds along its rocker panels, spraying back and forth. Two tires went flat with a loud puff. The rear one, still spinning under the excited driver's heavy foot, ripped apart and jumped off the rim. The screech of metal on concrete was deafening.

Bolan leaped free of the Vette to charge the Olds, the Ingram bucking as he ran. The passenger-side glass starred, then collapsed inward, spraying the inside of the vehicle with razor-sharp fragments.

Lee charged the van. He carried the Ingram in one hand, but held his fire. A handgun was the only way to capture the van in usable condition. He pumped three quick shots from his Coonan automatic. No hits. One of the men in the van's rear jumped down to the concrete, leaving his legs exposed below the door level. Lee dropped to one knee and fired twice.

The hidden man's left knee shattered. He howled in pain, falling in a heap to the ground. Lee fired again, this time punching a small hole over the man's heart and a fist-sized rupture in his back.

Bolan reached the Olds, just ahead of hellfire sprayed from a darkened corner of the warehouse. One of the van men was drawing a bead. The slugs ripped at the concrete to Bolan's left, sharp chips flying, mingled with sparks. The Olds heaved as the driver leaped free. Bolan dashed to the car's rear.

He got into a crouch, holding the Ingram like a handgun. He hosed the rest of his magazine into the dark corner, then yanked out Big Thunder. He sighted quickly and fired. The shot crushed through the driver's skull, punching the man backward.

Suddenly the warehouse was bathed in light. A whirring noise echoed through the upper reaches. Bolan turned in time to see the huge overhead door rolling toward the concrete floor. Now he knew where the other van man had gone. It was too pat. This had probably been the plan all along. Cardona was going to burn Buccieri.

Welcome to the club.

The two hardmen from the Olds had sought whatever cover was available. The crates of rusted machinery lay to the left, back toward one wall. In the harsh light flooding the warehouse, he could see a bright smear of color that could only be a Hawaiian shirt. The color winked and flashed in gaps between a gigantic crate and its muddy-red contents. Bolan aimed carefully.

The color moved again, this time sliding toward the other end of the crate. Watching the upper left-hand corner, he saw a forehead appear, then a pair of eyes. Bolan squeezed and the gap exploded into a red flower.

One man from the Olds returned.

Lee leaped to the roof of the van, nearly sliding off onto the floor on the other side. The man in the rear of the van fired three shots up through the roof, two missing completely. The third also missed, but narrowly. A flap of metal folded back by the slug pinched the piece of flesh between Lee's right thumb and index finger.

He yanked hard, felt the webbing tear away. The wound was small but bloody, and his thumb felt numb. He shifted his handgun to the left hand and sucked at the stinging tear. The blood was slowing, but still plentiful. A quarter-inch V of skin was missing entirely, and the ragged edges of the rip extended another quarter inch to either side.

Lee crawled forward on the van's roof, his right hand bloody and slippery on the smooth metal. He got to his knees and flipped, rolling once and landing on his feet, facing away from the van. He whirled and fired, his left hand bucking with the shots. His first went wild, the second on target. The van man pitched forward, landing facefirst on the concrete. The shot had smashed through his lower jaw, breaking the bone at the hinge on its left side. Blood began to mingle with the clotted oil on the floor.

Lee hollered to Bolan, "You get the other three, I'll take the driver."

Bolan nodded and slipped another full clip into his Ingram. The hidden SMG was a problem. The last man from the Olds was pinned in the corner, near his dead buddy. That left the man who had turned on the lights and closed the door. He'd take him last.

Bolan sprayed autofire into the pile of crates, slugs ricocheting off the rusted metal. The SMG was higher up, judging by the angle of fire. A metal stairway ran up into one corner of the warehouse, ending in a catwalk of orange-painted steel nearly forty feet off the ground. Stacks of boxes and leaning wooden shipping skids lined it intermittently.

The catwalk ran from front to back, with a small cubicle at either end. The cubicles were made of the same painted steel, with large glass windows making up their upper halves. The cubicle to Bolan's right, at the rear of the warehouse, was displaced forward somewhat. A dark green metal door was set in the back wall, which opened with a push bar set at waist level.

The SMG was somewhere up there, but before Bolan could get to it, he had to go through the Olds guy.

Leaping into the van, Lee charged the back wall of the driver's cab. The driver heard the commotion and turned to see what was going on. His eyes grew wide as he realized Lee was right behind him, only a thin sheet of glass separating them.

He reached to the seat beside him, but Lee had seen enough. He raised the Coonan automatic and held the muzzle a scant fraction of an inch away from the glass. He fired once, the report sounding overloud in the narrow confines of the van. As the glass imploded into the cab, Lee fired again.

The first shot had caught the driver high on the right shoulder, punching down through collarbone and, deflected, skidding along under the skin like a metal tick until it exited, burying itself in the driver's left thigh. But it was the second shot that killed him, crushing the temple and rending the cerebrum with whirling knives of bone.

Lee climbed out of the van, slammed the rear doors shut and locked them, then raced to the cab and yanked it open. The driver lay on his face in the front seat, blood pooling in the passenger bucket. Lee grabbed the dead man by his belt and tugged him out of the van.

He stripped the driver's jacket and tossed it onto the bloody seat, then climbed in. When he had arranged the jacket as best he could to cover the gore, he started the engine. He saw Bolan creeping toward the pile of machinery and threw the van in gear. Lee roared down the warehouse, cornering sharply and rounding the crates with a squeal. The crouching man leaped into the open. Bolan's gun cracked once, and the man fell.

Bolan gave the thumbs-up as the van sped past. Lee left the engine running, then bounced out of the cab. Pointing to the metal stairs at the front of the building, he ran toward the bottom step. Bolan sprinted toward the rear corner.

Lee waited, his foot poised on the first step. When Bolan reached the other staircase, he waved, and they began their climb. A slug pinged off the stairs above Bolan's head, and he heard the distant crack. The lone man at the other end of the warehouse was armed with a rifle. He wasn't much of a shot, but he was going to be a nuisance.

Bolan and Richards reached the first landing at almost the same instant. Each man turned and fired a short burst toward the other end of the building, just enough to keep the switchman honest. Bolan heard a rush of footsteps on the metal catwalk. They clanged dully, the reverberations traveling down through the metal staircase. He fired blind, aiming ahead of the sound, but heard nothing to indicate a hit.

On the second landing, Bolan stopped. Watching the play of shadows, he hoped to get a fix on the hidden gunman's location. But nothing moved.

He resumed his climb, now a flight behind Richards, who was on the final leg of his staircase. Bolan took the third flight two steps at a time. His heavy tread tolled like a bell in the huge empty arena. He was nearly at the top when he heard gunfire from Richards's direction.

A rush of steps headed toward him. The running man was obscured by the skids and cartons, but there was no mistaking which way he was coming. Bolan lay flat on the cold metal, concealed by a pair of skids leaning against the front rail.

He was about to peer around them when a burst from the SMG spit in his direction. The deadly hail clattered on the metal, then lost itself against the wall. Bolan ducked instinctively. The steps came on.

"Here he comes, Jim," Lee hollered. "Twenty yards."

Another burst from the SMG ripped at the fragile wood cover just above his head. Bolan held his ground. When the man had closed to five yards, Bolan made his move. He rolled out into the center of the catwalk. Lying on his back, he sighted upside down at the charging gunner. Big Thunder bucked twice, its motion unfamiliar in the inverted position.

The SMG clacked, then banged to the metal. It bounced once, clanging a death knell, then slid off into the air. It arced to the pavement below, shattering on impact. The charging man fell forward, his chest smashing into Bolan's averted face. Bolan shoved the body sideways, meaning only to get out from under its crushing weight. He felt the body poise, then seem to rise.

Bolan rolled to his side as the dead man slid over the edge feetfirst. The awkward angle pulled the corpse almost upright, and it hung like a hummingbird in midair, then plunged. It snapped to a halt, the back of the dead man's neck wedged against the lowest bar on the guardrail. The dangling legs swung grotesquely as Bolan reached out, but it was too late. The shifting weight broke free, and the man fell to the pavement below.

Lee ran up, panting. He was bleeding from a wound in his left shoulder. He gripped the injury tightly with his right hand, which also oozed blood.

"That worked out okay, man, but I must be out of shape. I'm really winded."

"Crank it up, Lee. We got one more play to run."

"Aw, Coach, gimme a break."

Bolan smiled. It was a cold and mirthless expression. Before he could answer, a slug slammed into the wall above their heads. The flattened bullet slid to the catwalk with a clang.

"Son of a bitch must be on your side, Coach, gettin' in my face like that. Time to teach these scrubeenies a lesson."

They raced down the stairs, keeping low to give the rifleman a smaller target. The warehouse echoed and magnified their racing steps, the metal clanging dully under their weight.

As they charged across the open floor, Lee noticed a figure high on the wall. The man was climbing a metal ladder toward the roof, where another door was set high in the metal wall. He stopped to look over his shoulder and Bolan fired. The bullet twanged away, glancing off the rung beneath the climber's feet.

Aiming higher, Bolan squeezed again. This time he didn't miss. The man struggled to keep his grip. His weight pulled him backward, and in an awkward dive he curled out over the catwalk below and plummeted to the pavement.

Lee reached him first, prodding the bloody pulp with one toe.

"Dumb bastard. S'posed to fill the pool before you practice diving."

CHAPTER THIRTY-EIGHT

"What are you telling me?" Buccieri ran a hand through his hair. His face was still blackened from the greasy smoke. He hadn't changed his clothes. "What the hell are you telling me? We lost the money? We lost the goddamn money? Is that what you're telling me?"

"Joey, I don't know what happened. The deal didn't go down the way it was supposed to. Dom never came back. I made a few calls. The money's gone. So's the coke. We got burned."

"Who told you? Who the fuck told you that? How do you know? Where's Dom? Get him over here, right now."

"He's dead, Joey...."

"Dead, what are you talking about?"

"Dead, man, all three of them. And Cardona's boys, too. I got to a guy in Vice. He told me about it."

"Why should you believe him? Tell me that!"

"Because we own him, Joey. He's in our pocket."

"And you believe him?"

"Yeah, I believe him."

Buccieri ran his hand through his disheveled hair again. The fingers caught in tangled curls and he angrily ripped them free, tearing a few hairs loose in the process. "I don't believe this. I don't. Somebody wastes Sally's yacht, blows Poggi away. Now you're telling me I'm out three million bucks. I don't fucking believe this. What am I going to tell the commission? If I don't believe it, you can bet your ass they won't."

"Joey, Joey, calm down. We got to think it through, that's all. We can fix it."

"Fix it?" Buccieri was shouting at the top of his lungs. "Are you going to make Poggi get up and walk? Huh? You going to do that? Fix it . . . my ass."

Tony Clemenza started pacing. He felt confined in the basement of Buccieri's home. The ceiling was too low for his six three height. The dark paneling seemed to press in on him like the walls of a closet.

When he spoke again, it was with restrained, reasonable anger. "Look, Joey, it's not just business with me now. You know that. Vinnie was my brother. I got an interest, now."

Buccieri sat down heavily on a sofa, careless of the sooty smudges his dirty clothes were leaving on its cream-colored suede. "Tony, I'm sorry about Vinnie. You know that. I don't mean I'm only pissed about the business. I'm just. . ." He spread his hands helplessly.

"Whoever blew the boat probably took us off, right?"

"Yeah, sure."

"And we know who blew the boat, right? It had to be Cardona."

"Of course it had to be Cardona. I know that. What I don't know is what we do now."

"What we do is we waste him. What's to decide?"

Buccieri was in a bind. He hadn't told anyone about his kidnap, or his terror. He was absolutely convinced that Cardona knew everything he was doing, before he even decided what he was going to do. It was as though Cardona narrowed the options, then forced him into the only logical choice. Cardona had someone on the inside, he was sure. But who?

And how do you mount a sneak attack on a man who controls everything you do? Or was that part of Cardona's plan, too? Joey had to think this out very carefully. He wasn't used to it. He didn't like it.

But he had no other choice.

Then he remembered something. It had slipped his mind, but now it came rushing back like a runaway freight. "Tony, get me the tape."

"What?"

"The tape. Get me the damn tape. Of the warehouse."

"There isn't any tape, Joey. For Christ's sake. What tape? It was vacant."

"No, not that warehouse. You remember, the one we watched with Sally, the explosion. The import warehouse."

"I didn't see any tape. I don't know what you mean."

"Sal, Sally had the tape. It must still be there. Go to his house. Tell Mrs. Maggadino you have to get something from the TV room."

"Joey...I can't. I mean, Jesus, he's only buried a few days. What the hell am I gonna look like if I do that? A goddamned vulture."

"Get it."

"Okay, Joey, okay. I'll get it. Take it easy. You got to tell me what I'm looking for."

"There was a tape of the explosion. There was a guy on it, coming out of the warehouse just before the explosion. Sally knew who it was."

"So?"

"So, he must work for Cardona. We find him, we find Cardona, for sure. Get the goddamned tape. Now."

Tony Clemenza stood mute. He shook his head, a messenger on a fool's errand. He walked to the stairs and started to climb. Halfway up, he bent, poking his head under the ceiling. "I'll be back as soon as I can."

Buccieri said nothing. He had covered his face with dirty hands, rubbing his eyes as if to blot out something he couldn't help seeing.

THE PHONE RANG for the third time. Cardona picked it up with distaste. There was so much to do, so many plans to make. He had given instructions that he was not to be disturbed. Now they were putting through a phone call, only an hour after he'd told them not to.

"What is it? I thought I told you not to bother me. When?... All right, yes, I'll talk to him.... José?.... What happened? All of it?... How?... Who was responsible?... No, no. It couldn't be. He wouldn't dare. And everything was gone? The shipment and the money?... All dead? You're sure?... Then Mr. Buccieri is a dead man. Yes. I'll let you know.''

How could it all come apart so easily? He had planned so carefully. But he had factored that into his calculations. It was too soon for Buccieri to have recovered his nerve. Someone had sold him out, that had to be the explanation. But who?

Perhaps...

Cardona left his study. He mounted the stairs to the first floor. Studying the things he had accumulated, the things he loved, one at a time, his anger mounted. And with it, a sadness. There was so much he wanted, so much he didn't have. The paintings, the money, they were as nothing to a man who needed control more than anything else. And that was exactly what he didn't have.

It had all been an illusion. When your plans fall apart as soon as they were made, you don't control anything. When people you trusted to perform simple tasks failed you so abysmally, you didn't have control. When all the money in the world seems insignificant compared to an imagined betrayal, you were out of control. Diego Cardona was out of control.

He climbed to the second floor, watching the white leather of his loafers crush the deep white pile of the carpet. They sank in so easily. Looking over his shoulder, he was appalled to see how easily the fibers sprang back. He was only halfway up the stairs, and already the impression of his foot had vanished from the first step.

Fascinated, he turned completely around, watching the carpet throw off all trace of his passage. The carpet rejected him, refused to accept his dominance. He was something to be ignored, something to bend before but not break under. He would move on, and it would be as if he had never been. Business as usual. Diego Cardona faced his deepest fear head-on, and it terrified him: he was nothing, he didn't exist. Not for the carpet, and not for the world. He was a passing phenomenon, a shooting star, a mayfly.

But it wasn't too late, not yet. He could still make his mark, still grab the world by its lapels and shake it until it had no choice but to notice him. That was what he had to do. But how? What could he do that no one—not peasants and not presidents—could ignore?

Like a frightened man backing away from a snake, Cardona climbed backward up the stairs. One foot, then the next, each placed squarely, each pristine loafer ground into the resilient fiber of the carpet, crushing it, forcing it to bend and accept him, his existence. And, slowly, each demonic, sole-ground impression vanished, more slowly than before, but no less certainly. At the top step he watched. And waited. And each footprint slowly disappeared.

Transfixed by the white expanse, his fingers groped blindly on the table beside him. The Ming vase tottered precariously. Its unstable rattle drew his eye. It teetered and, in slow motion, fell just ahead of his grasping hand. It shattered on the carpet, its incomparable beauty and delicacy erased in an instant, an invaluable creation rendered valueless, a pile of fragile junk.

Unable to feel even horror at his loss, he bent in silence to retrieve one of the larger fragments. He ran his thumb over the sharp edge again and again. His thumb began to go numb, then to bleed, and still he rubbed, caressed and teased the razor edge. Switching hands, he probed his palm with the point, boring in and drawing still more blood.

Enthralled by the silent, slow welling, he ignored the pain, willed himself not to feel it. Slowly, like a priest blessing his flock, he raised and lowered the bleeding hand. Small drops of blood showered down the stairs, each tiny globe swelling and slowly spreading, greedily absorbed by the thirsty carpet. And this sign was permanent, this stain could not be shaken off, would be there tomorrow and a year from tomorrow.

Drop after drop, blessing after grotesque blessing, he raised and lowered his hand. Laughing aloud, his voice losing all repression, he made his indelible mark on the stairs.

And he knew now what he had to do.

THE WOMAN WAS ASLEEP. She felt a presence, more like a shadow, in the open doorway. Her arm, draped over closed eyes, slid away. She opened her eyes. The figure in the doorway was motionless. The silk sheet, which had fallen to her hips, rustled as she sat up. Grabbing the slick fabric, she pulled it to her throat, felt its coolness grow taut across her breasts. She reached out for the light.

"Don't. No light." The figure moved forward, seeming to glide. "I don't want any light. Not now."

"What do you want?"

"I have been more than patient. And now I want what I have always wanted. I want you."

"We've been all through that. I can't, not now, not yet."

"If I leave it to you, I will be an old man. Is that what you are waiting for? Is that what you want? An old man's sagging, wrinkled gray skin to rub against yours? The scent of death snorting from hairy nostrils, labored breathing that smells of dentures, a slight drool at the lip, a slime left behind on your own lips, your breasts?"

"No, of course not." She was repulsed by the image, as he seemed not to be. He seemed almost to relish it, to wallow in it. "But . . ."

He glided closer. She felt his weight on the bed, as if the shadow were heavier than the man himself. He sat down to remove his shoes. She slid across the broad bed, pulling the sheet more tightly around her. He turned, and even in the dark she knew he wasn't smiling.

His hand grabbed the edge of the sheet. His closed fist bunched the delicate fabric. She thought of how it must wrinkle under such abuse. He pulled slowly, and she fought against the removal of this last defense, knowing it was over, that she couldn't win.

Her arms began to bend. His wiry strength belied his slender body. With an abrupt yank, he tore the sheet away, laughing.

"How easy it is," he said. "I just realized how easy it all is. The secret is knowing what you want to do. Doing it is easy."

She tried to get up, her skin clammy and cold, but he lunged, knocking her to the floor. He slid off the mattress, landing nearly on top of her. He was still clothed, the soft cloth an obscene affront to her own defenseless nakedness. His hands grasped at her flesh, the hands of a drowning man grasping at straws.

He kissed her throat, a wet, passionless kiss. His restless hands pinched and kneaded her, not brutally and not affectionately, but as if he were trying to make certain she was really there.

"Don't, Diego. Please don't."

"You think because I can have so many women, so many more voluptuous, more beautiful than you, that I have no need of your body? Is that what you think?"

She tried to slide back away from him, until her head cracked into the wall. He slid forward again, keeping pace with her.

"But you don't understand, not at all. The secret, you see, why it is so easy. I want *everything*. Especially what others tell me I can't have. You are an attractive woman, but not so attractive that I couldn't find a thousand replacements in a week. No. I want you precisely because you tell me no. Perhaps, if you had thrown yourself at me, it would have been different, but it's too late for that now. You have issued the challenge...and I have accepted it. Soon, we will see who wins, won't we, Miss Russell. Or should I call you Valerie, now that we are about to become such good friends, eh?"

Her hands scrabbled against the wall, and she felt the wire. She tugged, catching the lamp in midair, and brought it down hard on his head. He groaned and slumped to the floor.

Getting to her feet, she clicked the light on. It glowed in her hands. "The things I do..." she muttered.

CHAPTER THIRTY-NINE

Joey Buccieri watched the videotape in slow motion for the fifth time. Tony Clemenza sat quietly at his elbow. The tape meant nothing to either of them. The man running from the warehouse almost certainly was responsible for its destruction. You didn't have to be a genius to figure that out. But you had to be Sal Maggadino to know who he was. Or somebody who went way back, somebody as old as Sally, somebody who was around when Sally had met the big man on the screen.

"I don't get it, Joey. I mean, okay, the guy blows the warehouse. So what? We don't know who he is. We look for him. Maybe we find him, maybe we don't."

"No, Tony, it's not that simple. This guy is special. He meant nothing to the old man. He said so. He knew him, not just recognized him, you understand. He *knew* him. It was weird, like he'd seen a ghost. The old man was shook up."

"All right, all right. You told me. But Sally's dead. It don't do us any good to sit here and watch the damn tape over and over. His name isn't going to be on the screen if you look at it a hundred times."

"I know. Damn Sally, he kept too many secrets. He never trusted me. He didn't trust anybody. He never..."

"What? What are you thinking?"

"Sally...I said he didn't trust anybody, but that's wrong. He did. The old guy, what's his name, the fish guy?"

"Guarino? The old guy used to sell fish from the wagon? What could he know? He isn't even family."

"I know. That's the beautiful part about it. That Sally was a genius. He could trust the old guy because he *wasn't* a made man. He didn't have an ax to grind. He could be, you know, objective. Sally could tell him everything, not have to leave anything out, because it didn't matter to the old man. And Guarino, he could say what was on his mind without worrying that he was stepping on someone's toes. Maybe . . . maybe he knows.''

"You want me to bring him here?''

"No, no. That wasn't Sally's way. He respected the old man, you know, kept him out of things. They used to meet on the wharf, where the old man sold his fish.''

"He doesn't do that anymore. Not for years, Joey. Maybe he's even dead.''

"No, he isn't. Sally would have said something. Done something. He loved the old guy.''

"I'll make a few calls, see what I can find out.''

"And Tony . . .''

"Yeah?''

"Don't say nothing. Not to nobody. Maybe Sally's way was the right way after all.''

Clemenza shook his head in agreement, then left the Sons of Napoli Social Club.

IN THE CAR, Buccieri was silent. He stared out the window, finally rolling it down and shutting off the air-conditioning. His reflection was getting on his nerves. It had taken a few phone calls to find out where Gianni Guarino was living. The time had weighed heavily. Joey kept second-guessing himself. His head kept telling him Maggadino had been ready for the glue factory, but in his gut, he felt uneasy.

Part of him knew he'd made a mistake. You didn't turn an old guy like Sally—with all he knew—out to pasture. You kicked him upstairs, made him an honorary member of the board. Guys like that knew things nobody else did, valuable things. They made mistakes, but they got through. If you talked to them long enough, listened hard enough, maybe they would save you from making the same mistakes.

It was too late for that now, but maybe this one time there was something they could do, something they could use, just sitting there waiting. All they had to do was use it. Joey turned to the back seat and rested his hand on the VCR. He was sure the old man didn't have one. Hell, he might not even have a TV. But that they could fix easy enough.

Clemenza was driving fast, but not recklessly. He had been a wheelman in the old days, a damn good one. When he'd paid enough dues, they took him inside. But he never lost the touch, still taking the wheel for special occasions. He claimed the secret was his peripheral vision. He had been a good basketball player in Brooklyn because he could see a defender sneaking up from any angle. The same faculty was useful on the road.

The big car rolled easily, its powerful engine something felt more than heard at moderate speed. Buccieri felt the same quiet, sleepy feeling he remembered from his childhood, falling asleep on long trips, his head finally dropping into a corner in the rear seat, his legs curled. Things weren't that simple anymore, hadn't been for a long time.

Guarino lived in a quiet residential area on the outskirts of the city. Most of the homes were small, but neatly kept. Their modest lawns were close cropped and well watered. Flowers lined most of the front walks, small beds of them clustered at either end of the concrete porches.

Buccieri had his head on his arm, leaning on the car door, when it pulled to a smooth stop. His eyes were heavy. He heard Clemenza's door close, and shook his head to clear it. Clemenza opened the door for him, the VCR cradled easily under one elbow.

"Jeez, Joey, I thought you were sleeping there for a minute."

"Nah, just thinking. Remembering stuff, that's all."

"Sally?"

"Yeah," Buccieri lied.

"I know what you mean. I miss him, too. It's like I feel lost, or something, I don't know."

"He was just a man, Tony. Just a man who got old, like all of us."

"He didn't die of old age, Joey."

"What are you telling me, for?"

"Don't be so touchy. I didn't mean anything."

"Well, don't talk about it, all right?"

"Whatever you say." Clemenza followed the younger man up the walk. Something gnawed at the back of his mind, not exactly a suspicion, but not that far away. He watched Buccieri ring the doorbell, then stand fidgeting, the videocassette dancing nervously in his hands.

The inner door opened. The interior of the house was dimly lit, and the strains of an opera carried through the screen door, something by Verdi. Buccieri instinctively thought of Sal, how irritable he got when business intruded on his opera nights. It was one more reason to think the old man had lost it. Buccieri had no time for music, no passion for it. He wondered whether that little thing had cost him Sal's esteem, whether it had been another nail in the coffin custom-built for his future.

The old man leaned forward, pushing his glasses up over his forehead. "Yes, can I help you?"

"Mr. Guarino?"

"Yes, I'm Gianni Guarino."

"My name is Buccieri, Joey...Joseph Buccieri. This is my associate, Antonio Clemenza. We'd like to talk to you for a few minutes, if we might."

"Talk? What about?"

"May we come in?"

"Excuse me. This is my opera night. Perhaps if you could come back some other time...?"

"I'm afraid it can't wait, Mr. Guarino. It's very important."

"Well, just a few minutes, then." He stepped back away from the doorway, holding the screen door open.

When they were inside, the old man dropped his glasses back over his nose and stepped back. "Joseph Buccieri, you said? That name sounds familiar to me."

"I am . . . was . . . a friend of Mr. Maggadino's. Maybe he mentioned me."

"Perhaps he did. I'm not so sure. Anyway, what is so urgent?"

"I need your help."

"What can I possibly—"

"Please, Mr. Guarino, let me finish."

The old man snapped his jaw shut. His annoyance at the interruption was very close to the surface. "Please, go on."

"Before we talk, I'd like to show you something. Do you have a TV?"

"In the den."

"Good. Can we go to the den?"

The old man seemed baffled, but agreed. "Follow me."

They passed a wide double doorway. The music was a little louder. Buccieri glanced into the room as he passed. It was modestly furnished. The only sign of extravagance was the elaborate stereo setup. A sophisticated Teac tape deck, outfitted with ten-inch aluminium reels, was turning quietly. Evidently it was the source of the opera. A double bank of red diodes winked from the control panel of an equalizer.

"Salvatore gave me that equipment when I retired," Guarino said proudly. "He liked Verdi as much as I do. We used to listen together, whenever his work permitted the indulgence."

He pressed on into the den. "The television set is in the cabinet in the corner."

Clemenza set the VCR carefully on a sideboard and opened the cabinet. Easily hefting the nineteen-inch portable, he began connecting the VCR cables.

"While Tony gets it ready, let me tell you what I'm going to show you."

"Why don't you just show it to me?" Guarino smiled. "One picture is worth a thousand words, eh? What must a videotape be worth?"

"This is a very unusual tape. For a couple of minutes, you won't see anything interesting. But there is a man shown in this tape. I want to know if you know who he is. Look at him closely when he shows up. He isn't there for long. We'll play it a couple of times for you, if we have to."

"Why do you think I might know him?"

"Because Mr. Maggadino knew who he was. He said so, when he saw the tape. I think he might have mentioned him to you."

"Oh, no, I'm sure not. Salvatore and I never discussed his business."

More pleading than threatening, Buccieri grabbed the old man's forearm. "Mr. Guarino, look. Sally... Mr. Maggadino is dead. You don't have to pretend anymore. I know you liked him, and that you want to protect him. But this is very important. There's a chance the man on this tape may have killed Mr. Maggadino, and even if he didn't, he might know who did."

"I don't think it's very likely, Mr. Buccieri."

"Please, just look at the tape. You almost ready, Tony?"

"One more wire." He fiddled with the rear of the TV for a few seconds, then said, "There. All set. Give me the tape, Joey."

Clemenza turned on the TV, inserted the cassette and closed the VCR. He pressed the Play button. A red light came on, and the screen flickered for several seconds. The familiar warehouse came on the screen.

"Okay, Mr. Guarino, here it comes."

The shadowy figure loped into view. For a split second, light fell over his features, then they were plunged back into shadow.

Anxiously, Buccieri watched the old man. "Well?"

Guarino shook his head. "I don't know him. I never saw that man before in my life."

"Are you sure? Look at it again. Play it back, Tony."

"Mr. Buccieri, I..."

"Wait a minute now, here he comes. There...stop the tape, Tony. Back it up a little. There. Look at him closely, Mr. Guarino."

The old man removed his glasses and bent forward to scrutinize the dim figure on the screen. "No, I'm sorry. I don't recognize him."

"You're sure?"

"Absolutely. Why did you think I might know him?"

"Just a hunch."

"No, Mr. Buccieri. More than a hunch. There is some reason, something particular. You and your friend didn't come all the way out here at this time of night with all this equipment on a hunch. If you tell me more, maybe I can help you. If this man had anything to do with what happened to Salvatore...well, it would be the least I could do. I didn't approve of his business. This is not a secret. I tell you nothing I didn't tell him a thousand times."

"Of course, I understand."

"But a man does what he can. Salvatore believed in the old ways, like in Sicily. He didn't understand that the beautiful thing about America is that he didn't *need* the old ways. In the old country, they were useful, necessary, but here..."

Guarino turned to face Buccieri. "Now, do you want to tell me why you think I might know who this man is?"

Buccieri nodded. "Mr. Maggadino seemed shocked, upset, when he saw this tape. He recognized the man, I'm sure. He looked like he'd seen a ghost."

"And he didn't say who it was?"

"No. But he knew. There was something about this man, something Mr. Maggadino knew. He was afraid of him."

"Salvatore was afraid of nothing." The old man rose up at the insult to the honor of his dead friend.

"Maybe not, Mr. Guarino. But he was afraid of this man, or of what he represented."

"Do you know anything about mythology, Mr. Buccieri."

"A little."

"Does the name Nemesis mean anything to you?"

"Not really. What is it, a terrorist group or something?"

"You might say that. Many years ago, there was a man, but...it was long ago, and this could not be the same man."

"Why not?"

"Because he is dead. But if he wasn't, and if Salvatore was truly afraid, it would be of this man."

"What's his name? Who is he?"

"Now, I don't know. Then, he had many names."

"Who, damn it?"

"They called him the Executioner."

"Did he work for drug—"

"He worked for no one. And I will tell you this one thing. If this man is the same one, then you should forget about it. Let Salvatore rest in peace."

"No way."

"As you wish, Mr. Buccieri. You've heard the expression 'It's your funeral'?"

CHAPTER FORTY

"This is his place, huh?" Richards was incredulous. "The man must have money he don't even know about."

"He grossed over a billion last year alone."

"A what?"

"A billion dollars."

"You're jiving me. And here I thought *I* was making a killing."

"That's not funny, Lee."

"Uh-uh, but it's true."

"Come on, we're wasting time."

Bolan went over the wall first. Richards waited for the high sign, then followed. Cardona's place was more heavily guarded than Bolan had seen it. Whatever else the man was, he wasn't a fool.

"How many you figure we got to get through to get to him?"

"No telling, but we want him. If we can get to him without firing a shot, so much the better. I want him alive, if possible."

"I want his ass dead and buried, Jack."

"Not if there's another way."

"How come?"

"I promised somebody."

"His mama?"

Bolan didn't answer. He thought of Roberto Cabeza, and the strange promise the man had extracted. It ought not to have meant anything to him, and Cabeza would never know whether he kept it or not.

Human contact counted for too little, anymore. The affection that had prompted Cabeza's request was too seldom a motive for behavior. If people would think a little more about others, instead of indulging their own worst instincts, maybe monsters like Cardona would dry up and die, blowing away in the first breath of fresh air like so many dead weeds.

Maybe.

But Bolan, for whatever reason, had made a promise, and he meant to try to keep it.

He led the way to the single vulnerable point he had found in the building's defenses. As he approached the door, he remembered the look on Valerie Russell's face as she stared out into the darkness at him. He remembered the contorted face of the guard, fatally wounded by the poisoned dart. Their two faces were the flip sides of a two-headed coin, the shock of recognition and the shock of incomprehension. Sometimes it seemed there was too little certainty in life for it to be considered a successful experiment, whether from a scientific or religious point of view.

Now everything was coming together. Whether it would crystallize and make things clear—or blow up in his face, like a collision of matter and antimatter—was anybody's guess.

Nearing the glass door, Bolan raised a cautionary hand. They had to know it would be the first place he'd try to get in. And they surely knew he was going to try. The stakes had been increasing, every bet doubled then redoubled. There was no way either player was going to fold. The wheels within wheels had been turning at blinding speed. Bolan wondered whether he or Cardona knew which way was up anymore.

Stopping in the shrubbery fifteen feet from the window, Bolan whispered through cupped hands. "They're probably expecting me to make a move here. Maybe I can draw them out. Then we turn the tables."

"You can't use yourself as bait, man. They probably blow you away as soon as look at you."

"I don't think so. I've seen guys like Cardona before. They're unpredictable, but I understand how they think.

This guy wants me. Not by anybody's hand but his own. He won't give up the pleasure.''

"Hell, man. They shoot you, he come out and dance on your face. That's all he wants."

"I'm betting it's not."

"I hope you know what you're doing."

"I'm batting a thousand so far."

"You know what odds Jimmy the Greek would put on your next at bat?"

Bolan nodded. Without another word, he stepped forward and walked quickly toward the glass door. He was betting guards would be keying on the door from outside, rather than in. If he got in, it was too late, and the bedroom was no place to make a stand. It was too confined, and once the building had been pierced the odds would be against the defenders. The one reckless factor in such calculation was the arrogance of Cardona himself. A man who thought he couldn't lose, didn't believe in odds.

Bolan's senses were at a high pitch. He heard the leaves rustling as the wind blew through the high trees. He approached quietly, intently, unwilling to betray his expectations. The door was only three feet away.

The explosion threw his shadow into bold relief on the stone wall. The blast had come from behind and to his left, down by the main gate. Immediately the rattle of submachine-gun fire broke out. The squeal of rubber and the roar of an engine told him all he needed to know.

Somebody was coming in the hard way. A branch moved off to his right. A guard stepped into the open, a baffled look on his face. He couldn't reconcile Bolan's presence with the uproar at the main entrance. Nobody trying to gain stealthy entrance announced himself with fireworks like that. Bolan raised his Beretta. He watched the confused man sort through his options, eyes rolling like the wheels on a slot machine.

Bolan fired, the shot taking the guard in the center of the forehead.

Richards rushed up, almost as confused as the guard. "What the hell is going on, Jack?"

"Seems we have some competition for Mr. Cardona's attention."

"Who?"

"I'll give you one guess."

"Buccieri?"

"Who else?"

"So soon?"

"My guess is he was planning something like this all along. Our little charade just forced him to act sooner."

"The man is dumber than I thought."

"That just makes him a little more dangerous. And as far as he knows, we're working for Cardona. He's probably looking for us, too."

"What do you think?"

"We're here."

"Let's go, Jim."

Bolan stepped up to the glass and lifted it. Richards pitched in, and the panel was out of the way in short order. Bolan led the way into the house.

The gunfire sounded closer now. The cars had stopped, probably in front of the house. Bolan felt the vibration of heavy steps through the floorboards. Men seemed to be running in every direction. Some of the gunfire was louder than the rest, probably the security men returning fire from inside the building.

Bolan stepped into the hall, sprinting for the stairway to the gallery over the main room. He cleared the last step and turned into a hail of SMG fire. He dropped to the floor under a fine cloud of plaster dust from the wall behind him.

Hands grabbed his ankles, then he slid backward as Richards dragged him out of the hallway.

"That was close."

"Thank me later, Jack . . . if we get out of here. There another way to get where we want to go?"

"Not as far as I know. My guess is Cardona would head for the security room. It's got steel doors, and the walls are probably heavily reinforced. He can see what's going on and direct the defense."

"From the sound of things, he needs the Bears' front line to defend himself right now."

"Look, there's only one guy, I think. Let's draw his fire, and nail him when he reloads."

"You think I'm going out there, you crazy."

"Neither one of us is going out there. The guy's scared stiff. Has to be, or he never would have missed me. He'd have waited until I had no place to go."

"So, what you want to do?"

"Grab something, anything. Throw it into the clear. We'll see what happens."

Richards skipped down the stairs, returning with a large vase. "This pretty nice vase. Shame to do it, but..."

He rolled the ornate ceramic onto the landing above. It landed without breaking, but almost immediately shattered as the man at the other end of the hall opened up. The firing was relentless. Chips of the pottery flew everywhere, some hit again as they pinwheeled through the air. The polished hardwood floor was grooved and gouged by the onslaught.

"Wait till the man see his floor." Richards laughed. "He going to have a cow."

Bolan charged up the stairs as the firing stopped. Richards waited until he turned the corner, then dived onto the floor above, ignoring the sharp sting of the pottery fragments as he slid into the opposite wall.

He looked down the length of the hall, through Bolan's charging legs. A slender man in a three-piece suit was struggling to ram a new clip into his Uzi. Bolan continued his charge, then fired a 3-shot burst just as the clip slid home. The front of the suit spattered with blood as the guy crumpled to the floor.

Richards was up and running before the corpse stopped twitching. Bolan had already leaped over the fallen defender and turned a corner. Richards heard his steps on metal stairs. He snatched up the Uzi and rounded the corner in time to see Bolan fire another burst through the rapidly closing steel door at the bottom of the steps.

He thought for a second the big guy had missed. But only for a second. The door hung immobile, a band of light squeezing through, then sagged outward, propelled by the slumping figure of Bolan's target.

Bolan yanked the dead man aside and charged into the control room. Rapid handgun fire thundered in the enclosure as Richards bounded down the steps two at a time. In the corridor ahead, two men dived for cover behind a heavy oak sideboard. Lee held the Uzi at his hip and chewed at the wood, laying down a pattern of 9 mm stingers. The wood splintered, and one of the crouching men pitched onto his face in the middle of the hall. Richards ignored him, digging through the oak for his companion.

The corner of the sideboard sagged as the Uzi emptied its magazine. The remaining man reached over the top of the antique, firing blindly with a .45 automatic. Richards hit the deck, his eye fixed on the glittering arc of shells ejected by the pistol.

As the automatic clicked on an empty chamber, Richards charged. Ripping a Python .357 Magnum from his hip, he dived onto the sideboard headfirst, slid on over the top and landed muzzle-first on top of the cowering guard. He squeezed the trigger, his hand bucking at the detonation. Gore sprayed back into his face, the sticky blood running down his cheeks. The man beneath him stared up with vacant eyes, one hand desperately trying to hold in the bright red fluid staining the front of his shirt.

Richards stood and sprinted back toward the steel door. The room was silent. He stepped in, crouching, his gun extended in a two-hand grip. Bolan was getting to his feet, stepping out from behind a steel desk. Two men lay slumped over an elaborate control board. Over their heads, several smoking holes were all that remained of a bank of TV screens. The close air was heavy with the stench of death.

"Where to, Chief?" Lee asked.

"Cardona's office." Bolan cocked an ear toward the hallway. Sporadic gunshots confirmed the assault was still under way. "We'll have to watch out for the competition up there."

"Eyetalians aren't known for their shooting eyes," Richards said. "They do better with cement."

"The Mob boys aren't known for their sense of humor, either."

"Who's laughing?"

Bolan stepped past him and back into the hall. He had hoped to nail Cardona in the control room. When he wasn't there, Bolan was thrown back onto potluck. The drug czar could be any place in the house, if he was even there at all. Racing back up the stairs, he entered the corridor where Cardona's office was located.

It was the room in which Roberto Cabeza had made his last decision. And Bolan thought again of his promise. If things got any hotter, he'd be off the hook. It was the first time in his life Bolan hoped things got worse before they got better.

Pounding down the hall, he almost missed the frail figure on the floor at one end of the pool table in the recreation room. He thought at first it was a tablecloth. But something grabbed him, made him look again. He stopped in his tracks, almost colliding with the racing Richards.

He entered the room gun-first, scanning the dark corners. It seemed to be abandoned, except for the prostrate figure on the floor. The long white gown looked familiar. Maybe they had Cardona after all.

Bolan bent over the unconscious form. He took one slender arm and turned the body faceup. He was instantly sorry he had. Angry red welts and a mass of bruises nearly obscured the features of Valerie Russell.

CHAPTER FORTY-ONE

"What happened?" Bolan asked.

Valerie tried to sit up. Her arms gave out, and Bolan caught her. Through split and swollen lips, she said, "Cardona's out of his mind."

"I know that. And so should you have. What did he do to you?"

"He accused me of being a DEA agent. I thought he was going to kill me. Then you guys crashed the gate. Just in time."

"He's so far gone, he probably thinks everybody's DEA," Richards said.

"Only this time he was right."

Bolan's jaw fell. "What?"

"I said he was right, this time," Valerie repeated.

"We have to get you to a hospital," Bolan stated.

"Not now, the police will see to that. You have to stop Cardona before he gets to Plaza Murillo."

"It's too late for that. Besides, we can catch up to him soon enough. And we have a more immediate problem. Those weren't police who came in."

Startled, Valerie opened her eyes wide. They were glazed, almost vacant. She seemed to be staring into a great distance, seeing things no one else could see. She was getting progressively more disoriented.

"Who was it, then?" she asked.

"Bunch of Eyetalian dudes, pissed at Cardona, same as us. Only they also pissed at *us*," Richards volunteered.

"What's going on?" Valerie asked, trying again to sit up.

"Tell you later. Right now, we have to get you out of here."

Bolan turned to Richards. "Lee, see if you can find out what's happening. Maybe we can get out the same way we got in."

"What we going to do, bounce her over the fence?"

"You got any better ideas?"

"Not for a while, now. This whole mess is a bad idea, you ask me. You good guys got it harder than I thought, Jack."

He stepped cautiously into the hallway. A second later, he was gone from view.

While he waited for Richards to return, Bolan tried to get a fix on the current situation. Scattered gunfire still echoed through the huge house, most of it from the grounds. It was impossible to tell who was getting the better of the firefight, but Bolan really didn't give a damn. If they wanted to knock each other off, they were just making the mopping up he'd have to do a little easier.

He looked at Valerie, who had closed her eyes. Her lips parted, and he thought she was going to say something, but only a soft groan escaped. He didn't know whether to believe she was DEA or not. Until they got out, it wouldn't be possible to check out her story, and even if it wasn't true, she couldn't be left here. As far as he knew, the worst she might be guilty of was bad judgment. That wasn't a capital offense.

Usually.

Bolan heard sirens off in the distance. The police would be here before long, and his previous experience with Bolivian law enforcement was anything but reassuring. They had to get out, and get out quickly.

He checked Valerie for broken bones. Her limbs seemed in good order. He wasn't sure about her ribs. Her face was distorted, but the jaw was all right. A broken nose was likely.

When he finished, he took the tattered remains of her dress and tied it back together as best he could. The result wasn't going to win any fashion awards, but it hardly mattered. He heard footsteps in the hall and wheeled, the .44 AutoMag in his fist.

"Don't shoot, Jim, it's me." Lee was whispering. He ducked into the recreation room.

"What'd you find out?"

"The house is empty. Some fools running around in the woods out back. There's two cars out front, lights on and engines running. Probably the canolli cavalry. Think we can get one of them without too much trouble."

"I heard sirens. You see any police?"

"I heard 'em, too, but so far the coast is clear. Want to take a crack at it—so to speak?"

"Let's go."

Bolan hauled Valerie to her feet. She was heavier than she looked, her form more muscular than he imagined. He draped her over one shoulder. Pointing to the Uzi on the floor, he said, "You better take that."

Richards picked up the SMG, then looked at Bolan a long moment. "One thing you got to understand, Jack. Any cops out there, I'm gone. I ain't going to no burrito prison. Not now, and not ever."

Bolan said nothing.

"Just so you know," he said.

"Understood. And Lee, as far as I'm concerned, when this is over, I never even heard of you."

"How soon they forget." Lee grinned.

He slipped into the hallway, then waved Bolan on. The big man staggered a bit under his burden. Valerie moaned, trying to shift her weight. Bolan placed the flat of one hand on her back, patting her as he would an injured child. "Stay still. We'll be out of here soon."

Descending the main staircase, which swept in a huge semicircle, Bolan couldn't help but notice the wreckage spread out before him. The firefight had been furious. All four walls of the central gallery had been raked by fire. Bullet holes, in a drunken scribble, had shattered the pristine serenity. Plaster was cracked, and in some places had fallen away in chunks.

The defense had been costly, if not pointless. The firing seemed to have abated. If the visiting team won, they would be needing their cars. If not, the victors would be chasing down stragglers. Bolan tottered down the stairs just as a flare of light flashed through the main doorway, which was now thrown wide.

A squad of police burst through the entrance, carrying automatic rifles. Eight in all, they split into two teams of four. One team pushed on into the house, the other arranged itself across the entranceway. A ninth man, obviously an officer, strode in. His manner was more majestic than the situation required and than his rank, whatever it was, might have dictated.

Bolan had frozen on the staircase, Richards right in front of him.

"Buenas noches, señores, señorita."

Bolan shrugged.

The officer continued to speak in Spanish, a sneer too hammy to be credible twisting his pencil mustache. "You seem to be leaving in a hurry. Gasoline is expensive in La Paz, because of the OPEC, yes? You shouldn't leave your cars running. Oh, and please put your weapons down."

"They're not our cars," Bolan said.

"Would you care to put the young lady down?"

"She needs medical attention."

The officer strode across the polished wood floor, now littered with plaster and wreckage. His heels clicked on the hardwood. Bolan noticed the hand-tooled leather of his boots. They were not cheap.

Climbing halfway up the staircase toward Bolan, he continued. "She shall get all the attention she needs, medical and otherwise. Is there some reason you didn't call for an ambulance?"

"We wanted to take her ourselves."

"You are friends of Mr. Cardona?"

"Guests," Bolan said.

"What happened here?"

"I don't know."

"Diego is not here?"

"I haven't seen him."

"He is a good friend, to leave you here for all this excitement, no? Better than the TV."

"Look," Bolan snapped, "this woman has been badly beaten. She has to get to a hospital."

"Are you trying to tell me my business? I am a humble man. There is much I don't know, much I don't understand. But my business is one thing I understand very well. I think we *all* have some business to discuss at my office, hmm?"

"Can't it wait? I don't think Mr. Cardona would appreciate this sort of treatment of his friends."

"Perhaps not, but he is also my friend, and he understands that my business often requires difficult decisions." He turned on his heel to walk smartly back down the staircase. He crossed back to the entranceway to confer with one of the men at the door.

Bolan didn't like the way things were going. The guy seemed to mean it when he said he was Cardona's friend. That could mean one thing. He was in Cardona's pocket. The boots were all the evidence anyone needed that his income was more than a policeman's salary.

Two men climbed up the stairs. One gathered the assorted weapons while the other kept his rifle trained on the three captives. When the guns had been picked up, the man gestured with his rifle.

Bolan followed Richards down the stairs, Valerie bobbing on his shoulder. The rifleman indicated the door, telling them to hurry. Outside, they were bundled into a military truck. Two men armed with rifles climbed into the back after them. A moment later, the officer came down the steps and climbed into the front of the truck.

Another policeman took the wheel. The truck started with a jounce and rocked down the long drive to the street. Bolan noticed several other police vehicles, but they were in the only army truck at the scene.

Through the glass panel separating the cab from the rear, Bolan could hear the officer instructing the driver. They were laughing easily. It was just another routine job for them. The two policemen watched Bolan and Richards warily. Valerie lay on the truck bed where Bolan had propped her in one corner. Her head rolled loosely with every bounce of the tightly sprung vehicle.

"Don't think they taking us to no police station," Richards whispered.

"Wonder if they speak English," Bolan answered.

"Let's find out," Lee replied. He gestured to one of the riflemen. "Your mother know who your father is, my man?"

"No comprende."

"I asked you if your mother had to pay your father to get her pregnant."

The two riflemen leaned their heads together and whispered quickly in Spanish. Again, the first man answered, *"No comprende."*

Richards smiled at Bolan. "We don't say too much, I think we okay."

"They never searched me," Bolan whispered.

"You carrying?"

"A Beretta 93-R, under my coat."

"Nice piece." Richards grinned at the riflemen. "Get ready to make your move."

Lee mimed lighting a cigarette to the guards. He got a nod in response. He fished a pack of Camels out of his shirt pocket, then patted his pockets, looking for a light. Getting to his knees, he crawled slowly toward the riflemen. Planting himself to one side, he again mimed lighting up. The one nearer Lee dropped his guard just a little, and the muzzle of his weapon strayed off to one side. He reached into his pocket for a lighter.

Extending the pack, the young black man offered a smoke to the guard, who reached for it just as Richards let it go. The guard snatched at the pack, missing it narrowly. He cursed and bent to retrieve it. That was when Bolan shot his companion through the forehead.

Richards lashed out with his fist, catching the leaning guard in the throat. He swung again, connecting with the guard's nose. The crunch of collapsing cartilage and breaking bone was nearly drowned by the cry gurgling through a crushed larynx, as Richards stood.

He kicked out with his right foot, bracing himself against the side of the truck. The guard collapsed against the tailgate and Richards dived, grabbing the unconscious man by one leg as he pitched backward. If he had fallen out the driver would have noticed him in the rearview mirror.

The truck swerved suddenly, throwing Lee to the floor, but he hung on. Bolan rushed to help, grabbing the second leg. Together, they hauled the unconscious man back into the truck.

The lights of the city were gone. The truck was on the open road. It was grinding through the gears, downhill. The scrub pine was getting thicker.

Hurriedly improvising, they propped the dead guard against the side of the truck and the unconscious man opposite him, against the other side. Bolan found some cord in a loose coil on the floor and bound the man upright, lashing him immobile against the wooden struts supporting the canvas cover. There wasn't enough to tie both men.

Bolan stripped the belts from the two guards and fashioned a sling to hold the dead man upright. The truck bounced into a turn, rocking roughly in a rutted side road. It looked as though they were slated to be three more of the disappeared, a species that was very common in South America.

The vehicle lurched to a halt. Bolan and Richards sat against the front of the truck, their captured rifles ready. With a rattle, the tailgate fell away. The officer stood, hands on hips, painted a garish red by the taillights of the truck. The driver leaned in and muttered something in Spanish. Bolan and Richards fired simultaneously. The driver dropped like a stone, his head nearly severed by the sudden burst.

The officer looked surprised, but just for an instant. His sneer returned, as if by reflex, then slowly faded away into nothing. When Bolan hit the ground, the officer was flat on his back.

His dead eyes gazed wonderingly at the brilliant stars overhead.

CHAPTER FORTY-TWO

It was nearly 9:00 a.m. Valerie Russell's apartment looked like a cross between a hospital ward and a war room. Bolan watched the others and taking stock, he wondered whether he had finally run into the big buzz saw that would cut him to ribbons. He had always known it would happen one day, but never dwelled on it. But now, it seemed like he'd found the big one, the one he couldn't handle. Cardona was so slippery, so plugged in—and so unpredictable—he seemed invulnerable.

He looked quietly at Valerie and the others, who were more subdued than he was. She looked no better after her emergency treatment, but it was obvious she felt a bit better. She lay on her bed, pillows piled behind her to prop her up. Her hair was pulled back away from her face. It was apparent the beating had been brutal, but carefully administered. Cardona had wanted to hurt her, but not kill her.

Bolan wondered why, but only for an instant. Deep down he knew the answer. He had other plans, plans that had been interrupted by the assault on the gate. According to Valerie, with every blow he dealt, he had yelled at her. Each yell was another piece of his "master plan," as he called it. Valerie had protected herself as best she could, even provoking him once when she thought he had finished. She wanted to know everything.

Now, having told it all to someone else, she felt drained...and relieved. At least the secret was no longer hers alone. Someone else knew, someone, she had no doubt, who would be able to interfere, to stop him, before it was too late. She had told Bolan and he would do something.

Bolan wasn't so sure.

He looked at her, half in puzzlement and half in admiration. "You mean to tell me you knew who I was all along?"

She shook her head. She winced with the sudden movement.

"Brognola told you?"

"No. Someone else."

"Who?"

"I can't tell you that. It's part of an ongoing internal investigation. I can't compromise it."

"Was it Tommy Calabrese?" Callahan asked quietly. He and Richards had remained quiet during her narration. Dr. Gonsalves had warned the three men that she needed complete rest. Besides the broken bones Bolan had detected, she had a severe concussion, possibly a skull fracture, but she refused to be taken for X rays. Until Cardona was grounded, she wasn't going anywhere.

Valerie declined to answer the question, but Callahan already knew the answer. "It was, wasn't it? And he was also the subject of your investigation. You don't have to deny it . . . or answer it. I know it's true. And I was part of your investigation, too, wasn't I?"

This time she nodded.

"Well, Tommy's dead."

She looked startled, then turned to Bolan. He nodded his head.

"And you were right about him. I didn't want to believe it when Bolan told me, but you were right. About him. Not about me." His voice quavered with shame and anger. He couldn't decide whether it was worse to be suspected or to be innocent of those suspicions.

Bolan reached out a comforting hand. "Brian, it's over. Forget about it."

"For what it's worth," Valerie whispered, "I never believed you were guilty. But you and he were so close, so..."

Callahan walked out into the living room to stare silently out the window.

"We have to go," Bolan said.

"Be careful, all three of you."

"Be better'n that," Richards reassured her. "We be good, too." He stepped out to join Callahan.

"Be seeing you." Bolan patted her hair gently, tucking a few stray strands back behind her ear.

"You'd better be." She smiled weakly, her puffed lips twisting with the effort.

Bolan closed the door quietly. In the living room, he said to the others, "Time to go."

"We'll never stop him, you know that, don't you?" Callahan asked without turning away from the window.

"We'll see," Bolan said. "One thing's sure. We're going to do it alone or we're not going to do it at all. I'm damn tired of trying to figure who works for whom in this country."

"You think it's any different back home?" Callahan asked. "Shit, who did Tommy work for? Who do I work for, for that matter. It's gotten so I don't even know anymore."

"Hell, Callahan, you should be like the big guy here, and me. We work for ourselves."

"You proud of yourself, Richards? I wouldn't be, if I were you."

"You could never be me, Brian. Not in a million years."

"Why's that?" Callahan asked, interested in spite of himself.

"Hell, man, you too white. No soul, baby." He laughed uproariously until, remembering Valerie in the other room, he choked it off with one hand.

"All right," Bolan said.

He turned off the light and stepped out into the hall. They took the stairs down to the basement, each wrapped in his own thoughts. When they reached the rear door, Bolan asked, "You get everything we need, Lee?"

"Check. That Valerie, boy, she know some weird dudes. Some stuff's in the Bronco. The rest'll be there when we ready. I made some calls once we knew for sure what we need.''

"Brian," Bolan continued, "I don't want you to do anything except watch. You understand? You're still too weak."

"No way. I'm in all the way or not at all."

"Suit yourself, but you're on your own. Cardona's got two dozen mercenaries, and they're armed to the teeth. We can't afford any heroics. If you can't keep up, you'll get left behind."

"I'm a big boy, Mack."

Bolan nodded, then pushed open the fire door and stepped out into the alley.

"When he supposed to try this big play?" Richards asked.

Bolan waited until they were all in the 4X4. "Valerie didn't know. She wasn't even sure which building. All she knows is that it's a government building in Plaza Murillo. And he wants some high-ranking hostages."

"Shit, I thought the man owned the place, what he need hostages for?"

"Things have changed," Bolan said.

"How's that?" Richards asked.

"There are no rules, now. And he knows it."

The Bronco roared into life as Callahan turned the key. The blocky vehicle leaped forward, slipping easily through the alleyway and out into the avenue.

"You tell Brognola about this?" Callahan asked.

"No."

Callahan waited, but Bolan volunteered nothing further. The young DEA man looked at the man sitting beside him. "Mind if I ask why not?"

"No."

"All right. Why not?"

"This is my play. I might be legal again, but I never was a puppet. There are some things a telephone can't help. This is one of them. And at this point, I don't even *have* anything to tell him. The ball is in Cardona's court."

"Fair enough."

"Besides, this is personal now."

"Valerie?"

"Partly."

"What else?"

"Oh, I don't know." Bolan sighed. "Lee's brother, and all the kids like him. Kids who get caught in the meat grinder. There's always somebody like Cardona there, ready to turn the crank. The kids go in and out comes money. It stinks."

"That all?"

"No."

"What then?"

Bolan said nothing.

"I thought you said that wasn't all."

"I did. But it's all I'm going to say."

A siren sounded behind them. Callahan glanced in the sideview mirror, then at the speedometer. "Damn, I wonder what's going on. I thought it was me, but we're under the speed limit."

The police van continued to wail, growing larger in the mirror. Callahan slowed still further, pulling to the right a little to let the van speed by. Still out of sight, another vehicle was also screeching. It careened out of a side street and ripped past, catching the van in less than a block. Six policemen had crammed into the small car.

"Something's up," Callahan hollered.

"Follow them," Bolan ordered. "This may be it."

"If it is, we're too late," Richards said.

"It's never too late," Bolan returned.

"I hope you right. I didn't come all this way to watch no police grab my man right in front of my face."

"Your man?" Callahan asked.

"That's what I said. You want him, you get in line, Jim. I got dibs on this mother."

"Dibs my ass," Callahan snarled. "Finders keepers, Jack."

"Don't call me Jack, Jim."

Both men lapsed into silence. They felt foolish, but didn't give a damn. Callahan was back in the locker room before a big game, when all the pressure built and built. Finally, with no place else to go, it leaked out in snapping towels and jocks full of liniment. The game was one for big boys only, and big boys, when all was said and done, weren't very different from little boys.

Bolan knew the feeling, the way it teased and tickled you. He knew the single difference between little boys and big boys. The big boys played for keeps. And this game was already into overtime. Sudden death.

Winner take all.

The Bronco roared after the growing convoy of police vehicles. Entering Plaza Murillo, Bolan noticed a cordon thrown around the old stone fortress housing the Palace of Justice. The home of the Bolivian supreme court as well as local law enforcement headquarters, the structure was imposing more for its bulk than its height.

The van leading the parade careered through the plaza, which was nearly empty of traffic. It had already been closed off to the public. A pair of uniformed officers waved at them to stop, Callahan looking to Bolan for instructions before braking to a reluctant halt.

One of the pair approached the Bronco on the driver's side. He spoke through the rolled-down window.

"I am sorry, but the plaza is closed to civilian traffic."

"What's going on?" Callahan asked, every inch the curious tourist.

"I am not authorized to answer that. I am sorry. Please, turn around and go back to your hotel."

"But I have to see someone in the courthouse."

"That is not possible."

"What the hell am I supposed to do? I'll be in big trouble if I miss this appointment."

"Trust me, sir. Your appointment will be rescheduled. No business is being conducted today."

"But—"

"Sir, please, do as I ask. I don't want to have to arrest you, but..." The officer shrugged, palms up, to show that matters were out of his hands.

"Okay," Bolan said. "Brian, let's go."

Callahan waved to the officer and backed the Bronco into a U-turn, spinning around and going back the way he had come. Several other cars waited their turn to be informed of the same inconvenience, but Callahan wasn't interested in rubbernecking.

"What do you think?" he asked Bolan.

"Looks like Cardona's made his move. He's already inside. And if it was a normal day, he's got some pretty heavy hostages on his hands."

"Damn!" Richards exploded. "They never gonna let us near that place. Son of a bitch!"

"They don't have to let us," Bolan said. "All we have to do is wait until dark. By then, things will have settled down into a state of siege."

"So what? They still not gonna let us near the place?"

"One thing you should know about the night, Lee," Bolan said, turning to face the angry young man.

"What's that?"

"At night, you don't need permission."

"Do you mean what I think you mean?" Callahan asked.

"You bet your ass, he mean just that," Richards responded. "We gonna make our own rules tonight." He extended his hand for Callahan to slap, but the DEA man ignored it.

"Man don't know when he get a break," Richards mumbled.

"Save it, Lee," Bolan said. "They might be our rules, but they're still rules."

"Don't make no never mind to me, Jack. Long as I get that mother, I don't give a damn whose rules they are."

"There's one you should remember," Bolan continued.

"What's that?"

"I want Cardona alive."

"After we come this far? You jiving me?"

"That's one thing I never do," Bolan said. "I want him alive, and if you try anything, you deal with me."

"But why?" The question came from Callahan.

"Yeah, Jack. How come?"

Bolan said nothing. He didn't know how to answer the question.

CHAPTER FORTY-THREE

"The hostages are all on the fourth floor," Bolan informed them, putting down his binoculars.

"How can you tell?" Callahan asked.

"I've been watching the place for three hours. Besides, it makes sense. The higher they are, the farther the police have to go to get them out. They're easier to watch if they're in one place. Cardona can spread his men out to defend the place without worrying about watching his prisoners. They probably rotate guard duty."

"Gonna be a bitch to get in there, specially since we don't want to ask permission," Richards muttered. He was unhappy with the notion of trying to rescue the hostages. "I still say we take out the main man, the rest of them go home. They got no reason to stay, unless they getting paid."

"No way we can risk it, Lee." Bolan was adamant. "We have to take out as many of Cardona's men as we can, without him knowing about it."

"What are we gonna do, fly in the window?"

"Uh-uh. We're going in through the basement."

"How we do that?"

"Storm drain. You got that building plan, Brian?"

"Right here."

"That thing is forty years old. I wouldn't want to bet it's still right."

"It's the only bet we have."

Bolan spread the blueprint out on a table next to the window. With his index finger, he traced a broken blue line on the wrinkled paper. It had turned a deep ivory color with age, and the ink had faded somewhat, but it was still legible.

"Right here, this is the toughest part of the entry." Bolan indicated the junction of the storm drain with the Palace of Justice sewage system.

"Tough is right," Callahan observed, shaking his head. "The grate on that thing is at least forty years old, maybe more. It could have been installed long before the diagram was made. The bolts are probably frozen with rust."

"It won't matter," Bolan argued. "We don't have time to jerk around with a wrench, anyway. We don't have that much time at all. Cardona's ultimatum expires in four hours. We have to be inside well before then."

"So, what you gonna do? We can't blow it the hell out of the way. The man would hear it."

"Cut through it."

"Man, they don't make saws good enough to even try."

"No saw. Acetylene torch. We can cut through it in less than an hour."

"Where we get a torch? That's one thing I didn't ask for. And no hardware stores around here that I saw."

"Don't worry about it. I already took care of it. Valerie made the arrangements. It'll be there, with the rest of the equipment. We have to meet it right...here." Bolan shifted his attention to a street map of the city. He indicated a point four blocks from the rear of the court building.

"She some woman, that Valerie," Lee said. "She sending a welder, too? We could use one."

"You mean to tell me we have to lug an acetylene torch, and a tank through four blocks' worth of sewers? You have any idea how long that might take?" Callahan turned away in frustration.

"I know how long we've got," Bolan said. "It amounts to the same thing. If it takes any longer, we can all go home."

"I'm ready to leave right now," Lee replied. "I can wait. Get Cardona some other time. He can't stay in there forever. And I got lots of patience."

"Then show some now," Bolan snapped.

Richards looked at the floor. After a long moment, he faced Bolan squarely. "You right, Mack. I'm sorry. I'm so used to being my own boss, I guess this is getting on my nerves."

"Forget it." Bolan looked out the window one final time. It was evening, and the court building was virtually dark. Dim light showed in only two rooms, both on the upper floor. "Let's go."

Bolan led the way down the back stairs. Their vantage point was in a hotel two blocks away, across the plaza. Their view had been virtually unobstructed, but only of the front and one side.

Getting into Callahan's Bronco, he said, "Brian, just to be on the safe side, let's get a look at the building from all sides. Can you make a circuit without attracting attention?"

"Yeah, but we won't be able to see the bottom floor on one side. And it'll take time. The place is completely sealed off."

"Make it quick."

Callahan started the engine. He worked his way toward the court building, keeping as close to the police cordon as he could. It kept the media and the curious a block away from the building on all sides. Sweeping past the one side they hadn't seen revealed nothing new. It was entirely dark. Turning behind the building, Callahan crept along. A row of shops obscured the lower part of the building, but at the rear its three upper floors were also dark. In the early evening, the court building loomed like a blocky mountain of granite against the deep blue sky.

"All right, I guess we've seen everything we can." Bolan checked his map. "Let's get to our rendezvous."

"You got it."

Richards kept his own counsel in the rear of the 4X4. A less sensitive person than Bolan would have thought he was brooding. But Bolan knew better. Getting ready to enter a potentially fatal encounter involved more than a little soul-searching. The more often you did it, the more you thought about it. And no one who had never been there could understand it. It wasn't like police duty, which involved a vague apprehension of potential, one that lingered and rubbed away at the back of the mind like coarse sandpaper. Going into battle was the closest, and perhaps the only, analogy.

The feeling wasn't rooted in fear. It was more like an examination of conscience. The more violent the encounter was likely to be, the deeper the solitude, the more intense the scrutiny.

They found the corner they were looking for.

"Back there," Bolan pointed. "The van should be in back of the grocery store."

Callahan turned into a narrow alley. It seemed as if the fenders of the 4X4 were a whisker away on either side. His breathing was constricted and shallow. He felt as if he were suffocating.

At the end of the alley they found themselves in a small courtyard—walls on every side, an alley like the one they had just come through entering in the middle of each. A white van was parked nose first against the back of the grocery store.

Bolan got out of the Bronco. He walked to the van and leaned through the driver's window. He talked for a few moments, but neither Callahan nor Richards could hear the conversation.

Lee broke the silence in the Bronco. "That is one mean dude. Glad he's on our side."

"I heard about him for years," Callahan said. He spoke softly, as if afraid of being overheard. "Never thought I'd actually meet him. I never thought he'd live this long."

"Yeah, know what you mean. But dig it, I bet you he never worries about it. I mean, he thinks about it, sure. But he don't worry. Man don't know *how* to worry."

Bolan waved to the Bronco, and the conversation ended abruptly.

The two men got out as the van's rear door opened. In the dull glow of the interior dome light, they could see a small man struggling with two large cylinders. Bolan leaned into the van and grabbed a heavy crowbar.

"Help Juan with the gear," he said. "I'm going to get started."

Bolan walked to the center of the darkened courtyard. Dropping to one knee, he felt around with one hand. Locating what he sought, he guided the crowbar under the lip of a manhole cover and strained against the heavy metal disk. A grinding sound rasped in the darkness as years of accumulated sand and grit ground against the seat of the disk.

A hollow boom echoed in the courtyard as the cover slipped off the bar. Bolan repositioned himself and tried again. This time, already loosened by his earlier effort, the disk rose high enough for him to slide the bar under all the way. Letting it go, he slid the disk to one side with a rattle as the crowbar fell free.

The heavy cover slid with a deep grinding rumble. When it was clear of the hole, Bolan let it drop to the stone pavement. The others had removed the equipment from the van and were walking toward him.

"All set?" Bolan asked.

Callahan nodded in the darkness.

As if he had seen the gesture, Bolan said, "All right, let's get going."

He aimed a bright flashlight into the manhole, holding it below ground level to keep down the glare in the dark courtyard. Leaning over the hole, he peered in. "Looks like it'll do. Not that we have any choice."

He straightened and swung his legs around, then dropped to the first rung of a metal ladder. Waist deep in the manhole, he reached out for two coiled hoses dangling from Callahan's crooked elbow. "I'll take these. When I get down, lower the gas tanks."

"Right."

Bolan dropped out of sight, a shadow falling into a black hole. They heard his feet splash into shallow water.

"All right, send it down." The voice was muffled and echoed eerily from underground. Callahan maneuvered his tank toward the lip of the hole. Its wheeled carriage was awkward and resisted his steering efforts. Finally, wheels perched on the very edge, he whispered, "Here she comes."

He gave the tank a shove with his knee, conscious of Richards grabbing on to the rear end of the heavy rope sling. With a hollow clang, like a bell tolling, the cylinder swung free and dropped like a plumb weight. The second tank followed quickly.

Richards climbed down through the manhole. He was gone from view almost immediately. Callahan sat on the lip, letting his feet feel for the ladder. Turning his body, he descended until only his head remained aboveground. He looked up at the sky, framed like a picture in the ragged roof edges of the courtyard.

Another step, and the stars were gone.

CHAPTER FORTY-FOUR

The torch hissed then popped, its bright flame rigid in the darkness. Eerie colors bathed the walls as Bolan started on the grate. Rather than try to cut through the two dozen interlaced bars one at a time, Bolan went after the rusted bolts. Eighteen of them poked in reddish brown lumps through the mounting ring. Each one was an inch in diameter. They had been mounted from the other side, and Bolan aimed his torch at the first.

The rust heated and popped, sparking in every direction. The white-hot flame chewed hungrily at the corroded metal. An acrid stench filled the tunnel, as small plumes of smoke curled upward to hang at the ceiling.

The first massive nut glowed red, then orange, then exploded into white heat. Bolan moved to its opposite number on the other side of the huge circular grid. Callahan, wearing heavy gloves to shield his hands from the incandescent metal, held a two-inch cold chisel against the glowing metal.

Richards moved in beside him, a small sledgehammer in his hand. He rapped smartly on the chisel. The hammer nearly missed, sliding off the edge of the chisel. He swung again and this time got it right. The still-white metal flew free, landing with a pop and a gurgling hiss in the three-inch stream of water flowing through the bottom of the tunnel.

In two minutes, the next nut was ready. Bolan shifted the torch in his hand and stepped back. When Callahan and Richards had moved into position, Bolan started on the third nut. It had taken them five minutes for the first pair. With eighteen cuts to make, they were already going to be an hour closer to the deadline.

If everything went smoothly.

The three men settled into a routine, shifting from side to side and back again. The first nine were gone and Bolan lifted his goggles to check the time. They were ahead of schedule, but not by much. Flipping the goggles back down, he started on the second half. His technique had improved, and the flame was steady, burning like a small, insistent comet in the underground cosmos.

Their feet were wet, and the grime was accumulating on their hands and clothing. A persistent drip from overhead had soaked their heads and shoulders.

Finally all eighteen nuts were gone, as were the bolt tips on which they had sat. A dozen and a half charred circles had taken their places, the metal blackened, but brighter than it had been in years, smooth from the flame tip, full of shiny scratches made by the chisel's blade.

One hole, the last, still glowed dully. Bolan played his flashlight around the edge of the grate, where it met the heavy steel plate to which it had been bolted. He was looking for the four pry slots, located at ninety-degree intervals around the circumference. He stepped closer, bringing the beam in tight and spotted the first one, all but obscured by thick, greasy mud. He scraped the ooze away with a knife blade, then cleaned the other three grooves.

"Let's get to it." He stepped back, grabbing a heavy crowbar from a tool rack on the torch cylinder. It struck a tank and the metallic ring bounced from the hard stone walls and ceiling, muffled only a little by the moss and oozing mud clinging to them. As the knell-like sound died away, the steady gurgle of running water took its place.

Richards yanked the second crowbar free. Bolan positioned his bar and Richards took his place across the diameter. Callahan handled the light.

At the signal both men put their weight behind their bars. The heavy plate wouldn't budge under the steady pressure.

"Son of a bitch is stuck," Richards said, flexing his hands.

"Let's try something else," Bolan suggested. "Lee, get on this bar with me. We have to break it free, maybe work one bar in all four slots to unfreeze it."

Richards sloshed through the water to a position beside Bolan. Both men held the bar, maneuvering to apply maximum leverage at a right angle. They pushed harder, slowly increasing the pressure. But the grate held.

"We have to get it out," Bolan stated. His voice was quiet, but the edge of anger and frustration crackled in the confined space. "Once more, Lee. This time, let's snap it. Maybe the sudden impact will do the trick. Brian, count down. On go, we'll hit it hard."

"I got a better idea," Callahan said. He stepped into the narrow gap between them. "We need a little more muscle, and we don't need light. My shoulder's okay."

He stuck the light in his pocket, its beam pointing up at the roof. Their shadows danced in a grotesque knot on the laced bars in front of them.

"Ready?" Bolan asked. "On three, one...two...three."

The three men surged forward, putting all their strength into the effort. The heavy disk began to grind in its seat. Gritty mud and sand trapped between it and the seat began to sift down onto their hands.

"Hold it," Bolan gasped. "Once more ought to do it. Ready?"

Again they surged forward, and this time, with a hollow rumble, the grate began to move. "Watch your feet," Bolan said, the words forced between his gritted teeth.

Like the shell of a hungry giant clam, the disk hinged open a half inch, then two inches. Gravity began to take hold and the plate slid to one side and down. The three men leaped back as the huge grating dropped to the stone floor and tipped toward them, finally landing with an enormous splash into the stream.

"That's it. Let's get the weapons." Bolan snatched the light from Callahan's pocket and trained it on the tool rack. Three Uzi submachine guns, looking almost innocent, nestled amid the bars and wrenches. Tools of another trade. A small canvas sack, crammed with ammo magazines and assorted gear, was draped across the handle of a hammer, dangling down toward the water.

Bolan splashed to the carriage, then grabbed an Uzi and handed it to Richards. He passed the second one to Callahan and took the third for himself. Opening the sack, he reached in and tugged out four clips and combat knives for Callahan and Richards. Slinging the sack over his shoulder, he stepped toward the gaping hole where the grate had been. It was nearly six feet high, and Bolan ducked a little to step through.

The others followed, the beam of his light all but obscured by his broad shoulders. The splash of their feet diminished as the tunnel widened. The water was not nearly as deep, the circular floor flattening to a slightly concave surface.

Suddenly Bolan held up his hand. The two younger men huddled around him.

"It's only thirty yards away. As nearly as I can figure it, we just passed under the stairs of the court building. This tunnel goes right on through and out the other side. We're looking for a side feed. That's about five yards long. At the end of it, we go up a ladder. There's another grate, but this one isn't bolted in place."

"How you know all this?" Richards asked.

"Valerie has solid resources. And amazing connections."

"You trust her?" Callahan whispered.

"I have to." Bolan turned abruptly, resuming his careful plod through the ever-widening tunnel.

A minute later, he disappeared.

The beam danced back out of the side tunnel, and Callahan sprinted forward, Richards right behind him. Once in the side tunnel, the feeling of confinement pressed in on them. They could touch either side with extended arms. An oval tube, it was taller than it was wide, but the ceiling was uncomfortably close.

Bolan moved ahead, walking slowly. He was looking for the overhead opening, and after ten steps he found it. Pointing the beam upward, he noticed the lowest rung of the ladder, just above the lip of the tunnel.

"You guys ready?" Without waiting for an answer, he grabbed the ladder and hauled himself up. His legs swung twice, a human pendulum, then he was in. Holding on to the ladder with one hand, he aimed the light back down at the ladder. Callahan indicated Richards should go first.

"And how you gonna manage by yourself with that arm, Mr. Drug Enforcement?"

"Don't worry about me."

"I'm worried about me. You don't make it, I got to come back down and shove your ass up there anyway. I'd just as soon get it over with."

Callahan knew he was right. He nodded. Richards positioned himself beneath the opening and made a stirrup of his laced fingers. Callahan placed one foot in the cupped hands.

"On three," he said. He rocked on his legs, gaining momentum. On the count of three, he sprang upward, balancing himself precariously on Richards's boost. He grabbed the ladder, putting most of his weight on the good arm. He was surprised at Richards's strength, but didn't want to show it. He felt the pressure from below increase, as he rose steadily upward.

Bringing one leg as high as he could, he managed to get a knee on the bottom rung. One more push from Richards, and he was home free.

Ahead, starkly outlined by the flashlight, Callahan could see Bolan's shadowy figure. He scrambled up the ladder to make room for Richards. The three of them were now strung out like beads on a chain. The access tube had been built with smaller men in mind.

They would be entering through the basement. It was unlikely Cardona would have a man down there, but they were too close to take a risk. He extinguished the light. Feeling with his hands, Bolan found the metal grid at the top of the ladder. It was held in place only by spring clips. He found one clip with his left hand, then placed his right palm flat against the grid.

Pressing steadily, he felt the clip give and the grid rise up. He traced the outline of the metal barrier and found three of the four clips free. He shoved just in front of the fourth and it came loose. Balancing the grid on his open palm, Bolan continued up the ladder.

His head and shoulders now projected up through the floor of the court building basement. Gently maneuvering the grid, he placed it silently on the concrete floor and scrambled out of the access tunnel.

Bolan reached out and found Callahan's shoulder. He guided him up, whispering "Careful. Easy now."

Then Richards joined them.

"What now, Jack?" he whispered.

"The main event."

"Where to?"

In answer, Bolan clicked the light on, flashing it in a quick semicircle. He spotted a large metal door and doused the light again. "Follow me," he whispered.

"Can't follow what I can't see. Use the damn light."

"Too risky."

"Then we do this," Richards whispered. He placed his hand on Bolan's shoulder and Callahan's on his own. "You the boss, but you fall in a hole, we gonna land on your ass."

Bolan began to move, keeping his pace steady to maintain the contact. It felt strange having a hand on his shoulder in the darkness. He had to remind himself not to brush it off.

When his own extended hand encountered a cold surface, he chanced another quick burst of light. They had found the wall, six feet to the left of the door. Bolan noted

the handle and put out the light again. He groped blindly for
the door handle, seeing it in his mind's eye, and knowing it
wouldn't be where he thought it was. The doorframe met his
fingers. He slid his hand along it, finally hitting the knob
with his wrist.

"I got it."

"Now what?"

"I'll go out and see what's around. You wait here." He
glanced at his watch. "It's two-thirty. If I'm not back in
fifteen minutes, you're on your own."

He yanked the heavy door open. The corridor outside was
not quite as dark. He slipped through the door and closed
it behind him.

The light startled him when he clicked it on. One end of
the hallway ended in a blank wall. At the other, a narrow
flight of concrete stairs climbed to the main floor. That was
where it all would begin, where the first resistance would be
encountered.

Cardona probably had a handful of men strung around
the first floor. It was the front line of defense and an ideal
place to watch the street for signs of activity. Bolan checked
his watch. A little more than two hours left. And the going
would be slow. Gunfire would alert the entire building. That
left him with the suppressed Beretta and a knife.

Precious little.

Bolan padded toward the stairway. When he reached the
first step, he put out the light. Above him, a small bar of
light slipped through a crack under the door. He watched it,
holding his breath and climbing a step at a time, expecting
it to explode into full bloom at any moment.

Once on the landing, Bolan pressed his ear to the door,
not really expecting to hear anything.

He wasn't surprised.

He turned the knob, hoping like hell the door didn't
squeak. Easing it open a crack, he peered into a small vestibule. The light was a safety lamp, a single bulb overhead,
and beyond it was another door. Then he remembered they

had seen no lights on the first floor from the outside. He stepped into the vestibule, guiding the inner door closed with one hand.

It was just as silent beyond the second door. The defenders were no doubt sitting in the darkness, keeping back away from the windows. He unscrewed the safety light and slipped onto the main floor.

Bolan debated whether to go back and get the others. The farther he progressed, the less he could do. The fifteen minutes was steadily eroding. Down to ten and soon five. He was about to go back to the basement when he spotted a dull red glow about twenty yards away.

A cigarette.

Using the light was out of the question. Cautiously, he felt his way toward the glow. He found a wall with one hand, and followed it. The smoker was only ten feet away now, just out of sight behind a corner. Bolan hoped he was alone.

The red glow came and went yet again. Bolan's fingers gripped the corner of the wall, his knife in the other hand. He inched up to the corner and sprang, catching the man in mid-puff. The small glow of the cigarette's tip threw red light over a startled face, which was nearly hidden by a bushy beard. Bolan aimed the knife just below it, striking home and swiping sidewise.

The bearded man brought his hands to the gushing wound, blood and air gurgling in his severed windpipe. He slumped forward, dead, and Bolan caught him.

CHAPTER FORTY-FIVE

"We can't go after the hostages until we take out the men on the lower floors," Bolan whispered.

"How can we do that in two hours?" Callahan argued. "We don't even know where they are. It might take two hours just to find them. And we have to take them down without any noise. You must be dreaming, Bolan."

"If you got any ideas, let me know."

"Too bad we don't have some of them darts you were telling me about," Richards said.

"Yeah, too bad." Callahan didn't even try to conceal his sarcasm. "What the hell would we do with them if we did have them? Your people carried spears, not blowguns."

"Never can tell, Mr. Football, never can tell. Fact, your head look mighty fine on my mantelpiece, all shrunk up like a little bitty baseball. With blue eyes."

"You two knock it off," Bolan snapped. "You've been sniping at each other for two days."

"Bolan's right, Richards." Callahan stuck out a hand. "We are on the same side. I just can't forget how you used to make your living. But maybe in your shoes, I would do the same thing."

"No way, man. I can hide easy at night. Better'n you." He grasped Callahan's proffered hand. "But the big guy *is* right. We got better places to bury the hatchet than in each other's backs."

Bolan squeezed a button on his watch to check the time. "Look, I got one guy, but that was luck. If one of the lookouts hears something, he might get trigger-happy. There isn't much time before the deadline. They've got to be nervous."

"All you're saying is what I said before. It's damn near impossible, unless we get real lucky."

"Better to be good than lucky," Richards suggested. "Why don't you let me take a hack at it. I'm used to working in the dark. And I got this . . ." He flashed a light for an instant on his opened palm.

"What is it?" Callahan asked.

"A suppressed Coonan automatic, .357 Magnum," Bolan said.

"Pretty good," Richards commented.

"All right! Here's what we'll do. We'll take it floor by floor. Lee and I will sweep, and Brian will wait on the landing. We finish one floor then we go up a flight and take the next. My guess is the second and third floors might be deserted. The main floor lookouts can see everything in the street on all sides. The hostages are on the fourth. We have to check two and three, but it shouldn't take long. Any questions?"

"Just one," Callahan said. "How long do I wait before coming in after you?"

"You don't come in, no matter what. If we're not back here in thirty minutes, you go back through the tunnel and get the national guard in here, fast."

Bolan opened the door and stepped through, Richards right behind him. They split up, Richards taking the leg of the hall Bolan had already explored while Bolan himself took the other leg.

Both ends of the corridor glowed softly. Some sort of light was flickering outside the building, its reflected glow bouncing into the corners of the main floor.

As Bolan neared the end of his leg of hallway, the glow got brighter. Maybe they would get lucky after all. Ambient light, no matter how dim, was better than none. It would help the guards, too, but they were more concerned with action in the street and the Plaza Murillo. Unless and until they realized they had been penetrated, the edge was with the would-be rescuers.

A loud rumble shook the building as Bolan rounded his first corner. Metallic, more a clank than a rumble, it sounded vaguely familiar. It was muffled by the thick stone walls, and distorted by the mazelike course it had taken to reach him, but he knew he'd heard it before. He stopped to sweep the area ahead of him. For twenty yards it was a hallway identical to the one he'd just left, only less impenetrably dark.

The situation changed at twenty-five yards. Dramatically. The wall seemed to glow. It took him a moment to understand that it wasn't a wall at all, but a full-length window. The source of the reflected illumination was now apparent.

The police had moved searchlights into position on that side of the building. The shimmering effect was the result of the lights being swept back and forth across the wall. With every pass, the several lights occasionally intersected one another, causing the rising and falling of intensity.

When two beams entered the same window at the same time, it was as bright as day. And when they had passed on, it was just as suddenly pitch-black. The contrast widened the gap still further.

Now it hit him. The noise. It *was* familiar. It was the sound of metal treads on pavement. Either a tank or a half-track, maybe an APC, had entered the Plaza Murillo. Bolan hoped they weren't planning to attack the court building. All hell would break loose, and the hostages would be doomed. Bolan prayed it was just a psychological ploy, a show of force to throw fear into the hearts of Cardona's army.

And if he was wrong, he probably wouldn't live to realize how wrong he'd been.

A movement caught his eye. A blocky outline at the far end of the room seemed to shift position. Bolan stopped abruptly. For a second he thought he might have imagined it. A searchlight zipped past, and the shadow moved again. Bolan wasn't sure. It could have been a filing cabinet, or a piece of furniture. As the light passed by, it might have appeared to have moved.

He waited patiently. Another searchlight passed, this time from the opposite side of the building. The outline moved again. It was no mistake. A man stood pressed to the wall, keeping well back from the probing fingers of the searchlights.

Bolan dropped to the floor. Sliding in tight against the outer wall, he shinned forward. He kept well below the row of windowsills, stopping each time a beam passed overhead. He knew the instincts well enough to know that the eye of the watching man would be drawn toward the movement of the brilliant rectangles on the wall. No amount of discipline could control the light-starved eye. It would snatch at each flash like a beggar at a crumb.

As he drew closer, he was able to pick out more detail. The man wore camou pants and a flak jacket. Patches of white marked those areas of his T-shirt that the jacket failed to cover. Whatever else he was, he was too bright, and not smart enough by half. Those bright white patches were all a sharpshooter would need to take him down.

Bolan eased the Beretta forward. Creeping another few feet, he stopped for a passing light, then lay flat. He held the automatic securely and pushed against the wall with his feet, gaining another yard. The closer he got, the better his chances.

He wanted light. No time for a guess shot. The lights continued to sweep across the face of the building, and he waited for one moving toward his target.

A block of light slashed the wall beside him, then the window in front of him. Window by window it moved forward. One more. For a split second, the patches of T-shirt jumped out of the corner shadows.

Bolan squeezed. Once, then again, he heard the quiet spit of the Beretta, no louder than a cobra, and twice as deadly. The light was gone, but the figure had slumped. No groan, nothing.

Bolan slithered ahead. The lump of darkness in the corner flashed into a man-shape then back into darkness as another light slid by. Fifteen feet away, he was sure. Light danced in and reflected off the glass of a large framed map on the wall. Two dark red blotches smeared the man's chest. As if the light had been there just for confirmation, it was gone again.

That made two. Two out of twenty-four. Not counting the main man, Cardona himself. Bolan wondered whether Cardona was even there. Men like him rarely had the guts to stay around for the final play. But even as he wondered, he was sure Cardona was in the building. This was his show. The others were just hired guns. Without Cardona, they had no reason to be there at all. Unconsciously Bolan looked up toward the ceiling, as if trying to look through the stone and steel above him. They were no more impenetrable than the human motives that brought them all together in so bizarre and deadly a fashion.

Bolan turned the corner and moved on. He wondered how Richards was doing. So far there hadn't been a sound. If Lee had been discovered, there had been no commotion. The new corridor was short, opening into the broad main lobby. Higher ceilinged than the rest of the first floor, the lobby lay under the massive dome of the Palace of Justice. Four staircases spiraled from a second-floor gallery to the slick marble floor.

The play of light and dark was more frantic, beams spearing in from all sides. The light bounced crazily, mixing gray and black shadows together like a crazed painter searching for the perfect tone.

The polished stone floor bounced back light reflected from a hundred surfaces. And there was no way around it. Bolan had to cut straight through the open area to get to the next corner. He looked up at the gallery, wondering if anyone was there, and if so, how many. The movement was constant, and patternless, as the aimless, wandering light came in and died or speared out through a second window.

A chest-high circular receiving desk stood empty at the center of the lobby. At the very heart of the chaos, it was the brightest spot, receiving the most light most often. It was the ideal vantage point from which to examine the gallery above.

It was also the eye of the storm.

And the bull's-eye.

Bolan made straight for it, sprinting in a tight crouch, his soft-soled shoes soundless on the hard stone floor. The slashing blades of light cut this way and that, their passes over his body so harsh and abrupt that he felt as if they had cut him.

The desk was bounded by a moat of shadow, pooled at floor level. From ten feet away, Bolan dived, sliding on the stone and slamming into the gleaming mahogany shoulder first. The echo of the impact seemed to climb each staircase in succession, then spiral back down for another ascent. Bolan held his breath.

The echo died.

The gallery was railed in burnished brass, its gleam fragmented and intermittent. It added to the confusion banisters shedding slabs of shadow on the wall above, reflecting splinters of illumination from every angle.

Bolan crept along the circumference of the desk, feeling its surface with his free hand, clutching the Beretta tightly in the other. Halfway around, he found a hinge set in the wood. Sliding forward a bit, he sought the other edge of the door. It was a tight fit, and he almost missed it. Running his fingers up toward the top of the desk, he searched for the handle that would let him open the door.

He found a knob. With his thumb, he located a keyhole in its center. Holding his breath, he turned the knob. He exhaled when he found it wasn't locked. He opened the door slowly, sliding around to make room for it. Opened just wide enough to slip through, the door bumped his shoulder as he hauled himself forward by grabbing the edge of the doorjamb.

Bolan got to his knees and looked over the top of the desk. Instinctively he divided the gallery into quadrants. The first, second and third sections were deserted.

Something caught his eye as he scanned the fourth quadrant: a stationary light, a rectangle set in the wall. It was the only static thing in the lobby. Rigid, motionless and dim, it seemed unrelated to the circus swirl of searchlights outside.

Then he realized what it was. A doorway, backlit from a hallway or a room beyond. Before he could decide his next move, two figures flitted through and were lost in the tangled maze of shadows against the gallery wall. Bolan watched and waited.

At the head of the nearest staircase they reappeared. Bolan watched in fascination. Like children sneaking downstairs to catch Santa in the act, they tiptoed down the spiral. They hadn't seen him, or they wouldn't have exposed themselves so easily. Yet they weren't moving like people in undeniable charge of the situation.

Bolan slid back to the door and, crouching, headed for the bottom of the stairway. In the scattered splashes of light, he could see them looking around nervously, peering back over their shoulders as if running from something...or someone. Bolan reached the foot of the stairs as they tiptoed into the last bend.

They quickened their pace. The prod of Bolan's Beretta froze them in midstride.

"Buenas noches, señores," Bolan hissed.

CHAPTER FORTY-SIX

"Buenas noches, Señor Bolan."

The words startled him. He spun, uncertain where they had come from.

"Over here, Jim. It's me."

"Lee, I could have killed you."

"Man, you know, I'm getting kind of tired of all this mess anyhow." Richards slipped up beside the big man. Continuing to whisper, he asked, "Who the *muchachos*?"

"Two staff guards. They overpowered the man who was assigned to take them to the men's room."

Richards laughed. "Don't that beat all? This scene going down, and the man lets people go to the toilet. Maybe he too civilized to pull this off."

"Don't bet on it."

"They going to help?"

"Yeah. I already learned what we need to know. Let's get Callahan."

"He ain't going to be much help, man. Not with that arm."

"He's got a lot of heart."

"This ain't Valentine's Day."

"I know you don't like Callahan, but we're all on the same team. Try to keep that in mind."

"It's not that I don't like him. I don't even know the man. But I don't like putting my life in the hands of somebody who only has one working."

"He's done all right so far."

"You right." Richards paused thoughtfully. "I guess I just don't like him."

"Come on." Bolan led the way back to the basement stairs to hook up with Callahan. As soon as they entered the vestibule, Callahan bombarded them with questions.

"Let me lay it out quickly. According to these guys," Bolan said, indicating the two guards, "there were twenty-six terrorists altogether. I got three of them on the first floor. These guys took one out when they made their break. That leaves twenty-two."

"Twenty," Richards interjected. "Got my ownself a brace on the main floor."

"Okay, twenty. They're all on the fourth floor, now."

"Cardona there?" Callahan asked.

"He's there."

"Awright. It's party time." Richards rubbed his hands together. "How heavy is it going to be?"

"Very," Bolan said.

"These guys are disciplined and well trained. Cardona's paying the tab, but they take their orders from a big guy with a beard. A Mexican. He seems to be the straw boss. From what our new friends say, he was in Bolivia before, with Che. I wouldn't underestimate these guys."

"What kind of weapons are we talking about?"

"Kalashnikovs, mostly. A couple of Uzis, and one or two grenade launchers."

Richards whistled. "Not too shabby. Sounds more like a small army than a bunch of hired hands. How we going in?"

"From the roof. There's a balcony along the length of the room. Big windows all along. We'll drop to the balcony and rush the windows."

Richards looked pointedly at Callahan. "You ready for some rock climbing, man?"

"Don't worry about me, Lee. I can handle myself, okay?"

Richards persisted. "'Cause I got you up that ladder, man, but I'm tired. I don't know if I got the energy to keep draggin' your butt all over Bolivia, Jack."

"Look, Richards, give it a rest, will you? You worry about your butt, I'll worry about mine."

"Fine by me. Just asking, is all."

"Where are we going to get the rope to get down to the balcony?" Callahan asked, turning his back to Richards.

"There's a workroom on the third floor," Bolan replied, "just off the stairs. These guys say there should be plenty there. A crew has been working with scaffolds repainting the stairwells."

"We catch another break," Richards said.

"I got a feeling our luck is about played out," Callahan mumbled.

"Dig Reverend Peale, here. You got to think positive, Jack. Believe in yourself. How you expect to be happy, always looking to come out on the short end?"

"God has a sense of humor, Lee. He never made a stick with a long end."

"I hear you."

"Let's go." Bolan handed two captured automatic rifles to the escaped guards. "You'll need these."

Each rifle had two magazines taped together for easy reloading. "You see any more ammo for these AK-47s, you better grab it."

"If the Good Lord is willing, *señor*, we won't even need this much."

"Don't count on it. We'll take the stairs. And keep it quiet." Bolan opened the door leading out into the first floor corridor. The blackness immediately pressed in on him. He could feel it on his face, as surely as if it had been heat or cold.

The stairwell was darker than night, but it was a welcome relief from the circus play of sweeping searchlights in the central arcade. Bolan took the stairs cautiously, keeping one hand on the cold metal railing set in the wall.

The dark staircase smelled of paint and turpentine. Stopping on the first landing, Bolan inhaled deeply. The acrid bite of the fumes was sharp, clearing his head like smelling salts. Behind him, he could hear the deliberate tread of his small team. It was precious little to take into combat against a trained assault force. Whoever dealt the cards hadn't been in his corner this time out. He started walking, more quickly now, as if haste didn't make waste.

On the third-floor landing he stopped again. He placed one palm flat against the wall, feeling the cool, smooth surface of the new paint. It was dry, but just barely. Running his hands over the wall, he hit a tacky spot, his fingertips sticking as if to the adhesive side of old Scotch tape. The tackiness pulled, but didn't really hold him.

He brushed the sticky fingers against his pants, feeling the dirt of the tunnel crumble against the gluey deposits the paint had left. And it gave him an idea.

He whispered for the guards to step back down a few stairs. Hurriedly he grilled them on the layout of the fourth floor. His idea was not without its risks, but if it worked, it would save them time, and might buy them a little more. Finishing the conference, he told Richards and Callahan what he wanted to do.

"I don't like it," Callahan whispered. "It can backfire."

"Brian, anything we do here might backfire."

"The man's right, Callahan," Richards argued. "If we can mess with their heads, get 'em thinkin' about something else, we got a better chance. Right now, them dudes hold all the cards. They inside that room with the hostages. They got everything they need. If we can get them running around a little, upset the balance, we might turn it around easier."

"And what if it doesn't work?"

Bolan fielded the question. "If we handle it right, we don't lose a thing. They won't have a clue we're here. It'll look like an accident."

Callahan was silent for a long time. In the darkness, it was as if he had left altogether. Finally, with a reluctant sigh, he said, "What the hell, let's give it a shot."

"That's my man," Richards said, clapping him on the shoulder.

"Lucky for you that was my good arm," Callahan said.

"I know that. I ain't all bad, you know?"

"I'm starting to believe it," Callahan whispered.

Lee thought he might have been smiling a little. He chose to think so.

"All right, then, it's settled." Bolan hesitated, then whispered to the two guards again. When he had finished, he said, "We'll get everything set and then work out the timing. I'm going to cut through the third floor with Lee and Felipe. Brian, you two go on up to four. Get the rope and get it ready. Ricardo will show you where it is."

Without waiting for an answer, he stepped to the hallway door and opened it. At the far end, a dim red glow marked the emergency light over the opposite fire door. As the heavy metal barrier swung shut with a hiss of pneumatic hinges, he had the feeling they had just turned the last corner. He couldn't explain it, but something told him the tide was changing in their favor.

The three warriors whisked down the hallway, their feet thumping softly on the marble floor. Occasionally a dull block of light flew by as the glass window of an office door was struck by reflected light from the searchlights outside. Small rectangles of light appeared, flitted like geometric insects and vanished almost immediately.

At the far door, Bolan waited for his two companions. In his haste, he had gotten several yards ahead of them. He was starting to breathe deeply again, only now aware that he had been gasping, unconsciously responding to the tension with quick shallow breaths.

When the others joined him, he said, "This is it."

He pulled the door open, a sharp groan escaping from one reluctant hinge. The metal squeal died suddenly and the door swung wide. He ducked through, holding it for Lee and Felipe, then guiding it closed with one hand.

"You're sure there's enough stuff up there, Felipe?"

"Sí. Many cans, mostly full. They are only half finished painting."

"All right, we'll get as much solvent and thinner as we can, and take some paint if we need it."

"Ought to use some of the paint anyhow," Lee whispered. "Makes more smoke."

"That'll hurt us as much as it will them," Bolan answered.

"Maybe, but the less they can see, the better off we are. Odds are more in favor if they can't see us too good."

"Okay, we'll try it," Bolan agreed.

He padded silently to the fourth-floor landing. The holding area for the hostages was a third of the way down the hall, to the rear of the building. If there was a chance of discovery, it would never be greater than now. At the top of the stairs Bolan risked a light.

In the corner—just as Felipe had said—five-gallon cans were stacked three high. At least twenty cans. Bolan grabbed two cans of turpentine and lugged them down the stairs. He unscrewed the caps, then flipped on the light to pry the metal inserts from the mouths of the cans.

"You know," Lee whispered, "I think I got a better idea. Why don't I stay here?"

"Why?" Bolan asked.

"I can set the fire and maybe get a few when they come running out to see what's going on. I wait up at the top there, by the roof door, I can nail a few as they come through. They won't even know what hit 'em."

"It's too risky," Bolan argued.

"Uh-uh. Not really. I can get on the roof same as you guys. I just do it from here, is all. It's better than us all going over the wall to the balcony. Keeps them guessing. Two fronts, man. Divide and conquer. It's classic."

"It's also suicide, Lee."

"You telling me you underestimate my abilities, Jim? I don't feature that shit. Not at all."

"It has nothing to do with your abilities. You know what kind of firepower they have in there. They'll cut you to ribbons."

"No way. I got me fire *and* firepower. Long as I can see the door, ain't no way nobody gets out less I want 'em to. Come on, man. You know it's better this way. If we all bunched up together, we could be in deep shit."

"All right, you win. But at the first sign of trouble I want you on the roof. You hear me?"

"I hear you. Come on, let's slop some of this stuff around here. How you expect to make a fire?"

Richards tilted one of the turpentine cans until the combustible fluid sloshed out and down the stairs. Backing up the steps, he walled himself off from the other two men with a cascade of the volatile liquid. At the fourth-floor landing, he opened another can, this one benzene, and let a pint or so run under the fire door, then poured the rest onto the stack of cans in the corner.

In a harsh stage whisper, he called down the steps. "What time you got, Jim?"

"Eleven-oh-five."

"Check. You better get out, man. I feel the urge for a cigarette comin' on. I figure ten minutes, it gonna be overwhelming."   .

"Lee," Bolan whispered back, "be careful."

"Don't have to, Jim. I'm gonna be good."

Bolan stepped through into the third-floor hallway. For a second he didn't want the door to close. It seemed too final.

Felipe tugged at his sleeve. "Señor, the clock is ticking. We have to hurry."

The door latch snapped shut with a soft click. Bolan had never heard anything louder in his life.

CHAPTER FORTY-SEVEN

"We've got five minutes," Bolan said. "Everything ready?"

"All set," Callahan whispered. "We made five ropes. Only found four scaffold hooks, though. Two guys are going to have to share one. I figure Felipe and Ricardo. They're the lightest."

"Good enough."

"Where's Richards?"

"He's at the other side. He'll be coming through the other door to the roof as soon as he gets their attention."

"No, *señor*," Ricardo hissed.

"Why not?" Bolan snapped.

"That door doesn't open. It was welded shut two years ago. Security was more important than safety."

"What?" Bolan turned to Felipe. "Why didn't you tell me that?"

"I am sorry, *señor*. I didn't know."

Bolan looked at his watch. "Damn. I only have three minutes to get back there." He started to open the door to the hall.

"Or what?" Callahan demanded. He grabbed Bolan by the shoulder. "What's going on?"

"Lee's at the top of the stairs. Once he sets that stuff on fire, he'll be trapped."

"Mack, it's too late, you can't get there in time."

"I have to try."

"I'll go. You go over the edge on schedule. We have hostages to worry about." Callahan was gone, his final words trailing off behind him in the darkness.

He ran down the hallway, heedless of the noise. Grabbing the door handle, he tugged it open and stepped through. His eyes instantly fastened on the small flicker at the top of the stairs.

"Lee, don't—"

Callahan was knocked to the floor by a dark figure as the flicker exploded into a ball of flame. Instantly the fire licked down the stairs, following the cascading liquid. Callahan struggled to his feet.

The shadow was standing right behind him. "Damn, that was a close one." Lee laughed. "What the hell you doin' here?"

"Ricardo told us the door didn't open. I came to stop you before you made an ash of yourself. Again."

"Thank you, my man. But I checked it out myself. Couldn't get the damn thing open, so I had to rig up a little Lee Richards special. Let the thing set its own self on fire. But I do appreciate your concern, Mr. Football." He bowed deeply. "We best haul ass. The boss gonna be mad if we late for work."

He broke into a sprint, disappearing into the shadowy end of the hall, Callahan right behind him. They charged through the fire door just as Bolan threw open the door to the roof. Bounding up the stairs, they slung their SMGs over their shoulders.

Felipe and Ricardo were already in position, their ropes held in loose coils in one hand. The other three men quickly grabbed their own ropes. The five men climbed over the parapet, arranged like beads on a rosary.

Bolan looked over his shoulder to the street below. So far they hadn't been spotted, but it wouldn't be long before the national guardsmen knew they were there. He only hoped they wouldn't lose their cool.

On a hand signal they all leaped into space, rappeling down, each man using the rough-cut stone of the palace to control his descent. Bouncing out and away from the wall, Bolan could see into the large, well-lit room. The hostages huddled together against an inside wall, the women surrounded by a tight circle of men.

As he hit the balcony, Bolan saw his own shadow starkly outlined against the stone as a searchlight swept past. It hesitated, then stabbed back in his direction. For one frightening instant he felt the delicate press of cross hairs on his shoulders. Then the light was gone. It didn't move; it went out altogether.

Thank God somebody on the ground had some smarts.

He slipped out of the rope sling, tossing it aside, then checked his Uzi and made sure he hadn't lost the spare ammo clips. Pressing it against the stone wall to wait for the others, Bolan heard a shout from inside. He was certain he had been spotted, and waited for the window to be thrown open.

Instead he heard several cries, all mingling together. The deep voices of the men nearly drowning the soprano terror of the women. *"Fuego! Fuego!"* Someone had spotted the fire in the stairwell.

Bolan heard a door slam back, its knob crashing into the hallway wall and echoing through the empty building. Easing close to the edge of the window, he was able to see several men in camouflage fatigues running toward the hallway. The others were milling around, uncertain what to do.

The hostages collapsed into a more compact mass, individuals now indistinguishable one from another. They cringed into themselves, terrified of the fire and of their captors. And, most especially, of their captors' terror.

It was time. Bolan stepped away from the wall and dived through the window, shielding his face and eyes with his forearms. He felt the prickly rain of glass splinters on his bare neck, small points of pain as the shattered window buried itself in his flesh in a hundred places. He was rolling to his feet as the other windows crashed inward.

Bolan fired the first burst, sweeping a tight figure eight through a knot of the baffled mercenaries. The confused men had congregated in the corner nearest the door, waiting to hear what was going on in the stairwell. Bolan's fire put an end to their concern.

A bullet whined past his ear. He turned as Richards squeezed off a storm of 9 mm slugs. Two mercs stood in a doorway opposite the hostages, armed with AK-47s and firing short, choppy clusters. Bolan dived to the floor as Lee chewed the doorframe to pieces. One merc went down, blood smearing the splintered frame. The second ducked back out of the way.

"Callahan, get the hostages into another room," Bolan barked. He was about to charge through the ravaged doorway, when a thunderous wave of heat rushed into the room. He heard agonized screams in the hallway, their echoes rising in pitch like an engine pushed to its limit.

The rest of the chemicals had blown. Feet pounded on the stone floor. A cloud of thick, black smoke mushroomed in from the hall.

"I'll check it out, man," Lee shouted as he ran past. He disappeared into the smoke. Bolan plunged into the next room, landing on his hip and sweeping the room with the SMG muzzle. The dead merc was the only one there. In a side wall, another door yawned open. The room beyond was dark. The screams funneled through meant it connected to the hallway.

So far, neither Cardona nor the big Mexican had been seen. Bolan turned at the scrape of a foot on the door behind him. Felipe stepped over the prostrate body in the doorway.

"Felipe, come with me," Bolan shouted.

He dashed into the dark room, ducking to one side as soon as he got through. His knee banged against something hard. The crack sent a splinter of fire along his shinbone and he tumbled to the floor. A furious hammering erupted from a corner of the room. Bolan heard the wall above him pulverize and scatter hunks of plaster to the floor. He had tripped over a chair, and it had saved his life.

Something heavy landed on his legs. In the darkness, he couldn't tell what it was. His leg grew wet as he reached down. The weight was Felipe. The hidden gunman had

caught him from hip to shoulder. He was dead. The little
man was heavier than Bolan would have thought. He slithered out from under the dead weight, trying to make no
noise.

Another chair slammed into his head. He reached out and
grabbed it by one leg, yanking it clear. With one hand, he
raised the flimsy chair by its molded plastic seat and tossed
it back toward the lighted doorway. The clatter of its fall was
drowned by the hammering Kalashnikov in the corner. A
hellish glow spattered and sparked as the AK-47 stuttered in
the darkness. The chair splintered and banged into the wall
ahead of the relentless fire. But it had served its purpose.
Bolan had a fix on the gunner.

Swinging the Uzi around, Bolan emptied the clip into the
dark hole. He rammed a new magazine home, then stumbled to his feet. Smoke was belching through the darkened
room, clouding the dim light from behind him. Bolan
charged into the hallway.

Thick gouts of sooty smoke tumbled like waves, pulsing
down the long stone-floored corridor on thermal currents.
The rising heat from the stairwell had no place to go and
detoured into the hall. Bolan could see little in the choking
fog. He dropped to the floor to get some clean air. The
heavy smoke had already left a greasy deposit on the floor,
motes of gouted paint and sticky ash coating the pale marble with grime.

Holding his breath, Bolan got up and ran away from the
billowing smoke. He reached the open door to the large office where the hostages had been held. Ricardo swung
around as Bolan entered, letting loose a short burst from his
Kalashnikov. Bolan ducked to one side as the skittish guard
realized who it was.

Ducking into the next room, Bolan sighed with relief. The
hostages were all accounted for.

"Cardona?" Callahan asked.

Bolan shrugged. "Not yet. Haven't seen him."

"Where's Lee?"

"I don't know. The last I saw him was when he ran into the hall. I'll be back."

"Wait, I'm coming with you. Ricardo and Felipe can stay here with the hostages."

"Felipe's dead."

Callahan stopped in his tracks. For a second a blank look clouded his features. Bolan had seen the look before. When lead became real and death staked its inevitable claim, reality revealed its ugly grin. Callahan shook himself, as if the knowledge were a thin skin he could shed.

"Let's go get Cardona," he said.

Bolan turned and led the way into the hall. It was pitch-black and deathly still. Somewhere in the thick shadows welling up from below, Diego Cardona was still free.

"We'll have to be careful," Bolan shouted over his shoulder. "The national guard is certain to come in now. Make sure you know who you're shooting at. And remember, Lee is out there somewhere."

They barged through the door into the stairwell at a dead run. The door banged back against the wall, booming down into the lower depths. The landing below chattered. An Uzi. The 9 mm slugs whined into the steel door above them, glancing off the wall in a shower of sparks.

"That you, Lee?" Bolan called.

Another burst of fire chipped and chewed at the masonry.

"Guess not," Callahan muttered. "What do we do? We can't go down these stairs. And the other set's on fire."

"There's one way," Bolan grunted. "You stay here and keep him occupied."

He banged back through the doorway. Callahan threw a short burst down the steps, looking over his shoulder at the closing door.

Bolan ran back to the balcony. Climbing out through the window, he grabbed the nearest rope. Snaking a big curve in the cord, he jerked, sending the loop back up toward the parapet. The hook rattled, but stayed where it was. He jerked again and again, sending one sidewinding loop after another back up the rope. Finally the hook bounced free, clattering to the stone balcony at his feet.

Bolan secured the hook on the edge of the balcony and swung out and down, landing on a window ledge on the third floor. He kicked in the glass, then chopped the remaining shards free with the side of his foot. When the frame was clear, he launched himself backward and swung back in, dropping through the open window to the shattered debris.

He felt his way across the dark room, broken glass crunching under his feet. His groping hand found a wall, then a light switch. He flipped it on long enough to locate a door, then shut the light off again. Catfooting it through the outer room, he bumped against a desk, rapping his knee on a sharp wooden corner.

The outer door was directly ahead of the inner one, and he found it with no trouble. He turned the knob and pushed the door open, hinges squealing.

The high-pitched squeak vanished under the crash of breaking glass. A hammering Kalashnikov chewed the open door to pieces. The sharp tang of burning paint rushed in through the portal, as hot air spurted past and on out through the missing window behind him.

Bolan was stymied. He couldn't go out into the hall, and there was no point going back up to four. He could try two, but knew he might have the very same problem. As he debated what to do, the hallway in front of him was suddenly bathed in light. A pall of thick, choking black smoke hung in the confined space, whirling and swirling as the currents of hot air pushed and pulled at it.

The lights could mean only one thing. The national guard had gotten into the building. The master switch was in the basement, so were the individual controls for each floor's outside lighting. Bolan knew Cardona had clout with Emiliano Gutierrez, the commander-in-chief of the national guard. If they got Cardona, he was as good as gone.

Bolan had to find him first.

He ducked out into the hall, then pulled back.

Silence.

Whoever had taken the door apart was gone. Or patient. Bolan bet on gone. He ran out into the hall, racing toward the stairwell.

The chatter of automatic weapons broke out in the stairwell. Bolan yanked the door open. The noise was deafening. Somewhere above him, three or four guns hammered incessantly. The stairwell was brightly lit, but a thin pall of grayish smoke dimmed the bulbs a bit, fogging the air with small clouds.

On the stairs, four men in combat boots and fatigues poured continuous fire at the fourth-floor doorway. They climbed steadily higher. If Callahan was still there, he was unable to return fire. It would have been suicide to try.

With a metallic clang, the roof door banged open. Bolan filled the stairwell with 9 mm hail. The two rearmost mercs were still in the doorway. Bolan's onslaught chewed them to pieces. As he started to run, a clattering ball bounced down the stone stairs.

Bolan recognized the antipersonnel grenade as he hit the fourth-floor landing. He dived through the doorway as the deadly sphere bounced on past and down. It blew almost simultaneously, filling the passageway with red-hot, flying razors. The shrapnel ripped and clawed at the masonry, trying to chew its way through to Bolan's prostrate form.

He got to his feet and ran back to the doorway. Overhead, he heard the familiar *whup-whup-whup* of a chopper, its engine roaring as it swung in low. Bolan sprinted up the stairs and out into the cool, clear night air.

The helicopter roared again, this time swinging up and away. Through the glass bubble, he saw the grim face of Diego Cardona, his lips drawn back in a death's-head smile. Bolan emptied his magazine, but the slugs glanced harmlessly away from the bulletproof bubble.

A shadow rose from the gravelly tar of the roof. Lee Richards ran to Bolan's side, shaking his fist at the departing chopper. "What we gonna do now?"

Bolan ignored the question, staring at the ghostly figure of Cardona as it dwindled into the night. The pale features were chalky white, and in the uncertain carnival swirl of searchlights from below, it seemed as though the hellish grin was fleshless bone.

When the chopper was gone, Bolan whispered, "Now we go get him."

He looked up at the sky. The stars were all but obscured by the glare from below. He knew where Cardona was going. Roberto Cabeza had told him about the redoubt in the ruins. Bolan couldn't have imagined a more fitting place to finish it.

And finish it he would.

Tonight.

Viscachani _____

CHAPTER FORTY-EIGHT

One hundred miles due south of La Paz, Viscachani sits on a flat slab of stone, draped in moss and tangled vines. A few trees poke up through the fallen blocks. Walls meet at every angle, their chunky stones rough-faced and fitted as tightly as hand in glove. The jagged saw of the Andes hacks away at the heavens on all sides.

Diego Cardona and Marcellito Estrada watched the chopper climb, its shadow passing over them like a huge nocturnal insect. The chopper dropped down and away from the Inca ruins, veering out over the forest below.

Cardona waited, fondling a small black transmitter in his left hand. Two miles away now. He was satisfied. He pressed the small red button with his thumb, grinding it into the black plastic as if it made a difference how much pressure he applied. The chopper was transformed into a bright orange flower, instantly shedding fiery petals and dying in the moment of its birth.

The burning wreckage rained down on the forest below, like a shower of meteors or a storm of hellfire and flaring brimstone. Then it was gone.

Overhead the moon glided quietly by, its pale light coating the dark stone with silver. The forest turned shades of silvered green and greenish gray under the washed-out illumination. Cardona turned and led the way back into a maze of stone walls. Trapezoidal archways gave onto small courtyards and led from passage to passage in the stone labyrinth.

Finally, in the heart of the coiled passages, Cardona shone his light on a metal ring at the center of a large pentagon. Five fifteen-foot-high stone walls surrounded the court, a single trapezoidal arch centered in each. He knelt by the ring, grasped it with both hands, then tugged. The ring remained motionless, despite his apparent effort. Letting it go, he turned to Rivera.

"Maybe you can move it, Marcellito. It's too heavy for me."

He stood back, pointing to the ring. Estrada knelt and leaned forward. Grabbing the ring in both hands, he strained upward, his forearms bunching with knotted muscle. With a harsh grinding sound, a wheel of stone—so finely cut its margin had been undetectable—lifted free of the surrounding stone.

"What's down there?" Estrada asked, leaning over the edge to peer into an inky hole.

Cardona moved closer, aiming the light into the well. It revealed a set of stairs cut into the raw stone, spiraling into the darkness. "Security," he whispered. "Safety."

"It looks like a prison to me," Estrada returned, laughing.

"Sometimes I wonder if there is a difference."

"Then you've never been in prison, Diego."

The Mexican slid into the hole feet first, feeling blindly for the first step. When he found it, he was waist deep in the center of the courtyard. "Here, give me the light," he said, reaching out for the flashlight in Cardona's hand. His fingers closed over the cold metal and he began the descent into the ground.

A dozen steps down, he turned to play the beam beneath him. "Okay, I'm down," he called. He could see Cardona's shadow above him. He shone the beam up through the hole, its bright glow picking out Cardona's pale, moonwhite face floating just above the rim of the opening.

A rasp echoed in the hole and Cardona disappeared. A dark parabola slid slowly across the lip of the entrance, eclipsing the cold smile that had hovered in the dancing beam.

For a few seconds it didn't register. Then, with a shout that echoed back at him from all sides, Estrada began to climb the stairs. As he reached the middle step, a hollow thud reverberated through the chamber. The sky was gone. Cardona was gone. The stone lid fell home with an incontrovertible finality. He shouted at the top of his lungs, the bellow mocking back at him, then escaping down through a series of small holes bored into the stone floor and coming back diminished, feeble and futile.

He scrambled the rest of the way up the steps and put his weight against the stone lid and pressed upward. The lid refused to move. He felt the tendons in his forearms grow taut. His elbows creaked with the strain. Bending, he placed one massive shoulder against the rock. Putting his back into it, he groaned with the effort. Still, the lid remained immobile. It was pointless. He was trapped, entombed.

He heard a distant gurgle beneath him, so far away that he wasn't sure he heard it at all. Slowly it grew louder. It seemed to come from every direction. Running water, lapping at stone. It grew in volume, steadily coming closer. Estrada fell to his knees, pressing his ear to the stone floor. It seemed to vibrate.

Racing around the stone chamber, he was able to isolate the sources of the noise. It was coming from the holes in the floor. He aimed the beam down into one of the holes, but the light disappeared before it found the bottom. He put his ear to the mouth of one shaft. He felt a breeze on his cheek. Air was rushing up from below, and with it the sound of the water.

Fascinated, Estrada lay on his stomach, peering down the tube with the flashlight aimed past the side of his head. Now he could see a glittering silver disk. The water was coming closer. Like a full moon rising, its shining round face grew brighter. Nearer and nearer it came.

He dropped a small stone chip and watched it shatter the shining face of the water, rippling from center to edge and back. He could reach down now, feel the water with his fingertips.

And then it bubbled up and out, a small shining mound of silver, spreading on the floor. Frantic, he played the beam around the chamber, picking out another silver geyser, then a third. The water was an inch deep now, steadily filling the seamless room. Estrada climbed the steps, sitting with his head brushing against the stone ceiling.

It was just a matter of time.

CARDONA SPRINTED down a narrow passage in the maze, his shoulders nearly brushing the rough wall on either side. With Estrada out of the way, he was home free. No one knew of this bastion except Roberto, and he was dead. So far undiscovered by archaeologists, the ruins were the safest place in the world. No one knew to look for him here.

A stone archway loomed ahead, and he ducked to pass under the low lintel. Once inside, he stopped running in order to catch his breath. He felt for the wall, found a switch and pressed it. Instantly light bathed the compact chamber in which he stood. He stepped down into the sunken room and crossed to a rough-hewn wooden table at its center.

Two small men suddenly appeared in the archway behind him. Each was dressed in black and carrying a blowgun. Cardona turned to look at them impassively. After a long moment he waved them in. They walked to the table and sat, watching him expectantly.

"So, it's come to this," Cardona said. The two men said nothing.

It would take him months to put the pieces back together, all because of that bastard Bolan. But he could wait. He was a patient man. It hadn't been easy the first time, but he'd done it. Now that he knew how, he could do it again. He still had money, and they would make it so much easier. All he had to do was wait it out.

Tomorrow he would go back to La Paz and fly to Switzerland. One night in the mountains was a small enough price to pay to save his skin. Cardona stood and walked to a cabinet in one corner of the room. He opened it expectantly, browsing among the bottles. Selecting one, he rapped its neck against the stone, grabbed a goblet from a shelf and poured himself a glass of wine.

There were worse ways to spend a night. He took a long sip of the blood-red liquid, then stared into the mouth of the goblet as he swirled the remaining wine in its bottom. Somehow, Valerie Russell figured in all this. He should have killed her when he had the chance. She must have betrayed him to Bolan. That would be his first goal. Getting even. All those who had betrayed him would have to pay for their treachery. But she was going to be the first. A rare honor.

Cardona swallowed the rest of the wine in a single gulp. He threw the glass against the wall, smashing it to a glittering heap of splinters on the floor. He walked back to the cabinet and withdrew a large crystal vase, cracking it down on the wooden table. He removed its fragile lid and shattered it on the wall. It rained in pieces on the ruined goblet.

Reaching into his coat, he took out the carved ivory tube and stuck it into the mound of coke in the vase. Inserting it into each nostril in turn, he inhaled deeply. The rush hit him like a wall, burning his nose. Lights flashed, and he shook his head as if struck repeatedly by a fist he couldn't see.

His senses seemed sharpened, as if an extra set of circuits had been plugged in. Images were more sharply etched. He began to fidget nervously, his ears pricked for the slightest sound.

He was ready for another hit. He picked up the tube from the table and leaned forward. He inhaled, and a distant thunder rolled in through the stone labyrinth. He shifted nostrils and took another hit. And again the thunder cracked. It echoed and rolled and died away. His name. The heavens were calling his name.

Another rumble, its rhythm stately, ominous "Car-don-na-na-na." It rolled and rumbled, dying reluctantly. "Car-don-na-na-na." A third time. And then he knew.

It wasn't thunder at all.

It was Bolan.

Here.

For him. Roberto must have told him.

And he smiled.

Revenge would begin sooner than he thought. He gestured to the two silent men across the table, walked to the cabinet and removed a Skorpion machine pistol from the top drawer. It was already loaded. He pulled a couple of extra magazines from the drawer and stuffed them into his pockets. With a nod of his head, he sent the two Jivaro out into the night.

Cardona breathed deeply to calm his nerves. He took a final hit of the coke and walked through the archway into the maze. The moon overhead was slipping away, now balanced on the rim of the Andes. In a few minutes it would be gone, leaving nothing but the stars.

He hoped Bolan had come alone, but knew he hadn't. And knew it didn't matter.

Again, his name thundered through the labyrinth.

Bolan stood on the wall, straining his eyes into the puzzled darkness. His shadow stretched before him, seemingly to infinity, as the moon slid to the very edge of the horizon. He was conscious of the broad disk behind him and knew it made him too good a target to pass up.

He cocked his head to one side. A faint whisper seemed to tease out of the maze and back in, unsure of itself as a shy young girl. The sound rose and fell, now there, then gone, then back again.

Bolan jumped from the wall, landing in a crouch. A whispered rattle leaped out from the wall above him. A slender reed fell to the stone floor beside him.

"Lee," Bolan whispered. "Be careful. Cardona has his headhunters with him."

"How many?"

"Right. I be back. Gonna take a little walk, see what's shakin'."

Richards slipped away, his feet whispering over the stone. Bolan kept to his crouch and pushed straight ahead, into the maze. A clatter on top of the wall turned him. He raised the Beretta 93-R and fired a 3-shot burst in the same motion. The automatic spit its own whispered death. A cluster of shadow collapsed atop the wall and landed with a thud in front of him.

Bolan knelt to survey the damage. The Indian was dead, two bloody holes punched in his rib cage. The third shot had missed. Bolan ripped a pouch of darts from around the man's neck and threw them into the darkness.

"Look out, man!"

Bolan heard the shout at the same instant something struck him sharply between the shoulders. He went sprawling headlong, slamming his left shoulder into the wall. The arm went numb on impact, a nerve paralyzed by the blow. His legs were tangled beneath him, a heavy weight across the back of his knees.

Bolan lashed out and squirmed forward, hauling himself free with his good arm.

"Lee, you okay?"

Richards didn't answer. Bolan crawled back to the shadowy bulk against the base of the wall. Richards lay still. Bolan reached out to shake him by the shoulder. The faint crack told him not to bother. The slender reed snapped off in his fingers, the small tuft of cotton a faint smear of white in the darkness.

Lee was dead. He had shoved Bolan out of the way, but couldn't avoid the dart. It had struck him high on the back just below his nape. And the Executioner had another score to settle.

Bolan rolled to his left, the Beretta clutched tightly in his fist. He watched the wall above him, waiting for the first hint of movement. It wasn't long in coming. He aimed into the shadow and pulled the trigger. The spit of the Beretta drifted away on a rising wind. This time, Bolan didn't bother to check the corpse. He knew he'd made the kill.

Scrambling forward, he passed through a low arch and entered the pentagonal court. The last moonlight seemed to have collected here. The darkness of the narrow passageway had sharpened his vision. Across the courtyard, a white smear, as silent as a shadow, drifted toward him.

The figure paused, still blurred as the moonlight dwindled. Bolan saw the figure tilt its head back, and with a feral howl it bayed his name as the moon finally died.

Cardona ran straight at him, spraying slugs from the Skorpion. The hellfire whined off into the night, rebounding from the stone. Like a whirling saw, it chewed at the ancient stone, chipping away and flashing sparks.

Then the magazine was empty. With another howl, Cardona charged straight toward him. Bolan waited until he could see Cardona's features clearly.

Then he squeezed the trigger as Lee Richards's image briefly flitted through his mind.

The Beretta was empty long before he realized it, the echoing fire deceptively real in the winding maze of stone. He stepped forward and stood briefly over the fallen Cardona.

As Bolan gazed stonily at the body of the man whose enterprise had caused untold misery to countless people, he knew that it would only be a matter of time before others would rise up to take Cardona's place.

The druglord's death was no great victory—it was merely one small event in Bolan's everlasting war against the savages. And now it was time to seek a new front. He turned his back and walked away.

NIGHT OF THE RUNNING MAN

He never thought of himself
as a lucky man— until he found
a briefcase with $500,000 inside

LEE WELLS

BULLETS OF PALESTINE

Howard Kaplan

A Palestinian and an
Israeli agent hunt for the
devil called Abu Nidal.

"Right up there with the best!"
—CLIVE CUSSLER

The orders to the Israeli agent Shai Shaham are simple: find Abu Nidal, and kill him. But penetrating Nidal's terrorist organisation seems impossible.

Shaham's opportunity comes when it is discovered that moderate members of the PLO are also out to eliminate Nidal. Shaham finds, then kidnaps their assassin and manages to persuade him that only by working together can Nidal be destroyed.

As the Israeli and Palestinians' trust and friendship grows, their mission is constantly plagued by age-old suspicion and hatred, which threatens to destroy them both. *Widely available from Boots, John Menzies, W.H. Smith and other paperback stockists. Pub. June 1988. £2.95.*

CARL A. POSEY

GOLD EAGLE

Science reporter Steve Borg is chasing the best story of his career. The world wants to know where the space shuttle Excalibur, carrying a dead crew, is going to land.

What Borg discovers is that the crew were murdered and the nuclear reactor on board has become a deadly bomb locked on an unalterable course straight for the heart of Soviet Russia. Pursued by the conspirators, who want to silence him at all costs, Borg battles against time to prevent Armageddon and preserve his own life.

Widely available from Boots, Martins, John Menzies, W. H. Smith, Woolworths and other paperback stockists. Pub. August 1988. £2.95

GOLD
EAGLE